Aggressor

Volume I

FX Holden

D1528915

Contact me:

fxholden@yandex.com

https://www.facebook.com/hardcorethrillers

The first novel in the Aggressor series

Cover art by Diana Buidoso: dienel96@yahoo.com

With huge thanks to my fantastic beta reading team for their encouragement and constructive critique.

Gabrielle 'Hell Bitch' Adams, Bror Appelsin, Juan 'Pilotphotog' Artigas, Mukund B, Nick Baker, Marcus Brown, Robert 'Ahab' Bugge, Marshall Crawford, Ted 'Bushmaster 06' Dannemiller, Michael Elvin, Julie 'Gunner' Fenimore, Harry Garland, Jonathan Harada, Dave Hedrick, Tom Hill, Martin Hirst, Tim Jackson, Dean Kaye, Devin Kerins, Rob Kidd, Mary Beth Knopik, David John, Thierry Lach, Joe Lanfrankie, Wayne MacKirdy, Catherine Shone Mayfield, David Mccracken, David McCowen, Graham McDonald, Brad 'Bone' McGuire, Mitch McWilliams, Matt Latter, Supreet Singh Manchanda, Alain Martin, John Morris, Paul J Neel, Steve Panza, Barry Roberts, Rick Rairdon, Yoav Saar, David Saylor, Janice Seagraves, Andy Sims, C Gordon Smith, Claus Stahnke, Lee Steventon, Julian D Torda, Neil Tomlinson, Diana Vredeveld, Stewart Webster, Karla Sue Wilson.

And to editor, Nicole Schroeder,
alexandria.edits@gmail.com
for putting the cheese around the holes.

Also by FX Holden: The Future War Series
(though each is a stand-alone story the recommended reading order is below)
KOBANI
GOLAN
BERING STRAIT
OKINAWA
ORBITAL
PAGASA
DMZ

Ag•gres•sor

(əˈgrɛs ər)

noun:

A person, group, or nation that attacks
first or initiates hostilities.

©Wiktionary

When written in Chinese, the word
'crisis'
is composed of two characters.

One represents danger
and the other represents opportunity.

John F. Kennedy

US President Warns Chinese Invasion 'Imminent'

Associated International Press, 30 April 2038 — US President Carmen Carliotti warned Thursday morning a Chinese attack on Taiwan was "imminent," framing the current economic blockade as a pretext for war.

It was the latest sign of mistrust from the West at Chinese claims the country is seeking a diplomatic solution to the current standoff. Carliotti, while maintaining there was a "diplomatic path" that avoids conflict, nevertheless used stark language to predict imminent violence.

"It's very high," Carliotti said when asked by AIP's Paul Raleigh how high the threat level is for a Chinese invasion of Taiwan.

"It's very high because they say they are conducting a naval and air economic blockade, but they have troops and landing ships by the thousands marshaling along the coast," she continued, speaking on the White House South Lawn before departing for Ohio, where she plans to sell the Taiwan Support Act passed last year.

"They have moved more troops in, number one. Number two, we have reason to believe they will manufacture an incident at sea or in the air as an excuse to go in. Every indication we have is they are prepared to go into Taiwan, attack Taiwan," Carliotti said.

Carliotti has predicted a Chinese invasion of Taiwan before but has previously softened her warnings by saying China's leader hadn't made up his mind. She was more definitive on Thursday, a day after Pentagon officials said 70,000 more Chinese troops have arrived at Chinese ports along the Taiwan Strait, along with strategic bombers, contradicting earlier Chinese claims of a pullback.

Pressed on whether she believes an attack will happen—and what the US response will be—Carliotti said: "Yes. My sense is it will happen in the next several days. As to our response, China knows it will be swift, and resolute."

Contents

Area of Operations

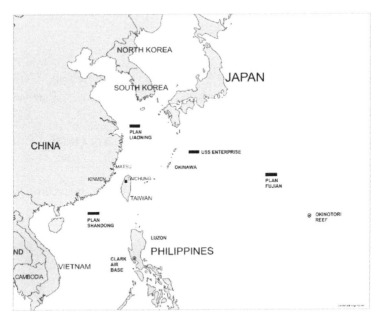

Map showing position of US and Chinese aircraft carrier strike groups at the outbreak of hostilities

© Mapchart

Cast of players in order of appearance

COALITION

Lieutenant Karen 'Bunny' O'Hare (USAF Reserve), Fifth-Generation Combat Aircraft Training Lead, Aggressor Incorporated

Lieutenant Colonel Kevin 'Salt' Carlyle (USAF Reserve), Chief Operations Officer, Aggressor Incorporated

Michael Chase, Pentagon Deputy Assistant Secretary of Defense for China

Carmen Carliotti, US President

HR Rosenstern, White House Chief of Staff

NSC ExCom members: Vice President Mark Bendheim, Homeland Security Secretary Emily Harvey, Defense Secretary Ervan Holoman

James Burroughs, Head of Defense Intelligence Agency China Desk, Chair of the Joint Wargaming Council

Captain Anaximenes 'Meany' Papastopolous (USAF Reserve), CO, 68th AGRS

Fleet Air Arm Squadron Leader Jules 'Two-Tone' Hamilton, *HMS Queen Elizabeth*

CHINA

Lieutenant Asien 'Shredder' Chen, Pilot Officer, Ao Yin Fighter Squadron, PLA Navy carrier *Fujian*

Second Lieutenant Min 'Maylin' Sun, Pilot Officer, Ao Yin Fighter Squadron, PLA Navy carrier *Fujian*

Colonel Wang Wei, Air Wing Commander, PLA Navy carrier *Fujian*

Major Tan Yuanyuan, PLA Navy Intelligence, PLA Navy carrier *Fujian*

Vice Admiral Li Zhang, Fleet Commander, East Sea Fleet

Captain Xi 'Casino' Bo, Ao Yin Squadron Commander

Major General Huang Xueping, Deputy Director for the People's Liberation Army Office for International Military Cooperation

Captain Yi Zhizhi, Commander of Water Dragon Commandos Detachment 23, PLA Navy

JAPAN

Takuya Kato, Marine Biologist, Japan Oceanographic Research Command

Captain Shinji Kagawa, Japan Self Defense Force Destroyer, *JS Haguro*

Empress Mitsuko Naishinnō, Head of the Imperial Family of Japan and Constitutional Head of State

Foreword

I hope you enjoy AGGRESSOR. Before we start, a word about the concept of a private military contractor, or PMC, providing military services to governments, which is central to this series.

This is not fiction; it is already a reality. You might be aware of the extensive use of PMCs to support Coalition Military and Intelligence security and ground operations in the Middle East during the Gulf, Afghanistan and Syrian wars. You might also be aware of the significant role played by the PMC Wagner Group in the Ukraine War. You may *not* have been aware that PMCs in the aviation field have provided Aggressor opponents (friendly aircraft playing the role of enemies in training and exercises) for militaries around the world, including the USAF and RAF. These contractors are equipped with some of the most modern fourth-generation fighter aircraft currently flying, including F-16 and F/A-18 fighters. The world's largest private air force is a US-based PMC that provides Aggressor services and flies three squadrons of F/A-18 Hornets.

The central idea in this novel, that a private contractor flying US-made fighter aircraft would be hired by Taiwan's government to help train its pilots, is not really a stretch.

As to the use of private Aggressor squadrons to support combat operations, that is a stretch, but only a small one in the context of future fiction. In 2022 the US Air Force confirmed that F-16s from the 18th Aggressor Squadron in Alaska had been used to fly armed interceptions of Russian aircraft off the coast of Alaska and advised it was normal practice for Aggressor squadrons to fill gaps in the USAF order of battle if active-duty units were temporarily deployed elsewhere.

So for this series, all I have done is combined the existing practice of using private military contractors to provide Aggressor services with the recently reported practice of Aggressor squadrons backing up active duty USAF squadrons where needed.

All it would take is a clause in a contract, and AGGRESSOR INC. would be a reality.

1. 'Any landing you can walk away from ...'

Luke Air Base, Arizona, April 1, 2038

"Uh, Luke Approach, this is Aggressor flight one ninety-four. I have a slight situation ... will have to go around."

Karen 'Bunny' O'Hare had more than a slight situation. What she had was a could-put-you-six-feet-under situation.

"Aggressor one ninety-four, Luke Approach, proceed southwest five clicks at 10,000 and hold over Aqua Caliente. You want to tell us about your 'situation,' pilot?"

Bunny checked the warning on her instrument panel and ran a quick diagnostic before she flipped the switch on her left that retracted and deployed her landing gear. Same procedure, same result.

"Yeah, Luke, I've got a 'neuromorphic chip reboot' kind of situation." She pulled up a checklist on her screen as she was talking, but she also had it in her head and was halfway through it already. "Can't get the nosewheel down. Need to dump fuel, and you probably want to wake up emergency services. This bird don't skid pretty."

It wasn't her first chip failure in the P-99 Black Widow II—there was a reason pilots unofficially called it "Widowmaker"—but it *was* the most inconvenient. A result of the US Air Force Next Generation Fighter program, the Black Widow had set a record for the fastest non-wartime speed from approval to first production. It had been "test flown" digitally in 2021 before a physical prototype was approved, and Bunny was learning that being a Black Widow pilot also meant discovering the bugs that hadn't been squashed along the way.

Especially the teething problems with its "state-of-the-art" neuromorphic central processing unit—a bunch of chips designed to emulate an organic brain, processing data in electrical bursts like synapses firing. When it worked, it could interpret data from the aircraft sensors and respond to it even if it hadn't been specifically programmed to recognize a particular image, sound or sensor reading: like a human realizing that a crocodile doesn't look quite like an alligator but that doesn't mean you can pet it.

So it was great at recognizing unexpected threats. But it sometimes sucked at the simple things, like lowering a damn nosewheel, because when it hit a situation it couldn't figure out, its default was to hand off processing to a legacy backup CPU while it rebooted—and that handoff was where things went sideways. Actions you were undertaking during the handoff got stalled or parked. Five years and 10 software upgrades later, and it was still happening.

"Alright, pilot, you can dump fuel beside Davis-Monthan Boneyard and get back to us to organize a low-level flyby so we can check if your nosewheel is maybe down and you're just looking at a system error."

Bunny had been through a neuromorphic CPU reboot before and she also had a feel for how the Black Widow flew with nose gear deployed, and it wasn't feeling right—but she flew to Tucson, dumped her fuel over unused ground at the air force aircraft storage facility, or "boneyard," and then got cleared in for a fly-past of the tower at Luke.

Her cockpit canopy was just a narrow, stealth-preserving sliver of Perspex above her head, and she could see all the way around the aircraft using the virtual view from cameras mounted in the aircraft fuselage. One of those cameras was showing her nosewheel hatch still stubbornly closed, but as the tower slid past her starboard wing at a leisurely 400 knots, she banked her machine to give the controllers there a good long look too.

"Uh, yeah, that's bad news, pilot. Nosewheel has not deployed, but your rear wheels are down. How do you want to do this?"

"Patch me through to Aggressor CO Colonel Carlyle, will you?"

The Aggressor Inc. operations commander, Kevin 'Salt' Carlyle, had already been alerted and responded immediately. "On my way out to the field now," he told Bunny. "What're you thinking?"

"I'm thinking I take the runway option, wheels down, glide it in nice and slow and then drop the nose right in front of a nice big fire truck."

"The owner will prefer that to you bailing and making a lawn dart out of our new Black Widow," Salt agreed. "But it's your call, O'Hare. You sure?"

"No. But I can't see a better option. Can you make that *two* big fire trucks, Salt?"

She circled again while the Luke controllers cleared traffic for her and got emergency services in place beside the runway.

"Aggressor one ninety-four cleared to land runway two one right, wind two six zero at one four. Good luck, ma'am," the tower said as she came around and lined up on the runway now visible on the horizon.

The coming crash landing would start deceptively smoothly, with a near-stall-speed rear wheels touchdown.

She'd practiced nosewheel-out landings in the Black Widow in a simulator, and what made them tricky was the machine tended to skew randomly left or right on landing. That hadn't been a problem in a simulator, but in the real world, if she started skewing, there was a very real risk of sliding off the runway, a wheel strut buckling, a wing digging in and the whole 15-ton plane flipping onto its back.

She had a sudden flashback to another aircraft, another time. Weird, where had that come from? She pushed it aside.

CPU_N online, a line of text flashed on her helmet visor, announcing the neuromorphic CPU had returned to the party. *Re-engage CPU_N?* "Hell no," Bunny said out loud. She was on her final approach. There was no time for another unexpected event. "You've caused enough trouble, buddy." She ignored the prompt.

As she trimmed her machine, checked the rear wheels were down and locked and adjusted her line for the slight crosswind, noting with probably misplaced relief the flashing lights of emergency vehicles beside it, all she could think about was the hundred ways this could end badly. She concentrated on the emergency landing checklist in front of her on a screen, letting it push thoughts of disaster out of her mind. And then she was over the runway and her wheels hit the tarmac and she stopped thinking completely.

Touchdown ... rear wheels down ... speed 140 knots ... 135 ... 130 ... half the runway gone ... brakes ... gently ... keep the nose UP ...

Bunny pitched forward as the nose of the Black Widow slammed into the ground, about as gently as if she'd been catapulted through the windscreen of a car in a head-on crash. Her harness bit into her shoulders, crushing her chest and knocking the wind out of her. She heard tearing, screeching metal, and sure enough, the machine swung first left, then radically right, and the entire plane was skidding sideways down the runway. Controls useless now, she dropped her hands to the ejection handle between her legs, ready to heave on it if the machine showed the slightest sign that it was going to flip.

The rear wheel struts held. She heard tires blow on her left, the whole aircraft heeled over to port, and the sound of metal on tarmac intensified as the rim of the rear wheel scraped across the runway, adding its protesting scream to the surrounding noise.

But it *held*.

Just as the machine was about to leave the runway, it ran out of momentum and, with a last sideways shudder, came to a stop and rocked to a standstill, port wingtip just inches off the ground.

The normal exit was through a hatch in the floor, but Bunny had her harness off and punched the emergency canopy release, not waiting for the mechanism to lift the canopy out of the way. It opened at the front, which meant it started lifting from behind her and she was up in her seat, back against the armored acrylic and shoving hard. When it had opened enough for her to squeeze through, she clambered out on the port side and slid down the canted wing like a two-year-old on a playground slide. She smelled smoke and hit the ground running, and only when she was a good 50 feet away did she stop, turn around and start pulling off her helmet.

A fire truck was moving in cautiously from about 50 yards away, another right behind it, and an ambulance behind them. She crouched down, panting.

The smoke was coming from her shredded starboard tires. But she couldn't see any flame, and while the nose of the Black Widow was a scarred mess, no flame or smoke was coming from up front. The Widow was a big machine, more missile truck than dog fighter, more like the B-21 Raider it had borrowed so much of its design from than its predecessors the F-22 and F-35. If anything, it looked like a big, fat, tailless paper plane, its smooth, downwardly-curved triangular shape disturbed only by the bumps housing its two engines and the rectangular slit of the cockpit canopy.

Dodged another bullet, O'Hare, she told herself, wiping sweat from her face. She stood, hands on hips, looking at her machine. *Airframe could be bent, wheel strut's just a stump, but definitely salvageable. At least they'll have an easier time working out what went wrong than if I'd climbed out at 5,000 feet and buried her in a state forest.*

The ambulance crunched to a halt on gravel just behind her and she turned.

A paramedic came jogging up to her. "How you doing, ma'am?" he asked in a cowboy drawl.

Bunny rolled her shoulders. "Pretty good. Just a few bruised ribs. You're going to tell me I need to get checked anyway."

He smiled. "Not your first crash landing, Lieutenant?"

21

Bunny turned and surveyed the bent nose section of the Black Widow ruefully. "Any landing you can walk away from is a good one, right?"

Colonel 'Salt' Carlyle walked into the sick bay as she was getting checked over by a medic.

"Breathe in …" the medic told her. Actually, his first comment as she had stripped off her flight suit and stood before him in briefs, socks and a cotton vest was, "Wow. That's a lot of ink."

"That's a lot of ink, *ma'am*," Bunny had chided him.

But she was used to that reaction from people seeing her uncovered for the first time. There was very little real estate on Bunny's body that didn't have some sort of tattoo on it. Every one of them was a memento of something she didn't want to forget, whether a person or a place, a victory or a defeat. And there had been plenty of all of that in her short life.

"Sorry, ma'am." He'd put his stethoscope in his ears and approached. "Uh, alright, please breathe in."

Bunny took a big breath, trying not to wince.

"… and out."

She let the breath go and stifled a cough she just knew was going to hurt. You didn't decelerate from 140 knots to zero inside a few seconds without a *few* bruises. But that was better than what might have happened to her if she'd had to punch out of the machine at altitude: concussion, spinal compression, contusions or fractures from landing in a tree …

22

"Why is it always you, O'Hare?" Salt asked, walking up beside the gurney she was sitting on as he shook his head.

"Not bad, thanks, Salt. Yeah, that *was* an amazing landing, thank you."

"I can see you didn't bruise your ego. Good news is we're insured for noncombat damage to our inventory." He coughed. "Uh, but also … I'm glad you got out of it in one piece."

The medic asked Bunny to lift her arms above her head and moved around behind her to check her back, lifting her tank top from behind and running his stethoscope across her back as she breathed in and out. Bunny gave Salt moon eyes. "Aw. I think that's about the nicest thing you ever said to me."

"Glad from a company, not a personal point of view. I've got a job for you," he said. Then checked himself. "I'm doing it again, aren't I?"

Bunny gave him a fake smile. "The thing where you ignore the person on fire in front of you and say what you were going to say anyway instead of looking for a fire hose? That thing?" The banter was an attempt to cover her basic disdain for Aggressor Inc.'s pedantic, punctilious and self-promoting operational commander.

"You're right. Sorry. What happened? Hydraulic failure?"

"Neuromorphic chip reboot," she said, rolling a shoulder to test it and wincing. "There's a reason Aggressor Inc. got a great deal on those Block 1A Widowmakers, Salt."

"They've had the same software updates as Air Force Block 2 Widows," Salt said defensively. "The airframes have had a bunch more hours is all. Besides, if your situation was caused by a neuromorphic chip reboot, it's still rare."

23

"It's the *second* time it's happened to me."

"So maybe we need to look at the pilot instead of the airplane, O'Hare."

Bunny let that one hang there. The look she gave him did all the talking. "I have a theory if you want to hear it."

"All ears," he said, in a tone that implied he was anything but.

"Both times the failure happened, I was on approach or in the pattern. I think ground radar is messing with the chip."

"Two data points don't make a proof."

She sighed and turned to the medic. "I think we're just about done. Aren't we?"

The medic straightened and came around in front of her again. He lowered the stethoscope and took out a pencil light, shining it first in one eye, then the other. "Now we're done. Looks like you got some bad bruising is all, but you need X-rays to be sure you didn't crack any ribs and probably a CT scan to check for spinal injury. I'll book you in."

"Right."

The medic nodded, picking up a chart from the gurney and reading off a page. "And in the meantime you call us if you experience any neck pain or stiffness, dizziness or confusion, headache at the base of your skull, muscle spasms in the back, arms or legs ... numbness or tingling in the arms and legs, radiating or stabbing pain down the arms and legs ..." He looked up. "Loss of mobility or limited sensation, such as the ability to feel heat or cold ..."

Bunny blinked at him and gave him her broadest Australian accent. "Mate, you just described the morning after a good night out, but I will let you know." As the medic

24

left, Salt handed Bunny her T-shirt, and she pulled it on and glared at him. "So what's this new gig?"

Salt closed the door behind the medic, then leaned back against the wall.

"You up to date on the Taiwan situation?"

She looked at him warily. "The situation where China issued Taiwan with a reunification ultimatum and Taiwan said screw you, so now China has the island blockaded tighter than a nunnery with Vikings at the door, trying to starve it into submission?"

"That was a coarse but accurate summary, and yes. That situation. Or more particularly, the Aggressor Inc. Taiwan situation."

"Of course. And now I am morbidly curious. What is the new gig?" Aggressor Inc. was a small and close-knit unit. So she knew all about the team trapped on Taiwan by the Chinese blockade. They'd won a contract a year earlier to provide F-22 Aggressor opponents to help train Taiwan's fourth-generation non-stealth fighter pilots in how to survive against the fifth-generation stealth opponents like the ones China would throw at them.

"Chicken and egg. I can't tell you the finer details until you sign a nondisclosure," he said. "But it's a straightforward job. Just another day at the office for you." His slight smile told her it wasn't. He was not in the habit of offering Bunny the choice jobs.

Bunny scratched the platinum stubble on her head. "Taiwan. It's never somewhere nice and peaceful, is it? Why don't you go and get us a contract to train the New Zealand Air Force, Salt? Six months zooming around the Land of the

Long White Cloud *not* worried about getting our asses shot down. How about that for a great idea?"

"We train fighter pilots, O'Hare. Does New Zealand even have an air force?"

"They don't need one, because they are friends with everyone. Unlike Taiwan, which is at war with the most powerful military in the region."

"Most powerful?" Salt raised his eyebrows. "You mean second most powerful, right?"

"No, I know what I said," Bunny said, climbing down from the gurney. "I said 'region.' So everyone else turned you down already, right?"

He balked. "Not exactly. You are our UCAV Training Lead, and there's a heavy UCAV angle to this one …"

She wasn't buying it. Yes, she was Aggressor Inc.'s UCAV, or Uncrewed Combat Aerial Vehicle, training lead. But while Salt tried to keep his professional and personal opinions separate, he had a poorly disguised dislike for Bunny O'Hare, which ranged from her preferred attire (torn) to choice of jewelry (piercing), taste in music (heavy rock) and general attitude to authority (deficient). She would not be his first choice for this sort of mission. It was one reason she was still in Arizona and not on Taiwan already with Salt's preferred A-Team. For which she had been kind of glad until now. "Yeah, nah, the others turned you down."

He shrugged. "You sign the nondisclosure agreement; I'll brief you and you can decide."

Bunny O'Hare had many flaws, one of which was a tendency to say yes quickly to dubious offers that she would then regret at her leisure. "Send me the NDA," she said. "I'll look at it when I get out of here." She knew enough to know

26

this was not a job she should rush into. China was pretty upset that six former USAF F-22 fighters were based on the rebel island for "training purposes," but since Aggressor Inc. was a private commercial entity registered in the Bahamas, all of China's protests to the US government had fallen on deaf ears because government officials just shrugged and said "nothing to do with us." Higher-level political realities had overtaken the protests. Since the Chinese ultimatum giving Taiwan's parliament three months to vote in favor of reunification or "face the consequences" had lapsed, China had thrown a ring of steel around Taiwan, allowing no commercial shipping or aircraft through. Chinese aircraft patrolled the skies just outside the 40-mile range of US-made Patriot missiles, and dozens of Chinese warships circled the island, stopping and inspecting every ship from the smallest fishing vessel to the largest freighter.

For nearly two months, it had declared the international waters of the Taiwan Strait a "military security zone," warning off and intercepting international shipping trying to transit the Strait. The US had forced passage through the Strait several times with ships of its Indo-Pacific fleet, but it had stopped short of trying to break the Chinese blockade and dock at Taiwanese ports or fly aircraft in. So the Aggressor Inc. aircraft and personnel on the island were trapped too. China had made it clear any aircraft trying to run its blockade, either inbound or outbound, would be intercepted and risk being shot down.

Salt reached for his phone. "No time like the present. I got the NDA right here."

While O'Hare was busy crash landing, Aggressor Inc. had already hit "send" on a press release announcing a new contract with the Republic of China Taiwan Government. While it was light on specifics, it contained enough detail to provoke a reaction on both sides of the Pacific Ocean.

Aggressor Incorporated, the Arizona-based military aviation training services provider, is pleased to announce a new $175 million contract with the Government of Taiwan. After intensive evaluation by the ROCTAF, Aggressor Inc. has been successful in winning a two-year extension of its existing contract to provide aircraft, pilots and related services to Taiwan.

The aircraft included in the contract are Aggressor Inc.'s fleet of USAF surplus fifth-generation F-22 fighters and newly leased Black Widow 2 pursuit aircraft.

While the announcement pleased Aggressor Inc. shareholders, not everyone who read it was quite as delighted. Inside the Pentagon, Michael Chase, deputy assistant secretary of defense for China, cursed and reread the paragraph.

He was alone in his office and swore out loud. "Who in the *gibbering depths of hell* authorized this press release?" he asked the walls around him. Chase wasn't up to date on every little private defense contractor with its hooks in the defense pie, but he was most definitely aware of Aggressor Inc. since it had already been the subject of several irate calls from his

Chinese counterpart because of its inconvenient presence on Taiwan. His cell phone was next to the laptop on his desk. He was willing to bet that in a few hours, when China woke up, it would run hot.

He was wrong. Fifteen minutes later, the laptop chimed with a video call and he answered. The uniformed army soldier on the other side of the screen spoke without preamble. "Call for you on the U.S.-PRC Defense Link, sir. Major General Huang Xueping."

Chase looked at his watch and wiped a hand across his face. The press release had been timed for a NY stock exchange audience, so it had gone out at 11 a.m. East Coast time. It was now 2 a.m. in Beijing. This meant that the Chinese officer on the other end of the call—the deputy director for the People's Liberation Army Office for International Military Cooperation—had probably been woken up to be presented with the press release. That he was calling Chase now instead of waiting for the morning was a sign the coming call would not be a friendly one.

The U.S.-PRC Defense Link had started its existence as the U.S.-PRC Defense Telephone Link, and had been set up by both countries after an incident in the South China Sea where a Chinese fighter collided with a US early-warning aircraft and the Chinese pilot was killed, while the US aircraft had to make an emergency landing on a Chinese island and its crew was imprisoned. Neither side had been able quickly to contact the other as the incident unfolded, so the communications link had been established to provide a channel for "resolving military misunderstandings."

In Michael Chase's experience, it had become a bullhorn down which the Chinese general staff vented constant outrage and hollow warnings, and as the US defense community representative, he gave meaningless assurances and restated public government positions. It had, however, proven its value the few times it had been used during actual military incidents—most recently during hostilities between China and the Philippines over a disputed island, in which US forces became embroiled. That particular fracas had cost Chase several sleepless nights, and he'd spent many hours on the line with his counterpart, General Huang, before it had been settled.

Chase sighed and straightened his tie. One thing he had learned over recent months, no matter what the time of day or night, General Huang always appeared on camera as though he had just showered, shaved and dressed in a newly tailored uniform. Damn him. He opened his laptop and slapped his cheeks, trying to shake off his pre-lunch blood sugar low. Then he tapped the icon on the screen that opened the video link. "Hello, General. It's early for you, so this must be serious."

The man on the other side of the screen was young for a senior officer in the PLA. In his early 50s, he had thick black hair, parted on the right, a high forehead and large glasses, with an overbite that made it appear he was smiling: a rare occurrence in his calls with Chase.

"Assistant Secretary Chase, a disturbing notice has just come to my attention," the General said.

And to mine, Chase thought, *if this is about what I think it is.* "And what is that, General?"

"That the US government intends to extend the presence of its fighter aircraft on the Chinese territory of Taiwan."

Chase ran his eye over the press release again. It said nothing about the US government. "I'm sorry, General, I'm not following."

"The American F-22s on Taiwan …"

"The *privately owned* F-22s on Taiwan, you mean."

"Do not dissemble, Mr. Chase. Your government has just announced these aircraft will remain on Taiwan beyond the life of their current contract. By extending their presence on the island, you are trying to achieve a de-facto military presence on Taiwan, which you believe will complicate the political situation for China."

In principle, what the Chinese officer was saying made perfect sense. There was a reason that diplomatic efforts to pull the Aggressor Inc. aircraft out of besieged Taiwan were not moving quickly. And of course, until he was briefed to do otherwise, Chase had to deny that.

"That was a private company press release, General, not a notice from the government of this country. I know this is a hard concept for a Chinese military official to grasp, but the US government is *not* involved here. I have no more information than you do about the commercial arrangements between this company and the government of Taiwan." That much at least was true. "This is a private contractor, providing training services as part of …" Chase did his best to hold some sort of line, but Huang interrupted.

"This is a US government contractor!" Huang said. "Do not play shell games with me, Mr. Chase. This company works for your government. Whatever it does is sanctioned by you. This is a dangerous provocation, and this 'contract' must be canceled! Those aircraft must be removed from that island."

Chase scanned the press release again. "I am a Pentagon official, General," Chase said. "You are talking about a private commercial arrangement. Perhaps you should take up your protest with the company itself, or with our State

31

Department. I'm not sure a political protest is the correct use of this operational link, or our relationship."

Perhaps it was the early hour in China, or pressures on him of which Chase wasn't aware, but Huang slapped the table in front of him with uncharacteristic anger. "Mr. Chase! China has declared a naval and air defense zone covering all of Taiwan. I have already warned you that China will *not* allow the US to sell any new weapons systems to the rebels or base any US military personnel or assets on that island. For 'training' purposes or otherwise!"

"And I can only repeat, General," Chase replied calmly, "that the US government does not recognize your illegal 'air and sea defense zone.' We reserve our right peacefully to transit international waters and fly in international airspace, or with its permission, the airspace of Taiwan. Plus, this is a private commercial arrangement, not a US government initiative." He was repeating himself. It was time to cut the call. "But I will look into the matter and convey your concerns."

"Convey *this*, Mr. Chase," Huang said. "This provocation will not be allowed to stand. If the US insists on going through with it, China's military will make a legitimate and necessary response using all the means at our disposal."

Chase paused, the General's words hanging in the air between them. Chase understood now why China was using the military deconfliction link for its protest. Unlike Chase, they had clearly been forewarned about negotiations between Taipei and Aggressor Inc., and the press release in front of him merely confirmed what they already knew. They had already prepared a response, and it was being delivered to Chase now. Via the military deconfliction hotline, which meant it was more than an expression of diplomatic outrage: it was a military threat. In these situations, the line he had been ordered to convey by the Secretary of Defense was clear. "The US government has no desire for conflict with China, General, but neither do we fear it. Your concerns are noted and will be passed along. Is there anything else?"

"No. Take this warning *seriously*, Mr. Chase. Good night."

Oh, Chase planned to take it very seriously, but perhaps not as the Chinese General intended. He picked up his phone and called an aide. "Get me the Deputy Under Secretary of the Air Force for International Affairs. I want a full brief on this new Aggressor squadron contract with Taiwan," he said, then changed his mind. "No, wait on that. First, find out who the hell the CEO of 'Aggressor Inc.' is." He read the contact information at the bottom of the press release. "They're based at Luke AFB in Arizona; details are on that press release you sent through. And when you get him or her on the line, tell them I am not a happy man and they better have a change of underwear ready before we speak."

2. 'That was yesterday'

It would have saved Michael Chase a lot of time if he'd been sitting at a table in the Sage & Sand Bar just outside Luke AFB with Bunny as Salt explained the mission to her. And his reaction would probably have been very similar.

"We're sending *more* aircraft into Taiwan?" she said incredulously. "I thought we were supposed to be trying to get them out?"

"That was yesterday," he said, putting the NDA back into his pocket. "It's a dynamic world, which is why we are sitting here now."

"But, since China put a blockade on Taiwan, nothing is getting in or out."

"Yes."

"Then how the hell are we supposed to …"

"… get more aircraft in so we can meet the terms of the contract? Good job identifying the challenge, O'Hare."

"So, the people we have on the ground already are staying?"

"The contact has been extended, so yeah, they're staying. Our people there have an opt-out. Those who don't like the new arrangement can ship back home at the first opportunity and we'll fly new pilots and crew in when the blockade lifts. But the machines are staying." He pointed a finger at her chest. "And we promised Taiwan we'd train them against drone command platforms like the Widow, which is where *you* come in."

He explained the basics to her.

"The mission is to sneak a Black Widow into Taiwan, *through* the Chinese blockade?" Bunny asked in a low voice. They'd taken an outside table and the surrounding tables were mostly deserted, but habit made her cautious.

"Sure. Think of it as a proof of concept," Salt said. "We promised them three Widows to win the contract. No one else has that kind of hardware. If you can get one Widow through, we'll send the other two."

"China will go apeshit if they find out. The P-99 Widow is a sixth-generation frontline stealth aircraft."

"They already know," Salt said, looking at his watch. "The press release just went out."

Bunny squinted at him. "That's a one-way trip, assuming whoever is dumb enough to do this even makes it through the Chinese air cordon alive."

"This operation is sanctioned at the highest levels of the US government," Salt told her. "Considerable assets will be put in place to ensure our pilot a safe transit. In *and* out."

"What kind of 'assets'?" she asked.

"Considerable. You'll have armed escorts on the way over, ordnance in your payload bay ..."

"What 'ordnance'?" she frowned. Aggressor Inc. aircraft almost never flew armed. Only when they were backfilling for regular air force units on short-term deployments, and that was rare.

"We'll be briefed when we get to Guam. You'll make your transit from there, with a shiny new Block II Widow we just leased from Air Force. That's got to make you happy, right?"

It didn't. "I've heard those kind of promises before." Bunny said, and held up the forefingers of each hand, about a foot apart. "There are four hours of empty sea and sky between Guam and Taiwan, Salt. If I even make it that far, when I get to Taiwan air space, I'll have to sneak through God knows how many Chinese combat air patrols and a PLA Navy missile destroyer screen ... China intercepts me, things could get kinda *kinetic*."

He gave her a cryptic look. "I told you, contingencies are being put in place. Look, you sneak in, put down and debrief on their defenses, then we'll get you the hell out of there again. You can take a long, well-deserved holiday with your special duties bonus."

"How about I take a long holiday *now*, instead? I assume I can say no to this job."

Salt looked pained. "You could, but then some other Aggressor pilot with fewer combat hours, fewer hours in the Black Widow, they'd have to do it instead. Anything happens up there, I know you couldn't live with yourself." He sat back. "You're the only one who can do this, O'Hare."

"You mean the only one stupid enough." Bunny cursed inwardly. Salt was playing on one of her weaknesses. Not the part of her that always thought she was the best person for the job, whatever it was. That was a given. But the part of her that hated hearing that the action was somewhere she wasn't. And the other part of her that couldn't help but take the side of a badly outgunned, outnumbered and shit-out-of-options underdog like Taiwan. A newly leased, factory-fresh Black

36

Widow? If the US Air Force was risking a sixth-gen fighter on this mission, it must be important.

"We. You said, '*We'll* find out on Guam.' You're on this mission too?"

It would surprise her if the Aggressor Inc. Chief Operations Officer was actually joining the operation. Salt did more than his share of the heavy lifting and he was no slouch with a flight stick. But for family reasons he rarely deployed overseas, preferring to stay closer to home and put in most of his flying hours on the Red Flag range at Luke. He was going to deploy to *Guam* for this one?

"Don't look so shocked," Salt told her. "I promised our Air Force contact I'd be mission controller on this job myself."

Bunny drained her beer. "Damn. This must be worse than I thought."

"The situation is not as we thought."

Colonel Wang Wei, squadron leader and air wing commander aboard the People's Liberation Army aircraft carrier *Fujian*, sat in his stateroom with his wing intelligence officer, a Major by the name of Tan Yuanyuan. Her fine-boned face looked more irritated than worried, but Wei had learned that Tan lived in a perpetual state of irritation. She was either annoyed at what she knew or what she didn't, annoyed if she was kept in the dark on anything and annoyed once she was informed about something that she hadn't been told earlier. But that irritation drove her curiosity, and relentless curiosity was something Wang prized highly in an intelligence officer. "No?" he asked. "How not?"

"Our intelligence on the American flight composition has changed. I have sent details to you."

Wang turned on the tablet in front of him. The *Fujian* carrier task force had just finished monitoring the activities of the ships involved in the huge Western war games known as RIMPAC 2038. One US carrier strike group, based around the *USS Enterprise*. One Japanese carrier group, based around its carrier, the JS *Izumo*. A recently refitted Australian carrier, the *HMAS Adelaide*. And unusually, a UK carrier strike group based around *HMS Queen Elizabeth*. Each of the Western carriers fielded variants of the F-35 stealth fighter. In addition, the *Enterprise* could launch conventional fighters, or low-observability F-47 Fantom, Sentinel and Stingray drones. The expanded RIMPAC 2038 war games were not just a military exercise; they were a political one, intended to show China the sort of air and sea power that its enemies could muster if it decided to invade Taiwan.

But RIMPAC 2038 was over and its ships dispersing to ports across the globe. *Fujian* Air Wing's new mission orders had come through as the ship was also preparing to return to its home port in Shanghai. Wang called up the new intel Tan had sent to him, then frowned. "A C-5 Galaxy, as expected. But now it has *two* F-15EX long-range escorts. How reliable is your new information?"

"I have no reason to doubt it." Tan was not an aviator. "This complicates the mission, yes?"

"Yes," Wang said, leaning back with his hands behind his head and staring at the ceiling. "If a single tree falls in a forest, and no one hears, it can look like an accident. If *three* fall, it looks deliberate. The Vice Admiral was clear that we cannot engage in open conflict with the Americans." He rocked his chair back and forth. "We have to find a way to execute this mission but still avoid accusations of deliberate foul play."

Tan was not so concerned. "I do not understand the dilemma." She pointed toward the flight deck overhead. "You have 70 fighters in your wing. There are three aircraft in the American flight. You can meet them with overwhelming force and destroy them before they even understand what is happening."

"All it would take is a single mayday call from our target to raise suspicion," Wang explained. "And the Americans call these F-15EX escorts 'missile trucks.' Each of them can carry up to 22 air-to-air missiles. My entire air wing, as you say, is just 72 aircraft. At any time, four to six are undergoing maintenance. I cannot send the rest against this target and leave *Fujian* unprotected. So remove another 18 from that total. I would only be allowed to send 36 aircraft against them at best. Depending on their configuration, those two F-15s could carry 44 missiles: more than one missile for each of my fighters. If they are detected and the Americans respond aggressively, *Fujian*'s entire air wing could be rendered combat ineffective."

"Surely *not* the most likely outcome."

Wang grunted and paged down to the Maneuver Unit tasks in the revised OPORD. Under the heading "Interdiction," he read the mission order out loud.

Intercept the American transport aircraft and destroy it with the utmost discretion. It must not make Guam ... He clicked his fingers as he continued reading. "Pull up a map for me." Tan did so and lay her tablet in front of him so he could see it, and tapped an icon to display the *Fujian*'s planned route. A circle radiating out from the carrier showed the attack radius of his aircraft, which overlapped nicely with the different routes the Americans would most likely fly on their expected route from Hawaii to Guam. "We should intercept them midway through their flight, after an hour of uneventful flight, when they are dozing," he decided. "Where are the RIMPAC carrier strike groups now? The Americans could call for help from any of them."

Tan tapped an icon on her tablet screen and four icons appeared over the Pacific and Indian oceans. "The nearest will be ..." She did some calculations. "... *USS Enterprise*; currently more than a thousand miles from the expected intercept point. The American Galaxy and its two escorts will be all alone up there and surprise will be on your side," Tan pointed out.

Wang smiled. He had been young once, and his voice had vibrated with the same unfounded confidence. His loyalty and reputation for faithfully executing his orders had earned him command of the air wing on China's newest and largest aircraft carrier. But with experience had come a healthy dose of realism.

"What intel assets do we have on or over Hawaii?" he asked.

"We have 24/7 satellite coverage, optical and infrared. I suspect we also have one or more human sources in or near Hickham Air Base keeping an eye on what is taking off and landing," Tan said. "I've been told we can expect to receive a flash warning the moment the US cargo aircraft takes off."

He nodded. The Lockheed Galaxy was one of the biggest cargo aircraft in any air force. It would be hard to miss. "I need to know more than that. I need to know the projected route, how many and what type of aircraft are in the total package, and what those escorts are armed with."

"You ask a lot, Colonel. I will do what I can."

Wang ran his finger thoughtfully along a line from Hawaii to Guam. "Our best chance is to take them here, halfway, but finding them without alerting them will not be easy. The Americans will have the entire western Pacific Ocean to hide in."

"Yes, perhaps," Tan replied. "But we have *Vortex*."

As Tan and Wang planned her demise, Bunny was in a cab headed back to her accommodation. *We've spent 10 years trying not to wake the Chinese bear,* she was thinking. *The whole world is wondering when the US will make a material decision to openly support Taiwan and challenge China, and now this—we're basing fifth- and sixth-gen fighters on Taiwan and acting like we're not?*

It felt like something a politician thought was a clever idea. But the Chinese would react the same no matter what badge the stealth aircraft were flying under. They. Would. Be. Pissed. And this mysterious "ordnance" she would be carrying, where did that factor in?

Sure, she knew Taiwan was in trouble, and desperate times called for desperate deeds. The latest reports Bunny had read said Taiwan's 14-day strategic oil reserve had now been exhausted and it was already experiencing shortages in foodstuffs like fish, dairy products, rice and sugar. Without the ability to put to sea, its huge appetite for seafood had exhausted local fresh and frozen seafood stocks, which was putting pressure on local chicken and pork supplies. The population of 24 million wasn't starving yet, but supermarket shelves were emptying, gas stations were no longer selling to private citizens, and electricity was already being rationed.

Bunny had also heard rumors that the US and its allies were considering how to get humanitarian supplies into Taiwan, including a Berlin Airlift-style operation, with aircraft flying out of US bases in Okinawa, Japan. When she'd heard about that idea, she'd sold everything in her share portfolio and bought gold, since China had only one response for anything to do with Taiwan now, and that was to threaten open military conflict with anyone who interfered in its "internal affairs." A "Berlin-style" airlift? Ask her, Western nations might as well go straight to declaring war.

Bunny heard an aircraft taking off from the base across the road and rolled down her window, recognizing the roar of the engines. A Widow, so it was likely one of their own. If things were going to get "kinetic" on the transit across the Philippine Sea from Guam to Taipei, she was glad she was going to be in the cockpit of a Widow, and not the older Raptor. The Raptor was smaller and stealthier than the Widow and orders of magnitude better as a dogfighter, but though it could pull data from nearby aircraft like drone Stingrays and Valkyries, an F-22 pilot couldn't command them with anywhere near the ease a Black Widow pilot could.

Ironically, the Black Widow was given a P for Pursuit designation, but the P-99 Widow wasn't designed to "pursue" its enemy at all. Its drone wingmen had that role. A product of the Air Force Next Gen Air Dominance program, the Widow set peacetime records from drawing board to production line because it was essentially a scaled-down version of the B-21 Raider strategic bomber—a long-endurance, bat-winged flying command center—and its role was to prowl invisibly behind the aerial front line, assimilating and relaying data and communications and using "loyal wingmen" drones and its own long-range missiles to engage aerial and ground targets. It didn't carry a cannon, since it had no chance to outmaneuver any modern fighter aircraft, and if the enemy got within guns range, the Widow pilot's best chance of survival was to wave a virtual white flag and eject.

But for a four-hour flight, Bunny also liked the Widow over the Raptor because its cockpit was *roomy*. OK, no, it didn't exactly have the in-flight toilet or sleeping compartment of a B-21 Raider, but having been adapted from a strategic bomber which did, it featured two reasonably large stowage compartments in the cockpit, which could be used for survival equipment, extra piddle packs or T-shirts, or most important of all, *snacks*.

She looked at her watch and groaned. Their flight to Hawaii via San Diego was at 0400, after which she and Salt would have to run to make the Galaxy that was taking them to Guam. She had just enough time to get home, pack, sleep a stomach-churning two hours and get up so she could make her flight.

Cheer up. You can sleep when you're dead, O'Hare, she told herself for the hundredth time. *Which could be very, very soon.*

Okinotori Island was the most southerly land formation controlled by Japan—a possession disputed by several nations including China, but for now, not one that was disputed with gunboats and Marines. It was part of the Palau-Kyushu Ridge in the Philippine Sea and had been little more than a coral reef before Japan built its first marine research facility there in 1988. It was upgraded to a radar and surveillance station in the 1990s, and then, starting in the 2020s, a small port and runway were added, against vociferous Chinese opposition. China had been busy through the early part of the century mapping the seafloor around Okinotori—not because of any resources they expected to find there, but because the island lay almost exactly halfway between Taiwan and US naval and air bases on Guam and would be a potential rest and refitting port during any conflict, not to mention a transit point for US attack submarines.

None of this interested Takuya Kato. He held a Ph.D. in marine bioresources from the not-particularly prestigious institution of Fukui Prefectural Public University, and all Takuya Kato cared about was … coral. More specifically, how to keep it *alive* when everything around it, from humans to climate change, was trying to kill it. His Ph.D. had been obscure enough to earn him two years of unemployment before he was offered a job trying to regenerate the coral formations at Okinotori, which had just about been wiped out by decades of abuse caused by the sporadic construction and increasingly permanent human habitation on the reef. When he read the survey report to prepare for his job interview, he had one question.

"Why bother?" he'd asked the naval officer and the government official from the prefecture that administered the territory. "It's all but dead thanks to the port you built on top of it and it's not particularly rare."

"It may not be rare, but it is important," the naval officer had said. "For our claim to an economic zone around the reef to be valid, there has to *be* a reef. We are about to go to the international Maritime Court again, and no reef, no claim and no economic zone. Do you see, Kato-san?"

Kato pointed out his Ph.D. was in a species that lived nowhere in the Philippine Sea. The naval officer said that to the Japan Naval Self Defense Forces, coral was coral. "Do you know how to regenerate coral or not?"

"Yes. But you really should find an expert in the species that grow around Okinotori."

"Yes, we really should," the government official agreed. "However after three rounds of advertising, you are the only applicant."

That didn't surprise Kato. The position required the applicant to live on-site for a year, with only one return journey to Tokyo in that time. He would join a "thriving and curious team of marine biologists" who he later learned were only curious because they included an alcoholic female whale specialist called Niko, and Yuzu, an agoraphobic specialist in nothing really at all who Kato was not even convinced was sentient. Besides the two other scientists, the station consisted of a detachment of marines, combat engineers who maintained the tiny port as well as the station's power and water supply and staffed its radar and communications station.

Right now, the station was deserted except for Kato. The entire complement of Marines and scientists had flown back to Japan for Golden Week, that glorious Japanese tradition in which most of the country clocked off and celebrated national holiday after national holiday with travel, jazz and car racing. When he had learned the entire population of Okinotori, such as it was, was planning to bug out, Kato had volunteered to stay behind to keep the lights on since the idea of having the place to himself was simply too tempting to pass up. He could get more work done in a week than in a month of tiptoeing around the booze-addled Niko or the aggressively antisocial Yuzu.

So he nearly fell out of his small Zodiac as he was preparing to snorkel on one of the outer reefs two days into Golden Week when the buzzer he'd stowed in the bottom of the fiberglass boat rattled loudly. It was only supposed to do that in very rare situations: the failure of the power or water supply, a priority communication alert or a surface contact on the station's radar. Not that Japan was particularly fussy about

45

international shipping passing by Okinotori, but another justification for its existence was the lighthouse and radio beacon mounted on the superstructure of the station that was supposed to keep shipping from running aground on the reef and surrounding sand bars, and it was his job as watch officer to ensure the warning systems were functioning if a contact appeared.

He dropped his diving gear back into the bottom of the boat with a sigh and started up the motor, pointing it back toward the concrete and rusted iron pier at the base of the main station building that the Marines humorlessly called the port. The research station was a single three-story white building and associated machinery plant on a rusted platform built from three shallow-water oil exploration platforms, and to get from the water level up to the main building meant climbing the equivalent of three stories of rusted metal stairs or summoning an even slower crane-engine-operated elevator.

So Takuya Kato humped his grumpy 32-year-old ass up the rusted stairs and then into the white building and up a further two floors, past the offices on the ground floor, past the living quarters, "recreation" and kitchen area on the second floor and up to the communications and engineering level on the top floor. The grandly named "comms hub" was a windowless hole off the central corridor lined with screens Kato had never had to look at and radio or radar equipment he had no idea how to use. He only needed to understand one screen, the one in the middle of all the others with a sticky note on it saying, "Watch This Stupid." On the other screens and consoles were similar sticky notes: DON'T TOUCH THIS, OR THIS, OR THIS.

The main screen was a wide flat LCD divided into different status windows that showed him key data from the radar, radio comms, lighthouse systems, ocean-thermal power generation unit and water purification plant. He leaned on the console in front of it and squinted at it.

Radar. It was showing a single blip about 12 miles out, moving across the top of the screen, so *through* their radar field, but not *toward* Okinotori. That was good. He checked the radio beacon since it was still daylight and the lighthouse was not relevant. It was reporting a steady broadcast signal, sending out a message that could be detected up to 10 miles away warning nearby shipping they should check their course and coordinates as they could be approaching a shipping hazard. Out of habit, he ran his eye over the other windows. Power, good, water, good.

He scratched the stubble on his chin and straightened. No drama. After grabbing a cold juice downstairs, he would get back to work. He was seeding the ravaged seabed with glauconite and foraminifera and needed to get it done while it was still low tide. He gave the radar one last glance.

Oh, come on. Seriously?

The blip had changed course and was headed directly for Okinotori now. Was it in trouble or something? It was possible it had picked up the station's radio warning and was coming in for help. Should he hail it? It had happened a couple of times since Kato had arrived at the station, usually small freighters with engine or other mechanical problems, but once they'd been called on by an ocean-going pleasure cruiser that had run out of water because its stupid owner had ordered the crew to use its last fresh water to fill his swimming pool.

He should hail it.

He picked up the radio handset from the console next to him and checked the VHF radio was set to the maritime safety frequency. Before he pressed the button, he said a couple of sentences in English, practicing them out loud.

"Uh, unidentified ship north of Okinotori Island, this is Japanese Maritime Research Station Okinotori. Your current heading is taking you toward an area of submerged sandbanks and reefs. Do you need assistance?"

He released the transmission key and waited, hearing only static.

Was it his English? "Uh, unidentified ship? This is Japanese Research Station Okinotori Island. You are approaching navigation hazards. Do you need assistance?"

He nearly jumped out of his skin as the loudspeaker above him crackled to life.

"Japanese Research Station Okinotori, this is People's Liberation Army Navy research vessel *Yuan Wang Three Zero*. No help needed. We will anchor off your northeast quarter about five miles out from your position for an indefinite period as we affect minor repairs. I repeat, this is PLAN vessel *Yuan Wang*, no assistance is needed, Okinotori. Thank you and out."

Oh, crap. A Chinese navy vessel here, now? During Golden Week, when the place was deserted? That *couldn't* be a coincidence. What was he supposed to do? He tried to remember what the Marine captain had told him, right after telling him to *bloody touch nothing*. "Touch nothing ... but if anything happens you can't handle by just restarting or rebooting, get on the Sat Phone to Oceanographic Support Command and tell them." He'd pointed at one of two sat phone numbers written on tape and stuck to a screen. "Number is here." He then ripped the other number off, rolled the tape it was written on into a ball and threw it into a waste bin.

"What was that number?" Kato had asked.

"That was *my* sat phone number," the officer told him. "Don't call me when I'm on holiday or my wife will hunt you down and kill you."

Kato pulled a chair over and reached for the sat phone, then hesitated. What was he going to say? "Some Chinese navy ship says it is anchoring in our exclusive economic zone?" They'll ask you for details, dumbass. What had the Chinese radio operator said? PLAN vessel *Yuan Something*? He couldn't remember. He reached for a keyboard and logged onto the internet, running a search for PLAN vessels with names that sounded similar.

Yuan Wang. That was it. *Yuan Wang 30.* He read the entry on the screen. Oh, double crap.

PLAN vessel *Yuan Wang 30* launched in Shanghai, China, July 2028. *Yuan Wang* class vessels are used for tracking and support of satellite and intercontinental ballistic missiles …

Triple crap. He looked at the photographs. The vessel was massive—the size and rough shape of a cruise liner—covered in radomes and with two massive satellite dishes mounted amidships. What in hell was it doing off the coast of Okinotori? Was there a Chinese space launch coming up? Kato quickly ran a search for news about Chinese space launches just executed or planned for the immediate future but came up blank. Well, maybe not a surprise. They wouldn't exactly advertise every launch and it made sense they might station one of their satellite-tracking ships near the Indian Ocean depending on what they were firing where.

OK. The database entry for the ship said it carried a mixed civilian and military crew. So China probably wasn't about to use it to stage an invasion of his little reef. But a ship that tracked ballistic missiles? He had to phone it in to Japan's Oceanographic Support Command.

He stood, looking out the window that looked northeast over the station's raised metal and concrete runway, in the direction the Chinese ship would soon be anchoring. It might be close enough for him to see with binos. The runway caught his eye. It was about 8,000 feet long and 100 feet wide, and he'd been told it was rated for large military cargo aircraft, but the heavy wood and metal piles anchoring the concrete and sand to the seabed looked just as rusty as the rest of the station. Eyeballing it balefully, he wouldn't like to be landing in anything bigger than the usual twin-engined, 10-seater light passenger aircraft that flew supplies and personnel in and out, that was for sure. He reached for the number taped to the screen and sighed.

His foraminifera seeding would have to wait.

3. 'Or die trying ...'

O'Hare was not good at waiting. In fact, she didn't *do* waiting. She did pacing, and grumbling. A little sighing, and a good deal of whining. But she'd learned early in her military career that there would be a lot of waiting ahead of her, so she always had a pack of cards on her and played mind-bogglingly difficult solitaire games to distract herself.

As she and Salt and a bellyful of crates inside the Guam-bound C-5 Galaxy bumped through the sky out of Honolulu, she'd already worn her card deck thin. Looking across at Salt just made her angry. Guy could sleep anywhere, it seemed, and he'd slept on every leg of their flight from Arizona to California and then to Hawaii, waking up only to eat, use the latrine or change planes. They had been forced to jog halfway across Hickam Field to make the Galaxy that was taking them to Guam, but he hadn't broken a sweat and fell asleep as soon as his ass hit the bucket seat against the fuselage wall. She put away her cards, reached out with a boot and kicked his foot.

He opened one eye and looked at her. "What?"

"You think China will try to stop me?"

He closed his eye again. "They're trying to stop everything else that flies or sails, why not you?"

"You're not just saying that to motivate me?"

"Most people would not find that a motivation, O'Hare." He crossed his arms across his chest and lowered his chin to his chest in a clear signal he wanted to keep sleeping. She kicked his boot again.

"You didn't answer."

Salt straightened, rubbing a hand across his face before turning to her. "You were at the same briefing as me. Anything that tries to enter their air defense zone, they are turning around. They fired warning shots alongside a *commercial* airliner ... so yeah." He winked at her. "But to stop you, they have to find you, right?"

Bunny remembered the briefing just as well as Salt did. "And they've got a hulking great carrier task force right in the middle of the Philippine Sea that can do that for them."

"*Fujian*? Pfft," Salt scoffed. "We've got real-time on their position; you can easily avoid any patrols they put up. Plus, Navy has a plan for keeping them busy while you're in the neighborhood."

"Navy has a plan," Bunny said derisively. "You don't see a flaw in those four words? Because I do."

"Relax, will you?" Salt said. "China talks a big game, but when it comes down to it, they're no match."

"No match? In case you haven't been keeping up, Salt, China's army is 10 times larger than America's, it has the same number of tanks, more artillery, the same number of fighter aircraft, more unmanned aircraft, the same number of missile frigates, more destroyers, more submarines, three aircraft carriers ..."

"We have 11," Salt pointed out. "And that's just the *big* ones."

"China isn't aiming for global domination, just the Pacific and its home waters, so three is *plenty*."

"Nukes. We have over 5,000. China has what, a few hundred?"

"More than enough to destroy anyone who threatens them," Bunny shrugged.

"And ..." Salt raised a finger. "It's not just about quantity. No one can match us for advanced technology. Communications, surveillance, electronic warfare, laser, hypersonics, radar, satellites, missiles, stealth ..."

Bunny crossed her arms. "China has *two* stealth fighter types and is ahead of us in AI. Satellites? China's military satellite network is as capable as ours, and they also have a ring of hunter-killer satellites in orbit that can take down Western satellites at will. China is the only nation with a functioning space station and it's about to be the first nation to put a man on *Mars*. You really want to keep going?"

Salt opened his mouth to speak but didn't get the first word out. Without warning, the Galaxy heeled over onto its port wing and started losing altitude until the pilot corrected with an equally violent right roll. Salt and Bunny were tossed around like rag dolls, pinned in their seats by the shoulder and lap harnesses but limbs flapping at the sudden maneuver. As the plane righted itself, Salt started swearing, but Bunny punched her harness release and started running forward. Ignoring the warnings of the loadmasters sitting further along the cargo bay, she weaved between pallets of equipment and supplies until she got to the stairs leading up to the flight deck and took them two at a time.

She came out into the crew compartment to the sound of more cursing. A flight engineer was sitting on his butt in the passageway, holding his left knee. In the cockpit, voices were also raised, but sounded more angry than alarmed. With another jerk, the aircraft corrected its attitude again and

Bunny gripped the wall of a sleeping compartment next to the fallen engineer to steady herself.

"You alright, mate?" she asked, helping him up.

He stood unsteadily on one leg, rubbing his head. "Kneecap's all messed up," he said, wincing. "I was on my way out of the latrine … think I slammed my head on the way down too."

Bunny sat him down on a bunk and helped him get his leg up. He had an ugly gash across the back of his head and she gave him a pillow to hold against it. She went forward to the cockpit. She knew better than to ask questions and the busy crew didn't even notice her standing in the gangway. Bunny kept quiet and listened.

"Where is he now?!" the pilot was asking. His voice was strained like he was trying not to yell and not quite succeeding.

The other flight engineer had his face against a cockpit side window. "Four o'clock, level. There's two … I see two of them. Line abreast."

"How far?" the copilot asked.

"One klick, maybe two."

"*Bastards*," the pilot said. He turned to the copilot. "How'd they jump us?"

The engineer sat back in his seat and noticed Bunny. "Back in your seat and strap in, Lieutenant, we have a situation here."

"And you're a flight engineer down," Bunny said, nodding at the empty chair. "I just laid him on a bunk with a busted knee and concussion."

54

The pilot shot a look over his shoulder. He'd looked at the passenger manifest and knew who she was. "I need someone to monitor control and safety systems. You capable?"

"Can do."

"Sit down, pull on a headset, and strap in then."

Bunny slid into the vacant seat, pulled on a wireless headset and surveyed the unfamiliar instrument screens in front of her. It took her a second or two to orient herself, but a multifunction display was a multifunction display and she pretty quickly realized what she was looking at: engine settings and temperatures, fuel flow and fuel levels, system status readouts, flap and control surface settings ... everything looked nominal.

The other engineer leaned over to her. "What do we call you?"

"Lieutenant will do," she said. "What happened?"

"We got buzzed. Instruments went wild, lost radio contact, jamming probably. Then these guys came out of nowhere, no radar warning," the engineer said, jerking his thumb over his right shoulder. "Chinese uncrewed fighters, looks like. Two CH-7s, keeping station off our starboard wing now. Our escorts were fast asleep. They scattered. Coming back up to altitude now, trying to get shit under control."

China's newest killer drones were bat-winged supersonic naval fighters that could launch from a carrier deck, carrying up to 1,800 lbs. of ordnance. Bunny was about to ask whether the Chinese fighters off their bow were armed when the F-15 flight leader's voice interrupted.

"Unidentified aircraft off our starboard side, this is United States Air Force flight out of Honolulu, flight designation FORTE-2, requesting you to back the hell off. We are documenting your actions and you *will* be reported to international flight safety authorities for that little stunt."

Documenting their actions? *Ooh, that will scare them away,* Bunny thought.

"Can they even hear us?" the engineer asked.

"They can hear us," Bunny told him. "Just as well as they can see us. Drone pilots might be back aboard their carrier, but they'll be monitoring comms. Give them a second ..."

But there was no reply from the Chinese fighters. The F-15 pilot repeated his message, a little more calmly the second time. Still no reply.

"Any reaction?" the Galaxy pilot asked.

The copilot had his neck craned over his shoulder. "I think ... yeah. One of them is moving ahead of us, the other is holding off our wing. I can't see the F-15s ..."

Bunny knew the situation would unnerve the C-5's crew. Their escorts would have pulled back, getting some separation and trying to lock up the aggressive Chinese drones in case the situation went kinetic. The Chinese aircraft were pilotless. There was no helmeted figure sitting behind a bubble of cockpit glass for the Galaxy crew to eyeball, just the smooth, featureless gray nose housing the distributed aperture cameras and radar that the Chinese carrier-based pilots were using to monitor the cargo plane. The mental advantage was all theirs.

"What the hell is he doing now?" the copilot asked.

Bunny could see the Chinese fighter now as it pulled ahead of them, still on a parallel track on their starboard side. It was ignoring the warning from the American fighters. The Chongming had a small radar cross section but was not a sixth-generation stealth fighter. It lacked the latest in radar-absorbent coatings and had to carry its recon instruments or weapons on pylons under its fuselage and wings. Bunny was relieved to see this one was clean—no visible weapons. That didn't mean it was defenseless though. It might be electronic warfare capable, able to do anything from jamming their communications to firing a microwave energy burst at them.

And the big, slow, fat C-5 was an easy target.

As though reading her mind, Bunny saw the pilot push the throttles forward and heard the note of the C-5's four turbofan engines rise. They couldn't outrun the Chinese fighters, but they didn't have to make the job of keeping pace easy for them either.

Bunny ran her eyes across the instrument panels in front of her, saw nothing alarming, then turned her attention back to the Chinese drone, her fighter pilot eyes watching its near imperceptible control surfaces, trying to read its intentions. It was only a half mile ahead of them and seemed to be getting closer. An optical illusion. It was closing lateral distance, not separation.

"It's going to pull in front of you," she decided. "You should change altitude in case it decelerates."

"Thank you, Lieutenant, I can see it," the pilot said. "You keep your eyes on your instrument screen for me."

He might be tetchy, but he wasn't a fool. Bunny saw him ease back on his flight stick, and the Galaxy climbed. He let his escorts know what he was doing. The Galaxy was already at 35,000, and could probably move up to about 40,000 in the kind of conditions she was seeing outside the window.

"Bastard is moving up with us," the copilot remarked. "Right off our nose now. No, he's moving a little higher than us."

Lifting herself out of her seat a little to look over the pilot's shoulder, Bunny could see the Chinese fighter directly ahead of them, still about a mile out.

Bunny saw the outline of the Chinese fighter blur slightly. "Break left!" Bunny called. "*Break!*"

But she was too late. The blur she'd recognized had been a cloud of radar-defeating metal foil chaff being released from the back of the Chinese fighter. Or *multiple clouds.* In seconds, a stream of tiny strips of foil enveloped them and then whipped behind them into their wake.

The Galaxy's pilot had reacted immediately to Bunny's frantic warning, but turning the Galaxy was like turning a supertanker at sea, and it had no chance of dodging the clouds of foil. Usually fired by a fighter trying to dodge a radar-guided missile, the globs of metal strips were sucked into the open maw of the Galaxy's GE turbofan engines and Bunny dropped her eyes immediately to the instruments in front of her as the pilot struggled to keep their machine from losing too much altitude as it turned.

"Son of a ..." the pilot muttered. "Engines, status!"

Bunny was focused on the engine readouts. "Engines one through three nominal ... uh, rotation speed anomaly on engine four, low-pressure turbine!" Another blinking icon caught her eye. "Temperature warning on four."

"Emergency shutdown, engine four," the pilot commanded.

"I got it," the engineer beside her replied. All Bunny could do was watch and listen as their outer starboard engine wound down. "Engine four powering down."

"Declare an emergency; get me Wake control. I'm taking us down," the pilot told his copilot.

Bunny had a navigation screen on her left and glanced at it. They were about 150 miles from the US base at Wake Island. She had no idea how much cargo they were carrying, but judging by how the Galaxy had handled during that last emergency maneuver, it was pretty heavy. Three good engines should get them to Wake with no problem though. Over the radio she heard their escort fighters react, locking up the Chinese aircraft with their targeting radars and ordering them to pull away or be fired on.

A blinking warning light caught her eye before a computerized warning started sounding in her ears. *Oh hell.* "Turbine shaft vibration on two," she called, voice raised above the voice of the copilot who was trying to contact Wake Island air traffic control. "Automatic shutdown initiated." Now she heard the note change on the inboard port engine as the engine's automatic sensor system cut fuel to that engine too. They were down to two engines … the only good thing being that they still had thrust symmetry, with one engine out on each side.

"I'll get Wake on sat comms," the copilot said. "We got enough power to get us there?"

"We got plenty," the pilot said, with a confidence Bunny wasn't really feeling. "Where are those Chinese fighters?"

Bunny released her harness and stood, looking out the cockpit window nearest her as the engineer rose and looked out the window beside him.

"I got nothing here," she said after a moment.

"Me either. I think they bugged out," the engineer said. He listened to the F-15 pilots' comms in his headset. "Escorts are following them away. Yeah ... they're breaking off."

"Alright, you two. Sit down, shut up, and keep your eyes on your screens," the pilot said. "We are 10 minutes out of Wake and I am going to land this mother flawlessly ..."

"Or die tryin'," the copilot finished his sentence and held out his hand for a high five, a routine they'd obviously delivered plenty of times before.

The engineer in the other jump seat smiled at her reassuringly. Bunny didn't need reassuring. She'd had engines flame out on her before, made unpowered landings, blasted out of her cockpit, ass on fire after a missile strike ...

No, Bunny O'Hare wanted to pull the pilot out of his seat by the collar of his flight suit and jump in behind the yoke. Being a *passive* crewmember in a plane declaring an emergency was wayyyy outside her comfort zone. Trying to deal with the rising frustration, she focused instead on analyzing what had just happened. What the Chinese fighters had done went beyond aerial high jinks, or even harassment. Falling just short of a direct attack, it was an aggressive act of stupidity that might still result in the loss of their aircraft. Unless it wasn't stupidity, but a deliberate act of geopolitical point-scoring. A little "screw you" just to reinforce China's current, or virtually permanent, state of displeasure with all things American.

In which case Salt's belief she could be in for a rough ride from Guam to Taiwan was looking more like a prophecy than an abundance of caution. The Galaxy was dropping through clouds now and hit a pocket of bad air, sending a shudder

60

through its airframe similar to the one going through Bunny's mind.

Of course, what China was planning to do to them on the flight from Guam was moot right now. They had to make it safely down on the tiny speck of sand and coral that was Wake Island first.

Or die trying ...

The pilot of the aircraft that had intercepted the American C-5 was at no risk of dying. He never had been, really. But he would have been very happy indeed if his actions had resulted in the loss of the American cargo behemoth. And its entire crew.

So he had been disappointed to see it turn slowly away to the south with one engine trailing smoke, but still apparently fully in control. He had achieved his mission objective—to intercept and disable the American C-5—but not his personal one.

His name was Pilot Officer Asien Chen, and a US pilot had killed his sister, Li. Asien had been presented with his sister's posthumous medal at a military ceremony, and had never been told the circumstances of his sister's death, only that she had died during an incident over the South China Sea at the hands of an American pilot, "heroically defending the sovereignty of her motherland." Whatever the "incident" had been, it had been a significant one. Chen was one of dozens of family members presented with medals during the closed-door ceremony.

As he had walked up on stage to receive his sister's medal from her commanding officer, Chen, a trainee naval aviator himself, had boldly asked the General to be posted to his sister's squadron in the PLA Navy when he graduated. The man had simply replied that he should apply himself to his training and accept that the PLA Navy would post him where it felt he could best serve his country. He had done as he was asked. But he couldn't help but feel the hand of the General at play when he saw he was going to his sister's squadron after all: the Ao Yin, or *Bull Demons*, and to serve aboard China's new flagship, the supercarrier *Fujian*. From that day forward, he had been trying to prove himself worthy of his sister's legacy.

His older sister, Li, had been among the last generation of pilots trained to fly crewed naval fighter aircraft; Asien, one of the first generation trained to fly China's new CH-7 'Chongming' drone. It had gotten its name from the Chongming Niao, a powerful bird in ancient Chinese folktales, capable of defeating beasts 10 times its size as it could see its enemies both in the present and in the future, with double-irised eyes.

The CH-7 Chongming flown by Chen could also see into the future because it had a direct data link to the top-secret *Yuan Wang* class "research vessel," *Three Zero*. A vessel with technology so advanced the pilots who were linked to it had been told only that it was a new type of radar.

Officially, *Three Zero* was a satellite tracking and communication vessel. Carefully planted intelligence leaks had convinced Western militaries that *Three Zero* was also used by China to track intercontinental ballistic missiles in flight and predict their trajectories so they could be intercepted. It could do these things ... and *so* much more.

Three Zero had no conventional radar of its own, but it could assimilate sensor and communications data from multiple sources simultaneously—satellite, drones, aircraft, ground units, even subsea sensors—and present it to the soldier, sailor or air officer who needed it, at quantum speeds, in easily digestible fashion. Most importantly it could do so over an area nearly 300 miles in diameter, compared to an American *Aegis* air warfare destroyer's radar range of about 200 miles. But *Three Zero* had an even better trick hiding inside a small and innocuous dome on its deck.

Asien Chen had not needed to use radar to intercept the American C-5. *Three Zero* had directed the Chinese flight of two Chongming fighters directly into the path of the C-5 Galaxy without either the ship or the interceptor aircraft even once using their own radar—by creating a tornado-shaped microwave vortex *and shooting it into the sky.*

High-frequency radar slid off the skin of modern stealth aircraft without picking them up. Low-frequency radar could detect them but worked too slowly to guide missiles at the targets it identified. *Three Zero*'s quantum radar shot electrons through a winding trumpet-shaped tube of magnetic fields and created a blast cone that bathed the sky, instantly detecting any object in a 20-degree arc up to the level of the ionosphere.

When scientists at Tsinghua University Aerospace Engineering School first announced their breakthrough in 2021, a prominent quantum physicist at MIT told Science Magazine, "There are just so many problems with this idea I don't know where to start." The Tsinghua research team soon went quiet and the science world assumed the project had died. But the reason the Chinese team went quiet was that their project was transferred to a facility run by the Chinese National Defense Commission for Science, Industry and Technology. They were given a virtually unlimited budget, and in 10 years, they had a working prototype. In 15 it had been scaled up and mounted on *Three Zero*, coupled with a shipboard quantum computing mainframe to sort through the hundreds of thousands of returns and classify them in microseconds, then hand off its calculations to China's *Type 055* anti-air destroyers, circling aircraft, or land-based defenses.

Sure, the moment it fired its microwave vortex into space, it radiated like a small sun, and any radar warning receiver in the area would light up like a halogen bulb. But the vortex jammed the avionics of anything in its arc while it was active, and by the time the target was unblinded, *Three Zero* had all the data it needed, and it was dark again, ready to move to a new position.

Three Zero could detect a swallow at a range of 100 miles, and a seagull out to 300. But even better, it could tell the difference between the swallow and the seagull, and plot a missile intercept trajectory for both. *Three Zero* was the hub of the baddest anti-air, anti-missile system afloat. But neither the captain, his crew nor the radar technicians aboard *Three Zero* had any idea how it worked. They were not indoctrinated into its secrets, only the instructions they needed to operate it. To them, it was simply "Advanced Sensor System 090: code name Vortex" and any of them who was curious enough to probe the Tsinghua technicians aboard *Three Zero* about the scientific marvel that was their new "radar" got the cover story that it was simply a copy of the American Aegis system. This satisfied them, as everyone on board *Three Zero* quietly assumed that anything American was of course superior to the reverse-engineered crap which Chinese engineers and scientists foisted on the People's Liberation Army Navy.

Located near Okinotori Reef, halfway between Guam and Taiwan, *Three Zero*'s Vortex crew picked up the lumbering Galaxy in microseconds, calculated a projected track for it and shot the data to Asien Chen.

Chen and his flight leader had orbited their drones above the interception sector for less than 10 minutes before their avionics blanked and automatically shut down to avoid damage from *Three Zero*'s microwave vortex. When it passed and their systems came online again, the American aircraft had appeared on their tactical displays courtesy of the PLA Navy radar, and optical-infrared sensors soon picked them up. They dropped on the unsuspecting American flight like the birds of prey their Chongmings were, completely undetected until they flashed across the nose of the lumbering gray cargo plane to take up station off its wings, ignoring the two escorts, who scattered like frightened pigeons.

The angry hail over the open guard radio channel from the escorts had been expected. And ignored. Aboard *Fujian*, the two pilots sat in racecar-like carbon shell cockpits deep down in the aircraft carrier's heavily armored bowels and prepared the maneuver they had been ordered to execute: the destabilization of the main enemy's aircraft by forcing it to fly in the vortex of Chen's Chongming drone.

But as he prepared to drop back on the C-5, a heat had risen in his chest. Was this *all*? That he should try to destroy the American aircraft by *indirect* means? To cause a moment of panic on the flight deck of the Galaxy and then withdraw? What signal would that send? What would his sister think of him, if that was all? It grated on him to do so, but he had dumped chaff into his wake as ordered and had been happy to see the American cargo plane spiral out of orbit toward the sea, only to watch in frustration as it recovered, limping away toward the safety of the American base at Wake Island.

And now he stood before his Wing Commander. Colonel Wang Wei had left him standing at attention for a good minute, not acknowledging his entry into his commanding officer's stateroom, reading through a report on the tablet PC in front of him before pushing it aside and lifting his eyes to regard Chen with ... what? Disdain? Irritation? No ... something else.

"So, Vice Admiral Bing's special favor finally comes to bite me on the ass," Wang said. "I have to admit I expected it might take longer before you made your auspicious presence felt here."

Chen held his head firm, staring at the wall over the Colonel's head. He had not been asked a question, and so he stayed mute.

"Take the boy under your wing, the general said. Don't draw any attention to him, but keep an eye on him. See that he gets a chance to prove himself. His sister was a hero of the motherland; he must be given the chance to honor her sacrifice, but make him earn it. 'Yes, General,' I said. 'Of course, General.'"

The Colonel stood and kicked his chair aside with explosive violence. Chen flinched but stayed silent.

"Good. At least you know when to shut your damn mouth. No protests or stupid excuses." Wang ran a hand through salt and pepper hair. "Your orders were to *bring that aircraft down*. Your performance up there did not honor the memory of your sister," he said. "I knew her. Did you know that?"

Asked a question at last, Chen lowered his eyes and looked into the Colonel's face. He saw sadness. "No, Colonel, I did not."

"She was the commander of Ao Yin Squadron when I joined the *Liaoning*. In the air she was cold, clinical. She was not a natural pilot. More technician than artist. But her pilots knew she would die on a flaming sword for any one of them and eventually, she did. Do you know what the other Bull Demon pilots called her? Her call sign?" He indicated the chair beside Chen. "Sit, boy."

Chen sat, back straight, fingers curled into knuckles on his knees.

"I asked you a question," Wang said, still standing.

"Mamma Bull."

"Yes, *Mamma Bull*. Tough. Aggressive. A leader. That's the legacy you have to live up to. Are you worthy of it?"

"No sir, I am not," Chen said.

"Damn right you aren't. Do you know how she died? I was in the air with her that day. Do you *want* to know?"

Did he? He knew she died a hero. But exactly how … yes, of course he wanted to know. "Sir, yes, I would like to know."

Wang looked down on Chen as though weighing each of the words he was about to deliver. "She died attacking an *inferior* opponent in an *inferior* aircraft and her death may have cost the motherland victory that day."

The heat rose in Chen's chest again. He could not contain himself. "Sir, my … my sister died a *hero*."

Wang leaned down and lifted his chair, righting it and setting it behind his desk again. He sat down in it and leaned forward, both elbows resting on the desk. "She did. But the homeland lost 70 heroes that day. Think about that number."

Chen blinked. *What?*

Wang leaned back in his chair. "Ah. They didn't teach you that at the academy, did they? The 'Pagasa Incident,' I think the Western press called it. Not even a footnote in the history of the conflict between our two great nations. The main enemy didn't want to talk about their losses either, so both sides have hidden the truth, but we who were there that day, we know the truth." Wang straightened a crease on his trousers, and brushed off an invisible hair. Then he fixed Chen with a hard gaze. "The People's Republic of China does not need more dead heroes, Pilot Officer Chen. It needs pilots who can execute orders."

Leaning forward, Wang tapped his tablet and a screen came to life on the wall beside them. "What do you see when you look at this screen, Chen?" Chen studied it. It showed *Fujian*'s current area of operations, from Taiwan in the west to the Philippines in the southwest, with Japan to their northwest.

"I see our carrier strike group, Colonel." Icons on the screen also marked the American bases on Hawaii, Guam, Wake Island and, of course, on Japan. Not to mention the separatists on Taiwan. "Surrounded by enemies."

"You see the obvious. Do you know what I see, Chen?"

"No, Colonel."

"Sadly." He rotated his chair and stared at the map for a moment. "I see a need for pilots who are not mindless robots, blindly executing orders. I need pilots who can *think*." He narrowed his eyes. "You were ordered to chaff that transport plane, to disable its engines, yes?"

"Yes, Colonel. I am sorry, I failed, Colonel."

"And tell me, Chen. Did you think beyond your failure to what you should do next? Your objective was to force that plane into the sea in a way we could claim was an unfortunate mishap. Did you do so?"

"No, Colonel."

"You were focused on your orders. A pilot with initiative would have seen his tactic failed, and adopted a plan B ..."

"Plan B?"

"Ram the American. Force an 'accidental' mid-air collision. Damage the adversary's machine so badly it could not continue ..." He shook his head sadly. "An officer should always be focused on the objective, not the plan. The 'plan' becomes ancient history the moment we set eyes on the enemy."

"But, Colonel ..."

"I know. You were not ordered to do so."

"I am sorry, I failed to ..."

Wang laughed bitterly. "Your expression of regret is pointless, Officer Chen. You would be on a helo off this ship and bound for a desk job if not for the legacy of your sister and the influence of your benefactor, Vice Admiral Bing. Is that clear?"

Chen swallowed hard. "Yes, Colonel."

Wang stood again, looking down at Chen. "I was ordered by Vice Admiral Zhang to destroy that transport, deniably. I assured him we would and I relied on you to deliver on that promise. You failed yourself, me, *and* the Vice Admiral today. You are dismissed."

Chen stood, saluted, turned and left the stateroom, his ears and cheeks glowing red.

4. 'A sky full of stars.'

As Chen retreated from his personal near-death scenario, Bunny and Salt were reliving theirs. True to their boasts, the two Galaxy pilots had landed their crippled machine at Wake, one engineer down and with two dead engines. With runway to spare.

What surprised Bunny was not that they had made it down. True, the Galaxy pilots only had one chance to stick their landing, without the power to execute a go-around if they screwed up, but they had a straight-in, straight-down run, and hell, nothing was on fire. No, what surprised Bunny was how shaken up Salt was. They'd agreed to stand the Galaxy crew to drinks on the tiny island's only bar after their debrief, and Salt had really gone at it hard. He'd challenged the Galaxy pilot to a game of darts in an Irish bar on Wake where every round of six darts that didn't score a bullseye meant a shot of tequila … and he hadn't thrown a good game. Bunny had helped him to the nearest bathroom where he'd spent 10 minutes steering the porcelain bus before she left a hundred on the bar for the Galaxy crew who were still going strong, and got Salt outside for some fresh air.

Salt had another heave in a back alley and then stood, wiping his mouth.

"You looking at?" he slurred at her, leaning against a wall.

"Dunno, boss, what am I looking at?"

He tried to focus behind her. "Find whatever passes for a cab here. We gotta get home. Shit gonna hit the fan tomorrow." He tried to push past her.

"Why? What do you know I don't?"

"Nuthin."

He pushed against her but she wasn't moving. "What's up, Salt? You feeling your mortality suddenly?"

Salt tried again to push her away and then stepped back, flustered. "Hell, O'Hare, you really are a stupid sunnabitch, you know that?"

Bunny wasn't fazed. "Yeah, people keep telling me that. But enlighten me."

Salt pointed at the dark sky. "You think that was a coincidence? Huh? What happened up there?"

Bunny shrugged. "We got buzzed. The a-holes wanted to make a point about who owns the sky over the Pacific, but the Eagles chased them off. It's not the first time, won't be the last."

He gave an exaggerated laugh. "Of all the flights crossing the Pacific in all 64 million square miles of sky they just *happened* to pick on ours?"

Bunny crossed her arms. "Whoa boss, check that ego. You think you and me being aboard that Galaxy had anything to do with what happened?"

Salt swerved around her. "You dunno nuthin. What happened up there wasn't … there are things that … forget it."

Bunny followed him out to the street. "Wasn't what? Things that are what?"

But Salt had seen what must have been the island's only taxi down the street and stepped out in front of it, waving his arms like a windmill. Bunny got him inside it and leaned up against a door with the window open, then told the driver to take them back to the airfield.

Bunny watched roadside stalls roll past her window. The airfield at Wake had been upgraded with the pivot to Asia of US forces, but it was still little more than a boomerang-shaped mound of sand and scrub in the middle of an enormous ocean. It housed airfield ground crew, a civilian administration, Army Patriot anti-air and High Mobility Artillery Rocket Systems, or HIMARS, anti-ship batteries. They would be sleeping in the Galaxy tonight, while another machine was dispatched to fetch them and the cargo from the one that had been damaged. Salt soon had his eyes closed and head back, either out of it, or pretending to be. On Guam they would be briefed on the next leg of the mission and she would check out the machine she was ferrying to Taiwan to make sure everything was in working order before a wheels-up at 1300.

Something didn't sit right in Bunny's gut. They were still well outside the 12-hour "bottle-to-throttle" time limit but she'd never seen Salt lose control like he had tonight. The guy was usually as buttoned up as a cat's butthole. She'd never been in combat with him, but she'd flown his wing in dozens of red-on-blue engagements and he'd never once blinked, even when things got hairy. But they get buzzed by a Chinese fighter and he goes on a total bender? It wasn't the first time she'd seen him drunk, but it was the worst. And it wasn't even midnight!

She shook her head and let it go. Guy probably had something private going on that she didn't know about. And if she was honest, she didn't want to know. As long as he did

72

his job, and got them to Taiwanese airspace without screwing up, she would wave him goodbye in Taipei and take the two weeks bonus leave she'd been offered for agreeing to this little "potentially kinetic" shitshow. Maybe jump a flight to Singapore—an RAF friend of hers who owed her a few drinks was stationed there now.

Salt was always having "family issues" of one kind or another, something she didn't have to worry about. Which suited her fine. She had no serious partner, no living relatives. Hell, she'd never even had a dog or cat. She had plenty of buddies though. Alright, a few. A couple she'd even call friends. Not that she didn't get lonely or want company, but somehow something she did inevitably pissed people off. A badly timed insult here, moody silence there, the occasionally impulsive punch to the jaw. People were so damned *sensitive*.

She rested her head on the back of the seat and began dozing as the cab bounced through the night.

Yeah, an in-room massage every day and mai tais on the balcony at Raffles. She looked over at Salt. She wasn't a total idiot. She had some idea what he'd been babbling about. The only things standing between her and a honey-colored furlough were the wreck in the seat beside her, and 1,700 miles of sky.

Plus, if the day's events were any guide, the Chinese People's Liberation Army Naval Air Force, which had just shown a personal interest in the activities of Karen 'Bunny' O'Hare.

<< Karen O'Hare was sitting at the bottom of a hole, knees drawn up to her chest, shivering, staring up at stars. Well, not a hole exactly.

A rainwater tank on a concrete stand, the top of it rusted away and the bottom littered with the dirt and debris of 20 years of disuse.

She was 13 and her grandpa had "tanked her" again. She was too big then, and he was too old, for him to grab her and throw her over his shoulder and climb up the side of the tank with her and bundle her inside it like he used to. But he could still get her in there, because the alternative was a belting and the wiry old man was still strong enough to dish one out.

The memory that flashed unbidden into Bunny's mind as she was crash-landing her Widow was the time she accidentally started his ancient Skyreach Bushcat and found herself taxiing down the dirt strip behind the machine shed on the family cattle station, as terrified as she'd ever been in her short life. She'd had a few turns on the stick and throttle when they were out mustering cattle or checking water holes—she couldn't start learning for her pilot's license until she was 14, but she'd bugged the old man ceaselessly to let her get started early. She watched his every move in the cockpit until she had the startup routine down pat, and that day she'd been messing about in the cockpit, flipping switches just like him, not thinking for a moment that the damn thing would actually start.

Until it did. Because the stupid old dope had left the master switch on from their flight earlier in the day.

The Bushcat was bumping along the strip, propellor whirling and engine popping as she tried everything she could think of to shut it down. The Bushcat had large Perspex panels in the pilot and passenger side doors so that they could get a good look at the ground just by tilting the aircraft, and suddenly she saw her grandpa there, arms cartwheeling, grabbing at the passenger door handle. She reached over and kicked it open for him with one of her feet and he reached inside, grabbing onto whatever he could, before half dragging himself, half being dragged inside.

He leaned over in front of her and scrabbled for the magnetos, killing the engine.

The machine had barely finished rolling before he'd hauled her out and was dragging her through the dirt toward the tank beside their homestead. He was panting from running after her, but he said nothing, which to Bunny was worse than if he was bawling her out. She'd rather take a belting than spend another night in the tank, but he knew that, the old bastard.

He dumped her, sobbing, at the base of the tank and stood over her. His face was a thundercloud. He pointed at the ladder up the side of the tank. "Get in there before I knock the living breath out of you." And she looked at the belt that held his jeans up over his skinny ass and knew he meant it. Because there was no one to protect her anymore since her parents died, and except during the muster, she was all alone with the sadistic madman, on an outback cattle station the size of the state of Delaware. So she climbed up the side and then down the ladder propped up against the inside, and he followed her up, pulling the ladder out of the tank, throwing it on the ground behind him, leaving her in there. Sometimes he came back as night was falling and threw a bottle of water in there for her to drink from and piss in, but that time he didn't.

So 13-year-old Karen O'Hare sat in the dirt and rust and shivered and stared up at the stars. She wasn't feeling sorry for herself. She was thinking now she knew how to start it, and she already knew how to fly it, so one day she was going to take that bloody Bushcat and fly it the hell out of here.

Michael Chase had a big day ahead as well. One he had dreaded from the moment he had laid eyes on the Aggressor Inc. press release. And dreaded even more as he dug into the dark game of geopolitical bluff that lay behind it. Because Chase was now one of the few people in the Pentagon who knew a truth that the American people did not yet know.

America was going to throw down the gauntlet to China over Taiwan. Plans had been made to supply a soon-to-be starving Taiwan by air. It had its own internal code name, but it would soon become public and the communications geniuses in the Pentagon had given it a media-friendly code name: "Operation Skytrain," named after the workhorse of the Berlin Airlift, the C-47 Skytrain.

Outside the circle of "need to know," it was talked about as a "contingency plan." Michael Chase had just learned it was much more than that.

Operation Skytrain would completely dwarf the 277,000 flights and 2.3 million tons of cargo flown during the Berlin Airlift. Supplies would be stockpiled on Okinawa and freighted over by heavy cargo aircraft, flying under the banner of a multinational coalition including the US, Canada, South Korea, Japan, the UK and Australia. A literal "sky train" of cargo aircraft would fly nonstop between Okinawa and Taipei, 24 hours a day, seven days a week. The coalition of governments committed to the operation had been told they would need to support it for *at least* one year, and be prepared for it to be extended.

All of this, Operation Skytrain planners were certain, China's spies would eventually learn. And China would try to signal the Western coalition partners that the idea was folly. Signals such as the recent and particularly unsubtle interception of a US C-5 Galaxy cargo aircraft off the coast of Wake Island, perhaps. Which was the subject of his now daily call with General Huang.

"No, General Huang, we are absolutely certain that the aircraft were Chinese," Chase was saying. "I can get clearance to send you the video, if you require it."

76

"I am afraid that will be necessary," the Chinese general replied. "I do not know about any such incident involving a Chinese military aircraft. I suggest you check with your so-called allies in the region. Perhaps they were playing games with you? The Indian Air Force has some long-range drones."

Chase did not rise to the bait. "Actually, General, if you tune into any news network tonight, I think you will see an edited version of the fighter escort camera vision we will be releasing to broadcast networks, along with our condemnation of China's action in causing such catastrophic damage to our aircraft that it was forced to make an emergency landing."

The Chinese general on the video screen did not bat an eyelid. "*Another* fake video, Mr. Chase? Do you never tire of trying to convince the world your Hollywood creations are reality?" He waved a hand as though swiping the screen right. "Perhaps you should be more careful where you fly your military transport aircraft. Accidents can so easily happen."

The threat was not even thinly veiled, and Chase knew it was probably triggered by China's rising unease about the intelligence it was receiving on Operation Skytrain. Or their pique over the recent announcement about the F-22s on Taiwan.

Chase did not rise to the bait. "This is just a courtesy call, General. We will make our protests through the usual channels and take measures to protect our cargo aircraft even better in the future. Please make a note of that last remark." He said goodbye and ended the call.

He closed his laptop and leaned back, staring up at the ceiling. People around the building he worked in thought they knew what Operation Skytrain was. After his top-secret, eyes-only briefing from the Under Secretary of Navy, Michael Chase was now one of the few people in the world who *really* knew. And more importantly, he had learned that with the imminent flight of the lone Black Widow aircraft from Guam to Taiwan, Operation Skytrain had *already started*. Depending on your definition of "humanitarian."

"We passed GICL two hours ago, O'Hare," Salt was saying.

Bunny had checked in one last time with her crew chief, and she and Salt were completing the walkaround of her aircraft as they talked. The "Good Idea Cutoff Line," or GICL, was the moment in a mission planning phase when no new ideas could be introduced. As Mission Commander, Salt drew his line a lot earlier than Bunny did. As far as she was concerned, you could keep having good ideas right until the moment an enemy missile stopped you from having any ideas at all.

"It's not a new good idea. It's just a good idea you said no to in the briefing. I'm just saying, think about it again," Bunny said.

"You are not going up there alone," Salt told her. His flight jacket had the Aggressor Inc. patch on one shoulder (*Aggressor Inc: We Bring It*) and a patch featuring a saltshaker on the other. He had not earned his call sign for the more obvious suspicion of throwing salt over his shoulder for luck, but for the habit he had of always reminding his pilots of their mistakes—salt in their wounds. "You were at the brief. China has multiple air defense assets along your route and you will be trying to thread a tiny needle." He slapped the belly of the Widow. "Air Force is kindly leasing us this shiny new machine, and we have promised to deliver it and its payload to Taiwan, so you will kindly accept any additional assistance you are offered."

"Yeah, and about that ..." O'Hare said.

On their arrival on Guam, Salt had shared the fact she wouldn't be flying with an empty payload bay. Bunny had done a double take when she was told what she would be delivering to Taiwan *inside* her Widow. The Hypersonic Attack Cruise Missile, or HACM, was probably one of the most powerful and least talked about air-to-ground weapons in the US inventory. Another phrase often used to describe the HACM was "carrier killer." China currently fielded three aircraft carriers, and nestled in her Widow's payload bay were three carrier-killer missiles, bound for Taiwan. It occurred to Bunny that if it found out about them, China might have an interest in those missiles not arriving on Taiwan.

The HACM missile could fly at speeds greater than Mach 5, or 3,800 miles an hour, could fly anywhere between 100 to 60,000 feet and reach farther than 300 nautical miles. More importantly, it could be launched from multiple aircraft types and cover that 300-mile distance in just *four minutes*. Autonomous targeting and terminal phase maneuvering capabilities made the HACM virtually impossible for conventional missile defenses to jam or intercept in the one to two minutes they might have to even detect it. China's three carriers, and the more than 150 aircraft they could launch, were a pivotal part of its blockade of the sea and skies around that island, and the US was about to give Taiwan's air force the capability to quickly destroy them. *All* of them.

When she had been told what she would be transporting, the mission had finally made sense. All this effort, just to sneak a Widow into Taiwan for training? That had seemed a bit cockeyed, but Bunny had seen stupider things in her time in the military. But sneak a Widow into Taiwan carrying strategic weapons that could change the balance of power in the Taiwan Strait? Yeah, *that* made a little more sense. And severely challenged her already hard-to-find inner calm.

Bunny had rounded on Salt. Now she understood his drunken rambling the night before. "Those missiles came across to Guam from Hawaii with us in that C-5 Galaxy, didn't they? Those crates in the hold ..."

"Yes. Welcome to the party at last, O'Hare. Still think that Chinese drone chaffing us off Wake Island was a coincidence?"

Yeah, no. She didn't. But if it wasn't a coincidence, it meant ... "China *knows* about this mission?" she asked.

Salt shook his head. "Doubtful. They may have known our Galaxy was transporting HACM missiles to Guam and decided to interfere with it. Hard to keep an ordnance transfer like that a secret with the logistics train it takes to move high-value weapons anywhere these days. A hundred different intel vectors—human or cyber—could have alerted China to what was on the manifest for that Galaxy flight. But the specifics of *your* mission ..." he'd gestured around the room, "... are known to just a handful of people in the defense establishment, and half of them are in this room right now." He had given her a look of scorn. "What? So you going to pussy out now?"

She hated to admit it, but that got under her skin, like Salt knew it would.

But she wasn't finished. There was also her issue with the rest of the mission package. Her Widow, its payload, and three Valkyrie loyal wingman drones she'd been allocated. Armed for bear.

80

She didn't care that the timeline for arguing about the mission parameters had passed. "No. But those Valkyries. Adding three escort drones to our package will not deter China or make this mission more survivable," Bunny insisted. "Up there alone, I'm nearly invisible. With three Valkyries in tow, there are three times the chance we'll be detected." She was right, even if he couldn't see it. Air Force mission planners had calculated that if Bunny's flight was detected on Chinese radar, China would think twice about attacking it, if it was more clearly capable of defending itself. Salt had agreed.

Bunny had most emphatically *disagreed*. She wasn't seeing any signs of China thinking twice about anything these days. The Valkyrie was a semi-autonomous drone that could be controlled by the aircraft it accompanied. It could be configured for air-to-air or air-to-ground combat, reconnaissance or electronic warfare roles, and in air-to-air configuration, each Valkyrie carried four short-bodied Peregrine missiles nestled in recesses in its fuselage.

Salt pointed across the apron to where the three Valkyries were lined up in front of a hangar, crews busy arming pulling pins from their missiles and detaching fuel hoses, power and data cables. Salt nodded in their direction. "You have been heard, pilot. Conversation closed. Now, I have to go make sure your three little buddies are ready to party."

Conversation closed? Yeah, not really. Three Valkyrie loyal wingman drones on any other mission would be a definite force multiplier, but when you were supposed to be flying in ninja mode, they were more of an encumbrance. They might take off with her, but she had no intention of trying to penetrate Taiwanese air space with them still glued to her Widow. That was a problem for the future though. Bunny fumed for a moment as Salt turned on his heel and walked off, then bent to finish her inspection by ducking under the

81

open payload bay doors and crouching down to check the ordnance that had been mounted there.

When she'd heard what it was, she understood why Salt had been so tight-lipped back in Arizona. She whistled. She wasn't looking at ten 1,000 lb. bombs. Or even 22 Stormbreaker glide bombs, which almost certainly would have made the Chinese flip their wigs.

Grouped in the center of the payload bay, leaving room for only six medium-range air-to-air missiles for her own defense, were *three* hypersonic land attack missiles.

Under the belly of her Widow, she warily eyed the red ribbons dangling from the arming pins still inserted in the warheads of the missiles hanging over her head. Ordinarily, they would have been removed before any mission, but her orders had been clear on this issue.

"You will, under no circumstances, remove the arming pins or otherwise attempt to interface with those missiles. Your mission is to deliver them to the Republic of China Air Force Taiwan," the Air Force Captain briefing her and Salt told her. "*In situ*. Understood?"

"Completely. But for self-defense …"

The captain clicked to the next slide in his briefing, expecting the question. "For self-defense, you have six Peregrine medium-range air-to-air missiles in the remaining mounts in your own weapons bay …" the captain said. He continued, "… and three Valkyrie drones, two in air-to-air and one in electronic warfare configuration. This package gives you 14 air defense missiles and advanced electronic warfare capabilities. You will not under *any* circumstances use those HACMs, so put them out of your mind. Think of them as inert."

"What are the RoE?" she'd asked.

The captain clicked to his next slide, anticipating her again. "Rules of Engagement. If you detect potentially hostile aircraft or radar, evade and avoid interception if possible. If you are actively intercepted, you will neutralize the situation and *not* the adversary. Only if you are fired upon can you neutralize the adversary, sacrificing your Valkyrie wingmen if necessary to escape." He gave Bunny and Salt a sweeping stare. "Is that clear, before we move to the threat environment, Lieutenant?"

Bunny nodded. No surprise there. *"Neutralize the situation"?* On this mission, that meant optimizing stealth, increasing separation from her drone wingmen, using them to distract a hostile force while trying to break the adversary's radar lock. OK, so, in two out of three scenarios, she was expected to turn tail and run. She didn't protest. They were standard peacetime RoEs and completely understandable given the mission parameters.

"Clear, Captain," she told him with a smile. Yes, they were standard peacetime RoEs, but once she was airborne, there would be gray zones in them big enough for her to shoot a missile through.

If she had to.

Aboard *Fujian*, Colonel Wang sat with Vice Admiral Zhang in his flag quarters. No other officers were present, not even the air wing intelligence officer, Tan. The old man was many things that frustrated Wang—a political animal, traditionalist, orthodox, risk averse—and he did not like to be challenged in front of his subordinates, but he was also one who encouraged his people to speak up and created a one-to-one environment where they could do so safely. Once any dialogue was done and orders were issued though, he expected total loyalty to his decisions.

He looked nervous, pushing a printed communique across the desk. He was also a man who eschewed digital communication, requiring everything to be printed for him still. Wang read it and understood why the Vice Admiral had called for him. "We are opening hostilities with the Americans? This is a shoot-down order."

The command from Ningbo Fleet Command was brief. *US Air Force aircraft taking off from Guam for Taipei, takeoff imminent. Type Black Widow. Escort 3 x Valkyrie armed drones. Intercept and destroy while in international airspace. ISR assets tasked: Yuan Wang Three Zero, PLA SSF Space Command units 1987C23-27. Report on completion.*

The Vice Admiral nodded. "I conferred with Fleet. The attack is to be discreet. All American aircraft are to be destroyed. No survivors, no witnesses. Deniable."

"This is not a transport flight, Vice Admiral," Wang warned. "The Black Widow is a potent aircraft, especially when teamed with armed drones. If the Americans choose to fight ..."

"That is my worry," Zhang said. "How would you execute this mission?"

Wang thought hard. "A beyond-visual-range engagement," he said. "No warning, a surprise attack. Otherwise, the Americans could capture audio or vision of our aircraft and upload it for propaganda purposes."

"It cannot fail. If the Americans escape ..."

"I will deploy two squadrons, 36 aircraft. One squadron, Ao Yin, for the interception. The other, Xiu Snake, 100 miles northwest as a blocking force in case the first interception is unsuccessful."

"*Thirty-six* aircraft against four. Is that necessary?"

"There is no guarantee, even with the ISR assets available, that the American flight will be easy to locate. There is a lot of sky between Guam and Taipei, Vice Admiral."

The old man nodded. "Very well. There is no time to waste; get your aircraft in the air. I will order the strike group to change course accordingly."

Wang stood. "Vice Admiral, if I may ask. What is so important about this flight that we are willing to open hostilities with the Americans now?"

Zhang hesitated, apparently considering how much he could share with Wang. "Our intelligence indicates the American crewed aircraft is carrying hypersonic missiles. They intend to base them on Taiwan."

"HACMs?" Wang asked, disbelievingly. Were the Americans insane? Hypersonic missiles were designated as "strategic weapons." To base such missiles on Taiwan would be a massive escalation in the American response to China's blockade. Just short of a declaration of war.

"Yes, I am told the Americans call them 'carrier killers,'" Zhang said. "Launched from Taiwan, their flight time to any target in the Taiwan Strait or Chinese mainland would be measured in seconds." His face looked suddenly grave. "So you can see why they cannot be allowed to reach Taiwan."

5. 'Not a snowball's chance'

April 3, 2038

As her machine spooled up, Bunny ran another quick avionic systems check. She'd never flown this particular Black Widow before, and it smelled factory fresh. She liked her rides with a few miles on the clock, gremlins already ironed out. But the Aggressor Inc. bird she'd done a face-plant in back in Arizona had been one of those, so that logic didn't really hold. Flipping through a maintenance menu, she clocked the software version for the neuromorphic chip and checked it was a newer version like Salt and the Guam crew chief had promised. Not that she wasn't the trusting type, but she was also the *verifying* type. And she didn't want to be in a clinch with a Chinese fighter when her Widow's central processing unit decided to have a brain fart. But then, what were the chances it would happen to the same pilot, twice in their career in the space of a week, right?

She checked again. She didn't like what she saw.

Bunny O'Hare was an avionics engineer's nightmare. She didn't just look at the fighter plane's avionics interface. She got into the diagnostics menus behind it and she dug around inside the plane's brain. And yeah, what she saw was that the P-99 Widow Block II was running new software on its neuromorphic chip. But it was the *same damned chip*. The chip that had given her a total loss of control for three potentially fatal seconds coming back from a Red Flag exercise. The same chip that had failed as she was coming in to land at Luke and forced her to grind her Widow's nose into the dirt. As far as she could work out, all it took was a solid blast of electromagnetic energy to take the chip offline, and there were a dozen scenarios in which that could happen, which she did *not* want to have to deal with.

So Bunny O'Hare flipped through the maintenance menus for the aircraft's combat AI and she *disabled* the neuromorphic chip. It was more dramatic than it sounded. The neuromorphic chip powered the AI that sent recommendations to the pilot about what to do in situations where pilot data overload was a risk. It could even take control of the airplane from the pilot if it detected that the pilot was dead or incapacitated. Bunny had never found herself in that situation—yet, touch wood—so she quietly killed the new Widow's neuromorphic chip and forced her machine to use legacy processing systems. Of which she was one.

Then she ran her eye across the ordnance data. She had green lights across the board on the weapons in her payload bay, including the three HACMs. Under the symbols on her ordnance menu for the HACMs though, a warning flashed: *Arming disabled.* She turned her attention to the menu that showed the status of her three Valkyrie drone wingmen.

One was fitted with a countermeasures and electronic warfare, or EW, belly pod. The second and third both had scanning array radars in their nose pods and Peregrine missiles nestled into recesses under their bellies: four of the medium-range missiles each. The way she thought of the Valkyrie was like a high maneuverability supersonic missile mothership. The first versions had been subsonic, but the latest variant could reach Mach 1.4 and either engage a target painted by the fighter controlling it, or patrol autonomously for up to an hour, looking for targets itself.

Carrying the three HACMs meant Bunny had space for only six missiles of her own. But if she got herself into a situation on this mission where she was loosing off her own missiles, she was in seriously deep shit. Speaking of which ...

Her Widow wasn't completely defenseless. A little larger than the old F-117 stealth fighter, but with a roomier cockpit, it had a smaller radar cross section than the F-35 Panther. It looked like a scaled-down version of the new B-21 Raider bomber, which itself looked like a scaled-down version of the venerable B-2 Spirit stealth bomber. She flicked through to the countermeasures menu on her multifunction display and checked her Air Trophy active protection system was online. She saw it was loaded and reporting for duty, then paged away again. Air Trophy was a defense of last resort, so Bunny knew if she ever heard the Widow's Air Trophy system firing, it might be the last thing she ever heard.

She flipped the toggle on the Valkyrie menu that put the drones into *takeoff: formation-keeping* mode. A fighter pilot didn't really "fly" a Valkyrie. He or she issued it with one of a hundred context-sensitive commands and the machine's combat AI did the rest, right up to the point of weapons release, which had to be confirmed by a human either in the air or monitoring an engagement on the ground.

Satisfied, she contacted Guam tower, led the three drones out to the taxiway and waited for permission to get airborne.

Twisting awkwardly, she reached for a compartment at her hip, unlocked it and sorted through the contents before choosing an item and closing the compartment again. She looked at it and reconsidered putting it back in the compartment but then shrugged to herself. She pushed up the visor on her helmet and took a bite of the chocolate bar.

It was going to be a hella long flight and she'd been told a few of the insiders on Guam were making bets she would not make it all the way to Taiwan. A message from the tower told her that her flight would be released in about five minutes. She took another bite of chocolate. Well, like her old grandma had once told her, there was no point dying with uneaten chocolate in your pocket.

A naval electronics rating stuck his head through the wardroom door of *Fujian's* level 3 aft subdeck and scanned the room. When his eyes found Asien Chen sitting at a table with a cup of cold coffee and an untouched bowl of noodles in front of him he called. "Pilot Officer Chen! Alert Five!"

Chen leaped to his feet, sending the contents of the coffee cup splashing to the floor, unheeded.

"What's up?" he asked the rating as he pushed past him into a gangway.

"Flash message from Fleet. Fighter aircraft sighted taking off from Guam," the man said, hurrying after Chen. "Heading for Taiwan."

"How many?"

"One ..."

"One?! Drone wingmen? Other escorts?"

"Three. It's a squadron scramble."

Damn. Chen hit a stairwell and flew down the stairs two at a time. Regulations said he was supposed to "hurry slowly" when called to readiness. That had never been Chen's style. He hit the aircraft command deck running and was nearly out of breath by the time he reached the large hangar-sized space that held their drone control pods. Six were already occupied by the pilots flying defensive patrols around *Fujian* and its escorts. The one next to his own pod was also occupied, his wingman for this mission, Maylin 'Mushroom' Sun, already in her pod and flipping switches. He heard the thud of boots and excited voices behind him as other pilots streamed into the squadron pod bay.

Since the intercept on the American transport and his humiliating dressing-down, Ao Yin Squadron had not been called on for anything but routine duties. A few pilots had been allocated to routine carrier defense patrols, but Chen's stick time had been limited to the on-board simulator system—an unspoken punishment for his performance in the last action.

From his pocket, he pulled out his personal communication device as he ran to the squadron briefing room. Their short-form orders were already posted:

Combat air patrol: Guam-Taiwan corridor. Foreign military aircraft in this corridor on a heading for Taiwan airspace can be intercepted and on the orders of Commander, *Fujian* Air Wing, destroyed.

No more warnings. No more hailing hostile aircraft on the open "guard" channel, politely asking them to change course. The gloves were off.

The briefing room was full as he dropped into a seat beside his fellow Academy student, fellow Ao Yin pilot and longtime buddy, 'Mushroom' Sun. "You flying my wing?" he asked her, glad to see her there. She was probably the best pilot in the *Fujian* Air Wing and he was often paired with her

90

at the front of a formation. His confidence in her wasn't matched by her own confidence in herself, which was *another* thing he liked about her. They were both competitive, but they weren't rivals.

"You bet," she replied, bumping fists with him. The briefing went by in a blur. He just wanted to get it done and get into his pod.

It was not a given that Chen would have been on duty when the alert came. He could have just as easily been fast asleep in his bunk. And there was still no guarantee of action. The alert could be a false alarm. American fighters took off from the US airbase almost daily. Usually just for flight checks, or a run over Andersen Air Base's aerial training range. But Alert Five status meant he was about to be handed control of a Chongming drone already locked into one of *Fujian*'s two electromagnetic catapults, engines warm, systems primed, ready to be fired into the air at five minutes' notice.

He settled into the seat of the pod and the same rating that had fetched him from the wardroom handed him his audiovisual rig. It wasn't a helmet, not really. It was closer to a pair of noise-canceling over-ear headphones attached to some seriously gangsta sunglasses. What made it a generation beyond the sort of rig a modern video gamer might use were the two small electronic nodes that the rating was sticking to the skin behind Chen's ears. They sent electronic impulses directly into his occipital nerve, giving him sensory feedback that allowed him to sense how close he was flying his aircraft to the edge of its performance envelope. He could be hundreds of miles from his machine, but he would feel a buzzing pulse that increased in urgency as the aircraft got closer to a stall, would be given a jolt of neck pain if he was overstressing its airframe, would feel a stabbing sensation in

91

his spine if he didn't immediately react to a missile launch warning or other danger.

The Chongming's combat AI was designed to take control of the drone out of the pilot's hands if it could sense they were entering a state of sensory overload, but the drone's engineers had discovered that human pilots performed better if they could "feel" the aircraft they were flying.

Going through his guided pre-flight checklist, Chen checked his squadron call sign. Lately, the operational planners on *Fujian* had taken to giving them football club nicknames. Sure enough ... he was Blade One. From the Chengdu Blades club no doubt. Ah well, it could have been worse. On his last flight he had been Athletic Two. Hardly a motivational name given Chongqing Athletic were league bottom dwellers.

Settling the wraparound glasses in front of his eyes as one of the last things he did, Chen initiated augmented reality vision and suddenly he was *inside* the Chongming's cockpit. As he swiveled his head, he looked across the flight deck at his wingman's sleek black aircraft, 50 feet away and behind him, crouched on its catapult like a jaguar ready to spring. At the rear of the flight deck, he saw two more aircraft coming up on the carrier's aircraft elevators even as those parked on the side of the catapult began spooling up. It was a full squadron scramble ...

The Chongming didn't have an actual cockpit. The view he was looking at was simulated by the aircraft's distributed aperture video system, which allowed him a 360-degree view around the aircraft if he wanted it and automatically drew his eye to other aircraft, targets or threats like enemy missiles.

He'd had a beautiful rearward view of that American Galaxy as he lined himself up slightly ahead and slightly above it before he triggered his chaff dispensers and sent it staggering toward an emergency landing on Wake Island through a cloud of silver foil. The chewing out he had received had been worth it. He'd heard a few of his fellow pilots had given him a new call sign. He'd taken a variation of his sister's call sign in flight school to honor her—Papa Bear—but he'd heard the others were calling him 'Shredder' after the Galaxy interception. He smiled. Papa Bear had been alright, but 'Shredder'? That rocked.

"Blade Two, ready for launch," his wingman, call sign 'Mushroom,' reported. She'd been given her call sign by her fellow pilots because of her habit of curling into a ball and burying herself deep under her bed covers when sleeping. She said it was to block the sound of the other pilots' snoring—on *Fujian* they hot-bunked in berths of four pilots to a room—but seeing her pale face emerge blinking into the light when she was called out of bed was just like watching a mushroom emerge from its bed of mulch.

He completed the checklist on his heads-up display, worked his controls and checked visually that the control surfaces on the fighter responded, then flicked the checklist away with a finger gesture, resting one hand on his throttle, the other on his stick. "Blade One, ready for launch."

Did Asien Chen care that he couldn't smell the aviation fuel or feel the wind across *Fujian*'s deck walking out to his aircraft? No. His visor told him exactly how strongly and from where the wind was blowing. Did he miss the jackboot kick in the spine his sister had told him she got every time her J-20 fighter was flung into the air from the deck of her carrier, the *Liaoning*? No. The sense of dizzying motion in his augmented reality glasses as the Chongming rocketed down *Fujian*'s deck was strong enough to make trainee pilots with weak stomachs lose their last meal. The synaptic nodes behind his ears buzzed the moment his wheels separated from *Fujian*'s deck and then he was airborne, one with his machine, soaring into the sky.

He'd flown piloted jets in training, of course. And he was fully qualified on the J-20. Would he trade his humble Chongming for his sister's J-20 Mighty Dragon stealth fighter tomorrow if he were offered?

Not a snowball's chance.

For all the PR surrounding it, Chen knew from open-source analyses on the internet that China's stealth fighter had a radar cross section nearly double that of its Western adversaries. That meant that in nearly all instances where the J-20 had tried to intercept the American F-35 Panther, the Panther saw it first.

That weakness had been seen in the aerial conflict known as the Pagasa Incident in which the American stealth fighter's kill-to-loss ratio had been far superior to the Mighty Dragon's. The first, admittedly limited, round of China's test of air strength against America had gone to the Americans.

But the *Fujian*, with its complement of deadly Chongming fighters, had not been available for the Pagasa Operation. And though he was not privy to top secret data about the radar cross section of the J-20 compared with the Chongming Rainbow 7, Chen had seen enough in Red Flag exercises against aircraft from China's other two carriers to know that his little Chongming might not pack the same missile firepower as the much larger J-20 and might not have the same stealth advantages, but *Fujian* had a huge advantage over its two older sister carriers. They could only carry 24 fighters. *Fujian* had space for 40 Chongming drones below decks and could park another 12 on its flight deck if needed.

And unlike the other carrier's piloted fighters, if *Fujian* lost an uncrewed fighter in combat, it did not lose a precious pilot. Its pilots were safely back on the carrier and could simply be assigned another drone and immediately return to the fight.

The Chongming had one other advantage over a crewed fighter. In a knife fight, a close-range merge in which the two opponents fought at visual range with guns or infrared missiles, the Chongming was near unbeatable. Without having to worry about the g-forces a J-20 pilot in his cockpit was exposed to, Chen had learned in Red Flag exercises he could sit comfortably in his pod and flip his Chongming on its axis, reversing on his piloted opponent with a flick of his stick, or send his machine spinning like a child's top to evade an incoming missile, without losing a moment's situational awareness. His Russian-made 30 mm autocannon locked automatically on its target and fired faster than Chen could even think the word "fire!"

Chen realized he was squeezing the throttle so hard with his left hand that his knuckles felt like they were going to pop. He lifted his hand off the throttle and flexed his fingers. *Take it easy, 'Shredder.'* Ready Five was not a guarantee of a launch. He could sit here for an hour, only to be stood down again. But the mass of activity on the deck around his machine told a different story.

If *Fujian* had been at sea during the Pagasa Incident, the Americans would have been given a different lesson in air power. And maybe his sister would still be alive. He pushed that thought to the back of his mind, focusing on the voices of the air officers inside *Fujian's* primary flight control center as they coordinated operations around the massive carrier. Minutes ticked by. He began to cramp, the tension in his body having no way to find release.

Then came the command he had been waiting for.

"Blade flight. Launch, launch, launch ..."

Takuya Kato was also on standby at Okinotori Reef. He had been waiting over 24 hours for someone to tell him if he should be worried about the bloody great Chinese warship parked right up alongside his research station.

Or, alright, not exactly alongside. Radar showed it was 10 miles out and though he had tried climbing to a high point on the station's lighthouse tower, he couldn't see the Chinese ship with his binos. So he'd sent a small commercial camera drone out to give him a look at it. It was a tiny drone he used to get optical and infrared images of the coral beds around the reef every couple of weeks so that he could see if they were growing or receding. Ten miles was about its maximum range, but he'd climbed the lighthouse tower again to give himself the best possible signal and then sent it in the direction of the radar contact. He figured with a ship that big, it wouldn't be hard to find.

It wasn't. It really looked like a passenger cruise ship where someone had ripped out the shuffleboard and pool decks and mounted satellite dishes and radomes. He didn't want to get too close in case the ship was armed. He couldn't afford to lose his only survey drone. But he started getting control signal warnings about a mile out from the warship so he stopped his drone there and zoomed the camera in on it. He'd drawn a deep breath. The ship was broadside to his drone and the three enormous satellite dishes on its deck were all trained on the sky in different directions. Mounted on a platform at the rear of the ship was a bright white dome about 100 feet around. It looked relatively new. Just in front of it was a smaller satellite dish and Kato couldn't help but get a chill when he realized that dish was pointed straight back at his drone. Or more likely, at *him*, on Okinotori Research Station.

It gave him the very distinct feeling that any communication that was going in and out of Okinotori would be sucked into that dish and relayed to someone in China before he even got the chance to read it himself. Theirs was at heart a civilian research station, not a military one, even though it fell under the authority of the Japanese Self Defense Forces Oceanographic Support Command, or OSC. Their communications all went via commercial satellite and internet providers or VHF radio. They weren't, to Kato's knowledge, even encrypted.

He'd pulled his drone back to Okinotori and resolved to be very careful about what he said and sent back to the mainland. But he had said nothing yet, except for a panicked voice message to a faceless duty operator at OSC alerting them to the Chinese ship and asking them for instructions. He'd received a very standard message back via the station's email. "Your message received. Please await our decision."

Now it was a day later and he'd received precisely nothing. He had to do something though. So he uploaded a few of his drone photos to an encrypted messaging app the station's researchers used to share data, and sent them off with a warning not to send plain text emails or messages to him and request the photos be passed on to the JSDF Navy. Maybe they would react a little more quickly to the idea a massive Chinese vessel like the *Yuan Wang* was parked off a Japanese reef.

After he sent the photos, he sat looking at them, comparing them to images of the ship he found on the internet. The photographic images didn't really show anything that wasn't already in the public domain, though the bright

97

white dome at the rear of the ship was definitely new. It wasn't in any of the internet photos. Another thing he thought was interesting were the infrared shots he'd taken. The drone had only a very basic infrared capability, but it showed different hotspots inside the hull and infrastructure of the ship. All the satellite dishes were showing hotspots at their base, indicating they were drawing power, so they must have all been active. A dome at the front of the ship was also a hotspot, though only a small one. Amidships by the ship's waterline, he saw a larger blurred hotspot, showing it was quite a large heat source and probably deep within the hull— maybe the ship's engines?

But right underneath the newer bright white dome was a bright yellow and red hotspot. Something under there was drawing a shit-ton of juice. Kato was no ship's electrician. He barely knew how to shut down or restart the station's own power system, but he'd taken infrared photos of Okinotori's power plant just for fun, testing out his drone's cameras, and whatever was drawing power on the *Yuan Wang* under that little dome was giving off a bloom maybe a hundred times brighter than Okinotori's little unit.

Kato sat in the station's central communication office, checked for about the tenth time his photos had been sent, no new message had been received, and then went back to feeling restless. He should go back to his research, but he felt that would have been a particularly sheep-like thing to do with the Chinese navy offshore. Like a sheep that looked up at a rumbling volcano and decided the best thing it could do was eat some more grass. He'd never spent much time in the communication center and as he looked at all the sticky notes posted on screens and switches saying "DON'T TOUCH THIS" he got quite annoyed.

He lifted one and looked at the buttons underneath it, which were mounted under a small LCD screen that was currently switched off. The label above the screen said *UFP release controls*. Under each of the three buttons were smaller labels: *UFP 1, UFP 2, UFP 3*. And then a red label saying: WARNING STATION COMMANDER AUTHORITY REQUIRED. Underneath the screen was a small keyboard and a joystick toggle. Interesting.

A thought came to him. Am I not the commander of Okinotori at this moment? Do I not have the authority to press any damn button I damn well want?

He let out a small laugh. Yeah, right. The authority to get his ass fired, probably prosecuted for misuse of State property, more like.

He put the sticky note back on top of the switches, checked the radar screen to be sure the Chinese ship was still there and got an idea. He'd dig out the station's Japanese flag and run it up the flagpole at the top of the lighthouse. Maybe play a Japanese radio station over the VHF radio. Let them listen to *that* with their big-ass satellite dishes. That would show China who the hell was boss here.

Bunny O'Hare was about an hour and 20 out of Guam when it happened. More importantly, she was only about 40 minutes from linking with the US Navy Stingray refueling drone that would tank her flight up and get them all the way to Taiwan.

Bunny's heads-up display started flickering and multiple alarms started sounding in her cockpit. Her first thought was "that damn processor again," but a quick glance across the flashing displays inside her cockpit and visor told her otherwise.

She tried to key her satellite radio to raise Salt back on Guam in his mission command trailer. All she got was static. She quickly tried a range of sensors and saw everything except her distributed aperture camera system was scrambled. Bunny was no stranger to what she was seeing. She'd seen it over Syria, over the Arctic and over the South China Sea. She was being *jammed*.

She looked quickly around the sky for attackers, saw nothing. Her three Valkyrie wingmen had moved closer and were still holding formation with her. When their radio or satellite links to her Widow were jammed, they moved within visual range if they weren't already and used a laser transceiver mode to send and receive data and instructions.

Screw this. If Bunny had learned anything in air combat, it was that straight and level got you *dead*.

She shoved her throttle forward and pulled her machine into a spiraling climb, trusting the Valkyries would follow. They were at 20,000 feet. She wanted 30,000. She locked the nearest Valkyrie on her optical-infrared tracking system so she wouldn't lose sight of it, and set the optics on all drones to help look for any airborne targets around them. She got nothing. Her search radar and comms systems were trying to frequency jump to break the jamming, but without luck. Whatever it was, it was powerful. A ship or airborne warning aircraft messing with them maybe? But she'd picked up nothing on her radar warning system before the jamming started. A tracking radar should have had to lock them up before it …

Her blood froze. What was it the Galaxy engineer had said? "Instruments went wild, lost radio contact, jamming probably ..."

Right before the small Chinese Chongming drones appeared out of nowhere.

Bunny quickly reran the rules of engagement in her head. She was not to initiate any attack if she was simply intercepted. But she could respond to Chinese aggression in kind, returning fire if fired upon. Could a jamming precursor to an intercept be defined as an attack? After what had happened to Bunny's Galaxy off Wake Island, her personal answer to that was a big "hell yes," but she knew a lawyer would probably say "hell no."

So she was limited from firing a high-explosive missile at her adversary until she had one already coming right at *her*. The Black Widow was not built to win that kind of fight. It was built to identify its targets at a distance and kill them before they knew it was there. To engage an adversary at close quarters with missiles already flying was suicide, and she had no intention of going to her death through sheer stupidity.

Not when she had perfectly ... alright, *probably* ... legal options.

With the flick of a switch on her flight stick, she brought her weapons systems online and selected her EW-configured Valkyrie, then set it to autonomous "search and engage." It didn't carry a warhead of its own; the nose-mounted payload was all electronics. So technically, she wasn't "firing" at her adversary, was she?

Bunny O'Hare did her best work in the gray zones.

Sending the Valkyrie out of visual range meant she may never get it back, and she wouldn't know what was happening to it until and unless she broke through the jamming energy she was still bathed in.

Another pilot might have hesitated, worried about losing ordnance they might need later. Another pilot might have waited for the jamming to resolve itself so they could be sure to maintain contact with a precious asset, or be worried they'd get chewed out for overreacting. Bunny O'Hare was still alive after multiple combat engagements because she was *not* that pilot. Mind you, she was also persona non grata with her own air force and flying for a private contractor because she was not that pilot too. But you had to take the sour with the sweet.

"Valkyrie away," she intoned to herself, giving the order for the drone to go autonomous and cover her six, before rolling her machine, pulling her stick back and diving for the sea 25,000 feet below at Mach 1.4.

At 10,000 feet she smoothed out the dive, heading for 1,000 feet but putting her machine into a banking turn and "going ninja." She optimized its stealth profile by minimizing its radar and infrared cross sections, though she stayed ready to maneuver radically if she needed to. There wasn't much she could do for the two Valkyries still glued to her wingtips, about 200 feet out on either side of her. They were not strictly stealth aircraft, but they were small and she was down so low now hostile radar would have a hard time finding them in the background clutter of the sea.

Leaving the Widow to fly itself, she turned her attention to her optical infrared scanners and began quartering the sky, looking for any sign of a threat. Her EW Valkyrie was already out of sight, the order she had given it telling it, "Search the

102

sky around you, and if you identify a suitable military target, lock it up and try to fry its electronics."

She completed one 360-degree optical scan. No missiles incoming, no distant specks in the sky ... But no sooner had she begun quartering the sky again than the static in her ears cleared and Salt's angry voice broke into her cockpit.

"... the hell O'Hare! I am showing your EW Valkyrie has gone active. Where are you?"

6. 'An atoll the world had forgotten about'

Bunny decided she would deal with Salt in a second. After all, he was sitting comfortably in a trailer on Guam while she …

Her Valkyrie had reestablished satellite comms and come back online, so she took control of it, canceled its last orders and ordered it to climb, executing the opposite of the maneuver she had executed herself, climbing to 35,000 feet. The Valkyrie had a radar only slightly less powerful than the one onboard her Widow, and she put it into a 360-degree spiraling search pattern.

Almost immediately she got a return.

"Salt, I am showing multiple unidentified fast movers bearing 170 degrees, altitude 30, range 56 miles. Vectoring my EW Valkyrie for an intercept," she said. "I'll pull the rest of my flight away in the opposite direction."

"Negative, O'Hare. Call that drone back. We cannot aggressively engage unidentified aircraft in international airspace."

Bunny cursed. There were times for meekly obeying your CO, but then there were times it could cost your life … "That jamming was foreplay, Salt. And this is my call. I'm going to let those bogeys on our six know what a lady means when she says no thank you. O'Hare out."

She pointed her aircraft west, increasing the separation between her flight and the pursuing aircraft, dropping her three machines down to wavetop height. She looked at the plot of the enemy aircraft being sent to her tactical display by the Valkyrie drone, which was fast closing on them, maybe 50 miles out. They had seen it now, were turning in on it, its wildly radiating radar acting like a lighthouse to moths. They had taken the bait; now to confuse them. She cut the Valkyrie's radar temporarily and lost the hostile aircraft plot, but it meant that until they got within their own radar range, they would be steering blind.

Seconds ticked past agonizingly slowly. Frozen on her screen where it had last been tracked at 40 miles was a cluster of dots that could only be Chinese fighters. The Chinese had headed straight for her EW drone. If they were worried they might have a supersonic fighter headed straight for them, they hadn't shown it. Any minute now they would issue a challenge on the open guard radio frequency, and order the drone they could see to turn away—standard Chinese procedure. Just as standard US procedure was to ignore them.

Bunny had been counting seconds in her head, multiplying them by the cruising speed of her Valkyrie. It would now be about 20 miles out from the approaching fighters and probably still on a direct intercept track. She hit a control on her weapons screen to bring the Valkyrie's radar online again, putting it in "targeting" mode. Time to let China know her bird had its fighters dead in its sights. The fact it wasn't carrying missiles … well, they didn't need to know that.

She'd noticed the ground crew on Guam had painted names on the noses of her Valkyrie drones.

Huey, Dewey and Louie.

105

"Say hello to your new friends, Huey," she said out loud and prepared the drone to execute a full-spectrum electronic warfare attack on the Chinese fighters. It just needed to get a *little* closer ...

A threatening icon in his heads-up display and audible warning in his pod suddenly grabbed Pilot Officer Asien Chen's attention. One of the American aircraft had broken away and was accelerating straight at them! Just as quickly, it dropped off his radar screen.

"Hostile targeting radar at 12 o'clock," Ao Yin squadron's 'Blade flight' commander Colonel Wang Wei said calmly. "Altitude 28, range 20." Chen had noted with chagrin that Wang was flying with his pilots on this mission, apparently feeling he could leave nothing to chance this time.

Chen smiled. The aggressive American fighter's approach was ... *unexpected*. But not unwelcome. Wang wanted a clean sweep on this mission. He had told his pilots as much. Four American aircraft, four kills. Chen badly wanted to claim at least one of them.

"Blade pilots, formation four, prosecute interception," Wang said.

Chen watched Maylin 'Mushroom' Sun, in the aircraft to the left of him, slide away to port, and he twitched his stick to follow. Wang was making his 10 aircraft harder targets for the approaching American machine, but their adversary was not deviating from their course. It seemed they wanted to test their Chinese counterparts, and Chen approved. He knew American fighter doctrine was for pilots flying with drone wingmen to sacrifice their drones first in any potentially

106

hostile engagement, so this aircraft was almost certainly uncrewed.

Not the kill he wanted. Only flesh torn from bone would satisfy Chen's need to prove himself.

He would soon find himself surrounded. And if he didn't comply with their orders to turn back to Guam, he would find himself dead.

On their interplane channel, Wang projected calm. "Blade pilots, hold formation; arm missiles but do not fire until my order."

First off the deck, Chen and Sun were flying at the point of the Chinese arrow and would be the first to engage. Chen had not waited for Wang's order. He had already armed his PL-15 air-to-air missiles, and as Wang finished speaking, he brought up his radar and locked it on the approaching American.

"Blade Leader, Blade One has target lock, requesting permission to engage," Chen intoned.

"Blade One, hold your fire," Wang said. "You will only fire on my order."

Chen ground his teeth. Wang was being typically cautious. What was he waiting for? For the American to fire first?

Chen flexed his fingers again and gripped his flight stick. He frowned. The American had closed to 20 miles and showed no sign of breaking off. Chen checked his Chongming's optical infrared sensors. They had not picked up the American yet, but it could only be a matter of moments. The American was closing at ... Mach 1.4? A speck appeared on the horizon, trailing vapor, and an auto-generated ID flashed on his visor.

It was an American Valkyrie and it was headed straight for him and Sun. *Come on, Colonel, what are you ...*

"Blade One, engage."

Chen felt none of the elation he'd expected to feel, closing on his first kill. It was, after all, just a dumb machine. "Target locked. Fox three!"

He launched his PL-15 Thunderbolt missile in active radar-seeking mode. As it dropped from his machine and accelerated toward the target, he knew it wouldn't even have time to get to its Mach 4 top speed before it reached the doomed American fighter.

The EW Valkyrie, Huey, *was* a pretty dumb hunk of metal and silicon, as such things went. Since he was expendable, he had been made simple. He had no sophisticated onboard AI, and certainly nothing resembling a personality. He had no sense of self, but he had a hard-coded, bloody-minded determination to stay alive and stay aloft at all costs if he was attacked.

Which his threat warning system told him was happening, *right now*. A hostile targeting radar had locked him up, which machine logic told him meant a missile would soon be on the way. He'd been waiting to reach optimal EW range before engaging the adversaries ahead of him, but the new scenario changed that.

Huey immediately amplified his radar emissions to maximum strength, engaged his pulse doppler engine to boost himself above Mach 2 and powered *toward* his attackers. Then he locked up and fired a beam of high-intensity energy right at the missile just milliseconds away from striking him.

The energy fried the missile's radar seeker and it flew right past Huey, spiraling wildly through the sky behind him.

He didn't celebrate still being alive. He was, after all, just a robot.

Huey immediately turned his energy on the next threat on his warning receiver—the Chinese aircraft that had fired on him.

"Target lost, missile going wide!" Chen said. *The American was nearly on him.* Chen stayed cool. The target was too close for a missile shot of its own, and the Valkyrie didn't have guns, he knew. So it was jamming; it would try to barrel past him in the merge and then circle behind him for a missile solution. Nothing aloft could turn tighter than his Chongming though, Chen was confident of that. He brought up his Russian-made 30 mm autocannon.

Let the American come. If he didn't kill him in the merge, he'd finish him before they even started to turn into each other.

He could see the American machine in his optical viewfinder now and his heads-up display drew a targeting box around it. Even though it was close, it seemed small, but things were moving too fast for him to worry. He gritted his teeth and kept his machine pointed right at the onrushing aircraft. They were heading toward each other at three times the speed of sound. Any moment the reticle around the target would turn red and *his cannon would* ...

A radar receiver warning was the first thing he heard. The next was white noise, screaming in his ears. His heads-up display turned to snow. Electronic warfare attack!

Now the American was coming straight for him and he was *blind.*

He tried his controls, but they didn't respond. He'd lost control authority too, the enemy electronic warfare attack cutting the satellite link between Chen on the *Fujian* and his Chongming.

No! What just happened?

O'Hare was still pushing her Black Widow away from the Chinese formation at a tangent. She could see it clearly now on her tac screen, lit up by the Valkyrie hammering toward it at the speed of sound.

"O'Hare, break off that EW attack!" Salt ordered.

"Roger that, Colonel," Bunny said reluctantly. Huey had blasted through the Chinese formation, scattering it to the four winds, and she ordered him to shut down jamming and to climb again, sending him zooming into the sky above the hostile fighters. "Just wanted to get their attention ..." As she watched, the Chinese drones started reforming, probably trying to reestablish contact with their base. Two Chinese fighters broke away from the larger formation and began pursuing Huey. "They fired at my Valkyrie and they've still got it locked, Salt. What do you want me to do?"

"Dammit, I ..." O'Hare could hear the gears grinding in Salt's voice as he adjusted to the reality she had presented him with. She'd done exactly as she'd been ordered, hadn't she? Neutralized the situation without actually attacking the adversary? "Very well. Sacrifice that EW drone if you have to, but you will *not* engage those fighters with missiles. Is that clear?"

"Crystal, sir," Bunny told him. She wasn't flying the Valkyrie, Huey. Just giving it orders. So she changed its orders to "evade and rejoin" and set herself a looping intercept course that would put her back on course to meet their refueling tanker. The Chinese fighters were falling away behind them now, focused on destroying her Valkyrie. Huey had bought them valuable time and airspace in which to escape their pursuers, so all she could do for now was wish him luck.

"Come back to momma, Huey baby," she said through gritted teeth, watching the Chinese icons on her screen close on her drone. "Hang in there."

"Blade Leader, Blade One. Jamming cleared. I have the target locked again, reengaging," Chen said.

The American machine, which his AI could still not identify, was pulling away from them. Chen's Chongming had a maximum speed of Mach 1.2 and he had pushed its throttle "through the gate," as far as it could go. As he had turned to follow the American machine, it had already stretched out to 10 miles separation and was now at 15. He would not lose radar lock for some time yet unless …

As though it read his thoughts, the machine nosed down and dived for the sea. There was a very real risk if it reached sea level they would lose it in radar clutter reflected by the waves below. His finger hovered over the missile trigger …

"Blade One, hold your fire," Wang suddenly ordered him.

Chen gritted his teeth. The target had leveled out now and was still pulling away. "Colonel! Separation is increasing, request permission to engage."

"Negative, Blade One, that was an EW drone and it might try to rejoin its mothership," Wang said. "We will track it for as long as we can and then search along the heading it gives us."

"Sir, I have …"

"You have your orders, Blade One. The Black Widow is our priority. *Rejoin*," Wang said curtly.

Chen slammed a fist into the Perspex roof of his pod. "Blade One, breaking off." As logical as the Colonel's orders were, a kill was a kill, and Chen had just been denied his first.

Wang continued. "Blade pilots, I am laying in a track that will keep us in contact with the American drone for as long as possible. I am ordering Xiu Snake Squadron to take up a blocking patrol to the north. But we will probably need to wait for another fix from PLA Navy support. Close on me."

Chen banked his machine and gave it a navigation order to pilot itself back to rejoin formation with Wang. He safed his weapons, shut down his tracking radar and paged away from his ordnance screen in disgust.

The Chongming hunted best if it was taking its targeting from other airborne or ship-borne radar platforms. If it used its own radar trying to find American aircraft, it risked alerting them to its presence and triggering a blizzard of missiles before it had a target itself. But why did they need to "request another fix"? Chen had assumed the PLA Navy support was being provided by one of their *Type 055* air warfare destroyers, the Chinese equivalent of the American Aegis. If the PLA Navy had picked up the American flight once already, why were they not continuously tracking it? Why could they not *instantly* update *Fujian* and its aircraft on the Americans' new positions?

Three Zero could not update Wang and his pilots on Bunny and her Valkyrie's positions because it could no longer see them.

The Vortex system was optimized for area air defense, scanning a predictable area of sky and identifying any threats within it—such as incoming missiles or stealth aircraft— for destruction. It was not optimized for the job being asked of it right now.

Although nothing could escape detection if it was hit by the Vortex energy stream, generating that stream took enormous amounts of electrical energy. That was one reason the system could only be fielded on a ship the size of *Three Zero*. And to do it, the massive gas turbines on the ship had to generate electricity and store it in a giant battery and capacitor system that could release it in a single 1-megawatt discharge.

Recycling the discharge took 15 minutes. By then, a fast-moving target had of course moved, and though its quantum computing AI support system was excellent at predicting where in the sky to look for its target again, it was not perfect.

The Vortex operators aboard *Three Zero* fired another burst of energy at an arc of the sky and got plenty of returns, but none were the aircraft they were looking for. They adjusted their array and prepared to fire again. It was not a question of whether they would find the Americans again, but a question of when.

And where.

Bunny was happier now than she had been for the last half hour. The Chinese fighters had seemingly broken off and her Valkyrie "Huey" had rejoined her. For as long as its fuel lasted—which she calculated would be about another 30 minutes unless they made it to the tanker rendezvous—it had parked itself off her wing like a friendly dolphin, bobbing along in the wake of a sailing ship.

But they were all still skipping over the sea at wavetop height, which burned fuel faster. They would get better endurance at altitude, and it was probably safe enough now to climb out again and make a beeline for that tanker.

Salt was *not* happy. Salt was furious. He showed it over the radio as only Salt could; in low, cold tones. "O'Hare, you showed reckless disregard for your rules of engagement. Try that again and you will be relieved of duty the minute you put down in Taipei and your contract with Aggressor Inc. will be terminated," Salt said.

Bunny opened her mouth to argue but shut it again. She weighed her answer, for once. "Your call, Salt. But I am still alive and personally, I would rather be alive and unemployed than still on contract to Aggressor Inc., but, you know, dead."

Salt couldn't contain himself now. "You have *no* idea what those Chinese fighters intended," he retorted. "They didn't fire on you, but you *provoked* them into firing on your Valkyrie. We were expecting to be intercepted but there was nothing in their behavior to show they were going to do anything except politely ask you to divert. Which we could have handled."

Maybe it was the tone of his voice; lilting, mocking ... patronizing. It reminded her of another conversation, a lifetime ago. She replayed the memory, enjoying it. To her surprise, it made her calmer and she returned her mind to the present. She cared whether she lived or died, that was given.

114

She also cared whether she got her machine and payload to Taiwan too, because deep in her democracy-loving heart, she kind of admired the plucky little island for facing down the Chinese behemoth for the best part of a century. But whether she ever flew again for Aggressor Inc., or more particularly for Salt Carlyle, *that* she didn't really care about.

Bunny O'Hare had what was known in the military profession as a "unique skill set." A borderline personality disorder also, yes, sure. But she could land her Widow, wave Salt goodbye and sign a new contract with a new employer before the sun even had time to set over Taipei. So threatening to fire her was no threat at all. Well, except for the fact she would be trapped on Taiwan with no job and the entire Chinese army about to invade.

Which was maybe not good for her future prospects. She decided to take one more run at Salt. "You happen to notice I was being jammed, Colonel?"

"You lost radio contact, there was some atmospheric interference. That's what I noticed," Salt replied. "Right before you went off reservation."

Bunny felt her aircraft bump in the unstable air over the sea. "Uh-huh. And a burst of 'atmospheric interference' came and went, right before the Chinese fighters appeared off the wing of our Galaxy off Wake Island and tried to knock our engines out." Bunny took her stick and eased her machine a few hundred feet higher, looking for smoother air. "Or you forget that?"

Salt was quiet a moment, then replied. "I remember."

"Well, it sure sounds to me like you forgot. There was no 'polite request to divert' back then either ..."

"Point taken," Salt admitted.

115

"So yeah, I deployed an *unarmed* Valkyrie." She looked at her altimeter and fuel flow; they needed to get off the deck soon. "And I am still alive, on mission, with payload intact. Wonder who will Aggressor Inc. and the USAF think did the right thing?"

Salt didn't like being lectured and rose to the jibe. "I'll tell you what they will think, Lieutenant. They'll think it was pure dumb luck you are still alive. And they'll decide you broke their carefully calculated RoE. One more wise-ass move like that, you're history."

Not the first time I heard that, Bunny thought. *Won't be the last.* But it sounded like she was getting the second chance she needed. She looked at her altitude and fuel-burn rate. "Well, you're the boss down there, Colonel. But I'm the boss up here. I'm taking my flight up to meet that Navy Stingray refueling drone."

Bunny heard voices conferring in the background over the open channel, Salt in animated discussion with whoever he was sharing the command trailer with. Eventually, he came back on. "Yeah, you won't be doing that, Lieutenant." Bunny could hear a smug timbre in his voice. "Sending you a new waypoint. Orders of the client."

It took a moment to download, but Bunny looked at the new destination on her nav screen. "We're putting *down*?" Bunny asked with undisguised disgust.

"The Chinese threat has been confirmed, and you probably just made it worse. Air Force wants you to put your machine down on friendly soil while it considers the tactical situation. There are other cards in this deck than just you."

Alright. Put down *where*? She was 700 miles out into the middle of the Philippine Sea with a quarter tank of fuel remaining. During flight planning they'd identified a couple of potential emergency landing options along the route between Andersen Airfield on Guam and Taiwan. She looked up the coordinates and scanned the data for the airfield there. It didn't look like much of an airfield to her. Probably some sort of abandoned World War II runway on an atoll the world had forgotten about. And the place she was about to die.

Okinotori Island?

It might be time to reevaluate your life choices, girl.

<< *Nearly 16-year-old Karen O'Hare was still on her grandfather's station. It was the June muster, the one time of year she wouldn't be anywhere else. The mobile mustering team had moved in for two weeks, six strong on bikes and horses, working together with Bunny and her grandpa in their fixed-wing aircraft, and a second pilot in a chopper, a two-seater Robinson R-22.*

On a good day, she was behind the stick of their Bushcat, but even on a bad day she'd be on a dirt bike, or spotting in the chopper. And this memory, this day, was one of the good ones. Her grandpa was two years older and two years weaker. His stomach was cramping, and he had blood in his stools. He told her this, but she didn't really know what it meant. All she knew was it laid him low and she got to do the flying with a stock hand in the cockpit with her as spotter.

They looked for the big mobs of cattle, marking their locations for the helo and the bikes to go after later.

The stock hand she was with was called Sam. She was the leading hand for the mobile crew, was about 30, had about a million freckles on her sunburned face and a little blue heeler pup she carried everywhere with her in a pouch around her neck. Even in the Bushcat while they were flying.

117

O'Hare asked her about it.

"Got to get him used to noise and mayhem," she told O'Hare. "Before we train him. Do it this way, he feels safe even though he's in a plane 200 feet over the ground with a pilot who isn't even old enough to legally buy a beer." O'Hare had the Bushcat tilted onto one wing, circling a water where they'd seen a big herd of Zebu a few days earlier, checking they were still there. They were, white bodies easily visible against the red outback dirt, clustered together in the scant shade of a few scrubby trees. Sam had her binos out, doing a count. "Sixty-eight, sixty-nine … about seventy, I reckon."

"I buy beer for grandpa when I'm in town," O'Hare told her, indignantly. "No one asks my age."

"Bet they don't. Too scared probably." Sam looked at her like she was weighing up a bad idea. "We're roasting wild pig tonight. You check on your grandpa, then come out to our camp if you like. Get a decent feed."

She went to the campsite after making some dinner for her grandpa and found Sam and her crew standing around a pig on a makeshift spit. There was already a small pile of empty beer cans in a washing basin by their feet. Sam handed her a can. It wasn't beer. It was rum and coke, premixed.

"I figure you more for a Bundy and Coke kind of girl," Sam said, putting an arm around O'Hare's shoulders and leading her away from the group a little, standing off to one side like they were watching the sunset turn from gold to purple.

"Thanks, you're probably right," O'Hare said, sipping the drink and wrinkling her nose. She'd never had rum before. She forced herself to take another sip and burped.

Sam laughed. "Attagirl. But a word of advice from Aunty Sam, especially around this crew: the secret of a good night out is always to be the least drunk person at the party."

"Really?"

"Yeah. Trust me on that one." She raised her own can to toast O'Hare, and they both took a sip. It tasted better the second time. Sam held her gaze on O'Hare. "But hey, changing the subject, I want to ask you something."

"Yeah?"

"The old man, he knocks you around, doesn't he?"

O'Hare felt the heat rising in her cheeks. She'd had a big argument with her grandfather a few days earlier and he'd lashed out, clipping her across the cheek. She thought she'd covered the bruise up. Apparently not.

"Sometimes."

"More than sometimes," Sam said. "You know this is my third muster here. Your grandpa is a total bastard. It's time you started thinking about what you want to do with your life, make some choices."

O'Hare felt ashamed. And angry. It was alright for her to think of her grandfather as a bastard, but it was another thing to hear someone else say it. "He's not that bad. He …"

"Total bastard," Sam said. "You need an exit strategy, girl. A way out of here."

O'Hare did have a … well, not a strategy. Or even a plan, really. More of a dream. "I have, sort of … I'm going to join the Air Force."

"How old are you?"

"Sixteen, soon."

"You can't join until you're 17."

"Really?"

"Army, Navy, Air Force, it's the same … 17. I know because I thought about it once." Sam sipped her drink. "Going to be a long year all alone here with that old swine."

119

O'Hare felt the heat rising in her face. And the blackness. She was sure she'd read 16 somewhere. She wasn't sure she could take another year.

Sam saw the look in her face. "Hey, cheer up buckaroo. Why I invited you here is I've got an offer for you."

"An offer?"

Sam pointed at the chopper sitting behind their row of tents. "I need a backup pilot for Don. Having two pilots will get us more jobs, and a better rate. You can fly a plane; he'll teach you to fly a chopper. Get your hours up, I'll sponsor your license. How's that sound?"

"This is like a job offer?"

"Nah, you'll be working for free," Sam said. "Yeah, stupid, it's a job offer. And your ticket out of here."

Suddenly the chasm in front of her didn't feel that wide. "I ... when?"

"Alright, now we're talking," Sam smiled. "We finish the muster here in a few more days, then we're moving north to Morney Plains. You come with us."

"Yeah, but no, I ..." She saw a hitch. "I've got exams. I can't just drop school." Bunny did her schooling via Alice Springs School of the Air, by satellite, over the internet with a dozen other outback students. She had two exams coming up in two weeks: math and computer coding.

"Who said anything about dropping out of school?" Sam asked. "You'll work, and you'll study, slacker."

She wanted more than anything to say yes. "I don't know," she heard herself say instead. "Grandpa ..."

Sam put her arm around her again, pointed her toward the barbecue pit and dragged her along. "Wrong answer. The right answer is 'yes, boss, I'll pack my stuff tomorrow.'"

"Tomorrow?"

"Yeah, you're moving into camp with us," Sam said. "Where we can keep you safe until we move out." She stopped by the barbecue and raised her can, and her voice. "Boys and girls, a toast to our newest crew member, Karen O'Hare!"

There was an enthusiastic cheer, and O'Hare realized everyone else was in on it already. It had already been decided, probably for days.

Three cans later, her head was buzzing. She wasn't the drunkest one at the party, but not the least drunk either. She was sitting on a stump by the coals from the fire, the helo pilot, Don, flat on his back beside her, staring cross-eyed at the stars.

"The hell kind of name is 'Karen'?" he slurred.

"It's my name," she said, defensively. "What's wrong with it?"

"Karen int no kind of proper pilot name," he said. "You're s'posed to be in the cockpit with me tomorrow, but I amt flying with no one called Karen."

"Well, what kind of name is Don?" she asked him back. "Maybe I don't want to fly with a Don? Donald. Donny … whatever you are."

"P'seidon," he said.

"What?"

"My Army aviation call sign. Poseidon. On account of I once landed my chopper on a bed of reeds I thought was grass. Had to fish my bird out with a crane. Stinking bloody reeds." He petered out, and Bunny hoped he had fallen asleep, but then he got a second wind, his voice welling up again. "No. You need a proper call sign, O'Hare. Hey … wait. I got it. O-Hare."

"No, stop …"

"Yeah, totally. I'ma call you 'Bunny.'"

"I really wish you wouldn't."

121

"Too late!" He drew a deep breath and bellowed at the stars. "Bunny O'Hare, kick-ass bush pilot! Yeah, that's a name."

His cap was lying in the dirt next to him, and she picked it up, laying it across his face. "Good night, Donny." She rose a little unsteadily to her feet. The others had all crawled into their tents, and she still needed to find her way back from the muster-crew camp to the homestead, in the dark. She checked the stars, worked out roughly where north was and started walking.

From behind her a voice slurred into the air. "G'night, Bunny O'Hare. Sleep tight. You got a big day ahead."

Takuya Kato was also reevaluating his life choices. Here he was, still very much a "newbie," his first time alone on the station, and already, almost on the first day, he had a crisis he did not know how to handle.

He had decided that although it would probably make him look like he was panicking, calling Oceanographic Command again, *twice* in 24 hours, about something as minor as a Chinese warship covered in antennas anchored right offshore was something he had to do. Right? Or lose his mind. Because, yes, he probably was on the edge of panic.

It just didn't seem normal to him that no one would call him back. Even if they thought he was being a snowflake, he had to talk to *someone*. Except … he couldn't. The station's satellite telephone had been showing "searching satellite" on its display screen for at least the last hour. The station's internet was also reliant on a satellite link, and that was also showing "signal not found." That kind of thing happened during thunderstorms or if there were sunspot events, but …

Kato was no military expert but the fact there was a warship sitting just out of view with four huge satellite dishes on it seemed like more than a coincidence to him. He decided to try the VHF radio. Maybe he could get a message to a passing merchant ship? He powered up the radio and reached for the handset, switching to the Maritime Safety frequency.

He was no radio operator. What was the protocol for what he should say? He'd have to wing it. "Uh, this is Japan Oceanographic Research Station Okinotori calling any vessel in range, do you receive?" he said, then released the button to listen for a response. All he got was static. He tried again, getting nothing but white noise. Kato tried changing frequencies, without luck.

Don't panic, a voice in his head told him. Another one shouted right back. *And why the hell not?*

7. 'A speck on the skyline'

Colonel Wang was still locked into the control pod of the Chongming drone he was piloting when there was a knock on the hard Perspex shell over his head. He jumped. As a pilot who had risen through the ranks flying crewed aircraft, it still shocked him when physical reality interrupted the augmented reality he was looking at through the Chongming's simulated cockpit views.

A simple message would just have been passed to him over the radio. Whatever the interruption was about, it wasn't simple. He checked the tactical monitor and saw no change to the situation of the last 15 minutes. They were still waiting for an update on the American aircraft positions. "Captain Bo, Blade Leader, I am putting my machine into formation-holding mode. You have command."

"Good copy. Blade Section Lead has command," his second-in-command, Captain Xi 'Casino' Bo, replied.

Wang pulled off his head rig and hit the release on the pod hatch to see his intel officer, Major Tan, standing there. She pushed a tablet at him. "Colonel, we have a developing situation."

"What is it?" he asked, trying to make sense of the icons on the map she was showing him.

She placed a finger on the screen. "A US Navy surveillance aircraft is on a path that will take it directly over

Fujian in direct defiance of our NOTAM military exercise warning. It is not responding to our hails."

He reviewed the data on the screen. And cursed. "A US Navy P8 Poseidon. Are we sure of the aircraft type?" The Poseidon was *not* just a surveillance aircraft. It could carry cruise and anti-ship missiles, torpedoes, mines or depth charges.

She nodded. "It has been intercepted by a patrol 100 miles north of *Fujian*. Our pilots are in visual contact. It does not appear to be armed." She tapped another set of icons, farther out from *Fujian*. "And a flight of four X-47B drones has also been detected here, holding station just outside our air exclusion zone."

The American Poseidon might not be carrying weapons, but unlike an uncrewed surveillance drone, which he might consider simply shooting down, it carried a human crew of nine. The greater concern was the flight of X-47B drones, which were not currently in a threatening posture, but that could quickly change, and they *could* be armed.

It was a very deliberate provocation that he did not have time for.

"Order that patrol to stay in close contact with it. If it reaches our outer picket line, they are to give it a final warning, and if it does not respond, alert me." He thought again. "Divert Xiu Snake Squadron to patrol between those X-47Bs and our picket line and launch six more aircraft to take up station where Antler was patrolling."

"Yes, Colonel."

He reached for the pod hatch to close it, then paused. "Push the theatre-level plot you just showed me to my tactical screen. Alert me on radio if there is *any* change to the situation. Clear?"

"Clear, Colonel."

He closed the hatch and pulled on his head rig, immersing himself in the Chongming's systems and data again before switching to visual augmentation and checking he was still holding formation with his squadron as expected. He took a moment to think before retaking control of the mission. The American intrusion to his north could not be an accident. The aircraft involved must be at the extreme limits of their range if they were operating from US carriers or land bases. They would have launched hours earlier, no doubt timed to coincide with the American aggressor flight's transit around China's exclusion zones.

To some extent, the action had succeeded in forcing him to react. The loitering X-47s were intended to put him off-balance. He had no illusion that the Americans would risk a hostile action against China's carrier task force—that would be a definitive act of war—but they would know he could not allow a US aircraft to fly unchallenged right over the top of China's flagship carrier. And they would know that standard protocol would force him to position fighters between the X-47s and *Fujian*. The American carriers involved in the recent RIMPAC exercises also carried F-35 stealth fighters. A niggling thought entered Wang's mind. The Poseidon and the X-47 drones were the aircraft he could *see* to his north. But what if they were not the only aircraft out there?

Dammit to hell! Reluctantly, he realized he could no longer stay with his pilots in pursuit of the American Black Widow. He had to take charge of the developing strategic situation. He reached for his radio. "Captain Bo, I am leaving the flight and moving to operational command. You have command of

Blade flight. As soon as you reestablish contact with the American aircraft, you will contact me for orders."

"Yes, Colonel."

He punched the release on the pod hatch and pulled the neural nodes from behind his ears, climbing out. Major Tan was talking to an officer a few feet away, and he called out to her. "Major! Join me."

She walked quickly over and fell into step with him. The carrier's flight command center was one deck above the pod hanger, but he didn't have to wait to get there to start relaying orders. Taking an earpiece from a pocket of his flight suit, he started barking out the instructions he had given Tan to the air boss in the Commander Center. When he was done, he turned to the Major.

"We lost them?" Wang asked. "Nothing from *Three Zero?*"

"It is a big sky, Colonel." She gave him a pained look. "The drone gave us a vector, but the Americans have apparently changed course …"

"You have a theory about where they are headed, I hope."

She looked grave. "They could have met up with an airborne refueling tanker … They must be low on fuel."

"Then why aren't we looking for *that?*"

"We are. But I have another theory." She told him about the tiny atoll and its airstrip.

"*Japanese?*" Wang picked up his pace. He did not need further analysis to know what the reaction to this intelligence would be. He reached for the comms bud in his ear. "Get me Vice Admiral Zhang immediately."

"We can't raise them," Salt told Bunny. Back on Guam, they had been contacting the Japanese airfield at Okinotori for several minutes, trying to alert them that Bunny and her drones would make an unscheduled landing, but they had received no response. She was still flying at sea level and burning fuel like there was no tomorrow, unwilling to expose them to whatever Chinese radar or directional jammer had locked onto them last time.

Bunny checked her starboard wing. Huey was still faithfully trailing along beside her, but the data stream he was sending her showed he was down to 15 minutes of fuel and change. He'd be going submersible pretty soon.

"Maybe there's no one home?" Bunny offered. After all, Okinotori Reef was a speck in the ocean hundreds of miles from anywhere. She had no idea what facilities Japan had there, though the data on the airfield showed it was operational and had water, power and commercial aviation refueling facilities.

"You're going to have to make a pass over the airfield, see if the runway is clear," Salt said. "You put down first. The drones can follow you in."

If they can. "Roger, heading in," Bunny said. For now, Salt was all business again, but she knew his anger over her actions earlier would not be forgotten, no matter how compelling an argument she had made.

She approached the reef from the northeast, about 200 feet over the ocean.

Her drones were flying 200 feet behind, a couple of hundred feet higher, staying out of her turbulent wake. She had her radar and radio switched off now, emissions at a

128

minimum, head on a swivel checking the sky and sea around her for threats, not trusting the Widow's optical detection systems to alert her. And that was probably why she saw it immediately.

A speck on the skyline. As she sped toward it, it grew longer, broader … and higher!

Bunny zoomed her forward lens. The object was clearly man-made. *What the hell?!* She already had back pressure on her stick, and her Widow jumped a few hundred feet higher, clearing the object with just a couple of hundred feet to spare because the ship—it was definitely a ship—was festooned with towering satellite receiver dishes. Her Valkyries followed her up and down again.

She craned her head to look behind her as the ship disappeared beneath her wing and got on her radio. "Uh, Guam. There is a ship lying off Okinotori. A bloody *gigantic* ship," she said. "Does Japan have some kind of satellite-tracking ship?"

"Unknown," Salt told her. "You got Okinotori airfield ahead? Once you put down …"

Bunny looked at Huey's fuel readout. "Guam, I have to put my EW Valkyrie down first, or it's going to run out of fuel." She got an itching feeling on her neck, which she knew was the thought that there was probably still a squadron of Chinese fighters looking for her. "Or I could send it back out to protect my six …" Bunny said.

"The drone is irrelevant," Salt told her. "Your payload isn't. You put your machine down first and …"

He never finished the sentence.

With chilling inevitability, his voice dissolved into white noise. *Jamming.* The hair rose on O'Hare's neck and she shoved her throttle through the gate, igniting her afterburners as she zoomed vertically into the sky, suddenly desperate for altitude.

She'd been ordered to land, sure ... but wheels down, burning off speed and altitude as a horde of Chinese fighters dropped on her? Not happening.

As she checked altitude, attitude and speed, a blinking warning alert began flashing in her heads-up visor.

Sensor failure ... multiple systems compromised ... sensor failure ... multiple systems compromised ... Multiple systems compromised? It took a neuromorphic AI to tell her that?

No shit, Sherlock.

The Vortex crew aboard *Three Zero* had an advantage in finding the American fighters that had nothing to do with the superiority of their technology. A Chinese Ministry of State Security human source inside the US military had provided them with the exact route the two fighters would take. Of course, they might deviate slightly, and the information was only useful until the first Chinese engagement, but it had been more than enough information to allow the Vortex crew chief to point his sensors at the right arc of sky each time.

Until now. Since the abortive engagement with their fighters, they had been reduced to guesswork about where to aim their arrays. He had been ready to fire another burst of microwave energy at the sky along the latest predicted route of the American flight when a warning came from the ship's combat information center.

"Four fast movers on *visual*, bearing zero niner zero, range five miles, low!"

The commander of Vortex didn't even try to bring his array to bear on the incoming fighters. In fact, he turned his array in the *opposite* direction to the threat. "Array to two zero seven. Azimuth zero to 10,000. Fire on my command!" How the enemy had found them, he had no idea, but they had made a fatal mistake if they thought a low-level supersonic pass would intimidate *Three Zero*'s crew.

"Array aligned on bearing two seven zero and charged!" his energy system control officer reported.

"Wait for my order." If he'd shot energy at them as they approached, the Americans would have flown through it in seconds. By hitting them as they pulled away instead, the storm of energy he was putting into the sky would give him one to two minutes of solid data.

The man cocked an ear to the ceiling and listened. Inside the steel-plated casing under the Vortex dome, he could hear nothing. But then the enemy was on them. A thundering rumble shook their metal housing as the American aircraft boomed overhead.

"Fire!" he had ordered and smiled with satisfaction as the hostiles appeared on his plot. Interesting. They had never tested what would happen to targets flying so close to their array when it fired. He hoped the pilots of those aircraft did not plan to have children.

"Targets reacquired," Captain Bo told his pilots with preternatural calm. "Blade flight, turn to one eight nine and make speed 700. Target area, Okinotori Reef."

131

Asien Chen checked his tactical display and watched it update itself with both the current and projected position of the American Black Widow. There were four targets on the screen again. So the jamming drone had rejoined its mothership after all. Good. More meat for *Fujian's* Chongming pilots. If they were let off their leash.

Chen guided his machine toward Okinotori as it accelerated, his eyes glued to the tactical plot. One of the Americans was staying low; the other three were breaking high. The radar plot could not differentiate the aircraft types. No matter. They would all soon be dead.

Let the order come, and I will make you proud, Li, he told his sister silently.

Bunny's two missile-armed Valkyries, Dewey and Louie, were locked onto her with their short-range formation-keeping lasers, and they followed Bunny up into the sky. She knew she was making herself visible to whatever radar was on that cruise-ship-sized vessel, but hiding was no longer an option for her. She needed fighting room. She could only hope the big ship was friendly. Or at least not carrying surface-to-air missiles.

She checked for Huey. He was down low, setting up to land as she'd ordered him to do. She'd briefly spotted the narrow runway rising out of the shallow sea around the reef and an idea had come to her. The Chinese commander would assume, just as Salt had ordered her to do, that she would desperately try to put herself on the ground first. And as per Chinese doctrine, he would default to trying to kill the piloted aircraft first, knowing that if you killed the mothership, you made it a hundred times easier to kill its wingmen.

Bunny checked her altitude. In the space of a minute, she'd risen from near zero to 10,000 feet and was still climbing hard. She pulled back the throttle and leveled out. Which direction would the Chinese fighters try to jump them from? She drew a mental line between their last contact and her current position and banked her machine to point it west, tangentially away from the likely threat vector and at an angle that would minimize her radar and infrared cross section.

For a few minutes, she had her hands full. Killing her emissions, blanking her infrared signature, pushing Dewey and Louie further out to make them harder to detect, monitoring her sensors in case they came back online, keeping a visual on the killing skies above and around her. Because any minute now …

Sure enough, the jamming stopped. Just like it had last time, and the time before. It could mean only one thing.

Chinese fighters inbound.

"OK, boys, this time it's for real," she decided. She was probably going to get sacked anyway, so she was *not* going down without giving as good as she got. Radio link to Huey restored, she confirmed the order to land. There was no point in Huey trying to hide. She wanted him radiating, drawing Chinese fighters to him like a lamprey in a dark ocean. She brought his EW suite online and cued up his search radar, putting it in broad sweep mode to give him a chance of picking up at target if the Chinese fighters were off his nose, where she expected them to be. "Light 'em up, buddy," she urged quietly.

At the same time, she armed the air-to-air missiles in her weapons bay and on Dewey and Louie. The Chinese were supposed to be a nation of traders? Well, if China wanted to trade *missiles*, she had plenty to trade.

"*Fujian,* Blade Leader. PLA Navy plot shows three fast movers headed our way from Okinotori," Chen heard Bo say. "And another attempting to land. Permission to engage?" His passive sensors were picking up emissions from an adversary, probably a radar searching for them, or an attempt at jamming them again. The passive reading was enough to give him a bearing to the target and a very uncertain range. He needed an active radar lock.

Chen heard Colonel Wang reply instantly. "Blade Leader, *Fujian.* Prioritize the aircraft landing. It must not be allowed to put down. *Fujian* out."

Chen felt the muscles in his stomach tighten. The pilot must have been in a hurry to reach the safety of the ground. The others were probably less important drones. *Was it really happening this time? Would he get his kill?* He and Mushroom were still on point, flying at the front of the Chinese formation.

"Blade One, Blade Two, Blade Leader. You will engage the fleeing aircraft at altitude. Blade Three through Ten, you will follow me. We'll take the target on approach to Okinotori." Bo wasn't taking any chances. He knew there would be no commendation for shooting down a drone and letting the crewed American craft land safely, so he was sending the bulk of his force after the target that was trying to make it down onto Japanese territory.

But damn! It meant he and Mushroom were being sent after what were probably drones. Chen quickly checked his targeting plot. The last known position of the overhead Americans was not updating. The PLA Navy radar had lost the track again. Either the American stealth was

134

extraordinarily good, or the Chinese radar was not. Every second since the target had been painted was a second in which it could have changed position in any of three dimensions.

"Shredder, we can fire our missiles in active seeker mode. They might see the targets before we do …" Mushroom suggested.

Shredder thought it through. It was his call as lead pilot in the element. "Only if we get the bearing right. We can't afford to miss. Accelerate to 680 knots, make altitude 20, take a five-mile separation, and go active. Broad search arc," Chen ordered. They would be spreading their radar's energy over a wide area of sky, meaning they would need to be closer to their target to get a hit.

"Blade Two going active," she confirmed. "Five-mile separation." As he watched through the lenses on his drone, she rolled her machine right and peeled away.

He turned on his Chongming's search radar. It made a couple of sweeps, coming up blank. But he knew the enemy was ahead of him somewhere. The one, the only, question on Chen's mind right now was *who would see who first?*

Bunny had the answer to that question. Even as she was powering away from the Chinese formation at 600 knots, the radar aboard her EW Valkyrie, Huey, had illuminated about six Chinese aircraft, right where she hoped they would be. Four were down at about 10,000 feet and maneuvering to intercept Huey approaching Okinotori, but the other two were climbing through 15,000 feet toward 20 and appeared to be on an intercept track for … Dewey, Louie and Bunny.

135

She rolled a little left and adjusted her course more northward to make the job harder for her pursuers. Could they see her? They were only 20 miles behind her. The other group was making a beeline for Huey and was already well within missile range if they wanted to take a long shot. If it were her piloting a Chongming, she'd want to get closer, get a solid lock before shooting.

Running out of fuel was suddenly the least of Huey's problems. He wasn't going to make it down.

"You may as well go out in style, mate," Bunny muttered to herself. She punched some commands into Huey's interface and hit "execute." She ran quickly through Huey's EW attack profile menu and picked a suitable algorithm.

Forget him. She had plenty else to worry about. She pulled up a tactical screen that showed the last known position of all combatants. Twenty miles to her South, Huey had just pulled out of his landing approach, ignited his afterburner and aimed himself straight at the larger group of Chinese fighters, approaching Okinotori from the east.

North of the Japanese reef, the flight comprising her, Dewey and Louie was up at 20,000 feet and pulling away from Okinotori again. She had the two drones trailing five miles behind and on either side of her, between her and the two Chinese fighters that had broken off the main group and come after her. Which showed one thing clearly … whatever ground or ship-based radar China was using was more than capable of detecting her Widow. That was bad news. The good news for her was that it apparently still relied on its air force to do the killing, and the radars on the Chongming drones chasing her were far less capable.

She was in ninja mode—all emissions dampened, drones operating on laser comms, engine exhausts shuttered, heading and attitude optimized to bounce radar energy away from her and not back at the pursuing fighters. Theoretically, she could sneak away from this engagement now, leave Huey to his fate and bug out. But Huey wasn't the only one with fuel problems. She was down to 16 percent … not enough to make the rendezvous with the tanker to the west and definitely not inside her comfort zone for a protracted fighter engagement.

She really was having a devil or deep blue sea moment. Stay hidden and keep heading north, but run out of fuel. Or try to sneak back south and try to get her machine down at Okinotori exactly like the Chinese were now expecting her to do, and where they would be waiting for her, having no doubt just dispatched Huey.

The devil it is. It wasn't even a decision, really. The only question was, would she sacrifice both of her trailing drones in the attempt, leaving her with no protection for the onward flight, or would she try to shepherd at least one of them down onto the runway with her?

Ah hell, the way things were looking, there wasn't likely going to *be* any "onward flight" unless she tried to even the odds, so she might as well burn both drones and give herself the best chance of survival. She cursed whoever had come up with the Valkyrie's names because as she cued up their orders, she actually felt a little bit bad that she was about to send Dewey and Louie to certain death.

Thankfully, she didn't give them their orders by voice or have to listen to them stoically reply, "Yes, Lieutenant!" They simply registered the pulsing light from her comms laser, fed the orders into their combat AI systems and, with no fuss at all, peeled away toward the last known positions of their targets.

Louie went toward the two Chinese fighters pursuing her, and Dewey toward the larger group that was currently and completely fixated on Huey.

OK, China, Bunny thought grimly. *This is your wake-up call.*

To the East, the four-plane element Bo was leading in pursuit of Huey finally got a missile lock on their target over Okinotori. He couldn't see what kind of aircraft it was, but its actions told him it was crewed—so it had to be their target, the Black Widow. And it was still airborne! It seemed to have aborted its landing approach and was now swinging around to face them. But if the pilot was planning to attack them, he was outnumbered and out of time.

"Blade Leader to Blade flight," Bo announced. "All aircraft, arm missiles. Prepare to ..."

"Targeting radar on our six! Missiles inbound!" came a panicked shout. His eyes flicked to his radar warning receiver display painted on his helmet visor, which confirmed the call. There was an enemy fighter right behind them. His tactical display showed four missiles inbound, still 20 miles out though. Only four missiles, but there was no way of knowing yet which of his closely grouped fighters they were aimed at. They'd been jumped, but the enemy had given them precious minutes in which to react.

"Blade flight, break!" he ordered, and like a starburst firework, each member of his flight peeled upward and outward, away from him, while he continued straight, pulling his machine into a screaming vertical climb. His mind raced. He was Blade Ten. Blades One and Two were engaged to the north. That left him several fighters to give orders to. If he

138

tried to do it by voice, he'd barely be halfway through by the time the enemy missiles were on them. And Chinese air fighting doctrine did not allow for pilots to be left to their own initiative in a dogfight. But the Chongming was a drone and, as such, capable of uncrewed semi-autonomous flight.

In other words, he could take his pilots "out of the loop." He jabbed a thumb onto a button on his throttle and tapped another on his flight stick to take control of all the aircraft in his flight. He could now issue simultaneous orders to every aircraft in his flight. It was a power only to be used as a last resort, but with an unseen enemy on their six and missiles flying, he judged *this* was that moment.

"Blade Leader has … Blade flight authority," he grunted, the virtual reality-enhanced images of his zooming aircraft in his helmet viewfinder giving him a completely physical sense of vertigo. Working the buttons on his flight stick and throttle, he sent orders flying through the ether and saw the machines in the sky around his react immediately.

Blades One and Two he ordered to continue searching for the larger American fighter group of three. It was probably one of the group that had broken off and attacked Bo and his flight, but that still left two up at 20,000 feet and unaccounted for.

Blades Three through Six he ordered to swing around and engage the threat on their six o'clock. It was likely a Valkyrie or Ghost Bat loyal wingman and had just spent all its missiles, but he couldn't take the risk that it was a different type with more ordnance. It had to be destroyed, even if it meant the machines he had tasked to do it would be destroyed too. The Chinese aircraft were, after all, just metal and silicon. No Chinese blood would be shed.

The four remaining Chongming fighters included his own, and he ordered them all to go defensive, to try to avoid or outmaneuver any incoming missiles that locked onto them and then regroup on him. There was still an American fighter over Okinotori to deal with.

"Blade Leader, releasing flight authority. You have your orders, pilots," he said, and hit the command release. His pilots were "back behind their sticks" now, their machines already executing his orders, but their flight controls responding again to their pilots' inputs. All they had to do now was reorient themselves to their new orders and get back in the fight.

The entire process, from assuming authority to handing it back again, had taken seven seconds.

He quickly scanned the block of orders posted on his helmet visor and returned his attention to his own situation. The targets of the American missiles were clearer now.

And one of them was coming for *him*.

Bunny watched with satisfaction the mayhem that Dewey's four missiles had created. The Chinese flight bearing down on Huey had scattered like startled pigeons. Having executed the first phase of her orders, Dewey moved to the second, flipping his powerful search radar into jamming mode even as he picked out a single Chinese aircraft, locked onto it and set himself an intercept course that would put him right on its nose. As he accelerated.

To ramming speed.

Chen almost shouted with jubilation as he finally picked up a warning on his radar receiver, showing a radar in search mode, right ahead of him. It was just a brief spike and then gone. But now he knew where at least one enemy fighter was. He ignored the fact that it probably meant the American fighter could see *him*. He'd registered Bo's confirmation of their existing orders. He and Mushroom were 10 miles apart—they had this new enemy pinned like a grain of rice at the end of a pair of chopsticks.

"Blade Two, Blade One, fire on emission bearing, active radar homing."

"Blade Two copies," Mushroom replied tightly. "Firing on bearing. *Fox three.*" In the distance, he saw a flash as the PL-15 missile under her drone's wing lit its tail and streaked away.

"Blade One, fox three," he said, releasing his own missile. They didn't have a lock on the target, but they didn't need it. Their PL-15 outranged any missile in the American arsenal. The American machine had stupidly shown them where it was. Now it ...

"Missiles inbound!" Mushroom called suddenly. "Evading."

Dammit. Their target had fired on *them*. Chen saw Mushroom's outbound missile tracks on his radar, saw the direction of the attack on his radar warning receiver as the inbound enemy missiles went active and started homing on him, but he didn't turn away. Not yet.

There was one missile coming at him; the other was targeting Mushroom, who was breaking away to starboard and heading for the safety of the sea. He still had seconds to play with. He narrowed his own radar search, trying to lock up their adversary.

There! A chime in his ears and an icon appeared on his visor, off his nose, 10 degrees to port. Close enough for an ID this time … *Valkyrie.*

Another alert. It was firing again, two more missiles, one at Mushroom and one at him.

He couldn't ignore the threat any longer. But he had the American fighter ahead of him locked now, and he fired another two PL-15 missiles of his own. "Blade One, *fox three.* Evading!"

He rolled his machine onto its back and oriented it toward the incoming missiles before he pulled back on his stick and pointed his nose at the horizon. The radical maneuver would force the nearest missile to turn hard to stay with him, and he fired loitering chaff and flare decoys into his wake.

Chen had learned early in his training that flying the Chongming was an out-of-body experience. Because you weren't actually *inside* the aircraft, and your life was not at risk, you could keep a cool head and process a crazy amount of input. He glimpsed the white smoke trail of the nearest missile diving on his fighter from overhead and calculated visually that it was going to miss. His attention shifted to Mushroom's machine, and he saw with satisfaction that she had also evaded the first American missile, even as his own missiles closed on the American machine, which was diving toward the sea now in a futile attempt to escape.

He switched his attention back to the second American missile. This was going to be closer. *Too close.* He was firing a stream of decoys out the back of his Chongming, but the missile wasn't deviating, and he was running out of sky as the sea below began filling his augmented vision from horizon to

142

horizon. *Ten thousand feet, nine five, nine one ...* He held his nerve.

When he judged the enemy missile was about 10 seconds away, he rolled his machine upright again and pulled back diagonally hard right on the stick, jamming his left foot on the rudder pedal and shoving his throttle forward. Defying gravity, the Chongming went from a screaming dive to a sickening climb in the blink of an eye. A human pilot onboard the aircraft at that moment would have been rendered immediately unconscious—that is, if their head wasn't physically wrenched from their body by the g-force.

The augmented vision from the simulated cockpit rotated so violently that Chen actually felt a moment's motion sickness.

No missile yet designed could have followed Chen's radical change of direction, and the missile tracking his machine lost him, plowing at supersonic speed into the sea below.

The problem with the maneuver Chen had executed was that he was one of the only pilots in the Ao Yin wing who had perfected it. It required precise timing and perfect execution or the pilot would lose all control authority and the g-forces on the drone would tear it apart. Mushroom didn't even attempt it. As the second American missile aimed at her closed on her machine, Mushroom tried a corkscrew reverse, firing a veritable typhoon of decoys into her wake, but to no avail. The American missile powered through them and buried itself in her Chongming's exhaust and detonated. The blast separated her engine from its housing, and Chen saw her machine tumble from the sky even as he noted one of his own missiles had slammed into the closing American drone and turned it into a tiny fireball on the horizon and curved down toward the sea.

"Splash one," Chen reported with satisfaction. It wasn't a crewed aircraft kill, but it was a kill. His first. For Li.

Mushroom swore. "Blade Two is down."

Chen checked his sensors. "Blade One has no other targets," he admitted.

Bunny no longer had any idea what was happening in the air around her. She had gone dark—no radio or radar signals out, and even her radio receiver and all ancillary avionics shut down—because electricity is heat and noise, and heat and noise draw unwanted attention. With her drones out of visual range, she could no longer command them with laser comms and no longer receive messages from them.

She was alone.

Her only sensors were the distributed aperture optical-infrared cameras scattered around the Black Widow's smooth fuselage, giving her a 360-degree view of the sky around her out to about 20 miles in current conditions, and her own Mark I eyeballs, which roamed restlessly from instrument panel to helmet visor to quarter the surrounding sky before returning to the instrument panel again and repeating ...

She had dropped her speed to 500 knots and was curving the Widow in an arc that would bring it around to the west of Okinotori.

The plot frozen on her tactical display was minutes old now but showed eight aircraft in the sky just east of Okinotori. Louie had attacked them from the east, so they should have eyes and radars pointed away from the Japanese reef, toward the drone, but all it would take would be one, *just*

144

a single Chongming, to swing around and point its radar west, at her. And at a range of under 10 miles, it could not fail to see her, ninja mode or not.

Or for that damn jamming radar to pick her up again.

All she could hope was that at least one of her little buddies was still giving the Chinese fighters hell.

Hell was exactly what Dewey and Louie had given the Chinese fighters.

Dewey had fired first, scattering the flight headed toward Okinotori. As Bunny swung her machine around toward a landing on the reef, the larger Chinese group was either skating through the sky trying to evade his missiles or lining up a missile shot of their own.

To do that, Bo had sent four of his fighters at Dewey and ordered them to ignore the incoming attack. They got three missiles away before two of Dewey's four missiles struck home, taking both Chongming targets off the board. Dewey himself had accelerated beyond Mach 2 and aimed himself at a third Chinese fighter, but its pilot, back behind the stick after Bo had returned combat control to her, had recognized the threat and taken Dewey out from five miles away.

He'd traded his life dearly, spoiling the Chinese attack and taking two Chongming fighters with him.

Louie had gone after Shredder and Mushroom and fired two missiles, one at each target. He'd missed Shredder but took down Mushroom's Chongming before the volley of missiles they'd fired back at him had hit home.

145

He'd only scored one kill before sacrificing himself, but like Dewey, he had drawn the Chinese fighters to him, allowing O'Hare to escape.

O'Hare knew none of this. All she knew was that she had clear air and a runway off to her port side about three miles away and clearly visible now.

She was side-slipping toward a landing, skating in at about 2,000 feet and 400 knots. Wind from the east; at last something going for her. It would be on her nose, helping her keep her landing speed down, which was probably a good thing because the runway over her left shoulder looked *pretty bloody average*.

She had time to look at the Japanese installation properly for the first time and was not impressed. A three-story white building on pontoons, a sea-level dock that barely looked big enough to berth a decent-sized fishing boat and, running along what might once have been a coral ridgeline, a single runway on raised concrete. It couldn't be more than 2,000 feet long, maybe 100 feet wide. You could just about put a 10-seat turboprop down on it, but her jet-engined Widow, payload bay loaded for bear, needed 2,200 feet.

She needed to lose some weight, fast. Dump the three HACM missiles? *Hell no, that would give China the win.* She still had 3,500 lbs. of fuel though, so she quickly vented all but 1,000 lbs. It left a trail of white vapor in the sky behind her that a blind person could see from miles away, but what choice did she have?

She was about a minute away from what was looking like another crash landing.

8. 'Defender of Okinotori Station'

'Casino' Bo's voice was dispassionate. "Blade flight, regroup on me over Okinotori. We have orders to cover the airfield there."

His mood was rather more troubled than his voice conveyed. His arms still ached from wrestling his machine around the sky to avoid the American missile, but the fool had made the mistake of firing from too far out. Bo thanked his ancestors for the American pilot's mistake. He'd gotten behind Bo's flight undetected—Bo's fault for being so fixated on the target over Okinotori—and could have gotten much closer before showing his hand by lighting up his radar and firing his missiles. Launching from such a distance, he'd given Bo precious time to react.

But ahead of him lay almost certain ignominy. He'd lost three fighters and would probably be disciplined for it. He assumed the American Widow they had been about to engage over Okinotori had made it down. Another reason he expected a dressing-down. At best, he would be reduced in rank and pay and demoted from flight leader. At worst, he'd be taken off the roster and sent for retraining the next time *Fujian* docked. Miserable at the thought, he saw a lumbering Shaanxi cargo plane in his future.

It was so unfair. They had claimed *both* of the attackers … the kill-to-loss ratio was within acceptable norms. It was their first combat engagement, and the much-vaunted Americans had been given a smack in the jaw they surely could not recover from. The combat vision showed the two aircraft they destroyed were Valkyries. If their intel was correct, that meant the Americans had only two remaining aircraft, maybe fewer. It was hard to know with missiles inbound and outbound during an engagement that had lasted barely minutes. Perhaps they had achieved *more* than two kills? If so, his career might be saved.

Bo was not a glass-half-full person. He'd screwed up the intercept on the Widow. He was doomed.

Chen felt for his doomed friend Mushroom. On the one hand, she was still alive. Flying a crewed aircraft she would now be dead, or hanging from a parachute about to drop into a shark-infested sea. On the other, she was not only out of the fight, but she would also immediately be called into a debrief where she would have to account for every one of her actions during the dogfight, as every byte of data from the Chongming was streamed in real time to cloud-based servers during such engagements. The review would be a brutal second-by-second dissection of the engagement, and no pilot emerged from such a process with their confidence completely intact, least of all a pilot who had just lost their aircraft.

He brought his machine around and oriented it toward the other Blade flight aircraft, now nearly 30 miles distant and closing on Okinotori. He had not yet reacquired the fleeing American Black Widow.

"I'm sorry, Mushroom," he told his wingman, then offered the mutually unsatisfactory consolation. "Next time."

"Thanks, Shredder," she said with obvious pain. "Blade Two, moving to debrief."

He went to wave at her through the smoky glass of his pod and realized his hands were shaking. The adrenaline of combat still washed through his blood. He held them in front of his face and stared at them until they steadied a little, then looked at the mission timer on his fuselage. Fifteen minutes since they had been sent in pursuit of the Americans. Five since they had come under attack and returned fire. Three since Mushroom's Chongming had plunged into the waves below his aircraft.

The speed of air combat was insane. Hours of flying your machine off the deck of the carrier until you were in position to start your patrol and then minutes later, literal minutes later, you were "dead" or "alive," your enemy victorious or vanquished, and you were either on your way to a career-ending debrief like Mushroom, or still airborne, like him, hands shaking, wondering how the hell you had gotten through.

Chen turned his thoughts to the sea and sky ahead of him. Okinotori Island was technically Japanese territory. One of the Americans had put down there. They had detected no air defenses on their pass over the reef. What would they find there? Would the island's defenders be awake now, and aiming a missile battery at them?

Defender of Okinotori Station, biologist Takuya Kato, had been working on the platform that ran around the lighthouse, trying to get a radio signal by holding a crude wire antenna in the air as he hopped around on one leg, when thunder rumbled in the sky. Except ... it *wasn't* thunder. It was a long,

149

continuous rumble that soon resolved itself into four large jets, screaming across the waves.

Straight at him!

There was no time to think. Instinctively he threw himself flat as they blasted overhead. One started a flat turn to the south while the others screamed into the sky with engines spewing blue-white cones of fire.

First a Chinese warship and now this?! The jets were Chinese too, he guessed. They had to be. Who else would be so bold as to fly so low over the station that if they'd been any lower, they would have blown its windows out? He rose slowly to his feet. Three of the aircraft were just tiny dots rising higher into the blue sky. The other had swung far out to sea to the south, still down at sea level, and he could barely see it but … *was it coming back?*

Kato was beginning to seriously regret having stayed at the station for Golden Week.

As he watched the jet get closer, it seemed to him it was slowing down. Maybe he shouldn't be standing gawping if it was going to fly right over and try to get a look at the station, which is what he assumed it planned to do. He ran for the ladder down the side of the lighthouse tower and slid down it by just holding the side rails and using his toes on the rungs to slow his descent. He hit the deck at the bottom hard, but he was already running for the station's communication center, where he would be out of sight but still have a good view of what was going on around the reef.

It was also where the weapons locker was located, though Kato had no idea what the hell kind of weapons would be inside it. Who would trust any kind of weapon to a bunch of scientists and bureaucrats was beyond him, but he'd been told there had once been a rampaging seal that went amok and the

150

crew had been forced to attack it with a fire ax, so after that, they'd been issued with some kind of firearm. But even thinking about it was overreacting, right?

Or maybe not. He had run to the window that looked south over the sea at the approaching aircraft, and it *was* slowing. Not only slowing; it was lowering its *wheels!* He looked over his shoulder at the runway on the other side of the reef. The jet was planning to land? Was Okinotori being invaded?

No, that was stupid. You didn't invade an island with a jet. Kato had seen enough movies to know you brought troops in landing ships, or at least rubber boats, or dropped them from a helicopter, right? You didn't send a lone pilot or two in a jet.

But this one was definitely shaping to land. Kato had never seen a warplane up close like this before. It looked more like a missile than a plane. Long, sleek, with stubby wings. Then he wasn't thinking about much anymore, as the pilot seemed to change his mind. The engine note rose with the nose of the machine, and once again, it thundered overhead. He spun around and ran to the windows on the other side of the comms center to see the machine curve away toward the horizon, so low over the water he soon lost it in the afternoon heat haze.

That had been what … 15, 20 minutes ago? Kato had stood there staring out over the empty sea, looking around at the empty sky, listening to the hiss of static from the station's VHF radio, just waiting for something else to happen. Fully expecting it would. Not quite believing it hadn't. The lack of developments only served to increase his anxiety.

He needed a plan.

151

Weapons locker! He looked around, trying to remember where the hell it even was. There was a row of cabinets on one wall, and he ran over, pulling open the doors, but only found miscellaneous stores, tools and clothing. Beside the door leading out to the galley, there was another smaller but more solid-looking cabinet. That was it!

A small, solid-looking cabinet ... with a combination lock on it. Of course. People were people, and scientists got moody too. Who wanted a depressed and lonely individual on a station in the middle of the Philippine Sea to have easy access to a firearm, right? His manager hadn't left him any instructions about the combination either, of course. He rattled the door in the vain hope it might have been left unlocked, but it didn't open. There was a fire ax and extinguisher out in the corridor, and he tried each in turn, but all he managed to do was dent it.

And what would you have done with a bloody gun anyway, Kato? he asked himself. *Take the pilot prisoner? A military pilot wasn't a seal. He probably had a gun, too, and knew how to use it, and you'd end up full of holes.*

OK, he had to hide. But where?

Her wingmen were gone, and O'Hare was alone ... for now. Long enough to get herself safely down on a runway that was at least 200 feet too short? That remained to be seen.

She lined up the Widow's nose on a point about 100 feet short of the runway and dropped her airspeed, working the throttle to keep her machine just above a stall. Every time her airspeed dropped too low, warnings sounded in her ears, but she blocked them out, focusing on keeping her nose above the horizon and her airspeed low.

Wheels down, throttle forward ... stick getting mushy ... more throttle ... too much ... back off!

The start of the runway rushed up to meet her. She was nose-high and floated in over the runway as a blast of hot air from the tarmac took hold of her Widow and tried to push it *higher.* She chopped the throttle, dropping the 70,000 lb. airframe onto the tarmac with a thud that jarred her teeth in her skull. She dropped the nosewheel and then shoved both toe brakes to the floor as every control surface on her Widow deployed to increase drag and pull her up.

It would not be enough.

She could see that as the far end of the runway continued to rush toward her, with nothing but sea and sky at the other end of it. She'd touched down too late and too fast.

OK, she had one play left. The twin-engined Widow had a split throttle, which meant that she could apply power differentially to each engine. Leaving her right engine at idle, she gripped the left engine throttle tightly in her left hand and her flight stick in her right. On the ground, she controlled the nose wheel by twisting the stick, but for what she was about to attempt, just twisting the stick wasn't going to be enough ...

Three hundred feet ... two twenty knots ... not yet, Bunny baby ...

She twitched her flight stick a little, pointing her nose toward the left-hand corner of the runway.

Two hundred ... one eighty knots ... one sixty ... one fifty feet, one thirty knots ... get ready ... NOW!

She shoved her left throttle forward, hearing the roar of her left engine behind her as she lifted her left foot off the brake and twisted her stick hard right, trying to give the Widow as much portside thrust as she could and spin it around to the right on the narrow runway. It was the sort of maneuver you'd hesitate to do at 20 knots, let alone at 120, and the Widow didn't like it at all.

It staggered right, lurched left as though trying to correct, and then began to turn right. Slowly ... *too slowly.*

Then faster, as the engine thrust kicked in. Her nose swung wildly right, slamming her helmeted head against the portside cockpit glass. *Whoa, Nelly!* She pulled the port engine throttle back and saw the horizon swing wildly in her vision, the Japanese research station building coming into view now ... then runway ... sea again ... nosewheel to port ...

She jammed both feet forward on the rear wheel brakes again and ...

Her Widow juddered to a halt. She blew a huge pent-up breath out of her lungs.

She was still alive. And on the runway. Pointing diagonally across the runway, more or less, but at least she was on the ground and not in the sea. She looked over her right shoulder. She'd pulled around in a crazy half circle with just 50 feet of solid ground to spare.

Damn, that was pretty, girl, she commended herself as her stomach tried to settle. *Let's never, ever do that again, alright?*

With a blip of her engines and a twist of her flight stick, she lined her nose up on the runway center line again and began taxiing at speed toward what looked like a large hangar entrance on the sea-level floor of the Japanese research base.

It looked like it was made to take something like a commercial twin-engined transport, so the entrance should be high and wide enough to take a single sleek, streamlined Widow. She wanted to get her bird out of sight if she could, and …

And what?

She had no bloody idea what. Probably try to get back in touch with Salt somehow and work that out. She started thinking furiously as she made for the probably illusory safety of the hangar maw.

She had experienced the Chinese electronic attack enough times to form a theory. The jamming coming and going like that made no sense if it was intended to blind them and let the Chinese fighters sneak up on them. Because in that case, why did it come and go? If you could blind an enemy, you wanted them to stay blind, so you would keep jamming. But the pattern was the same each time … heavy interference that screwed up radio and radar operation, and then the Chinese drones appeared. So if it wasn't deliberate jamming, it could just be a side effect. Something somewhere—and of course she couldn't help but think about that massive ship down there with the crazy big satellite dishes—was blasting insane amounts of energy into the sky. Energy enough to drown out any other radio signals out there, but also energy enough that even a sixth-generation stealth fighter like hers could not stay invisible.

She'd never heard of anyone, let alone China, possessing such a system, but that didn't mean squat. All it meant was she and Salt were probably the first ones to come up against it. And if she was right, it made sense that you couldn't keep up that kind of transmission for very long. It would probably require the equivalent of a small nuclear reactor if you wanted to keep transmitting anything more than a few minutes, and, well, she hadn't heard of China putting reactors in any of its ships either. She was pretty sure something like *that* wouldn't have gone under the radar. So it was a new type of radar, had to be. With the nifty side effect it blinded its target.

How could they beat it? Well, like most radars, the curvature of the earth might defeat it. There were some low-frequency radar systems that could bounce waves off the ionosphere and back down again to detect low-flying aircraft, but they were too slow to direct fighter interceptions like this one was doing. So it was high-frequency energy, which meant if it was being sent from ground level, your best chance would be to fly nap of the earth and use sea clutter to help you hide. That wouldn't help at all if the radar was being fired into the sky from an aircraft at altitude, but in a game like this, you had to play the odds. The odds a system that burned energy like that could be mounted inside a plane? Low. Odds it was probably mounted on a hulking great ship covered in antennas? High. Flying nap of the earth all the way from here to Taiwan though made it even more important to hit that tanker because she would burn more fuel. And it made her a sitting duck if she was spotted visually because she'd only have two directions in which to maneuver: up or sideways.

It was a whole chocolate bar's worth of speculation, and she threw the packet back in the storage locker and took another sip of water. The darkened entrance to the hangar was resolving itself now, and she eased back on her throttle again. It was empty, thankfully, with what looked like some basic maintenance, refueling and electric charging dollies lined up against one wall.

She pointed her nose at the left side of the hangar to give whatever passed for a flight crew on this station room to drag her nose back around and point it down the runway again, was just about to coast into the hangar when ...

An icon appeared in her helmet, flashing and demanding her attention. Her blood froze, expecting a missile warning to follow. She was down on the deck, still out in the open, a sitting bloody *duck* ...

Wait. Not a missile. A *friendly?*

And then she smiled, reading the text scrolling across her multifunction display. *Valkyrie 1 requests emergency landing routing authority. Fuel at three percent estimated. Valkyrie 1 requests emergency landing routing authority. Fuel at three percent estimated.* Huey! The little guy was still alive somehow and making a beeline for Okinotori with fumes in his fuel tanks.

She hit the command to clear him to land. His AI would do the rest. And landing on the Japanese installation's runway would be no drama for him. He weighed a fraction of her Widow and could land on half the length of the runway, even fully fueled. She quickly pulled her machine in under the cover of the Japanese hangar and dropped the hatch in her floor, sliding through the cockpit exit as her machine rocked from its sudden stop. The ladder from the cockpit was still deploying as she dropped, fell four feet to the ground and tried a superhero-style three-point landing, which just dumped her painfully on her ass.

She ran to the front of the hangar just as Huey hit the tarmac, puffs of white smoke drifting from his tires as he gracefully rolled to a gentle stop and then began a shuffling, hesitant turn. Bunny smiled, imagining what she'd be hearing if he could speak. *What the hell kind of runway is this? You think I am a goddamn hobby drone I should have to turn around on this narrow-ass piece of tarmac? And what the hell kind of act was it leaving me up there on my own with fuel lights flashing while you got your machine down here nice and safe? Thanks a lot.*

157

But of course, he said none of that. His laser comms system had locked onto her machine again, and he was programmed to take up a landing position 20 feet off her starboard side, assuming there were no obstacles. Failing that, he'd simply taxi to a safe holding place within 100 yards and wait.

There wasn't enough room in the small hangar for Huey too, but she watched with genuine affection as he taxied as close to the hangar as he could and then simply shut down his engines and sat there, hot engine ticking in the tropical sun.

She felt like going out and patting him on the nose and giving him a treat, like a faithful dog that had just performed a neat trick.

But that would have to wait. She needed fuel and power. Looking around the hangar, she realized she needed more than that.

In the distance she heard the roar of jet engines, and in seconds, they were overhead. She shrank back into the shadow of the hangar. Then looked around her. She needed a Japanese-speaking ground crew who could help her sort jet fuel from avgas and get her two machines hooked up. Where *was* everyone?

Well, the day hadn't gone like she expected, so why should now be any different? But then, it's funny how a single day, or a single conversation on a single day, can change your whole life.

<< *O'Hare was 17 and had just finished high school. A year with Sam and her crew, and she'd put away enough money to get her to*

158

Melbourne, in southeast Australia, to look for work. She knew exactly what she wanted to do, but the guy sitting opposite her was having trouble understanding.

"I want to fly jets," she told the "Career Coach" at the Royal Australian Air Force's "Unlimited Opportunities" Center.

"Uh-huh," he said, looking and sounding bored, reading her application. "So you want to be a pilot."

"No, I'm already a pilot," she told him. "I want to be a fighter pilot."

Now he looked at her properly. Then down at her application. "You're 17. Flying planes in computer games doesn't make you a pilot."

It was the condescending tone that riled her. He was only about 10 years older than her, and not even in uniform. He was a civilian recruiter, a contractor. Her year on the mustering crew had changed her. She'd learned a few things. Like the cattle don't come to you; you have to go get them.

She looked around the room, where most of the desks were empty and most of the staff were drinking coffee or looking at their phones. The place wasn't exactly overrun with applicants. Then she saw what she was looking for. At the back of the room by a photocopy machine was an officer in a blue uniform. He didn't look like a pilot, but at least he was Air Force.

She reached over, ripped her application from the hands of the guy reading it.

"Hey!"

She ignored him and walked over to the Air Force officer, tapping him on the shoulder. "Are you in charge here?"

He looked surprised, then annoyed. "If you have an appointment, speak to the receptionist."

159

"I already spoke to him, and then I spoke to that guy there," she said, pointing at the Career Coach. "I want to speak to someone who knows what they're talking about."

He smiled, leaned his back against the copy machine and crossed his arms. "Alright, young lady, you have five minutes of my precious time."

"I want to fly jets," she said. She handed him her application. "I already have my light aircraft and rotary aircraft licenses."

That got his attention. He looked at the application and, as he read, held out his hand without looking up. "Got them on you?"

She pulled her licenses out of the back pocket of her jeans and handed them to him. He looked them over.

"Recreational." He said it like it was an insult. "Navigation Endorsement?"

"Didn't bring it, but I have it."

He handed back her licenses but hung on to her application, which she took as a good sign. "You must have started young."

"Got my fixed-wing license at 14, rotary at 16," she said.

He sized her up, from her short mop of dusty blond hair to her scuffed, steel-toed boots. "You grew up in the outback."

"Near Katherine."

"On a station?"

"Yeah. What do I need to do if I want to fly jets?"

"You finish high school?"

"Uh-huh. Top grades in math and computer science. The Air Force puts me through university, right? Then I can go to pilot school?"

"Defense Academy first, yeah, then Flying Training School," he said. He looked at her application again, where she filled in her school grades.

"Even if you cruise through, ace everything, you know how many make it through ab initio training into fighter school?"

"Don't care."

"One in a hundred and … you don't care?" he frowned.

"You're going to tell me how hard it is, how it's going to take years and I probably won't make it no matter how good my grades or how good of a pilot I think I am. I read what other applicants wrote online. I don't care because I'm going to be the one who makes it."

"Oh, you are?"

"Yeah. So my question is, the fact I already have my pilot license, with navigation endorsement, does that get me any credit at pilot school, or do I have to start at the bottom with all the newbies?"

'Casino' Bo's Chongming circled over Okinotori as the rest of his flight held offshore. "*Fujian*, Blade Leader. I have one target on the ground at Okinotori Reef. Repeat, one target has now landed at the Japanese airfield. Looks like an uncrewed drone, type … Valkyrie. Blade flight holding over Okinotori and awaiting your instructions."

Colonel Wang had reached *Fujian*'s flight control center and was watching multiple developments unfold as the request for orders came from his Chongming fighters over Okinotori.

The American Poseidon surveillance aircraft, a turbofan-driven aircraft based on the 737 airliner, was refusing to respond to any hails over the radio and had just overflown one of *Fujian*'s air warfare destroyer picket ships 20 miles out from the carrier. Two of his fighters were flying wingtip to wingtip with it, but the Poseidon was ignoring them too. The

161

Chinese ship below it had not just warned the American plane that it was entering a military exercise zone and risked being shot down; they had also locked it with their missile-targeting radar to remove any doubt that they could destroy it in the blink of an eye if they so chose. It had continued on its way, its crew not even deigning to look at the fighters in the sky beside them, and was now on a heading that would take it just north of the carrier itself.

Further north, the US X-47B attack drones that had been flying a lazy racetrack-shaped circuit around the sky had broken off and started heading back to their carrier, wherever that may have been. Wang did not have perfect information on the position of the US carriers at that moment and he had relaxed a little, only to have his irritation rise again when six new X-47Bs appeared on radar and took up patrolling where the other group had left off.

The squadron he had placed to his north to serve as a blocking force if the two American fighters evaded their pursuit would soon be in position to intercept the American drones if they made any threatening moves toward the carrier task force, but the six aircraft he had just launched from *Fujian* to take the role of blocking force were still forming up and wouldn't be in position for another 30 minutes.

And he had lost three drones! A lesson for future engagements—these Americans will fight back if threatened. He had ordered the first pilot who was shot down to report to him personally for debriefing.

The US actions were a series of provocations that would have him incandescent with fury on any other day, but he had a very clear-eyed view of what his priorities were. First, he would deal with his primary mission target, the American Black Widow bound for Taiwan. Then, he would drive off the American Poseidon and attack fighters to his north, which he could not believe were doing anything more than trying to distract him and split both his attention and his forces.

He had already partially succeeded in his mission. They had destroyed two and forced one of the American escort aircraft down. Of the Black Widow though, there was no sign. Yet. He needed the PLA Navy's wonder radar to find that for him again. In the meantime ...

He picked up the telephone in front of him and punched a number. "Vice Admiral, Colonel Wang. We have destroyed two of the American fighter's escorts and forced the third to land at Okinotori Reef. The crewed American aircraft has evaded us, but we expect that PLA Navy sensors will soon pick it up ..." He did not mention the loss of his own fighter yet; that detail would best be shared when he had achieved mission success. "I recommend we destroy the escort drone on Okinotori while we wait for an update on the position of the American Widow. Your orders?"

Vice Admiral Zhang sounded uneasy. "What about the threat to *Fujian*, Wang? How will the Americans to our north react if we attack a civilian Japanese research station? How will Japan react?"

"The US escort drone is out on a runway, on its own—a single missile would eliminate it as a threat. Any damage to the Japanese station would be minor. And the threat from the American aircraft to our north is insignificant, Vice Admiral. Easily contained. It is intended only as a distraction."

The voice on the line changed, becoming cooler. "Was it an insignificant threat that caused the loss of your fighter aircraft, Colonel?"

163

Wang balked. Someone in his staff had already ... but of course they had. "I have not been fully briefed on that action yet, Vice Admiral." It was the truth.

"You do not need a brief to see that the loss of our aircraft means the Americans are prepared to fight their way to Taiwan if they must, Wang," the Vice Admiral said. "Did you not expect this?"

"We did, Vice Admiral. As you know, we have more than sufficient forces ..."

"As do the Americans. I have just been advised two of their carriers in the Pacific have changed course and are now headed west again, toward Taiwan. Your operational window is closing, Wang, and you will only make matters more difficult for yourself if you provoke the Japanese to intervene by attacking Okinotori. You must pursue and destroy the American fighter that is still in flight. You will not attack targets on the ground at that Japanese research station, is that clear?"

"Yes, Vice Admiral. I assume I may intercept if the drone is refueled and attempts to take off again?"

There was a curious silence at the end of the line before the Vice Admiral replied. "No. I do not expect that to be necessary. Other assets are in play."

I do not expect that to be necessary? Wang concluded the call and, frowning, turned to his air boss. "Blade flight to continue its search along the last recorded heading for that Widow. Orders unchanged; locate and destroy."

Where the hell was the PLA Navy wonder radar now that he really needed it?

"Fast mover detected at two six eight degrees from Okinotori, 32,000, range 24, heading two niner zero," the Target Classification Officer in *Three Zero's* command center announced. "Designating Target A2. Probable Stingray."

The air warfare sensor officer in command of *Three Zero's* Vortex system nodded with satisfaction. The target they had just identified didn't look like the one they had been looking for. But it might be just as important. It took a moment for the new contact to be analyzed and correctly classified. When it came back, the Vortex commander could see they had struck gold.

"Get a message to *Fujian*," he told his comms officer. "Contact A2 is patrolling in Sector H231, and our classification is for a US Navy Stingray refueling aircraft."

Three Zero had just solved the question of how the American Black Widow flight was going to refuel on its journey to Taiwan. And they were about to present their friends aboard *Fujian* with a new tactical opportunity.

Kill that Stingray, and they would not need to find the American Widow. It would simply run out of fuel, and it and its pilot would become shark bait.

Wang had not hesitated to grab the opportunity the Vortex commander presented him with.

"*Fujian* to Blade flight, split your squadron; leave two aircraft on combat air patrol over Okinotori in case that drone tries to take off again," he ordered. "Send the rest of the flight after Target A2. Target is a US Stingray refueling drone. Engage and destroy." His voice was grimly determined.

The American was a ghost. You had him, then you didn't. The hit on their radar was still fresh. The American *must* be headed for a rendezvous for the refueling drone.

He watched the tactical screen on his wall with satisfaction. It showed his Chongming fighters were about 15 minutes away from being able to illuminate and track the American Stingray themselves. If he was lucky, he'd catch the American Widow nearby too. But that would be a bonus. One way or another, his mission was going to conclude in the next 20 minutes.

Chen looked at his mission timer and then his fuel gauge. He had about 30 minutes of fuel before he would need to pull his machine back to *Fujian*.

"Blade Leader to Blade Five and Blade Eleven, target is A2. Turn to bearing with me and prepare to engage," their captain, 'Casino' Bo, ordered.

"Five copies."

"Eleven copies."

"Blade One and Three, maintain combat patrol over Okinotori and stay alert. Report any ground, air or naval activity immediately."

"Blade One copies," Chen replied. Chen watched without jealousy as the two aircraft at the rear of their formation peeled away and headed north to attack the US fuel drone. To Chen, another drone kill was next to meaningless. Puerile target practice. For his sister's honor, only a crewed aircraft kill would do now.

They did not know what air defenses Japan might have on their small station, and they had detected no radar, but Casino had played it safe and set up their patrol about 10 miles offshore. Now Chen swung his machine around and oriented it on Okinotori Island again and prepared to overfly it at an altitude that would give him room to maneuver if the Japanese had anti-air defenses targeting them.

"Blade Three, formation five, radiate," Chen ordered, as he switched on his own search radar and set it to sweep the skies around them for any threat. Not that he expected to find one. The American Widow was long gone, and its only remaining drone escort was on the ground somewhere below. If for any reason it took wing again, they'd quickly swat it from the sky.

Something had been bugging Chen, a tickle at the back of his mind. He reached for his radio key.

"Three, who did Casino order to follow him to that Stingray intercept?"

"Uh, Five and Eleven, I think," the other pilot responded.

Chen frowned. The pilot flying Blade Eleven had been male. But the voice that had just responded to Casino was female. And familiar. *But it couldn't be* ... He could find out easily enough. He switched his multifunction display to show combat net data for the remaining aircraft of Blade flight and checked for ...

Well, hell. *Mushroom?*

Maylin 'Mushroom' Sun was as surprised as Chen to find herself back at the controls of a Chongming about to rejoin Ao Yin's Blade flight.

She'd been intercepted on her way to debrief by a flustered airman and ordered to follow him to *Fujian*'s flight control center. She had been certain she was going to be ordered to confine in quarters and face a court martial as soon as they docked. Instead, she found herself at attention in front of *Fujian*'s Air Wing Commander, Colonel Wang.

He was in the middle of intensive discussions with his air boss and barely glanced at her, so Mushroom waited with her hand to her forehead in a stiff salute until he was finished. Then he turned to face her. "At ease, pilot. Your machine was destroyed. Tell me how."

She drew a deep breath. "Colonel, the enemy sent a Valkyrie towards us. We picked it up on our radar warning sensors and fired our missiles in home-on-emissions mode, but it got its own missiles away before we destroyed it." She averted her eyes. She could not look at him. "The American missile ignored my decoys. I could not evade."

"Are you saying our defensive technology is deficient, Pilot Officer Sun?" he asked her sharply.

Sun felt like she was watching her brief fighter career careen to the ground in flames, just as her Chongming had done. It was unfair. She had done exactly as she had been trained to do, but the American missile had ignored all her decoys. Words rose unbidden to her throat. "Yes, Colonel. Respectfully, I did everything I was trained to do. The American missile ..."

"Silence. I have reviewed the engagement," he said. "Officer Chen was able to evade the American missiles. You were not."

168

He was right, of course. "Yes, Colonel," she said. "Officer Chen is the better pilot."

He was standing and looked down his nose at her in her chair. The *Fujian*'s air boss had returned and was waiting for a break in the conversation to interrupt. Wang held up a hand to stall him.

"As long as you believe that, he will be," Wang said. "The People's Liberation Army has given you every opportunity to be as good as the best pilot in any air force, has it not?"

"Yes, Colonel," she said miserably. *Here it comes.*

"You fly the most advanced combat drone; you fly alongside the best-trained pilots off the deck of the most advanced aircraft carrier in any navy. Why do we not fly *crewed* fighters off this carrier, Sun?"

Mushroom knew the reason. "Because the pilots of crewed aircraft can be killed in combat, Colonel," she said, reciting her training rote. "Dead pilots cannot learn. And they cannot *teach*."

He nodded. His face showed signs he was having a debate with himself before it settled. "You will return to the pod deck, Officer Sun, and relieve Blade Eleven in his machine."

Mushroom blinked her trademark blink. "Colonel?"

"You have learned. Now, go back to Ao Yin Squadron and teach."

She was being returned to active duty? She could still not comprehend it. When she did not move, Wang tilted his head and looked at her. "Are my orders unclear, Officer Sun?"

"No, Colonel, sir. I will report to the pod deck to relieve Blade Eleven." She turned, ready to go.

"But, Pilot Officer Sun …"

She turned back. "Yes, Colonel Wang?"

"In the future, you will not blame your equipment for your own mistakes."

She flushed. "No, Colonel."

"And if you lose another aircraft without good cause, you will be transferred to noncombat duties, is that clear?"

"Yes, Colonel."

"Go."

She'd spun her chair, trying not to hurry until she left the flight center and entered the gangway beyond, headed for the elevator to the pod deck. Only then had she started *booking.*

Now she was closing on the American refueling drone at 32,000 feet, on the wing of her flight leader, Casino, who it seemed was just as surprised to hear she was back behind the controls as she was to be there. They weren't using radar— the PLA Navy radar had given them a pretty good fix, and they didn't want to scare it off.

She kept her machine in formation about 100 feet behind and above Casino's starboard wing and turned on the formation-keeping laser before kicking in autopilot. Her face and neck were still sweaty from her sprint back to the pod bay, and she took a rag out of a pocket beside her seat and wiped the sweat away. Casino had earned his call sign after he was banned by his fellow officers from playing mahjong at the officer's mess after a suspiciously good run of luck and taken his next liberty in Macau, where he lost a fortune.

She sincerely hoped he hadn't used it all up. "Eyes on optical sensors, Mushroom," Casino told her. "We'll move into the target area, locate the drone, kill it before its pilot knows we're there."

170

Wang's last words came to her. *You have learned. Now, go back to Ao Yin Squadron and teach.*

"Blade Leader, Blade Eleven," she said, and hesitated. "That is not a good idea, sir."

The US Navy Stingray II had eyeballs of its own. Unlike the big, crewed tankers of previous generations, it was small and expendable. But Navy didn't send a Stingray up without a plan for getting it back down again, and they hated losing either a machine or its fuel load.

The Stingray carried its 1,360 lb. fuel tank on its centerline. Under each wing, for defense, it carried two medium-range Peregrine missiles. Under attack, its pilot could launch the self-guiding missiles and scoot. There was no room in the small drone for advanced radar, but it had optical-infrared sensors that could pick up moving aerial targets at up to 20 miles distance in the right air. And at 32,000 feet over the Philippine Sea, it was in the right air.

Circling around its holding waypoint, waiting for Bunny's Widow and Valkyries to show, it didn't know Mushroom and Casino were in the neighborhood yet, but they were about to make their presence felt.

171

9. 'Launch permission granted'

There was nothing Bunny could do now to hide Huey from the aircraft overhead. She turned to the back of the hangar, a door behind her Widow leading into the building above—a staircase probably. She expected angry Japanese scientists or Marines or whoever was stationed here to come bursting through it and demand to know what in the name of the Empress was going on.

And they might be armed.

But she saw nothing and no one. That was no guarantee they weren't here, or that if they were, they were friendly. Especially if that ship offshore had been Chinese. She thought about the small survival kit in her cockpit compartment: a compass, a flare and a five-inch knife, as well as a pistol and ammunition. Should she go back for her sidearm? No. After all, it was a friendly facility, right?

There was a rumble in the sky to their north and she turned her head, shading her eyes against the sun, searching for the source of the sound. Her friend the Chongming again. She needed some way to get a message out. If China was jamming her aircraft radio, maybe there was some other way to reach the outside world. Was it too much to hope the Japanese station was tapped into an undersea optical fiber internet cable? *Well, standing here scratching your ass will not answer that, O'Hare*, she told herself. *Get moving.*

Kato had decided he'd better move. He'd stood at a window watching the two aircraft land before turning away in a panic when a third Chinese aircraft boomed low overhead. The pilots of the aircraft that landed would come for him soon, that was for sure.

Kato's one advantage was he knew the station better than the pilots, or he hoped he did. The communication center was also known colloquially as "the penthouse" because it sat atop the long, white three-story building that was their research center, raised on pontoons over the sea. Japan had built it bigger than needed to make a statement: that this was their reef, and they were willing to put this bloody enormous building on it to prove it. It had around 30 large offices, a galley, a gym, two rec rooms, a cinema they used for their monthly meetings with a big screen but no projection equipment, and dormitory space for 50 people.

There had never been over 20 stationed at Okinotori at any one time, and in the week before Kato had been left alone, the station's total complement was ... 12.

But it meant he had a *lot* of space to hide in. So where should he go? The pilots would probably start at the bottom of the building, where the runway turned into a workshop and engineering space, and work their way up, right? Perhaps if Kato hid well enough, they would think the place was deserted and would stop looking? Then Kato remembered the dirty cups and plates he'd piled in the sink in the galley below because, well, there was no one else around he had to worry about and plenty of time to clean up before the others were due back. Any idiot could see someone was living here.

Plus, if the pilots were Chinese, the ship offshore could tell them they'd been in radio contact with someone at the reef, so there was that.

"Radio. I should check the radio one last time, see if I can ..."

Takuya Kato had never been a very decisive man. It had taken him several minutes to make his plan, and another few to try the radio for about the hundredth time before deciding no, the satellite link was still down, and the VHF was just static. As he reached for the switch to flip the console power off, he heard a voice in the doorway.

"Hey there, is that a satellite link?"

He turned slowly, raising his hands in the air, expecting to see the pilot standing there with a pistol in his hand. Instead, they were holding up a hand in greeting. "G'day. Easy there. I'm just asking."

It was a woman? A little hard to tell in the flight suit, and the cropped platinum hair gave him no clues, but the voice, the voice was definitely female. And ...

"You're not Chinese," he said, stupidly, in English. International researchers frequently visited the station, so he'd had plenty of opportunity to practice his English.

"Nope. Flying for the US of A," the pilot said with a smile, not making any move to come closer, which suited Kato fine. "You can check the markings on the wings." Now she took a couple of steps forward, holding out a hand to shake. "Lieutenant O'Hare," she said. "You can call me Bunny."

Kato shook her hand and frowned. "What is ... Are those aircraft overhead American too?" he asked hopefully.

174

"Ah. No." She shook her head and pointed at a chair. "Can I sit? Is it just you, or are there others here? I should probably speak to the person in charge …"

Kato looked at her properly now. She was still smiling but didn't exactly look friendly—under her cropped hair he could see a skull tattoo, and there was another tattoo that looked like a vine creeping up her neck to one ear—but she didn't exactly look threatening either. What should he say … the others would be "back soon"? He might have lied if she was Chinese, but if she was American, what was the point? "It is Golden Week in Japan; the others are on holiday. I am here alone."

She looked … disappointed. "OK. So you *are* the person in charge." She looked around the room at the consoles and equipment. "This looks like a radio room, so are you a communications technician or …?"

"I am a coral biologist," Kato told her.

"Coral."

"Yes, I am regenerating the reef," he explained. "It is why I am here. But why …"

"Am I here?" the pilot finished his sentence. "Well, those other aircraft you mentioned?"

Kato nodded.

"Chinese fighters. They were trying to shoot me down. And they are still up there."

Kato paled. "Has a war started?" It had once occurred to him that out here, in the literal middle of nowhere, a nuclear war could be raging and he would have no idea until his hair started to fall out.

"We've been at war for decades, my friend," Bunny told him. "It's just no one had the balls to declare it yet." She shrugged. "In the grand scheme of world events, our situation is not that dramatic. And kind of top secret, so I can't really say more."

"I understand. But I am sorry if you want to call for help; since the Chinese ship arrived, the communications have not been working."

The woman had walked over to the radio and computer consoles behind Kato, looking them up and down. "Fat, ugly, big satellite dishes, that one?"

"Yes."

She flicked one of the sticky notes Kato's bosses had fixed to a screen. "What do these notes say?"

Kato stood and looked at the one she was pointing at. "That says 'don't touch.' They all say 'don't touch.'" Kato felt himself blush. "As I said, I am a biologist. My boss did not want me to break any equipment."

Walking along the desk, the pilot was still examining the equipment when she stopped and leaned forward. "Whoa. And no wonder. You have UFP defenses around this station?"

"Yes. No. Sorry, what?" Kato asked. He saw the pilot standing in front of the switches he had seen earlier: *UFP 1, UFP 2, UFP 3*, etc.

The pilot pointed. "UFP. Upwardly Falling Payloads," she said. "You know nothing about this?"

"No."

She took a step back. "Probably best we keep it that way then."

Now she picked up a satellite phone handset, turned it on and off, listened to the static and sighed. "Well, this is more complicated than I hoped."

But Kato was no longer looking at her. He was looking over her shoulder, through a window, at the rib boat full of dark-uniformed men that was making its way over the surf break and toward his station.

"Sir, please listen," Mushroom was saying before Casino could repeat his order. "When my machine was destroyed, it was because we did not use the longer range of our PL-15 missiles wisely. We tried to close on the Americans, but they had already seen us, and they fired first." She held her breath. Had she been too bold? They were still 80 miles out from the last known position of the target, but their PL-15s had a range of 120.

Casino throttled back, and she heard the note of her own engines die off as it matched speed and kept formation. "You are suggesting we fire in target-seeking mode ..."

"Down the bearing we were given," she said. "One missile, monitor the data stream. If it doesn't find the target, try a second, yes."

"It is a refueling drone, Mushroom. What are you worried about?" he asked.

"I am worried, Captain, that we can't know *what* it is for certain, but we can try to kill it from here so that it does not matter."

They continued flying side by side for a few moments and Mushroom resigned herself to the idea he disagreed. But she was right, she knew that she ...

"Very well, I will fall back and cover you. Break formation. Set up the launch," he said and immediately rolled his machine left. She cut the laser link to his aircraft and went to work, selecting a PL-15 missile and giving it an aim point down the bearing to the target's last known position. When she was satisfied, she got back on the radio.

"PL-15 in target-seeking mode. Missile armed. Satellite link ... green. Permission to launch?"

"Launch permission granted."

"Launching ..." she intoned.

She wished she could have felt the mechanical thud of the payload bay doors opening, the missile dropping out into her slipstream and then the booster cutting in. She couldn't, of course, but she could see it, and watched with satisfaction as the tail of fire became a trail of smoke that sped into the distance.

As Casino pulled up alongside her again, she checked the data feed the missile was bouncing off a satellite and back down to her Chongming, which relayed it back to her pod on *Fujian*. It was hunting now.

"We'll hold station here," Casino told her. "Engage formation keeping."

She did so, flicking on her laser station keeper again. "I have missile sync," she said. "No target."

The radar seeker on the missile was small compared to the radars on their fighters, but the missile was much, much faster. In seconds it had reached Mach 2, and in under a half minute, it was at Mach 4.

She watched it count down the range to target. "Missile range to target, 30 miles. We should pick up a return soon."

But her target display stayed stubbornly blank. It looked like her missile had nothing ahead of it but sky.

As Mushroom's missile closed to within 20 miles of the Stingray, its infrared sensors picked up the missile's exhaust bloom. The onboard combat AI reacted before the pilot back aboard the US aircraft carrier who had launched it could even sit forward in his chair. It locked up the incoming missile and sent a message to the pilot's visor.

Incoming missile. Attempt interception?

The pilot jabbed the missile launch button on his flight stick in confirmation. Two Peregrine missiles fell off pylons under the Stingray's wings, igniting their rocket engines. But they were pointed nearly 90 degrees to the right of the Chinese missile and had to both accelerate and turn hard at the same time.

Evasion protocol?

Again, the Stingray's pilot jabbed buttons to confirm the order for the Stingray to bug the hell out. Without needing further orders, it rolled onto its back and begin pulling G's, pointing its nose toward the sea below and tightening the angle to the incoming missile.

"Target identified!" Mushroom said, unable to keep the excitement from her voice. "Missile tracking!"

"Counterfire," Casino said. "Two missiles. Interesting ... Their tankers have teeth. Arm a second shot in case we need it."

She split the screen in front of her, one side showing the engagement playing out 80 miles ahead of them, the other showing her ordnance as she cued up a second missile, armed and targeted it. She had a true position on the enemy aircraft now; no more guesswork.

The Stingray's defensive missile shots never really had a chance to hit the PL-15 coming at their mothership at four times the speed of sound.

Nor did it have a hope in hell of evading it.

It had no decoy flares, no tinfoil chaff. It could only rely on its own gravity-boosted acceleration as it aimed itself at the sea 30,000 feet below, dropped its fuel tank and fell like a comet.

Mushroom's missile simply aimed itself where it expected the Stingray was going to be in five seconds' time, and with tiny corrections of its thrust-vectoring nozzle, guided itself right into the center mass of the fleeing drone.

Then had a brain fart. It saw the drone. It also saw the fuel tank separating from the drone. The fuel tank gave a bigger radar return, and the PL-15 was designed to fall in love with big radar returns. *You, baby, I want you*, it sang to the 1,350 lb. conformal fuel tank, just before it detonated.

180

The fuel tank turned into an angry red and black fireball 100 yards across.

"Good kill, good kill!" Mushroom exclaimed. She'd watched the TV feed from the front of the missile all the way onto its target. It could not have missed.

"Alright, let's follow it in, confirm we have clear air over the target area," Casino said. "I'm already in the black book for our earlier action. I can't afford another screw-up."

"No sir," Mushroom said, trying to calm herself. Her first combat kill! Her strategy! It had worked!

"Going active on radar," Casino told her. "I'll sweep high, you sweep low."

She set up her radar to search the sky ahead and below her. But she expected to see nothing until they got over the kill zone. What would be there? An oily smudge on the waves below? She wanted to see that. Get a photo of it maybe.

A couple of hours ago she was certain she would be confined to quarters and face a court martial as soon as *Fujian* docked. Now she had her first kill. *Hell yeah.*

The Navy Stingray had been shoved off course by the blast wave from its fuel tank detonating, but it didn't lose control, and it wasn't damaged. It was, however, no longer mission capable.

Pulling out just above sea level, flying lower than any human pilot would dare, it swung around and oriented itself toward its mothership, 1,000 miles to the north.

Aboard the carrier it had launched from, the air boss was already readying a second Stingray. If they got it off the deck in the next 20 minutes, it would take another 90 to get on station. But they'd have to give it an X-47B fighter escort this time, give it more of a chance.

The Air Force Black Widow they were supposed to be refueling would have to survive nearly two hours, and he had no idea if it had the endurance, or the will, to do that. But he would not be the guy who left it high and dry in case it did make the rendezvous. He couldn't set the same rendezvous point where he'd almost lost his last bird though, so he moved the waypoint 100 miles west, but 50 miles closer.

Best he could do. Now the rest was up to that Air Force pilot.

That Air Force pilot wasn't exactly worried about the problem of refueling her Black Widow at that moment.

She was more worried about the guys who looked like Chinese naval special operations forces who were about to disappear under the overhanging building and pull up at the sea-level dock below it.

They were carrying what looked like automatic weapons. She was armed with an empty chocolate bar wrapper and a terrified Japanese scientist. It was not a tactically defensible situation.

"Anywhere we can hide?" she asked him. "Quickly?"

182

"I was about to go up to the roof when you came in," he said. "There is a weather station up there. They might not look in it."

She didn't like that. "And downstairs?"

"The Chinese soldiers are downstairs," he pointed out.

"Good point. Alright, up it is. Show the way," she said. But he wasn't moving. "What?"

"The weather station is too small for two people," he told her.

Hell and damnation. She could send him up top, take her chances trying to get past the Chinese troops, hide somewhere else. Make a run for her aircraft, try to get to her pistol, or even better, get airborne and then … run out of fuel. Or … get down to the boat dock, steal or disable their damn boat, see how they liked that.

Or they could do the smart thing and surrender. Surrendering bought you time, especially from people who underestimated you. As long as it didn't buy you a bullet first.

Psychologists say we react to stressful situations by reliving what worked for us in the past. Fight, flight, playing dead or taking the hit right on the jaw. Whatever got us through last time, we'll do it again. It's dumb instinct, and if you only survived the last few times through plain dumb luck, it's not much of a survival strategy.

But buying time in hopeless situations had worked for Bunny in the past. So …

Kato was looking at her optimistically. She was military; he expected her to have an escape plan. It almost hurt her to disappoint him.

183

"OK, play it cool," she told him. She ripped off her boots, started peeling off her flight suit and was soon standing in front of him in briefs and a T-shirt. He stood gawping at her. She preferred to think it was her full body tattoos that shocked him, rather than anything else. She clicked her fingers in his face. "Kato ... concentrate. I need jeans or something, quickly!"

He was still staring, but then came to his senses. He looked around. "The crew quarters are down on the first level. There would be clothes there ... or there are firefighting overalls in one of those lockers," he said, pointing to a row of lockers up against a wall beside a defibrillator and a fire extinguisher. She ran over with her flight suit, pulled out the smallest set of overalls she could find and shoved her flight suit into a bucket at the bottom of the locker, throwing a pile of cleaning rags on top of it.

She pulled the drab green overalls on, slipped on her boots and tucked the legs into the top of the boots before lacing them up again, then pulled the overall straps over her shoulders. She grabbed him by the shoulders. "Alright, say after me, you never saw any pilot."

"I saw no pilot?"

"Those American aircraft that landed, you never saw a pilot get out of them. You don't think there was a pilot in them. You have seen *no pilot.*"

"Who are you?"

"Systems engineer," she said. "I work here."

"You are not Japanese."

"You never have international staff here?"

"Only scientists."

"They don't know that," Bunny said. "Now, sit at one of the desks and keep your hands in plain view."

"What?"

Bunny showed him, taking a seat at a nearby console. "Like this. Hands on a keyboard or something. Men with guns are about to arrive, and we don't want to give them any reason to shoot us."

He copied her, sitting down, hands on the console in front of him. She pushed her chair back a little so that she was between him and the door the Chinese soldiers were most likely to come through. It was a token gesture, really, since they could just as easily come through the door behind her and Kato, but it made her feel better.

She looked across at him. "Who am I, Kato?"

He looked pained. "Systems engineer uh, I can't … I can't remember your name."

"O'Hare. I'll try to say it before they ask you what it is." *If we live that long,* she thought.

Now they just had to wait. There was about to be a lot of shouting, and if things went badly, some unfortunately one-sided shooting.

'Shredder' Chen watched with satisfaction as the PLA Navy rib boat made it through the reef and pulled up at the dock that ran alongside the Japanese station.

He'd spotted it several miles out, coming from the direction of the *Yuan Wang*-type vessel that was anchored offshore. He didn't need to be a military genius to work out that the same mission planners who had sent Ao Yin

185

Squadron after the American Black Widow had also worked out that if it evaded destruction, there was only one place for it to land. So they had parked a huge space communication and electronic warfare ship offshore, with a detachment of Marines or special operations troops aboard for contingencies.

Chen had never seen a *Yuan Wang* ship up close before and took their Chongming fighters for an overhead pass at about 5,000 feet, cameras zoomed on the ship below. The three massive satellite dishes lined up in the middle of the deck were pointed at targets in space, but there were several other dishes on the superstructure and radomes that no doubt hid other antennas as well. As he approached the ship, his radio automatically changed to a new frequency, telling him the ship below was probably jamming VHF signals in the area.

He checked his Chongming's fuel. He was about 20 minutes from "bingo," when he would have to return his fighter to *Fujian* or risk losing it. "Three, fuel state?"

"Forty-three minutes to bingo, Blade One," his wingman replied. He'd seen less action.

Chen could see the black-uniformed figures scrambling out of their rib boat now, two of them covering the metal stairs that led into the station building.

Not long now. All would be resolved. He'd have to be satisfied with his single drone kill today, but it would do. He had opened his ledger. He had no doubts that he would add to it soon enough.

O'Hare could see the Japanese biologist was on the edge of panic. He was gripping the console in front of him with both hands and his fingertips were white. There was a metallic clang outside, and his head snapped around, but when nothing more happened, he faced forward again, staring at the desk. His right leg started bouncing up and down.

"So where you from?" Bunny asked casually.

He turned to look at her, the question taking time to sink in. "Where am I from?"

"Well, Japan, obviously," she said. "But, like, Tokyo or what?"

"Nagoya," he said tersely.

"Not Tokyo then," she prompted.

"No. Nagoya is ... southeast."

"You studied in Nagoya?" she asked.

He didn't answer, turning away from her to look at the door. Bunny had heard nothing. Yet.

"Kato? University? Where did you study?"

He turned back, frowning. "Why?"

"Just asking," she replied. "It kills time."

"Fukui University," he said. "It is on the coast, west of Tokyo."

"Good diving there? Lots of reefs I guess?"

"Reefs? No ..."

That was as far as they got.

Two black-clad soldiers stepped into the room on each side of the door in front of them, their short-barreled bullpup assault rifles leveled at Kato and Bunny.

10. 'A meat locker?'

Commander of Water Dragon Commandos Detachment 23, Captain Yi Zhizhi, had split his eight men into two teams of four and sent them into the building with orders to subdue any civilians they encountered and dispatch any military. Except for the pilot or pilots of the aircraft outside. They would be needed.

He sent one team in at the base of the big white building, and with the other, he scaled fire stairs on the outside of the building up to the top floor, intending to work his way down to meet his men coming up. He waited out on the landing as two of his men went through the open door at the top of the fire stairs to clear the room beyond.

"Two civilians, unarmed," his team leader reported on voice comms. His team's comms used frequencies not affected by their mothership's signal jamming. Yi entered the room, sweeping it with his Type 95 assault rifle to his cheek, taking no chances.

Two civilians at what looked like communication consoles. Both looking shocked. One in jeans and a T-shirt, thick glasses. Looked like a scientist. The other in overalls, a woman. Some kind of mechanic or technician. Not military. No one armed.

He lowered his gun.

"Who is in charge here?" he asked in Chinese. They stared at him blankly. He sighed. It was worth a try. Foreign language proficiency was a requisite for the Water Dragon Commandos. In his team he had French, Japanese and English speakers. His Japanese-speaking soldier was inconveniently in the other team, making its way upward. Yi had learned his English in college. In Idaho. "I asked, who is in charge here?" he repeated.

The woman looked at the man and nodded in his direction. "He is. Professor Kato-san."

The man was staring at their guns and started raising his hands in the air.

The woman spoke again. "What do you want?"

Yi couldn't place her accent. British? South African? "Who are you?"

"Karen O'Hare," she told him. "Systems engineer. *Please*, what is happening?" She looked like she was about to cry.

Australian. He had the accent now. Not American, so not their pilot, which was the important detail for now. "Be quiet," he said, dismissing her. He motioned to his men to cover the doors leading out of the room, then turned back to the man. "You, how many people are on this station?"

The man appeared to recover his composure somewhat as fewer guns were pointing at him now. "Just us," he said. "The others are gone."

"Gone? Where?" Yi asked.

"It's the Golden Week holiday in Japan," the woman said. "Everyone has flown out for the week, except us."

"You will be quiet unless I speak to you, is that clear?" Yi told her. "Put your hands behind your head."

She quailed and slowly raised her hands to fold them behind her neck. Yi saw her hands were shaking. *Good.* There would be no trouble from her.

He gestured with the barrel of his rifle at the console. "What were you doing here?"

"I was trying the radio," the Japanese man said. "It is dead. It ..."

"Your role here?"

"Biologist," he said.

"Who else is here?" Yi repeated his earlier question.

"No one," the Japanese scientist said. "Like she said, the others have all returned to Honshu for Golden Week."

Yi stepped closer to him and raised the barrel of his rifle, pointing it at the man's gut. "You are lying. Where are the pilots of the aircraft outside?"

Bunny took in the scene. She hadn't gotten a count as the rib boat was coming in, but there were five here, so maybe another four or five elsewhere on the station. Clearing it room by room, maybe. Bunny had been around special operations troops before, and these guys smelled of spec ops. Which set alarm bells jangling ... a spec ops unit, aboard a Chinese navy ship that just happened to be moored offshore of the only facility with a runway in about 500 square miles?

That was way too much coincidence for Karen O'Hare to swallow. Something was starting to stink, and it wasn't just the manky overalls she was wearing.

She tried to focus. The squad leader asking all the questions had asked "where are the *pilots*," plural. Not a man familiar with aircraft then—he hadn't recognized that at least one of the aircraft was a drone. Good. She could use that.

"No pilots," Kato said, faithfully playing his role. "We saw no pilots. The aircraft landed, but no pilots came up here."

Bunny took a risk. "They're *drones*," she said. "I watched them land. One has no cockpit as far as I could see, the other one had a cockpit but no pilot in it. It was empty."

The Chinese commando turned toward her. His hand tightened on the stock of his rifle, and Bunny shrank away from him as though afraid he was going to strike her. Which was getting more and more likely. "How do you know they are drones?"

"I know nothing for sure, I'm just telling you what I saw," she said. "There were no pilots. Someone was flying them by remote control. So, drones."

He looked skeptical, but he didn't question her further. He lowered his jaw to his lapel as though about to speak into a throat mic when more soldiers entered the comms room through the rear internal door. Bunny counted four more. Now there were nine in the small room, plus her and Kato. The Chinese began conferring.

OK, party people in da house ... Bunny thought silently. *What's your next move?*

Yi took the newly arrived squad leader's report. The building was clear. At least on the first sweep. He had to be sure.

"Take your squad and go through the building again. Check every single locker, trunk or cabinet where a person could hide," he told the man. Yi had taken what the woman had said with a grain of salt. Yes, he'd heard the Americans had "optionally crewed" aircraft, so it was just possible the machines in the hangar and on the runway downstairs had both landed themselves on some kind of autopilot.

Possible, yes. Likely? He didn't think so.

He called his other three men to him. One was carrying the field radio they needed to contact their mothership. He had nothing to report, yet. "You four, search the outside of the facility. Every stairway, every ramp, railing, roof or tank. Look in the water; check under the dock."

"What about these two?" his radio operator asked.

"I will deal with them," Yi said, adjusting the grip on his rifle. "Get moving."

Something had been decided. Eight of the soldiers left, and Bunny and Kato were alone with their commander.

Bunny did not like the way he had just jacked a round into the breech of his assault rifle. She tensed.

He pointed his rifle at Kato. Bunny measured the distance to him. She was a good four to six feet away, and seated. Kato would be dead before Bunny got to her feet and she would probably be dead a second later. But she was right out of other options. So much for buying them time. She tensed the muscles in her legs ...

192

"You, Professor," the man said. "You will show me a room which can be locked from the outside, big enough for the two of you. No windows."

Bunny untensed. So apparently his orders did not include murdering "civilians." For now.

"Stand," the commando ordered. "Both of you." He kept a few feet from both of his captives, gun covering them both, but addressing Kato. "Well?"

"I think ... yes, there is a room, off the station mess," Kato said. "It locks from the outside, no windows."

"Lead the way. Walk in front of me," the commando said.

They walked out the rear door into a white-painted central stairway Bunny had not seen yet. It seemed to go down through the middle of the building.

Kato hesitated at the stairs. "The mess is one floor down," he said.

"Then go down. Slowly," the commando said, gesturing with his rifle. He was still a couple of feet behind Bunny. Out of reach, not that she knew the kind of ninja moves that could disarm a Chinese commando who had a rifle against your back.

They followed Kato into the mess—a small room with a few benches and trestles and a galley at one end—where he pointed at a white door set into the wall. "That's it."

The commando walked around them, keeping his gun on them with one hand as he tested the door with the other, opening it, checking inside and locking it again. It locked with a knob under the door handle. He didn't look very impressed, but he gestured with his rifle for them to go inside.

Alright, Bunny thought. *Step aside. Because it's just you and us, and if you give me one chance …*

Colonel Wang was repositioning his forces.

His pilots confirmed they had knocked down the US refueling drone and had successfully forced the US Navy Poseidon aircraft to deviate away from *Fujian.* The PLA Navy had sent a message to *Fujian* to advise they had taken control of the Japanese maritime station and secured the American Black Widow. Somehow it had gotten down and out of sight during the last engagement. But Navy special forces had quickly deployed to the island, which must have been the contingency plan *Fujian's* carrier strike group flag officer, Vice Admiral Zhang, had alluded to.

The fact they had been in position to do so told Wang their intelligence on the American Widow's mission went deeper than his intel officer, Major Tan, was letting on. It would have taken considerable advance notice to get a ship like the *Three Zero* in position to use its radar to locate the American flight, let alone with the foresight to include a detachment of commandos in case the American tried to make landfall.

He still had a swarm of damned American X-47 Fantom drones holding to the north of the *Fujian* carrier group's position, but he had moved Xiu Snake Squadron into a blocking position to intercept them if they dared move any closer, and launched more aircraft to reinforce them.

He still had Blade flight of Ao Yin Squadron patrolling around the Japanese reef, but they were low on fuel. It was

194

time to call them back. He contacted the Vice Admiral to confirm the order.

"Yes, bring your machines back. I have ordered the group to make speed north. I want *Fujian* between the rebel island and the two American carrier groups. We have the *Liaoning* carrier group holding the north end of the Strait, and the *Shandong* carrier group in the south. We will make the US Navy choose whether to go around us or go through us …"

"Yes, Vice Admiral," Wang said, thinking fast. "Vice Admiral, what are your orders regarding the American fighters to our north?"

"Dammit, man, can you never think for yourself?!" Zhang barked at him. "You are commander of the air wing!"

Wang blanched. With their flag admiral aboard the vessel, it was normal procedure to refer any major decisions to him, and Zhang usually embraced the role. For him to snap at Wang like this told him Zhang was under greater-than-usual pressure. "Sir, I would recommend to keep a patrol within range to engage them if they show any sign of moving closer. Otherwise, I would return carrier operations to standard protective posture," Wang said.

"Do it. A shame, Wang, that our ground forces had to conclude this mission for us. Your pilots did not impress with their performance today," Zhang said.

My pilots forced that Black Widow down where it could be dealt with, Wang thought. *Without them, those commandos would have had no role.* But given Zhang's mood, he had the sense to keep his mouth shut. "They have learned, Vice Admiral," he assured his superior officer. "They will do better next time."

195

"A *meat* locker?" Bunny O'Hare said, looking around her new accommodations. "An entire maritime research station with, like, a hundred lockable doors you could choose from, and you suggested a meat locker?"

"Yes," the Japanese scientist said. "The soldier said it must be lockable from outside but not be able to be opened from the inside." He looked sheepish. "I did not want him to shoot us." The small walk-in refrigerator had an inside light but a thick metal door with no handle on the inside, only a small latch to keep it from swinging shut, which the commando had pushed back into place against the wall.

He had given Bunny no opportunity to crash tackle him and had not been able to resist a pun as he closed the door on them. "Very good. As they say in the West, you can just stay in here and chill."

"Not sure this is better. At least a bullet would have been a quick death," Bunny said. She pointed at a fan high on the back wall of the room that was pushing out cold air. "A *refrigerated* meat locker." She gave the whirring fan another baleful glare. It wasn't a freezer, but it was about 40 degrees in the room, say about five degrees Celsius. The shelves on one side of the locker held vacuum-packed chicken, pork and fish. The other side was stocked with vegetables in wooden crates.

Her maritime survival training had taught her she could survive anywhere between 10 and 20 minutes in five-degree waters before her muscles started losing coordination and strength. Would it be longer or shorter in refrigerated air? She didn't know, but she doubted it would be more.

She regarded the Japanese scientist with disapproval. Of course, she might live longer if she cut him open and crawled inside his warm, blood-wet carcass. It was an option Bunny would seriously have considered if she'd brought even a knife with her. But she couldn't exactly gut him with an empty chocolate bar wrapper.

Then she noticed that Kato the coral grower wasn't actually looking sheepish. He was looking kind of ... *pleased* with himself. That just made her even more irritable. "Kato. Don't get me wrong, I am glad we didn't get shot and turned into shark bait, but at this temperature, you and I are going to be dead inside a half hour anyway."

"No, we can ..."

"Do *not* suggest we cuddle up, friend," Bunny warned him. "Because if that's your best idea, I ..."

He blushed. "No. I have been locked in here before."

Bunny blinked. "You what?"

"I came in to get some beers and the door closed behind me," he said. Now he *was* looking sheepish. "The others were on the sun deck on top of the building and they could not hear me yelling for help," he said. Now he was moving toward the shelves on one wall and put a hand on it. "I got so cold I thought, maybe if I could at least stop the fan, it would not be so bad." He grabbed a wooden crate full of vegetables. "So I started pulling these crates out and ..."

Bunny saw where he was going. Stopping the fan might raise the temperature a degree or two and buy them some time. But they were still locked inside a metal box with no door handle. She grabbed hold of one of the shelves, trying to see if she could rip it off the wall. But it was welded on.

"What are you doing?" the scientist asked.

"Thinking we might be able to bash our way out that door," she said, tugging at the shelf again. "You got a better idea?"

"Yes," he said. Kato lowered the crate to the floor and pointed at the wall behind it. "When I moved this crate, I saw the big red button behind it," he said with a smile and showed her. It was indeed a big red button, with Japanese writing underneath it. "It says, 'emergency door release.'"

Bunny stopped tugging at the shelf and instead turned to the Japanese man, giving him a high five. "Takuya, this is the start of a beautiful friendship."

Despite the temperature, he went into a total body blush. "Shall I trigger it?" he asked, reaching for the button on the wall.

Bunny put a hand on his arm to stop him. "It just opens the door, it doesn't set off an alarm?"

"No, just the door."

Good. Bunny was pacing. They didn't know where the Chinese commandos were right now, but she had a pretty good idea *why* they were here, and eventually they would move to secure her Widow. Loaded with high tech and ordnance, it and the Valkyrie accompanying it would be quite the prize. She had to get to it and stop that happening, but she couldn't fly it out without fuel, and fueling wouldn't be possible with people shooting at them. She'd have to destroy it somehow. "Alright. I need to get to my machine before the Chinese start pulling it apart." She clicked her fingers. "But the building could be full of commandos. Any ideas?"

He frowned, thinking, then brightened. "My Zodiac. It is tied up at the dock. We could paddle under the main building to the runway and get into the hangar from the outside."

"Genius! I guess that's why you're a professor."

"You said that. I never said I was a professor …"

Not enough time had passed since the commando had pushed them into the locker. He and his men could still be in the comms center, or just about anywhere else on the station, including right outside the meat locker, in the kitchen, fixing himself a sandwich. Bunny looked around at the boxes of food, and on the floor, boxes of bottled beer. Taking up a beer, she held it by the neck, jimmied the bottle cap off on a shelf, and chugged it.

Kato stared at the Australian pilot in confusion. They were planning their escape from the meat locker and she had decided she wanted a *beer* before they broke out?

But after she drained the last mouthful from the beer, she reversed the bottle and smashed it against a nearby shelf. She was left with a dagger-bladed handle of glass in her fist. "Armed and dangerous," she said, wiping her mouth. She nodded at him. "Do it, Kato."

He reached up and palmed the red button. The Australian pilot was facing the door, crouched on the balls of her feet, one hand against the flat metal surface, ready to push.

Nothing happened.

She turned to him. "I thought you said …"

Kato felt a moment of terrible doubt. "I … it …"

Then there was a click, and the woman was rolling through the door.

Bunny landed in the kitchen in a crouch, broken bottle up, ready to charge at anyone in her way.

There was no one. But right in front of her on a benchtop was a very large, razor-sharp Japanese fish filleting knife. She threw the broken bottle aside and grabbed the knife, testing its weight.

No one makes knives like the Japanese, she thought with satisfaction.

But escape and evasion were their priority. The Japanese scientist was emerging from the meat locker, looking around the room as though expecting an armed commando to appear from under a sink or out of the washing machine any second. Bunny grabbed the scientist and pulled him into the room, whispering, "Boat deck, where is it?"

"This way." He started running for a door that led off the kitchen area, and she followed.

Captain Yi Zhizhi had just delivered his report to the executive officer, or XO, aboard *Yuan Wang Three Zero.* His men had searched the entire station, inside and out, and found no one except the two civilians. He had inspected the aircraft himself and could see that one of them was very clearly a drone, with no cockpit. The other did however have a cockpit. And they had *not* found the pilot. That was an inconvenience, but the pilot was not their mission, the aircraft was—or more precisely, the munitions the aircraft carried in its payload bay.

His orders were simple. Secure the American aircraft, gain access to its payload bay and remove the ordnance inside. Then disable it with a thermite grenade in each of the engine intakes. For that, they had brought with them a very specialized technician, and he was down in the hangar right now, inspecting the aircraft.

"Very good," *Three Zero*'s XO said. "How much longer to complete your mission?"

Yi relayed the question over tactical comms to the ordnance expert down in the aircraft hangar, frowning at his response before returning to the radio. "Unknown. We have not been able to access the aircraft payload bay yet. If we can't trigger it to open electronically, we will need to use brute force. I would say at least another hour, plus time for transferring the weapons. Two hours, minimum."

"We will keep jamming incoming and outgoing radio signals until your next report," the XO said. "Waste no time. The American carrier to our north will probably send a long-range patrol to check out the situation here. The tactical window is already closing."

"Understood. Yi out," he said.

He should go down to the hangar level and supervise the effort to get access to the aircraft's weapons bay. But ... the missing pilot, that loose end was bugging him. And there was something about that woman nagging at the back of his mind. She didn't look military, was heavily tattooed on her neck and forearms, even under the fuzz that passed for hair on her head. But ... *now he had it.* He pictured her again in his mind. The overalls, old and oil stained. But on her feet, camel-colored combat boots. The Japanese scientist had been wearing sneakers. Who would wear heavy combat boots on a tropical station?

He looked around the comms room, saw the lockers up against one wall and walked over, pulling them open one by one. Sure enough, in one of them, he found a rack of overalls like the woman had been wearing, and in a bucket under some rags ...

Yi pulled out the flight suit, the patch on it screaming out to him: an aircraft on a blue lightning-riven background and the words *"Aggressor Inc., We Bring It."* He held it up in front of him. Too small to belong to the Japanese man, so it must be hers. The Australian. He threw it to the ground and ran to the nearby console where he had lain his weapon, snatching it up.

First, he would get her to open the payload bay door on her machine.

Then, he would shoot her.

'Shredder' Chen was also reflecting that he would have felt enormous satisfaction if he had been able to shoot Bunny O'Hare. Not that he knew her name, of course. To him, she was just "that American pilot." Of course, he couldn't know if it was the same pilot who had attacked him and Mushroom in their first engagement, or from whose missiles he had been forced to flee in the second. But the attacks and the pilot's subsequent evasion had a similarity about them that, to Chen, marked them as the actions of the same pilot.

That predictability was something he could use against the American if his ancestors would just give him one more chance to go up against them.

And Shredder was in pain—because Ao Yin Squadron had reformed, and its aircraft were headed back to their carrier.

Fujian had altered course and was sailing north now. New aircraft were being launched to cover the returning drones, and he was about to be relieved by the pilot who would take over the landing. Chen saw the man's shadow through the smoky Perspex wrapped around his cockpit.

"Ao Yin Blade flight, Blade Leader. Your relief has arrived," Casino ordered. "You can tap out."

"Blade Four, tapping out."

"Three, tapping out."

Chen put his machine into AI formation-keeping mode and unbuckled. "One, tapping out." The need to strap in might seem unnecessary for a remotely piloted aircraft sitting in a pod bolted to a deck deep in the guts of an aircraft carrier, but *Fujian* could lean up to 20 degrees in a powered turn, and then there was the risk of explosion either from an accident or hostile attack.

He cracked the pod shell open and climbed out, giving the other pilot a fist bump as he jumped in. The tension of their combat patrol now behind them, a few of the pilots began replaying the action on their way to debrief, with the highlights being the destruction of the American drones, especially the prize that was the Stingray refueling tanker. Casino said nothing, indulging them. No mention was made of the loss of their own aircraft, of course.

As Chen waited for the debrief to start, his gaze landed on the tactical map on a huge screen on the wall in front of them. It showed the position and new heading of the carrier strike group, and from the icons on the map, Chen could see that the mission that had been so all-consuming just minutes ago had already been relegated to history. To their west lay the rebel island of Taiwan, and northeast of them were two US carrier strike groups a few hundred miles apart. The projected track of their own carrier group would place them directly in the path of the incoming Americans.

Mushroom parked up next to him and then held her nose. "Phew. Did you shower today?" she asked.

"Like you smell any better," he fired back at her. "You probably shat yourself when you were shot down."

"I deserved that," she said, shoulders slumping.

He leaned over and put an arm around her. "It was not your fault," Chen said, trying to console her. "We should not have closed on them. That was my call."

"We both had missiles coming at us," she said miserably. "But I was the one who lost my machine."

"Stop moping," he thumped her between the shoulder blades. "You got a Stingray, dammit!"

"Only because Casino let me," she told him. "He knows I'm hanging by a thread."

The rest of the squadron had filed into the debrief room, and Chen noticed that none of the other pilots sat next to him. Or more precisely, as he was sitting next to Mushroom, none sat near her. It was as though they were afraid her luck might rub off on them.

Bunny and Kato's luck was holding.

Bunny was flying down the stairwell that corkscrewed through the middle of the building behind Kato, three steps at a time. They didn't meet any Chinese commandos. When they hit the bottom Bunny saw they had emerged onto a metal-grilled deck attached to a floating platform that bobbed on the waves about five feet below. Kato took the vertical ladder with surprising athleticism, landing on the platform with his feet spread before he ran for the Zodiac that was tied up at the end of it.

Bunny was right behind him, but something struck her as he started untying one of the ropes holding the little rubber Zodiac against the dock. It was built to hold about six people and had a single electric outboard on the backboard, plugged in and charging.

"Wait!" she said, grabbing his arm as he was about to jump in. "What happens if we get up alongside the runway and that hangar is full of Chinese commandos?"

He looked at her, puzzled. "I don't know. This is *your* plan."

"Yes. No. I mean, I was thinking we get in there and I find some way of destroying that Widow. My idea was to get into the cockpit, take control of my Valkyrie, taxi it right into the hangar and take out both the drone and the Widow. But I'd have to get out of the Widow before everything goes boom and I can't control the drone if ..." She saw the look on his face. "You have no idea what I'm talking about."

"No." She noticed Kato was looking at an open cabinet mounted on the rails near them, holding oars and life jackets.

"What are you thinking, Kato?"

He opened his mouth, closed it again, then said, "No, it is a dumb idea."

"The best ideas are often the dumb ones," Bunny said. "Come on, spill it."

11. 'That way be dragons'

Yi had arrived in the station mess to find the door to the meat locker open and the locker itself empty.

How the hell? He wasted time looking at the locking mechanism, unable to understand how it had been opened from the inside.

He lifted his weapon off his shoulder and held it at the ready. He put his finger to his earbud. "Two-Three Leader to all personnel. The prisoners have escaped their confinement. The female is the American pilot. Team One, check the building, Team Two, the surrounds. Order is still capture, not kill."

For now.

He looked at the floor, hoping for wet footprints or … *What the …?* A movement out a nearby window caught his eye. More shadow than substance. Something hidden behind a corner of the building. Down on the water.

He walked to the window quickly and saw it. A Zodiac, emerging from the pontoons that held the facility over the water. It was moving fast and after a few seconds was already 100, maybe 150 yards away. He squinted. He could see two figures in the boat, hunched over as though they expected to be shot at any moment, life jackets at their feet. He briefly thought about running up to the observation level above and trying to squeeze off a couple of rounds with his rifle. After all, he just had to puncture the boat's thin skin to turn it from a speeding boat into a buoyancy vest.

But they were already nearly 200 yards out now, and he watched—half in annoyance, half in curiosity—as the boat powered away from the reef and out into the open sea.

Where in hell did they think they were headed? The Zodiac was an elongated dot now, and he was losing it in the glitter of sunlight reflecting from the waves.

"Two-Three, cancel those orders. All personnel meet me at the rib boat. Get it ready for pursuit. Subjects are trying to flee by boat."

One of his team leaders came on the radio. "Shall we leave a couple of men behind with the American aircraft?"

"No, the only personnel on this facility just left it. I want a full team on the water for their recovery. We need that pilot."

He took a last quick look out the window. The Zodiac had disappeared into the humid haze rising from the afternoon sea. There was nothing in that direction for hundreds of miles except the *Yuan Wang Three Zero*.

Good luck with that, he thought as he started running for the stairs. *That way be dragons.*

That way be dragons, Colonel Wang Wei was thinking to himself. His intel officer, the indomitable Major Tan, had just relayed to him the latest data on when *Fujian*'s defensive air patrols, and the patrols being put up by the two American carriers to his north, would risk "interacting."

Four hours.

Meanwhile, his tactical advantages were fast disappearing, but what he was being asked to achieve was increasing.

He had just been tasked to provide air cover for the withdrawal of the PLA Navy vessel, *Three Zero*, from Okinotori Reef. He tapped a pencil on his desk; someone was apparently afraid it might become a target for American retaliation after earlier hostilities. Or perhaps, once they discovered what had become of their Black Widow and its cargo. The challenge was its underway time.

Three hours.

Any aircraft he sent back to that damned Japanese island were on a one-way trip, without enough endurance to both maintain station over Okinotori and make the return trip to their carrier mothership, which was steaming away from them at 30 knots. *Fujian* would cover 100 miles in the space of the next three hours. Once they got on station over *Three Zero,* his aircraft would have a short period in which they could cover the retreat of the big electronic warfare vessel.

Two hours.

Then the aircraft he had just launched would run out of fuel and fly themselves into the sea. It meant that unless he launched more aircraft to replace them, there would be a gap between when his aircraft ditched and when the *Three Zero* would meet with the anti-air missile cruiser that had broken out of *Fujian*'s carrier group to escort it to safety.

One hour.

Whatever aircraft he sent to plug that one-hour gap would be doomed like their predecessors, so he would be throwing away precious airframes that might be needed if *Fujian* was challenged by either of the American carriers to their north.

A problem shared was a problem solved, Wang believed. He threw his tablet down and fixed Tan with a bleak gaze. She had the broad cheekbones and wide eyes of her Mongolian ancestors, and Wang found himself imagining what kind of man would be brave enough to ask the intense Major Tan on a date. He would love to meet that man because he was surely without fear.

Sitting across the table from him, Tan read his mind. "You are worried about the resources we are wasting," Tan said. "But that mission was critical. Stopping that American aircraft was paramount for our efforts to isolate the rebels on Taiwan. Maybe even for the defense of our mainland."

"So you say. But your critical mission cost me three precious aircraft. Now I am being asked to sacrifice more, even as the American carriers to our north are closing on us with over *150* fighters."

Tan bit her lip and Wang could see she was weighing her words. She stood and closed his stateroom door. Perhaps he had spoken his mind too freely. As she sat, he prepared himself for a political reprimand. But it didn't come.

"Perhaps, Colonel, but the action today *was* critical," she said. "Have you not wondered why the Vice Admiral is willing to devote so many resources to bring that single American Black Widow down? Why the resources of a *Yuan Wang* class vessel, satellites and a PLA Navy special operations team were positioned at Okinotori without being certain they would even be brought into play? I can tell you this, they were not the only vessels deployed between Guam and Taiwan in support of this mission."

Wang narrowed his eyes and lowered his voice. "Of course I have wondered. The decision to move those assets into place must have been taken weeks ago …"

"Six weeks, actually," Tan said. "When we first received intelligence about the payload the American aircraft would be carrying ..."

"Hypersonic missiles?" Wang asked, seeing that Tan had not expected him to know. "The Vice Admiral told me. Yes, the threat they would pose, launched at such close quarters, is grave but ..."

She held up a hand to interrupt him. "I should not be telling you this. And I will deny I did. But I want you to be convinced of the importance of today's actions so that you do not doubt your orders in the future."

"I would not."

She smiled stiffly. "Of course not, Colonel. Our intelligence strongly indicates that the missiles aboard that Black Widow are hypersonic, yes ..." She hesitated, glancing at the door over his shoulder as though reassuring herself it was closed. "... and they may be carrying *nuclear* warheads."

Bunny looked at the flare gun Kato had just handed to her. It didn't exactly feel like the kind of weapon you could use to take on a squad of Marines armed to the gunnels, which is what she was certain they would face very soon.

But Kato's idea had been a good one. She and Kato had loaded the Zodiac with life jackets in two roughly person-shaped piles, fixed them in place with oars and rope, draped some oilskin jackets from a wet weather locker over them, put a couple of safety helmets on top of the piles and ...

"That look to you like two people hunched down in a boat afraid to get shot at?" Bunny had asked, regarding it critically.

"Yes," the Japanese scientist had replied. "No. I am sorry. This was a stupid idea."

"Well, it's better than anything I can come up with," Bunny told him. "Start it up." The boat was tied alongside a sea-level pier, pointed roughly east, toward the moored Chinese ship.

Kato jumped into the Zodiac. It had a 50-horsepower electric motor that could drive it at up to 40 miles an hour, and Bunny wanted every one of those horses kicking. When he had it running with its screw out of the water, purring gently, she untied the bow rope and called to him. "OK, check the rudder is dead ahead, crank the throttle up to full speed, and jump out as you drop the propellor into the water."

"Crank? What do you …"

She slowed down, grabbing the stern rope. "Sorry, set the rudder so the boat goes straight ahead. Set the throttle to full speed, lock it there and then sink the propellor into the water," she repeated. "*Then* jump out. You got that?"

"Yes, I got it," he said, not sounding at all confident. But he did more or less as she asked. He checked the engine and rudder were pointed perpendicular to the stern, rotated the throttle until the engine was screaming and dropped the propellor shaft into the water as Bunny braced herself on the stern rope. The Zodiac dug itself stern down in the water, bow rising under the power of the engine. She grunted, holding the rope, waiting for him to jump.

He jumped.

Not onto the dock, but into the water.

OK, that works too, I guess, she thought, feet dug in against the pull of the boat engine. *I would have gone for the dock, but to each their own.* As she saw his head emerge well clear of the boat, she let go of the stern rope, and the big Zodiac bolted away, headed out to sea. One of the piles of life jackets had collapsed a little and looked more like someone leaning nonchalantly on one side of the rubber boat, but as the boat got further away the piles looked more like a couple of people and less like a couple of coats draped over some life jackets with safety helmets on top.

Bunny reached down to pull the sodden Kato out of the water, and then the two of them watched as the Zodiac pulled away. In a minute or two it was 100 yards out, then 200. There was a small line of breakers around 250 yards out, and she held her breath as the Zodiac hit the waves, half expecting it to be bunted off course, but it crested the waves in a single not-so-graceful leap and kept going east.

She stood watching, hoping that someone in the building above them was doing the same.

"What are we ... waiting for?" Kato asked, wet and panting beside her from the exertion of his swim.

"A shot," she said. "Someone could try to put some holes in it ..."

But no shot came.

"Alright, phase two," she told Kato, pointing at the Chinese rib boat that was also tied up at the dock. It had been tempting to slash its rubber hide open with the kitchen knife she had taken, but she had other plans for the rib boat. "We get back up to that comms station before *they* come down here."

They went back up, then outside to some rear fire stairs on the side of the building opposite the hangar and comms center. Which led to her asking Kato if there were any

212

firearms on the station, and him showing her to the safety locker at the end of the pier with the flare gun. She regarded it again. It was, technically, a gun, with blue, white and red flares: one of each. She loaded one flare into the breech and snapped it shut again, looking at it doubtfully.

"This is it? A flare gun?"

"I think there is a rifle and ammunition upstairs," he said. "In a weapons locker."

Now was as good a time as any to retrieve it. The commandos' attention would hopefully be focused on the boat. He couldn't fail to see it, could he? They needed to make the most of the potential distraction. "Alright, so can you think of a way to …"

"It is on the wall of the communications center, where we last saw the Chinese commandos."

"Ah."

"And I was not trusted with the combination."

"Damn." The only other weapon was her pistol, still in her machine, no doubt now under Chinese guard.

They kept moving up the stairs, a floor at a time. They could have hidden and hoped for a lucky break at the hanger, but instinct told Bunny to go on the attack. The Chinese would either fall for their ruse, or they wouldn't. Either way, an attack would catch them off guard. Bunny fully believed the best defense was a balls-out offense. Whether in a dogfight, a bar fight, or a gunfight.

As they reached the top landing, they heard a noise. An engine? Definitely a high-powered motor. She moved to the edge of the metal fire escape landing that looked out over the ocean to the east. Sure enough, the Chinese rib boat soon came into view. She did a quick count. Nine black-clad soldiers were crouched at their stations, sheltering from the spray coming over its bow as it powered through the water in pursuit of the little Zodiac.

Outstanding.

They got to the comms center level. Bunny gripped her flare gun in one hand, her knife in the other. She had a vague plan if they found any Chinese commandos in the room—something like firing the flare into the room and following it in, screaming at the top of her lungs as she elegantly filleted anyone in sight—but since that was sure to end up with her dying in a hail of 5.56 mm gunfire she wasn't disappointed when she sneaked a look around the external door to see the room was empty.

On the way up the stairs, Kato had asked her, "Do you still need me? I think it might be safer if I hide in the weather station."

"I need you," Bunny told him. "For another few minutes. Then you can go hide, I promise."

Now she motioned him to follow her as she ran over to the console she'd seen when she first came onto the station. From the screen labeled UFP, she pulled the paper label he had told her said "Do Not Touch." All the switches on the console in front of the screen were also labeled in Japanese. "I need you to find the switch that powers this on."

"I don't think we …"

"*Now*, Kato," she said. "With everything that has happened here, you think anyone is going to be upset you did what you could to defend yourself?"

"I guess not."

Bunny took his head in both hands and turned it toward the console. "Power. On."

"Alright, alright ..." He started running his eyes across the switches.

While he did, she ran to the east-facing window. She could just make out the rib boat, leaving a white foam wake as it powered toward the horizon. How long until it caught up with their Zodiac and realized it was just a decoy? Five minutes? Ten? She bet on five.

"I found it," he said, pointing at a button under a plastic cover. "'System Initiation.' Does that sound right?"

She returned to his side. "That sounds perfect." She lifted aside the plastic cover and, asking no more, pressed the button down. The screen over the console buzzed and then winked to life. It looked like a monochrome radar screen from the last century.

"Green screen? Are you kidding me?" she said, watching as text on the screen showed the system booting up. "When was this system installed? During the Cold War?"

"The research center was built in 1988 and renovated in 2020," he told her. "So I guess it could be either?"

"I'm betting they repurposed a screen from 1988," she said. "The rest from 2020. UFP technologies didn't exist in 1988."

With an audible click, the screen refreshed and showed a ghostly green, glowing map of what had to be the wedge-shaped reef. Around it were three concentric circles, with Japanese text running around them.

"This, what does this say?" Bunny asked, jabbing a finger at the inner circle.

Kato leaned forward, tilted his head and squinted to read it. "Uh, it says 'Defense Perimeter: 1 kilometer.'" He slid a finger over the next circles. "This one says 5 kilometers, and this one 20 kilometers."

"Good. Excellent. Does it say anything on there about what *kind* of defenses?"

He studied the screen. "No, sorry. What is UFP?"

Bunny returned to studying the switches below the screen as she spoke. "Upwardly Falling Payloads. Ordnance parked on the seabed of coastlines or sea lanes that can be remotely triggered and float to the surface."

"Ordnance?"

"Stuff that goes boom," she told him. Her eyes fixed on a small rollerball with two buttons underneath it. "This text, what does this say?"

"Control Interface."

"I need an arming switch, Kato. Something that is going to wake the Kraken."

"Kraken?"

"Whatever your navy put on the seabed out there as a last-ditch defense for this place. Just read out all the labels to me."

His eyes scanned the console, and he ran his finger left to right across three prominent switches. "UFP 1 toggle, UFP 2 toggle, UFP 3 toggle. And this one here says UFP Disarm." He looked at the switches again. "That's all."

"That's enough," Bunny said. Defending Kato and the Japanese station from the returning special operations troops was her main concern. Without hesitating, she flipped the toggle for the inner one-kilometer perimeter from the "down" position it was in to "up." Disappointingly, there was no audible signal that anything had happened. But text started flowing across the green screen, and the inner concentric circle began pulsing.

"It says 'Warning. Coastal Defense System Activated. UFP 1 Armed. Automatic emergency broadcast initiated.'"

"Emergency broadcast?" Bunny reached over and tried the radio again, flipping across a half-dozen frequencies, including the maritime emergency band, getting nothing but static. It made sense though—if you had just triggered a "coastal defense system" centered on the atoll, you should probably start broadcasting either a warning or a mayday. The designers of this system just hadn't foreseen it might be jammed.

A blue diode near the trackball had lit up though, which caught Bunny's eye.

As she moved the trackball, a small mouse cursor appeared on the green screen, centered over the representation of the reef. A vivid memory came to her, but the blue diode pulled her away from it again.

Interesting, Bunny thought. *And what do you do?*

<< *Bunny O'Hare graduated from the Defense Force Academy with a computer engineering major and was fast-tracked to intermediate pilot training. It was soul-destroying. More simulation than real-world cockpit time, with a focus on formation and low-level flying. The low-level stuff was cool, but the formation stuff, not so much. She was still 10 weeks away from transitioning to Advanced Training, which would be her first taste of a real jet: the RAAF's Boeing Red Hawk.*

For Bunny O'Hare, 10 weeks was a lifetime. She was not doing well. It wasn't the flying; it was … hard to say. Stuff kept triggering her. It started at the Academy, a stupid girl there who used to call her name in a sing-song voice from the back of the classroom, and when she called her out on it, she made the mistake of doing it out in the parking lot when no one else was around.

Before she knew it, the girl had her face down across the hood of her car, face mashed into the metal, and she froze. "Get off me …" she heard someone whimper pathetically and realized it was her own voice.

"Get off me," the girl mocked, mashing her face into the hood even harder. She felt something in her nose give, and could smell blood. Felt her legs shaking uncontrollably. It was like she was a child again, getting whaled on by her grandpa, and she was paralyzed.

The girl let her go and walked off. "Bunnnnnny," she called as he walked away, swinging her car keys. "You don't belong here, Bunnnnnny."

She'd broken her septum, but she'd broken something else as well. Not her determination to succeed. Her grandfather had beaten that so deep into her it was part of her now. But maybe the green shoot of faith in humanity that had started to regrow after her year with Sam and her crew. And that little thermostat most of us have that stops us from doing things we know are patently self-destructive.

The next day, she got up, looked in the mirror at her busted nose and shaved off all her hair, leaving only a 3 mm fuzz over her scalp. She got her first tattoo that day too, across her upper arm in a flowing font: I belong. She ignored the taunts she got from the girl and her friends the next day, and the days after that.

Soon it was their final simulation session. They had to complete a close-formation circuit in a simulated Red Hawk cockpit, with two loyal wingman drones. It was task-intensive work keeping the two loyal wingmen in place without laser formation-keeping systems, which the Red Hawk of course didn't have. The trick was to have the two wingmen fly

218

waypoints, while you, as the human pilot, held your position between them. The loyal wingmen were controlled by command buttons on the flight stick, but fine adjustment of their nav waypoints was done with a trackball and buttons beside the throttle. Bunny finished the circuit, entered the simulated landing pattern and put her two wingmen down, then followed with her Red Hawk. She was nervous, and bounced the landing a little, but it was good enough. She was through. The next plane she flew would be a fast jet!

As she got up from her seat, she hit a three-key combination on the flight stick before she stood.

The girl who broke her nose was next up and sneered at Bunny as they changed places. "Looks like you 'hopped' that landing, Bunny?" Bunny went to the back of the room, took a fist bump from a couple of the others in her course and settled in to watch on a 2D overhead screen. The girl's first circuit was near perfect, but as she came out of the fourth waypoint, she was struggling with the trackball. She tried to lock in the next waypoint, but it kept drifting, like the trackball was moving in the opposite direction to what she rolled. She finally got it locked, but one of her drone wingmen fell out of formation. She got it back on her wing, made the turn, looked like she had her act together again and went to set the last waypoints, but struggled again, the cursor un-steerable, so she aborted her run.

"Damn trackball is screwing up," she insisted, almost in tears. "It's glitching. It's not me."

The instructors gave her the benefit of the doubt. They did a system reset, made a circuit themselves, declared the trackball nominal, and the girl got back in the seat.

Bunny just looked at her watch and smiled. Programming the trackball to glitch with a key combination on the simulator's flight stick after the first circuit was kid's stuff. Getting it to do it again after a system reset—that wasn't easy. She'd coded her hack to detect the reset and start a timer. Worked out how long a system reboot would take and *added the time it might take for the instructors to do a check flight. She'd only been out by a few minutes.*

When the girl tried to set her third waypoint, it started drifting again. She let go of her flight stick, tried putting both hands on the trackball, and things went sideways from there. She lost flight authority over one of her wingmen when it got within danger range, and its autopilot kicked in to force it out to a safe distance. Alarms sounded in the girl's cockpit, she threw her hands in the air in frustration, and the instructors called it.

She might still have been given another chance, except she lost her mind at one of the instructors when he told her she'd failed. It wasn't her first outburst. "Girl has anger management issues," Bunny whispered to the student next to her as she was led out. Bunny looked at her watch, satisfied her hack would wipe itself from the system again in a few minutes.

Then she got back to her dorm and had some long-overdue shuteye.

As Bunny moved the mouse over the inner ring on the screen, a series of equally spaced dots lit up. Two or three had crosses through them. UFP stations that were not responding maybe? She moused over one that was and clicked on it.

A menu in Japanese appeared on the screen. Looking over her shoulder, Kato read it out loud. "It says *1) Deploy, 2) Disable, 3) Detach.*"

"That's all?"

"Sorry, yes."

"Well hell, that makes the choice easy," she said. On the keyboard in front of her she hit the "1" key. A box appeared around the dot. She moved the cursor around the circle, doing the same to all the others.

"What does that do?" Kato asked her.

"Deploy something, I assume," she said. "Hopefully something fatally inconvenient to Chinese commandos." She stood back, looking out a window. The inner perimeter ring was supposedly just a kilometer from the facility. Bunny had seen UFP systems that comprised small canister-launched recon drones that drifted up from the seabed and then got punched into the air with a burst of compressed gas. She doubted Japan had put that kind of tech in concentric circles around its base—it would be easier to launch a recon drone from the station itself.

No, her money was on *mines.*

She stood up from the console and clapped Kato on the shoulder. "One last favor, if you're up for it?"

Yi Zhizhi's rib boat was closing on the pilot and the professor. The pilot and the professor; it sounded like the title of a bad romance.

The rib boat was made to ride standing up, with three-by-three rails that could take nine passengers behind the two at the wheel station and a demountable .50 cal up front, which wasn't intended for use while the boat was in motion, as the bucking and jarring as it hammered across the waves at 40 knots made aiming impossible, if not downright dangerous.

They had reeled in the fleeing Zodiac more slowly than he expected, but as they got closer, he saw why. It wasn't weighed down by two humans. It wasn't weighed down at all. It was riding high, almost skipping across the sea.

The figures in the Zodiac ahead of them had shown no reaction to their approach. They were still hunkered down in the bottom of the boat, as though trying to make themselves the smallest targets possible. If they'd found themselves a weapon though ... the next few minutes could be problematic. He needed that pilot to give them access to the weapons on her aircraft. His orders were to recover them intact, and he didn't want to risk damaging them by breaking open the payload bay doors manually.

He was standing next to the driver and shouted in his ear over the roar of the twin engines, "Throttle back, pull us up parallel, 20 feet out." The two figures in the boat had still not moved. He had a bad feeling in his gut, but he had to be sure. He turned and called over his shoulder, "Xi, get on the .50."

As his man ran forward and released the harness holding the .50 caliber machine gun in place, Yi followed him forward and stood at the bow, legs bent to absorb the bucking of the boat as they slid in over its wake and alongside the small rubber dinghy, which was still going full speed. For the first time, he got a good look at the passengers inside.

Life jackets, oilskin coats, oars and safety helmets. He slapped his hand on his thigh in anger and turned to the man on the gun. "Sink it."

As the gun began its heavy clatter, he fumed. It was the second time the pilot had fooled him.

There would not be a third.

12. 'A shark that had just smelled blood'

On the seabed, about 200 yards behind Yi Zhizhi and his men, the Upwardly Falling Payloads triggered by Bunny had just started deploying.

They had been buried in the sandy ocean floor off Okinotori for nearly 20 years, and the last time they had been checked by Japan Self Defense Force divers had been five years earlier. Not all were still functional. Repairing the dysfunctional units had not been a priority at the time, as no one ever really believed they would be used.

They comprised a box tethered to the sea floor with cables, floating about a meter above it. Bunny had been right. Inside was a basketball-sized "self-propelled acoustic mine." As the sides of the box holding it dropped open, the mine inside woke up and started listening for the sound of engines. It was programmed with acoustic signatures for tens of thousands of vessels, from submarines to aircraft carriers. It was smart enough to know not to attack Japanese vessels. But a large part of the mine's acoustic database was made up of PLA Navy vessels and included the Chinese-made twin 75-horsepower engines that powered the Type 075 rib boat favored by the PLA's Water Dragon Commandos.

Hearing the distinctive sound of the rib boat nearby, and discounting the higher-pitched whine of the Zodiac's single screw farther out, the mine calculated a distance to its potential target and decided it was within its capture zone. Then it calculated an intercept trajectory and began its deceptively gentle upward fall, using water jets in its base to put itself right into the path of Yi's boat.

The Type 075 was a ridiculously maneuverable boat, but Yi wasn't using any of that maneuverability. He'd ordered his driver to make a straight-line, maximum-speed return to the Japanese facility. If the pilot and the professor were still back on the atoll, they would almost certainly be either preparing the aircraft to take off again or preparing to destroy them so that they would be of no use to China. Either outcome would be a failure of his mission and the blame entirely his.

He looked through the heat haze over the water. Was that the facility he could see now? They were about a kilometer out and moving fast. Not much longer until …

He heard a shout from behind him, left side. "Object in the water!"

It was the last thing he heard. The next moment, the deck rose beneath him, and he was flying. Blackness rose to meet him.

Bunny and Kato had run for the station's hangar.

"You spend any time in here?" she asked.

"Just when I was getting off the transport flight, or helping to carry boxes from supply flights," he said.

She walked to the rear wall, where two small electric tanker trucks were parked, and slapped one of them. "I'm hoping one of these is jet fuel. Can you read the text on the side for me?"

"It says 'Jet A,'" he said. He looked over at the other truck. "That one says, 'Aviation Gas 100LL.'"

"Bingo, first time," she said, moving to the back of the first truck. "Alright, let's get this over to my machine first, and if we have time …"

There was a sharp report outside, and they both snapped their heads around. To Bunny's ears, it sounded like it was somewhere out to sea, to their east. They were inside the hangar, so the noise was muted, and they had no view.

"What was that?" Kato asked. "Was it …?"

"Some kind of explosion," she told him. "Which may have bought us the time we need."

Michael Chase, Pentagon deputy assistant secretary of defense for China, was going to try to buy time for Operation Skytrain. But the question was whether Major General Huang Xueping of the People's Liberation Army Office for International Military Cooperation would buy the line he was about to spin him.

Operation Skytrain had gone sideways before it had even started. When he'd been briefed on the idea to deploy hypersonic cruise missiles to Taiwan as a "weapon of last resort," he'd deemed the idea crazy. The US could have smuggled the HACM missiles into Taiwan any time since they were first widely deployed in the early 2030s but had not done so since hypersonic missiles we regarded as "strategic weapons," akin to nukes, and if their presence on the island leaked, it could have provoked a kinetic reaction from China. But now that the decision had been taken, it was the multiple layers of the operation that had struck him as making it doomed to fail. The mission planners for this first phase of Operation Skytrain had not only planned to smuggle the strategic weapons to Taiwan; they had ensured that China's Ministry of State Security would also learn of the plan by leaking it to a known Chinese agent. And intimating that the missiles might be *nuclear* armed.

"A deterrent isn't a deterrent unless the other guy knows you have it, and fears it," Chase was told.

Chase wasn't briefed on what warheads the missiles were carrying, but it was just about the dumbest thing he'd heard since Khrushchev decided it was a great idea to put nukes on Cuba.

It was all intended to ensure that China didn't interfere in the second phase of Skytrain, which was the genuine effort to provide a continuous supply of food, materiel and medicines to Taiwan via air. That phase of the operation was cued up and ready to launch. Ten C-17 Globemasters from the US, Canada, Australia, India and the UK had been loaded in Okinawa and were ready to depart on two hours' notice. It was critical for that effort to succeed if the blockade was to be broken, and Pentagon war planners had decided that there was a big chance China would just shoot down any transport aircraft approaching Taiwan, no matter whose roundels were on the wings. They would be forced to think twice about the wisdom of that though, knowing America had pre-positioned hypersonic carrier-killer missiles on the island.

So went the twisted logic of Operation Skytrain, Phase I.

And it all presupposed that the lone aircraft they'd sent from Guam carrying the missiles would make it through. A submarine had been considered, but the speed of events had made that option unattractive. Taiwan was now just days away from fuel and food shortages that would provoke civil unrest. A lone stealth fighter was deemed the best option, and the Black Widow was the only one that could carry three of the carrier-killer missiles. It was a long shot, and planners had wanted the extra layer of deniability that came with using a contractor like Aggressor Inc. If it failed, they could stay hands off and let the company wear the blame.

But then the Black Widow had disappeared from radar and comms halfway through its flight to Taiwan. Now, over two hours had passed since anyone had last heard from it. US Navy surveillance of the *Fujian* carrier strike group had detected unusually high levels of fighter activity just before the disappearance that could be related, but nothing had been confirmed until the Aggressor Inc. representative on Guam had reported that his pilot had been engaged by Chinese fighters near the Japanese island of Okinotori and was presumed lost.

The question of just how China had been able to detect and intercept one of America's next-generation stealth aircraft was one that would need investigating, later.

Okinotori was supposed to be a crewed maritime research station, but all attempts to contact the station had been fruitless. There was a one-in-a-million chance their pilot and cargo had made it down on Okinotori intact, but until Space Force got a satellite overhead, they would not know. And even then …

Now Chase was supposed to get on the line to the PLA's General Huang and double down on the deception. It was desperate, and the desperation would be transparent if Huang was up to date on events over the Philippine Sea. Chase was certain he would be, and if Chinese fighters had been in action, he would almost certainly be better informed about the fate of the Black Widow than Chase was.

There was no simple way to play it; he just had to bluff his way through. He decided given the circumstances, the bigger the bluff, the more chance it would have to succeed. But he was still on a hiding to nothing.

"I am sorry, Mr. Chase," the General on his screen was saying. "You say there has been another incident involving one of your aircraft?" He looked about as innocent as a cat with a bird in its mouth.

"Yes, General Huang," Chase said. "The pilot of one of our aircraft on a patrol out of Guam reported their aircraft was intercepted by Chinese fighters in international airspace near the Japanese island of Okinotori, and a missile was fired at them."

"Ah, but is that island *really* Japanese, Mr. Chase? That is a discussion for another time. I have no report of such an incident," Huang said. "This sounds very regrettable in the current circumstances. I am certain it cannot have been one of our patrols. It was more likely Japanese. Tell me, was your aircraft damaged?"

"No, not this time," Chase told him. "The pilot was able to evade the missile and continue on their patrol. But these incidents have become too frequent, General. If your pilots continue with this irresponsible behavior, a fatal incident is inevitable. And that could have terrible consequences, as you know."

"Yes. Let us talk about terrible consequences, Mr. Chase. What is the status of the American stealth fighters still based on Taiwan? I have been authorized to tell you we can make a temporary exception to our air traffic restrictions to allow them to be withdrawn."

Chase paused. "You should have this discussion with the company involved, General, I have tried to explain that. Not with me."

The General let a flicker of anger cross his face but then recovered, measuring his next words. "Then let us talk about something else. We have received intelligence that the US also plans to covertly position air-launched cruise missiles on the rebel island. Nuclear-capable *strategic* missiles."

"I know nothing about ..."

Huang held up his hand to stop Chase. "Please. We do not expect you to confirm or deny it. You can tell your State Department to expect a high-level contact from our government demanding a meeting between your President and our Chairman. But I can tell you the message he will be delivering. What you are doing is lunacy, Mr. Chase. You must withdraw your stealth fighters *and* your missiles. Or there will, as you predict, be terrible consequences." He looked theatrically grave. "Goodbye, Mr. Chase."

The call ended. He immediately called his contact at State to pass on the information and then replayed the call in his mind. Did Huang appear completely confident the American Black Widow had been destroyed? Actually, no. *Tell me, was your aircraft damaged?*

He didn't know. Which meant Chinese commanders didn't know. Hence, they were still worried about the prospect of the missiles making it to Taiwan. Which made perfect sense, considering the threats that followed.

He stood and walked to the window of his office. He had an anonymous office on the third floor in the third inside ring of the building, with a one-way window that looked out across featureless air to another reflective window 50 feet away from his. He saw nothing staring back at him, not even his own reflection, which struck him as a great metaphor for his current situation. Operation Skytrain was like that famous quantum physics conundrum about the cat in the box, which was hypothetically both dead and alive until you looked inside the box and saw that it either was or wasn't.

Somewhere out there, halfway between Guam and Taiwan, there was a pilot flying a stealth aircraft loaded with illicit weapons. Right now they were either dead, alive, or for all intents and purposes, both. Eventually, someone would look inside that box and tell him which.

Shredder and Mushroom had debriefed, written up their combat reports, showered, wolfed down some food in the *Fujian*'s mess and then tried to snatch some fitful rest on their cots.

Fitful for Shredder because he only ever slept lightly, and right now he still had the adrenaline from the day's encounter coursing through his veins. Fitful for Mushroom because she would normally just burrow into the middle of her bed, under her sheet, and fall straight asleep … but this time, she couldn't. She kept replaying the first engagement in her head, from the moment they were attacked to the moment her machine exploded.

So she was up and out of her cot before Shredder and waiting in the ready room when he walked in, blearily rubbing his eyes.

"I know they say there is plenty of research saying you can survive on two hours of sleep between sorties for up to five days," he grumbled as he poured himself hot water from an urn into a tea pot. "But I call bullshit."

He sat down heavily next to her, smelling of the Western cologne he used. A pilot across the other side of the room theatrically held his nose, but Chen ignored him. It had struck her as more than ironic that he hated Americans with a vengeance and yet doused himself with Calvin Klein knockoff aftershave after every shower. But she hadn't mentioned it to him. Partly because Chen was one of the few other pilots who bothered talking with her socially, and also because he didn't seem to notice or care that she was ... different.

It was like he couldn't even *see* her wheelchair.

"Berserkers played Warriors yesterday," she told him as he wearily sipped his tea.

He sighed. "You wouldn't be mentioning it unless Wuhan won."

"Three to two," she smiled. "You owe me a crate of San Miguel."

"Double or nothing on the next game," he said quickly.

"We started betting a bottle. You're up to a crate now. You really want to keep going?"

"Stop bitching and take the bet, unless you want to pussy out."

"Oh, I'll take it. Wuhan Berserkers are ..."

But she'd lost his attention; he was looking over her shoulder at the rating who had just appeared in the ready room doorway. Before he even said anything, the man had the attention of every pilot in the room.

His eyes fell on Mushroom first, of course. "Officers Sun and Chen, you're up."

Mushroom pulled her chair up alongside the drone pod, popped the hatch and pulled aside the safety harness on the pilot seat so she could lever herself across and into it. She'd lost the use of both legs in the accident that had killed her parents, so she first had to throw her legs into the pod and then follow them by holding onto the hand grips her flight crew had installed on the frame that held the pod hatch. It was the only bit of custom work needed on Mushroom's pod so that she could fly. Every other adaptation she needed, like hand-operated vertical stabilizer controls, was achieved by software. And yeah, every time she climbed into the pod, it gave her a bit of a buzz, she had to admit. Not as she was strapping herself in, but in that moment when the virtual reality rig settled over her head, and she started seeing what the cameras on the drone were seeing, simulating the feeling of sitting in the cockpit of her Chongming up on *Fujian*'s windswept deck.

It was like she was *there*. She turned her head and saw the launch crew slotting the catapult bar into place behind her front wheel. She could hear the sounds of people calling out, of jet engines roaring as landing fighters hit the deck, or the whine of push-pull trucks shoving aircraft around *Fujian*'s deck like chess pieces on a massive floating board. Her nostrils flared as she buckled herself in and began her startup checklist. Okay, maybe it was just a little more satisfying than grinding online games.

Going through the checklist was something she could do in her sleep, and she did it robotically as she replayed the mission brief in her mind.

You will take up station over Okinotori Island to replace the aircraft currently patrolling there. You will fly a combat air patrol to protect the PLA Navy space-tracking ship *Yuan Wang Three Zero*. You will intercept and redirect any aircraft whose approach threatens the PLA Navy ship and stay with it until it joins successfully with the *Type 055* destroyer *Dalian* north of Okinotori. Any aircraft refusing to change course away from PLA Navy vessels can be targeted with air-to-air radar. Uncrewed aircraft refusing to deviate may be destroyed on pilot initiative. Any attacks on crewed aircraft require express authority from the Wing Commander, *Fujian* Air Wing. In all situations, pilots may return fire if fired upon first.

The orders gave her and Shredder considerable autonomy but also contained an obvious catch. The only way they could determine if an adversary aircraft was crewed or uncrewed was to close within visual identification range. Which would make them vulnerable if the adversary's rules of engagement allowed them to engage from beyond visual range. As had already happened today.

But it was a fact of a combat pilot's life that rules of engagement only mattered until the missiles started flying. As she had learned to her chagrin once already.

There was another troubling element to their mission. The two aircraft they were replacing were not returning to *Fujian*. The Fujian had been heading away from the Japanese island at flank speed for some time now, and the island was outside the return range of a Chongming fighter. Their aircraft over Okinotori right now would be ditching in the Philippine Sea when they ran out of fuel. Shredder and Mushroom had been ordered to do the same. It told her that their mission was high priority. Very high.

She shook her head and returned her attention to her checklist. Call sign? Their call sign on this mission was Egret. A change in theme, at last.

She heard Chen's voice in her ears. "Egret One, ready for launch."

She had just finished her own checklist too. "Egret Two, ready for launch."

She swiveled her head, "looking" at Chen's aircraft across the *Fujian*'s deck. She loved this part. There was no gush of steam as the catapult fired, like on older carriers, but instead a building hum as the electromagnetic catapult built power … before the plane captain down on the deck shot his arm forward and the fighter beside hers rocketed down the deck and into the air.

She gripped her stick and throttle, knowing her machine was next.

She looked across at the plane captain. It was his job to check her machine was physically ready to fly, hers to fly it. He looked behind him at the catapult officer, to the side to the launch officer, waited for her to indicate she was set …

She clicked a button to flash the green LED on the side of her Chongming that was the equivalent of a snapped salute from a piloted fighter. His arm shot forward, and she shoved her throttle through the gate.

Her flight suit simulated the pressure of a takeoff, electrodes causing the skin on her back to tingle, making her feel as though the g-force of acceleration was pushing her back in her cockpit seat. Her stomach actually lurched from the wraparound vision of the fighter screaming down the deck, dropping and then swooping into the sky as she pulled up the wheels and trimmed it for a steady climb out to 5,000 feet. She banked around to put herself on Chen's wing as he circled patiently overhead.

"Egret One, Egret Two. Formation-keeping mode activated," she said as she fell into formation beside and behind him and let her flight AI take over the tedious task of holding her machine in place.

Once they had settled into the flight to their first waypoint, Chen came on the radio. "Okinotori," he moaned. "Why is it always Okinotori? I thought we were done with Okinotori."

"That place is jinxed," Mushroom agreed. "I'd rather be facing off against the two carriers to our north than making another trip to that bloody island."

"Amen, sister," Chen said. "But at least we're only babysitting a fat-assed spy ship on this mission, not chasing that damned Black Widow and its hellhound wingmen."

The damned Black Widow and its last remaining "hellhound wingman," Huey, had been fueled and plugged into power. Bunny had climbed into the cockpit to check everything was set for an engine startup and then dropped out again.

She showed Kato the port on the side of the fighter near its starboard air intake with the electrical cable running into it, and pulled a set of ear protectors from a nearby wall. "Alright, when I get back inside, put these on. It's going to get *loud*. When I've got the engines running on both machines, I'll give you a thumbs-up, you pull these cables out, and then you get the hell out of the way." She pointed at the Widow's exhaust ports. "And for God's sake, don't run behind me."

"Thumbs-up, pull out the cables on both machines, and get out of the way," he repeated, nodding nervously as he settled the ear protectors around his neck. "Yes. I understand."

He was taller than Bunny by about four inches, but she stood on her toes, took him by the shoulders and gave him a hug. He stood with his hands awkwardly by his sides, not returning it, but hey, what did she expect? She'd dropped in out of nowhere, got him locked in a meat locker, taken over his station to launch an attack on a Chinese commando team, and now she was leaving him again. He had every right to wish he'd seen the last of her.

She was about to disengage when suddenly he gripped her in a bear hug and lifted her off the ground.

As he dropped her to the ground, she felt her side gingerly. "OK, should have told you I cracked a rib about a week ago."

"Sorry. It has been … interesting … meeting you, Bunny O'Hare," he said, giving her a formal bow. Now it was her turn to awkwardly return it. "Perhaps I will see you in Nagoya one day. In less stressful circumstances."

"I'd like that," she told him genuinely. "I owe you a sake or three. And remember to send the invoice for that fuel to the US Air Force."

Kato watched as the Australian pilot climbed into her aircraft through a belly hatch and reappeared in the cockpit to pull on her helmet.

They'd used an electric pushback tug to turn the smaller drone around and line it up along the left side of the small runway, with the bigger jet fighter alongside it on the other side. As he watched, the twin engines on the fighter whined, and then flame burst from the exhausts. The sound quickly became deafening, and he put his hands over his ears, but then the engines fell to an idle and he could lower his hands again. Across from her, the smaller machine started its single engine, the engine note rising to a high-pitched roar before dropping away again.

Kato saw the control surfaces on the wings of the American fighter flex, first on the right wing, then on the left. The drone's control surfaces did the same. The bigger fighter looked like a fat-bellied bat, while the other looked more like a large missile than an aircraft, only the short stubby wings and V-shaped tailplane giving it the appearance of a plane. Kato had never seen such machines up close before, and if he was honest, they were quite … terrifying. They were designed for war, for meting out destruction. He realized some people looked at them as things of beauty, but to him they were horrors. He much preferred the silent beauty of life under the sea, of tending his reefs.

He was lost in that thought and hadn't noticed that the pilot was waving to get his attention. The roar of the machines' engines was, as she had warned, quite overwhelming. She gave him an exaggerated thumbs-up and he ran across to her machine, pulling out the electrical cable there and pushing the port shut. Then he ran around the front of her machine, ducked under the nose and sprinted to the drone, repeating the process. As he kicked the cable out of the way he realized he had done the aircraft in the wrong order and left himself out on the runway without an easy way back into the hangar. So he had to raise his hand in the air, make sure he wasn't about to get run over, and sprint back in front of the woman in her fighter again and into cover at the side of the hangar.

Panting, he turned to watch the two aircraft take off, certain they would either set fire to something or break some windows in the building above as the roar of their engines built.

Bunny watched with a smile as the skinny academic ran around in front of her machine and then back again, frantically waving his arms around to let her know where he was.

They'd made a deal that he would keep an eye out for new intruders, and be quicker to hide next time if he saw any. She tried to impress on him that any Chinese visitors would almost certainly be less polite the next time. "Don't do anything stupid," she told him. "Just tell them who you are and tell them I've gone. Tell them everything that happened was the crazy Australian pilot's fault. They might leave you alone."

She took a last look at him, standing in the lee of the hangar with his hands holding his ear protectors against his head. Would they leave him alone? That would depend very much on what had happened to the commandos out on the water.

But there was nothing more she could do about that. She turned her attention to her instrument display and locked in navigation waypoints before checking Huey's status. The station's fuel reserves had only been sufficient for a quarter tank each. Not enough for them to make it to Taiwan, but enough for them to find some clear air where they could get a satellite signal back to Guam and request tanker support. She doubted the Stingray they were supposed to meet with earlier was still on the wing, but it was possible there was another in the neighborhood.

Unless everyone had given her up for dead, which was entirely reasonable.

She brought up her radar warning receiver, or RWR, checking for radar emissions in the area.

Damn ... The RWR showed radars in search mode off her starboard quarter. The signal strength indicated they were within five to 10 miles. And right now, they were between her and where she wanted to go. *Damn damn damn.* The bastards never gave up. Her stealth protection should keep her invisible if she was careful, and Huey was so small there was little chance they'd pick him up, but she'd have to take off slow and stay low—flying-fish kind of low—down among the clutter of the waves, steering away from the Chinese fighters, but also steering away from Taiwan, wasting precious fuel.

And there was that damned Chinese radar to contend with. If that was still online ...

There were so many ways the next few minutes could go horribly wrong that she decided to focus on what she could control. Her machine, Huey and their takeoff.

The radar signatures Bunny O'Hare was picking up belonged to Shredder and Mushroom. They had arrived on station to the northeast of Okinotori and set up a figure-eight-shaped patrol 20,000 feet over the big PLA spy ship. It meant they could cover 360 degrees of sky every few minutes.

Their radars were set to broad search mode, enabling them to cover large swathes of sky for threats, but the price was their radars couldn't reach as far, nor were they as powerful as if they were shooting a narrow beam of energy at an arc of sky just a few degrees wide.

"They're going down now," Chen said, watching the aircraft they had replaced on his tactical display. The data they were sending was bounced off a satellite and back to him, so he could see their exact speed, altitude and position. "Down to 10,000 now."

It felt strange. They were just machines. There were no pilots in them. But they still had to be flown to the watery graves and ditched at exactly the right angle of entry so that they and the ordnance they contained would sink straight to the bottom of the Philippine Sea, not break up or float for unfriendly navies to collect.

"Such a waste," Mushroom observed.

"Ours not to reason why," Chen told her. "Five thousand-five."

A few seconds later, the signals from the two Chongming fighters disappeared. "They're gone," Mushroom noted. "That'll be us in a couple of hours."

"Weird thought," Chen agreed. He shuddered involuntarily, trying to imagine what it would really be like. Your machine out of fuel, dropping lower and lower, the sea rising to meet you. Of course, if you were flying a crewed machine, you wouldn't fly it all the way in, you'd punch out at a safe altitude, but then you'd be hanging under silk watching the water below, trying to work out if that shadow you could see, was that a *shark* ...

240

Yes, he had a thing about sharks. For some people it was spiders. For others, snakes or rats. Asien Chen had a fisherman uncle who had died in a shark attack, which had been captured on video and shared widely on social media. His parents had shielded him from it for as long as they could, but the video was ubiquitous, and all it took was an internet search for the younger him to find it. And a single viewing for the older him to develop galeophobia—an irrational fear of sharks—which had nearly disqualified him from service in the PLA Navy.

He turned his attention back to his sensors. "OK, Mushroom, enough spectating. We've got a job to do up here."

"Alright, ladies and gentlemen, our job is done. Set your systems to underway mode. Get everything locked down and ready for the cruise."

Aboard the *Yuan Wang Three Zero*, the commander of the Vortex system had been told to prepare to get underway and was taking his system offline. It was just as time-consuming a task as bringing the heavy power plant, capacitors and arrays online and would take them at least 30 minutes. But they had time; *Three Zero* would not be leaving until it recovered its away party.

Vortex could not be used while the ship was underway. The amount of juice it pulled from the ship's main turbines could only be sustained if the turbine power was not needed to drive the ship through the water. But as his crew went about their tasks with practiced ease, he sat back with his hands behind his head and reflected in the warmth of a day in which everything had gone their way.

They had picked up the American stealth fighter and its escorts, not once but several times. They had been commended by *Three Zero*'s captain for the speed with which they had reacted when the American flight had overflown them, enabling their air force to get a quick lock on them and dispatch two, forcing the others down on Okinotori.

Had the Americans tried to intimidate them with their low-level overflight? If so, it was an exceedingly stupid bit of bravado. No, more likely they were just as surprised to see *Three Zero* as the Vortex crew had been surprised to see, and hear, the jet fighters they had been tracking suddenly blasting over their heads.

"Capacitors discharged," one of his engineers reported. "Vortex is blind."

He didn't like that terminology. The crew had come up with it, but it sounded more dramatic than it truly was. With a call to the bridge, he could have power diverted from the engines to his Vortex system even while they were underway and get his array working again inside 10 minutes. It would mean the ship would quickly lose steerage way, but it was possible in emergencies—for example, if the fleet they were protecting was under missile attack. Vortex could give fleet air defenses perfect information on the incoming missiles to increase the likelihood of interception. Vortex was also one of the only systems able to confidently detect and predict the trajectory of hypersonic sea-skimming missiles.

The Americans thought their hypersonic weapons were unstoppable. Vortex made a lie of that belief. With perfect information, hypersonic missiles were easier to intercept. Yes, China's only active Vortex system was right now mounted on *Three Zero*, but now that they had proven the concept, soon every carrier task force in the fleet would be Vortex equipped, he was confident of that. And the vaunted American "carrier-killer" missiles would be rendered all but impotent.

Bunny and Huey blasted off the short Okinotori runway on full power and slid gently away to the west, with Bunny keeping them both so low she was getting spray off the larger whitecaps on her cockpit glass. She kept their rear quarter toward the radar signals of the Chinese fighters and put Huey in the shadow of her own machine to give him secondhand protection from her own stealth.

After 10 nail-biting minutes, the Chinese radar signals dropped off her RWR, and she began to hope she'd gotten away clean. She put her machine into a banking turn that would bring her back on course for Taiwan and trimmed for 10 degrees of ascent. Her satellite link was still being jammed by the Chinese ship back at Okinotori, but she'd soon have clear air and could get back in touch with Guam.

If anyone was home.

As she leveled out, her RWR blinked briefly. A ghost of a signal, it was gone as quickly as it had come.

"OK, baby," she said out loud, talking to herself as much as to her machine. "There has been way too much turbulence on this flight. Let's get some clear air and set our sails."

"Egret Leader, Egret Two, contact bearing two eight three degrees!" Mushroom said urgently. She flipped her radar into tracking mode and focused it down the bearing of the return she had just received, but the contact she had just seen flit across her radar screen had just as quickly disappeared. "No further data. Contact lost."

"You get a range or altitude on that?" Shredder asked dubiously.

"No. It's gone," she said. She was working her radar furiously, trying to narrow the search to the bearing on her screen. But without an altitude, it was like shooting a BB gun at a hummingbird. "I lost it," she admitted.

"If it was ever there," Shredder said. "Ghost return?"

Yeah, I don't believe in ghosts, Mushroom thought. *But I do believe in Black Widows.*

"Permission requested to explore the contact," she said.

"Check it, Mushroom," Shredder replied. "You have good instincts, girl. I'll hold here over the PLA vessel. Don't stray too far."

"Good copy. Two breaking west-northwest," she replied.

She felt her cheeks glow. Did he really think that? And did *she*?

She could detour over the island, see if the American plane was still there. But she would lose valuable time. She pushed her throttle forward, the "virtual acceleration" sending a tingle through her suit to her spine as she pointed her nose at the bearing her RWR had given her. Somewhere out there was a stealth fighter that had just taken off from Okinotori; she *knew* it, even though that was impossible. And it was headed for Taiwan, even though that was improbable.

As impossible and improbable as it was, she felt it. She really did. She swung her nose five degrees further north. If this really was their Black Widow and it was headed for

244

Taiwan, she had to fly where it was going, not where it had just been.

She cut power to her radar, her airspeed rising through 800 knots. She was a shark that had just smelled blood in the water.

13. 'This day is never going to end'

Bunny reached 20,000 feet and checked her satellite connection. Like the bars on a cell phone, it told her whether she had a good link to a US defense communication satellite overhead or not. And it was giving her the equivalent of five bars.

She drew a breath, framing her report. The last time she contacted Salt she had just spotted the Chinese spy ship and was lining up to land on Okinotori. *Before* she had been forced to abort her landing and fight her way out of another engagement. In which she lost two of her Valkyries. Followed by landing, the whole being-captured-by-Chinese-commandos thing, and getting airborne again. Yeah, *way* too much information.

She had learned a long time ago there were things your mission commander needed to know, and things they didn't. The art of war was in not telling your superior officers more than they could deal with but enough that they gave you permission to do what you were going to do anyway.

She opened a channel. "Uh, Aggressor flight to Guam. You there, Salt?" she said. "Aggressor flight Philippine Sea to Guam Mission Control. Come in, Salt."

She had to repeat herself a few times. Seriously? The guy had given up on her or what? Finally, a voice came back to her. "Aggressor flight, Guam Mission Control. Wait one."

She liked to imagine that her radio call had created at least some minor chaos somewhere. After all, she had been off the air for hours now.

"O'Hare? That's you?" Salt's voice came through at last.

"Alive and still breathing," O'Hare told him. "Sending you my position. Had a minor disagreement with more Chinese fighters. Lost two Valkyries. Got some fuel from our Japanese friends but still need to tank if I'm going to make it to Taiwan. What have you got for me?"

"You were supposed to remain on Okinotori until you got further orders," Salt said, sounding irritated. Seriously, the guy should be glad to hear from her at all; instead, he was getting ready to chew her out again? She didn't have the bandwidth for his shit.

"That wasn't viable," she said curtly. "Salt, I want to keep emissions to a minimum, so you'll excuse my brevity, but do you have a bloody refueling option for me?"

There was a brief pause. "Alright. Navy has a Stingray moving in west of your … no, northwest your current position. Sending you the rendezvous data. O'Hare …"

"Data copied. Aggressor flight out," she said, cutting the satellite link. "Asshole."

Signal energy, Mushroom thought jubilantly. Northwest of her. She now had two data points on the contact, and she drew a line between them, projecting it out ahead of her. She adjusted her track further north until it intersected the projected track of her contact. The signal was weak but most definitely real. Her contact was not a ghost.

"Shredder, Mushroom. I just picked up radio signal energy northwest my position. Pushing data to you," she said and waited. "Let me know when ..."

"I have it, Mushroom," he said. "Calling it contact M1. You are authorized to pursue. I will remain here. Checking for known commercial traffic, just in case."

It was a prudent check. Manila to Tokyo flights often took a route that went over or near Okinotori. But they flew with commercial flight identification beacons and would have shown on her radar with a big commercial aircraft warning label on them.

"Nothing," Shredder told her. "And no known friendlies. If it's there, it's military and it doesn't want to be seen. Stay on it. I'm going to get orders."

"It's our Widow, Shredder; it has to be," she told him.

"Easy tiger," he said. "It could be one of our own fighters. A J-20 from *Shandong* we haven't been told about. Don't make this personal. Keep your head while I check. Egret One out."

Don't make this personal? Just because the American had already shot her down once? Like *that* would affect her judgment.

Much.

Sure, it could be one of ours, she thought. A Chinese stealth fighter on a patrol they hadn't been alerted to. But what were the greater odds? That the American stealth fighter that had landed on Okinotori had taken off again, or that a completely different stealth fighter had wandered into the sector? She knew which bet she would take.

She pulled up her nav screen and zoomed in, then made a calculation. In five minutes, her track would put her in detection range of the unknown contact.

In three minutes' time, she would light her radar up again. *And she would know.*

The outer reefs of Okinotori Island were exposed at low tide, and it was low tide now.

The seas generally ran east to west, dumping low breakers on the reef, sending foam into the air that could fly all 500 yards to the Japanese maritime research station. It made cleaning the windows on the eastern side of the building an absolute salt-caked pain in the ass.

It also made the reef quite an obstacle for a swimmer coming from that direction. Especially when that swimmer had just been blown into the air by an acoustic mine, awoken 10 feet underwater and scrabbled to the surface to find himself surrounded by the dismembered remains of his squad members.

Which quickly began to attract sharks.

Yi Zhizhi had cautiously kicked himself away from the carnage before the feeding frenzy started and then struck out for Okinotori, which he could see whenever a swell lifted him high enough. He also felt like he'd broken a rib. Maybe even more than one. Letting the tide carry him around the reef, he looked for a break. He was not about to let a broken rib or a single saw-toothed reef stand between him and his new all-consuming goal.

Which was to reach the Japanese research station. And kill *everyone* he found there.

Takuya Kato had made himself some udon noodles with seaweed, tuna fish and oyster sauce. It was hard to believe he was alone again.

Probably because he wasn't. He'd taken his noodles and some bottled water up to the comms center and tried the satellite phone for about the hundredth time, getting nothing but white noise. That told him the Chinese ship was still out there. He stood and looked out a window to check the position of the sun. It was falling toward the sea now, maybe another three hours to twilight. Had it really only been this morning he'd seen the Chinese ship appear on the station's radar screen? It seemed like days had passed.

He stood there, thinking it was going to be weird trying to sleep tonight. He'd have to find himself somewhere, maybe that weather station he'd been thinking about, where he could safely hide without worrying about Chinese commandos shooting him in his sleep. He'd probably dream about them though; he was resigned to that. Kato was a vivid dreamer, his dreams so real sometimes he woke up not sure what was real and what wasn't.

Even his daydreams were vivid. Like now. He was looking out over the atoll to the east, where the low-tide waves were washing over the outer reef, sending fluffy gobs of foam into the light breeze. And if he squinted *just so*, well, he could almost imagine he was looking at a black-clad Chinese commando clambering over that reef.

His chopsticks froze on the way up to his mouth from his bowl. It wasn't his imagination. There *was* a black-clad Chinese commando clambering over the outer reef.

Kato wasn't a man given to swearing, but he swore now. It seemed this day would never end.

Mushroom was at 25,000 feet, 20 miles out from the point her track would intersect with the track of the unidentified contact, when she lit up her radar.

She had armed her PL-15 missiles and put them in semi-autonomous mode. As soon as she got a target, the data would be passed to her missiles as she was asking for permission to engage, and assuming she got it, they would fly, guided by both her radar and their own onboard seekers. A kill was almost certain.

Except she got no return.

Nothing but empty sky off her nose, 40 degrees left and right. She adjusted her radar search pattern, scanning both high and low. Desperately, she put her machine into a tight banking turn, completing a full 360-degree sweep.

Nothing.

Had she calculated wrongly? Mistimed her interception? Seen a ghost where there was only empty sky?

No! It must have been the Widow.

"Egret One, I've drawn a blank here," she admitted. "We're going to need Navy's help again."

251

Bunny wasn't where Mushroom had assumed she would be because Mushroom had very reasonably drawn a line between the two hits she got on Bunny's Widow and guessed that Bunny would follow more or less the same line and velocity toward Taiwan.

She hadn't. The refueling rendezvous point that Salt sent her had required her to deviate nearly directly east, ironically in the direction of the PLA carrier *Fujian*, though she didn't know it. The second Stingray that had been launched to support her mission was at that moment about 92 miles north of Okinotori. Counterintuitively, meeting up with the tanker actually took her further away from Taiwan, but the most important thing was she and Huey would leave the rendezvous with full tanks, more than enough to get them the remaining 835 miles to Taiwan.

Even limited to Huey's 600-knots cruising speed, she'd be inside Taiwan's air defense identification zone within an hour twenty.

Eighty small minutes.

She was relying on optical-infrared sensors for information about the battle sphere around her but saw nothing but beautiful blue afternoon skies.

And there it was. Or rather, *they* were. She'd picked them up at about 25 miles, so it was probable they hadn't seen her yet. She had expected a single aircraft, but her Distributed Aperture Sensors picked up three and quickly classified them, sending the data to her visor. One was the beautiful wedge-shaped outline of an MQ-25 Stingray tanker. The other two had triangular wings and a central air intake, where a cockpit would normally be, that marked them as X-47B uncrewed combat aircraft. She quickly checked the data Salt had sent her and tuned her radio to the Stingray flight's frequency.

"Viking flight, this is Aggressor Black Widow out of Guam, approaching at 25,000 on your six, looking for some of that blue wine," Bunny said.

"Aggressor, Viking. Jeez, don't creep up on us like that, Air Force. Wait one, we're just checking your credit. We'll be setting up a north-south orbit at 26,000 … alright Aggressor, looks like your credit is good, you can make your approach, take left-wing, park your drone under our right …"

"Thank you kindly, Viking."

As she closed with the Stingray, she could see refueling drogues lowering from the left and right conformal tanks under the tanker's wings. The Widow was designed to be able to refuel from either Air Force or Navy assets, so she deployed her Navy-style refueling probe. The two X-47s had peeled right and left and were circling in opposite directions to provide protection while the three aircraft involved in the refueling were at their most vulnerable.

"How much do you need, Air Force?" the Stingray drogue operator asked. He sounded like he was in the air with her, but of course, he was on a carrier hundreds of miles to the north.

She checked their fuel states. "Uh, 8,000 lbs. for me, five for my little friend … should be plenty."

"You got it."

"Closing now," Bunny said. "Going auto."

What used to be a hair-raising manual process was largely automated now, with the laser formation-keeping systems on both the Widow and the Valkyrie pairing with the Stingray and guiding the two aircraft right onto the trailing fuel hoses.

"Widow first ... 50 ... 20 ... 15 ... 10 ... got you. Now your buddy ... 20 ... 10 ... both locked... transferring ... How's your day, Aggressor?"

Bunny smiled. For the boom operator back on the carrier, this could be the highlight of the day. Bunny's day was only half over, and still likely to end with her dead. But what could she say?

"All the better for seeing you here, Viking," she said.

"Aw, I bet you say that to all the boys, ma'am," he replied.

The commander of *Three Zero*'s Vortex unit knew something was wrong as soon as he heard the throb of the ship's engines change. The throb increased in tempo, which was normal in a ship about to get underway, but they didn't start moving.

One of his engineers picked up a handset and spoke briefly with the person at the other end. "Turbine power has been redirected to Vortex," he said, putting down the handset. "Coordinates on the way. Our friend the Black Widow may be airborne again."

"Crash system-wake protocols," he announced in a loud voice. "We have work to do, ladies and gentlemen!"

The burst of interference hit Bunny's machine while it was still hooked to the Stingray's refueling drogue with pressurized fuel pouring into her tanks at the rate of hundreds of gallons a minute. Communications with the

Stingray were cut immediately, but the laser formation keeper had her and Huey locked into place.

What would happen now? Satellite links were down, just like before. Thank the gods she had disconnected that neuromorphic chip. There was no telling what the kinds of energy she was being hit with would have done to it. The Stingray pilot and boom operator had just lost contact with their machine, as had the two X-47B pilots. They should all default to "return to mamma" mode, but she and Huey were still hanging from umbilicals attached to the Stingray's wing tanks!

"Come on, come on ..." she said through gritted teeth. Her screens were covered with digital snow, but despite the strength of the interference she had never lost flight authority, so she hoped the systems related to refueling were also shielded against damage from high-energy pulses.

Agonizing seconds went by before a blast of vapor spat from the vent on the nose of her Widow and the Stingray's drogues undocked and withdrew automatically. The same over on the right wing, with Huey.

They were free. She ordered Huey back into close formation. They'd been hit by that Chinese radar again, and she knew it meant China's fighters now knew exactly where she was. And the Stingray. She held her stick hard over and rolled away from the Stingray, leaving it to its fate.

There was nothing she could do for it. She pointed her nose west, aimed directly at Taipei, and pushed her throttle forward. Her airspeed started creeping up. Huey could stay with her until she hit Mach 1, then the laser comms system would drop out due to sonic and heatwave interference. She'd have to give him orders before that, because as she'd decided earlier, there was no way she was going to try to penetrate the

Chinese cordon trailing one or more non-stealth Valkyries. But what orders? She was like a rabbit running for high grass with a fox on her tail. It was just a question of who was faster now.

To be honest, she was more like a *blind* rabbit, running from an all-seeing fox.

"Egret One, Egret Two, contacts!" Mushroom exclaimed. "Five fast movers, bearing zero four five degrees, altitude 26, range 40." She hadn't been inside the field of the PLA Navy's powerful radar and hadn't lost comms. The data from its radar had been passed from whatever ship it was mounted on, up to a satellite at the speed of light and then back down to her again. She zoomed the plot on her tactical map, trying to see what she was looking at, knowing every second that passed, the data was degrading since the PLA Navy's wonder radar only gave them a couple of minutes of detection time before it stopped tracking. When it worked, it was amazing; no stealth aircraft built could hide from it. She just wished it could generate a continuous return.

"Got them, Two," Shredder said. "I see three bogeys heading north, two heading west on a beeline for Taiwan. Waiting for IDs."

Mushroom didn't need to wait for an AI to classify the contacts she was looking at. The three heading north were a tanker and its escorts. The one heading west *had* to be her Widow.

Shredder came back on. "The bogeys heading west are a type P-99 Black Widow II and loyal wingman, type Valkyrie. I'm calling it your contact from before, M1."

"Laying in an interception course for M1 now," Mushroom told him. She shoved her throttle through the gate, and the pressure pads in her back pulsed as the acceleration of the distant Chongming drone began to build. "Two is buster for M1. Request permission to engage contact M1?"

"Checking with *Fujian* ..." Shredder said. Painfully long seconds ticked by. "Permission granted. Go get him, Mushroom."

The American would know she was coming. There was no point trying to hide now. She powered up her radar, narrowed the beam to a small cone 10 degrees to each side, above and below her, and glued her eyes to her sensor screen. But she was not going to wait for a return on the elusive stealth fighter.

She had learned.

Her Chongming fighter maxed out at Mach 1.2. The Black Widow had a similar top speed. She would never catch it in a straight foot race.

But the PL-15 missile had a top speed of Mach 4, four times the speed of sound and nearly four times the speed of a Black Widow. And the Widow was only 40 miles away; a PL-15 would reel him in within *half a minute.*

She armed a missile and aimed it at the last known position of the American fighter. Then she did the math in her head and adjusted the missile trajectory further west, to where she calculated the American would be when her missile reached him and started tracking him with its own radar. She wasn't unrealistic, didn't expect to get a kill with this long-range shot, but if she could force the American aircraft into evading, she could catch up with them herself.

In 30 seconds' time.

The missile leapt from the pylon under her machine's wing and streaked away ahead of it. "Fox three, *swine*," she said quietly to herself.

Bunny hadn't waited for the Chinese fighters to drop on her again. She engaged her radar to scan the sky ahead of her while she sent Huey on a high, looping reverse track so that he could cover her six.

He immediately got a hit on his radar warning receiver and sent the warning to her visor. *Missile: 174 degrees; altitude 28,000; speed 3,123; impact 23 seconds. Jam (J) or evade (E)?*

Bunny immediately punched the order for Huey to jam the incoming missile. It would not only try to overwhelm a missile's radar but also dazzle an infrared seeker head with its laser. Deal with the missile, then deal with the fighter that fired it.

She had altitude, so she dropped her nose a little to build up speed. She was nudging Mach 1.3 now. If the machine behind her was a Chongming drone, and if Huey did his job, she could just about outrun it.

Which was a lot of ifs.

"Egret One, I have a large radar signature ahead, signal strengthening," Mushroom said. "Suspect another EW attack, like last time."

258

"Must be that drone that landed on Okinotori," Shredder said. "We should have been allowed to destroy it while we had the chance."

"Missile has a lock!" Mushroom exclaimed. She was watching the data from her PL-15. It had locked onto the drone coming straight at it, but … *dammit.* The link went dead. The missile had flown into the jamming energy being pumped out by the drone and she had lost contact with it.

Would it burn through or run haywire like before? She had to assume the latter. And bitter experience told her she would be the drone's next target. What should she do? Send another missile downrange in a Hail Mary attack? Decision paralysis gripped her, and she hit the radio to try to break it.

"Orders, Egret One?" she asked desperately.

"Push through it, Mushroom," Shredder urged her. "That Widow is on the other side of the drone coming at you. It can blind you, but it can't kill you." He was talking calmly, like a man discussing the next move in a chess game, not a hot dogfight. "Set your machine up for autonomous engagement, but get ready to take back control the minute you can."

"Yes," Mushroom said. It was a tactical situation they'd trained for a hundred times, but her mind had blanked. *Focus, Mushroom!* she told herself. "Egret One, Egret Two, executing."

"You'll lose comms with your machine," Shredder warned her. "You've got this, Mushroom."

Her RWR showed the jamming energy was still coming from about 10 degrees off her nose, starboard side. Her missile had missed. The signal strength readout in her visor rose exponentially as the American drone closed on her. She still hadn't picked up the drone on her own radar, and as she watched, the screen dissolved into green and white static, and white noise from her radio filled her ears. She lost everything: radar, RWR, satellite link and comms … even her ordnance menus were glitching. She tried calling up her missile-arming menu and just got a flickering screen.

Just before her machine went offline, she issued her last orders to it. Her screens and controls went dead.

She might be blind, her machine was still in the fight.

Huey was faithfully and efficiently executing the protocols he'd been programmed to execute. He'd successfully jammed the missile that had locked onto him and forced it to fly wide. It was no longer a threat to either him or the Black Widow he was teamed with.

Now he had identified a new target. He'd tagged it as a Chongming Rainbow 7 uncrewed combat aerial vehicle and tapped into his onboard database for the optimal EW attack profile for degrading the Chongming's ability to engage in offensive operations. In other words, he carried in his silicon mind the recipe for scrambling the Chongming's avionics so badly, it could not find, lock or fire a missile at him or the Black Widow.

All he had to do was keep a narrow beam of high-powered radar energy focused on his target at the right frequencies to disrupt its external and internal communications. To do it effectively, he had to get close but not too close. So he didn't fly directly at his target; he stayed several miles distant and flew at a tangent that enabled his radar to stay focused on the target at the limits of its off-boresight capabilities, without putting himself in danger. While he did that, ideally another aircraft like the Black Widow would lock the target up and kill it.

That was the theory.

The theory really only worked on ground targets, like radar installations or mobile anti-air units. It wasn't designed for fast-moving targets like jet aircraft, which didn't just sit still while you circled around them.

14. 'Down among the fish'

In the early 2020s, Chinese and Western AI had diverged considerably, without either side realizing. While Western AI programmers were concerned with the ethical dilemmas of allowing artificial intelligences to make life-or-death combat decisions and preferred to keep humans in the loop, Chinese AI programmers were not given the same guardrails, except regarding strategic weapons like nukes or hypersonic missiles. So it was that, having lost contact with its pilot immediately after being given autonomous engagement authority, Mushroom's Chongming continued to pursue its primary target—the fleeing American Black Widow.

It was fighting at a significant disadvantage, with its scanning array radar out of action thanks to enemy jamming.

What Huey *couldn't* scramble though was the Chongming's Distributed Aperture System, the network of cameras spread over the fuselage of the Chongming that gave it 360-degree vision out to 20 miles in clear air. Mushroom had pointed her machine at the last known position of the fleeing Black Widow, and its AI continued searching for the American machine with its optical infrared sensors.

And found it.

A tiny black speck, 18 miles distant, trapped in a box on its DAS. Without hesitating, the AI brought the aircraft's nose around, armed its missiles …

And launched.

Bunny was pulling data from Huey even as she was fleeing the scene of his crime. So she saw him electronically chew up the missile fired at him, saw him successfully engage the Chinese fighter, and then saw with consternation that it was continuing its pursuit. Falling behind still, yes, but … a missile alert sounded in her helmet.

Five missiles? Seriously?

How was its pilot still able to control it with Huey jamming at full power?

The Chinese pilot was no fool. He had fired his homing missiles in a fan-like spread that started with just a couple of degrees separation but soon covered a huge area of the sky ahead of them. And in that spread was Bunny O'Hare's Widow.

She saw the Chongming change heading as it went for Huey next. She lost signal from her Valkyrie as he no doubt was forced onto the defensive by the Chinese fighter.

Her RWR demanded her attention next, showing at least two missile radars had locked onto her machine and were converging at her from behind. She looked at the closure rate. This wasn't Hollywood. She couldn't outrun them.

The Black Widow II was not a Chongming drone fighter. Based on a strategic bomber design, it was about as maneuverable as a fourth-generation, last-century fighter. In modern terms, that meant *not very bloody maneuverable at all.* So she had a snowball's chance of dodging them. *But a snowball's chance is not zero, O'Hare,* she told herself.

The missiles were approaching from high on her six. So she chopped her throttle, rolled her machine onto its back and pointed it almost vertically at the sea below. Her brain was giving her a running commentary on her impending death, supplemented by the icons in her visor and the warnings in her ears.

She had her focus on one thing and one thing only: the cue in her heads-up display that told her where to steer her machine to give herself the best, the only, chance of surviving the next few minutes. A small cross bobbed in her visor, and with throttle, yaw pedals and flight stick, she tried to keep the little cross inside the box her AI was telling her was her only chance of dodging the incoming Chinese missiles.

She had her throttle back, but her velocity was rising as fast as she was falling. Her altimeter was spinning crazily as it counted down to the moment she and the waves below would be the same height ...

Fifteen thousand two ... 800 knots ... fifteen ... 820 ... fourteen six ... 830!! ...

The numbers told her a story that ended with her death. The Widow began shaking violently, so hard she had to clamp her jaw hard to avoid biting her tongue off. The Chinese missiles didn't need to kill her, because the maneuver her AI was telling her to execute was either going to fly her right into the waves or tear her machine apart around her!

Two minutes to impact ... decoys to auto ... shit shit shit ...

She was going to die. She had gambled the Chinese fighter would go for Huey, gambled it would take the easy prey first, giving her time to slip away, gambled she could outrun it ...

You killed yourself, O'Hare, you could have stayed on the ground, you heard Salt, you could have just ...

264

One minute to impact. She couldn't see the missiles vectoring in on her, but her visor told her where they were.

Ten thousand one ... 840 knots ... nine eight ... 850!!

She relaxed the grip on her flight stick. The little cross in her visor drifted out of the box. What did it matter? She watched suddenly meaningless numbers and icons drift across her vision. If her neuromorphic chip had been enabled, it would have taken control of her machine at exactly that moment.

But it wasn't. She had killed it.

Time slowed. She could feel the last seconds of her life stretching out. She realized she'd never been more alive, never more *in the moment* than she was now, when she was about to die. Ironic much? She'd been shot down before and lived. But this felt different. When that had happened, she'd reacted out of instinct mixed with hope and saved herself. But she'd been in a machine that *gave* her hope. Now, as the last seconds before missile impact ticked away, she felt without hope. She was in a machine that was not made to survive alone. It was supposed to be surrounded with other, more nimble and capable allies: in the air, on the ground. It was supposed to stand off, punching at its enemies with its long reach, directing other, more capable fighters into the gaps it created while it stayed hidden.

"Do you believe in God?" the instructor who had qualified her on the Widow had asked her when they got to Defensive Fighter Maneuver training.

"Let's say I think there's Someone up there who has been watching over me, but I probably wore out Their patience by now," she'd told him.

265

"Well, in that case, you're screwed," he told her. "And that concludes the most important lesson on Defensive Fighter Maneuvers in the Black Widow II."

Remembering that conversation, a small spark lit her gut. Not a flame. Not really. More of a grudging, smoldering, stupidity-fueled resentment.

Her hands gripped throttle and stick again. Without thinking, her finger flicked an icon on the weapons screen in front of her. She didn't even register the text that flashed onto the screen.

AIR TROPHY SYSTEM: ARMED

Her smoldering resentment burst into a flame. *You want to kill me? Alright, mother. Try.*

She ignored the little AI cross wandering across her visor and its infuriatingly small box and pulled gently back on her stick. She was headed toward the waves at greater than the speed of sound. Any violent maneuver would tear her machine apart. But at the same time, as she eased her dive, she pushed down on her yaw pedals to put the Widow into a flattening supersonic skid that slammed her head against the cockpit glass and blanked her vision for a second. Through blurry eyes, the numbers in her visor registered again …

Eight thousand four … 850 knots … eight three … 860 …

The time for thinking ended. She felt a series of rapid-fire thumps as decoys fired automatically into the air behind, telling her the missiles were on top of her. She felt the gut-wrenching force of her Widow slowing as it flattened out its suicidal dive, and then a sound she had never heard before, and never, ever *hoped* to hear …

THUNK THUNK THUNK … *BOOM!*

The Air Trophy active protection system was designed to protect main battle tanks, then adapted to ships. It created a "neutralization bubble" around a vehicle, rapidly detecting, classifying and engaging anything from recoilless rifle rounds to anti-tank missiles, rockets or supersonic uranium-cored penetrating artillery warheads. And as the American B-21 Spirit stealth bomber and its little sister, the Black Widow, were being developed, the designers of those aircraft watched with interest as the Israeli-designed Trophy system proved itself on tanks and ships and thought to themselves ... *wait, if you can mount it on a tank, why not* ...

From the fuselage just behind Bunny's head, a small, dome-shaped turret popped up. It had already used the millimeter radar sensors embedded in her Widow's skin to lock onto the incoming Chinese missiles. The Air Trophy system piggybacked on the Widow's neuromorphic processor chip to identify the projectiles as missiles and decide if they were threats. It quickly decided one missile was not. It had been pulled off target by one of her loitering decoys and was flying wide.

The other was still flying *right into her path*. So the tubular Air Trophy launcher inside the dome swiveled toward the threat and ... coughed. Three times. Each cough fired a hundred explosively formed penetrators in front of the incoming missile.

Bunny heard the Chinese missile detonate in her wake and flinched. Her head was still jammed against the cockpit glass, and she felt, more than saw, the horizon in front of her sway downward as the nose of her Widow finally started rising and sea separated into green water and sky again. She was still skidding wildly through the air and eased her right foot off the yaw pedal until her machine was flying straight and level and she could unstick her helmet from the cockpit glass.

1,500 feet ... 600 knots ... alive and ... what next, O'Hare?

That was an easy question to answer. Lower. She had to get lower. Down among the fish, where neither that Chongming nor China's damned super radar could see her.

"What next?" was exactly the question Michael Chase was asking himself.

He'd just received word that the stealth aircraft carrying the carrier-killer cruise missiles *hadn't* been destroyed after all. So he'd been right—the Chinese General was not sure what had happened to the American flight. The problem as Chase saw it was one Isaac Newton had foreseen, and it was just as true in politics as it was in physics: for every action, a reaction.

He'd just been debriefed on the call between China's Chairman Xi and President Carliotti. He wasn't cleared for the detail, just the summary. Xi had warned that any attempt by the USA to position *either* stealth aircraft or strategic missiles on Taiwan would be regarded as a hostile act and met with a commensurate response. As a result, he was putting his Eastern Military Command, including his strategic nuclear forces, on high alert.

President Carliotti had not quailed. That did not surprise Chase. He hadn't met the woman, but he knew she was from a Sicilian-Bronx family and had earned her political kudos successfully fighting street crime as Governor of New York. Privately, in a bare-knuckle brawl between Xi and Carliotti, he'd have his money on Carliotti. She'd bite the guy's ears off and spit them onto his unconscious body.

Since coming to power, and taking the learnings from previous administrations that had failed in dealing with autocratic states, Carliotti had shown a bloody-minded determination to reverse decades of softly-softly diplomacy regarding China. Her administration had taken China to task in the World Trade Organization and started a trade war that was still ongoing. It had moved several times to expel China from the UN Security Council and other UN bodies for blocking votes on human rights issues. It had banned Chinese telecommunication and internet companies from operating in the US because of their refusal or inability to abide by data protection laws. It had provided massive subsidies to US electronics, robotics and chips manufacturers to reduce US reliance on Chinese suppliers. And it had taken a position in reunification talks with North Korea that neutralized China's ability to maintain North Korea as a buffer state against the South.

Carliotti had gotten off the phone from the blustering President Xi and *moved up* the timetable on Operation Skytrain.

It was a plan they had been ready to pull the trigger on anyway, so it required no additional planning. Five nations had ensured that the necessary assets were already in place on Okinawa, and more were on the way. All it needed was a green light from the US President, and she had given it.

Chase checked his watch. In 30 minutes, Carliotti was going to address the Washington press corps personally and announce a US-led coalition was going to start relief flights into Taiwan. Chase had seen a draft of the speech, and it was heavy on historical references to its namesake, the Berlin Airlift. But the most important detail would come in the last minutes of the speech.

The airlift had already started. The first C-17 Globemaster had—he checked his watch—already taken off from Japan's Kadena Air Force Base, loaded with medical supplies, of course. Flying time from Okinawa to Taipei was 90 minutes. Camera crews in Taipei were on standby to film the first cargo plane's arrival. The whole show was staged so that the President's speech and live footage of a C-17 breaking the Chinese blockade to land in Taipei could both be shown on 6 p.m. news bulletins across the nation.

One hour from now.

Chase picked up his phone and ordered a sandwich, bottled water and iced coffee to be delivered to his office. It might be the last chance he would get to eat anything for the next 24 hours. He should probably also call his wife.

General Huang Xueping, deputy director for the People's Liberation Army Office for International Military Cooperation, was about to totally and completely lose his shit.

Guns guns guns, the automated voice in her helmet said in a detached monotone as Mushroom's Chongming swept in behind the zigging and zagging Valkyrie drone and centered it in its Russian autocannon crosshairs.

Once it had gotten behind the American, she had regained control, since it was no longer in the Valkyrie's EW area of effect.

The crosshairs in her helmet visor went red, and the 30 mm cannon fired automatically. A stream of tracer spat from the nose of her fighter and filled the air where the Valkyrie had just been, stitching a line of foaming holes in the Philippine Sea.

The dogfight had taken them down from 25,000 feet to about 100 feet, with the Valkyrie twisting and turning like a rattlesnake while Mushroom patiently got her machine into position to take a killing shot.

But it wasn't a fight, not really. Not when the other machine wasn't capable of shooting back. If the Valkyrie had a pilot, she'd be hailing him on the open guard emergency channel and urging him to surrender. But there was no pilot. The Valkyrie was just titanium, aluminum, silicon and plastic, and killing it dead was the last thing between her and a victorious end to her mission. She'd killed the Black Widow—with the Valkyrie on the defensive, she'd regained the data feed from her missiles and had seen two of them follow the Widow all the way down to sea level on her tactical screen before they merged with the contact that was the American stealth fighter. A certain kill.

Taking a deep breath, she stayed on the Valkyrie's tail, waiting for it to make a mistake and swim back into her sights.

Guns guns guns.

The death of the Valkyrie was underwhelming in the end. It took the full three-second burst from her cannon in its exhaust port and flipped nose over tail through the air, then plunged into the sea, disappearing like an Olympic diver into a pool, with barely a splash.

Two kills! Mushroom felt like pinching herself. That took her tally for the day to three kills! She had gone from total disgrace to the highest-scoring pilot in the air wing. She

271

trimmed her machine to climb back out and opened a radio channel to Chen. He would also have been watching every minute of her engagement.

In fact, it was strange he hadn't already come on comms to congratulate her. She felt like she could float out of her drone pod on angel wings, and he didn't even come online verbally to give her a pat on the back?

"Shredder, Mushroom. Come back, Egret One?" She tried twice more, with no answer. It was annoying, and a little ridiculous. She could just about pop the hatch of her pod and yell at him if she needed to.

Nothing. Now she started to worry. She switched channels to the direct link to the air operations control room several decks above. "*Fujian* Control, Egret Two. Egret Two is returning to Sector E3, Okinotori Island. I cannot reach Egret One …"

"Mushroom, Shredder. I'm here," Chen's voice said at last.

"About time. You aren't mad at me for …"

"Mushroom, shut it. We're dealing with a situation. Release your machine and exit your pod for debrief and re-tasking. I'm doing the same. Okinotori is not the main game anymore."

Her blood chilled. "What? What is it?"

"The American carriers to our north—they just launched everything they have. I mean *everything*."

"The USS *Enterprise* battle group is here," Major Tan told *Fujian*'s assembled senior officers, among them Vice Admiral Zhang and his air wing commander, Colonel Wang Wei. A huge map of the Western Pacific covering Okinawa, Taiwan and the Philippines was projected on a wall, and she pointed with a cane to an icon east of Okinawa. "The *USS Gerald R. Ford*, which sailed from Pearl Harbor three days ago, here." Now her cane rested on a point further east, near the Japanese Ogasawara Islands in the Western Pacific.

"They hide their carriers under the skirts of their Japanese allies," the Vice Admiral said derisively.

"How close is *Enterprise* to our bases in Nanjing military district?" Wang asked. The Americans' newest supercarrier was also the closest to Taiwan, and therefore China.

"500 to 550 miles," Tan said. "Within strike range of our aircraft in Fuzhou and Wenzhou, with refueling. But protected by the entire USAF 18th Air Wing, 50 aircraft, plus the three Aegis anti-air missile destroyers in its battle group."

Wang furrowed his brows. Satellite, electronic and signals intelligence indicated the US carrier had just launched about half of its fighter complement of 70 crewed and uncrewed aircraft. Further east, near the Ogasawara Islands, the older *Gerald R. Ford*, first of the *Ford* class carriers, had launched nearly two-thirds of its crewed and uncrewed fighters, accompanied, it seemed, by early-warning aircraft and refueling drones.

More importantly, neither ship was making any attempt to hide the fact. The radio and radar emissions being generated by the two American air wings could probably power *Shanghai* for a week.

All along China's east coast, air defense fighters that had been marshaled in advance of any decision to invade Taiwan were being scrambled to meet what looked like a massive US air offensive. *But targeting what? Where?*

273

"What are they doing?" Zhang wondered out loud.

Major Tan hit a key, and smaller icons appeared on the screen, showing the position of individual flights of American aircraft. "The lead elements launched from the *Enterprise* are already here. They appear to be flying a combat air patrol between Okinawa and this point halfway to Taipei, Taiwan. Just outside our no-fly zone. The bulk of *Ford*'s fighters are well behind them." She switched to a second screen, showing a large mass of aircraft moving from the carrier *Ford*. "*Ford*'s aircraft appear to be heading to Okinawa. Human intelligence sources on Okinawa have reported Kadena Air Base is making ready to house up to 50 US Navy aircraft in the next 24 hours."

"It is flying its aircraft off and basing them on Okinawa!" Zhang said. "This is a precursor to an attack!"

"Or an attempt to deter one, Vice Admiral," Wang pointed out. "We have been moving our forces into position for several weeks now. We've been expecting the Americans to flex their muscles sooner or later. It looks like this is it."

Tan zoomed out. "The US will soon have the equivalent of three land-based air wings in the theatre. One in the Philippines, one on Okinawa and a third on Guam. Then its carriers can be withdrawn and replenished."

"Not to mention all of those damned cargo planes it has moved in," Zhang said. "Cargo? Paratroopers are more likely."

"And B-21 stealth bombers based in Guam, Hawaii and Darwin," Wang pointed out. "Let us not forget those." He contemplated the map. "How close are we to the *USS Enterprise*?"

Tan stretched a digital ruler across the map. "Four hundred twenty miles."

"Easily within range of our Chongming fighters, and we would not have to deal with American air defenses until they reached the *Enterprise* battle group."

Zhang and the other offices in the room looked at him. "What are you thinking?" Zhang asked.

"I am thinking, Vice Admiral, that the reason they are holding their carriers close to shore-based missile batteries is that decades of war gaming has taught them how vulnerable they are. Perhaps we can persuade them that no matter under whose skirts they hide, we can still threaten them."

Zhang smiled. "Send them scurrying all the way back to Pearl Harbor and Yokosuka?"

"Something like that."

"Prepare an air tasking order," Zhang told him. "I will speak to Fleet Command Ningbo."

Wang was about to turn to one of his staff officers when an out-of-breath naval rating appeared in the doorway. "Vice Admiral, Colonel … the …" He pointed at the screen Tan was standing next to, but didn't have the breath to finish his sentence.

"Take it easy, boy," Wang told him. "Breathe. Then speak."

He drew a deep breath. "On the news channels … The American President …"

Major Tan didn't need to be asked. Reaching to the screen controls on a lectern beside her, she turned the screen input to Hong Kong's CTV network. It would be in Cantonese, not

Mandarin, but at least it would stream the US President direct and uncensored.

She was standing behind a lectern in her press room, the lapdog media seated in front of her. She had already started speaking, and Tan turned up the volume.

"... the US government will lend every available resource to this multinational endeavor, and just as we broke the back of tyranny in Berlin in 1948, so will we break it again in 2038. And let China take note of this: The combined air cargo resources of the US and allies will dwarf what was marshaled for the Berlin Airlift. We already have the capacity in place to sustain the delivery of 10,000 tons of supplies to that beleaguered island, every day. Within the month, we will increase that to 20,000 tons. Per. Day ..."

President Carliotti paused for dramatic effect. "... for *as long as it takes.*" She looked down at her notes. "And I am gratified to be able to announce that 'Operation Skytrain' has already begun," she said, looking up again. "As I speak, the first of what will be thousands of humanitarian aid flights to Taiwan has already left Okinawa in Japan and will land in Taiwan within the hour."

A few journalists could wait no longer and started shouting questions, but she held up her hand.

"Please. Needless to say, we do not expect China to interfere in this humanitarian relief effort, but we have also put in place the assets to protect our aircraft and those of our allies. If China attempts to use military force to interfere, make no mistake, it will be met with force."

She looked down the barrel of the camera. "Now I wish to address the leadership of China directly. Chairman Xi, if you seek prosperity for all of China, if you seek prosperity for mainland China, for Hong Kong and for Taiwan, if you truly seek to create 'One China,' lift your blockade and let the people of Taiwan decide for themselves. Start by opening your skies. Chairman Xi: *Lift. This. Blockade.* If you do not, the democratic nations of the world will."

Vice Admiral Zhang turned to Wang. "I need to speak with Fleet immediately. How soon can you …"

"By the time you are off the satellite link, should *Fujian*'s air wing be needed, we will have begun generating the strike package, Vice Admiral," Wang told him, saluting.

As he watched the old man go, he lowered his arm and looked at the screen again, where the American President was speaking. Tan had shared the intelligence about the Americans' "Operation Skytrain" with him, but he didn't really believe they would … *dare.* Nonetheless, if he had been hearing the rumors about an American relief operation for several days, Beijing would have been aware of it for weeks. And hopefully in much more detail.

Wang knew China had been moving air, land and sea forces into its Eastern Military Command for months, in anticipation of the need for military action to back up its blockade. Plans would have been prepared. Assets moved into place. And a response readied.

Colonel Wang Wei had little doubt that China's *Fujian* carrier strike group would be a central part of that response.

Bunny was not taking the direct route to Taipei. She had refueled but was flying nap of the earth, using the earth's curvature to hide from Chinese radar behind her. Having done her math on fuel burn rate and distance to objective, she had plugged in a waypoint north of the island, inside

Japanese airspace near Taketomi Island, part of its Okinawa prefecture and the closest major Japanese island to Taiwan. She was still leery of that bloody Chinese radar, and if it caught her again, she wanted to be *inside* Japanese air defense territory.

As her nav system announced with an all-too-subdued dotted line across her nav map that she had arrived inside Japanese air space, which more or less flowed seamlessly into Taiwanese airspace, she tensed again. It should have been a moment to celebrate, but the next 20 minutes were probably going to be more, or as, dangerous as the last several hours.

She was about to move from relative safety into the dragon's lair. Ahead of her—she had been told in the mission briefing that seemed like weeks ago but was in fact less than a day earlier—China had deployed a ring of *Renhai* class surface-to-air warfare cruisers. It had seven of the ships, a Chinese equivalent to the vaunted American Aegis cruisers, and they were designed to detect and destroy everything from aircraft to ballistic missiles.

Classified test flights by US stealth fighters testing the *Renhai*'s ability to detect their fifth-generation airframes, with radar cross sections the size of ball bearings, had been inconclusive. Sometimes the reaction of the Chinese ships showed the Chinese cruisers were successful, sometimes not. But US war planners could not be certain whether their opponents were showing all their cards.

The *Renhai* cruisers were only a small part of her problem. Bunny had just pulled down satellite intel on their last known headings and positions, only hours old, and they did not move that quickly. The bigger problem for her was the air patrols China had established around Taiwan. The island was easily within range of land-based fighters from Fujian, Guangdong and Zhejiang provinces. The estimates she had been provided in her mission briefing were that, in any 50-mile radius around the island, she could expect to meet up to 20 Chinese fighters. Most would be decades-old fourth-generation fighters with inferior radars that her stealth tech should be able to defeat, but at least 10 percent were fifth-generation J-20 fighters with scanning array radars, or PLA Air Force Sharp Sword drones, similarly equipped. All carried the latest deadly infrared/optical/radar seeker version of the Chinese PL-15 missile, which she now, unfortunately, had firsthand experience against.

The PL-15 was, to use Australian vernacular, an absolute *bastard*.

She had maintained emissions discipline since escaping the last Chinese attack and ignored all hails from Guam. Salt had become increasingly strident in tone, but to reply to him would be like sending a "here I am, kill me!" flare into the sky ahead of her if there was an electronic-intelligence-gathering Chinese ship or aircraft anywhere nearby. She had to assume there were.

But now, she had to risk it. She would not be able to make it in alone. She opened a satellite channel.

"Guam, Aggressor flight. About to begin ingress to Taipei. Position uh ..." She read the numbers off her visor. "... 25.0212, 123.8088. Altitude ... call it zero. Bearing 270. What can you tell me, Guam?"

A voice she didn't recognize came on the line. "Wait one, Aggressor. We are ..."

"Guam, I don't have 'one,'" Bunny told the voice. "I am about to enter contested airspace. You talk to me now, or you send me prayers. Those are your options."

279

Seconds ticked by. Bunny reached forward to kill the radio. That was it. She was going in blind. Then the same voice came back. "Alright, Aggressor, we cannot reach your mission commander. I have a download for you …"

Couldn't reach Salt? What the hell, he was taking a freaking *nap*? She listened hard.

"… report is as follows. Allied forces have initiated Operation Skytrain, the mission to provide humanitarian supplies to Taiwan. Expect heavy Chinese air activity your position and north, northeast. Advise you to deviate south, go feet dry at Hualien. Repeat, Hualien. We are showing a *Renhai* cruiser 10 miles offshore Hualien, but Chinese combat air patrols are being redirected north in response to allied air operations in the Okinawa-Taipei corridor …" It was a lot of information to process, and the operator at the other end paused. But he had no more to offer. "Passing your sitrep to Carlyle. God be with you, Aggressor," the voice said.

Bunny O'Hare didn't know which particular god the man believed in, but at that moment, she'd welcome *any* god to her team.

"Good copy, Guam. Aggressor out."

Bunny cut the sat link and rolled her shoulders, then lifted her hands off her controls and flexed her fingers. It was game time. This was her comfort zone. She began to recite her mantra. It was different every time she went into action, but then again, it was always the same. It had been since the day she entered RAAF fast jet training.

Alright, girl, you are a supersonic, bat-winged mofo out of hell. No ship can touch you. They try, you will laugh. Anyone lights you up with a missile radar, you will laugh. Anyone gets between you and the tarmac at Taichung Air Base, you will laugh. THIS is where you live. THIS is your time. You OWN the sky. You are a freaking NINJA, and your shadow will be the ONLY thing anyone will see.

15. 'It gets real'

Colonel Wang Wei, Air Wing Commander, PLA Navy carrier *Fujian,* was well out of his comfort zone.

He had just launched every available Chongming fighter that was not already airborne flying defensive patrols around *Fujian.*

Fujian had lost three aircraft in the various actions over Okinotori. He had 12 aircraft on defensive patrol, protecting the carrier. Six aircraft were undergoing repair or maintenance. That left him with 59.

He had been ordered by the Vice-Admiral to launch them *all.* As was often the case, one of *Fujian*'s three catapults was nonfunctional and could only be repaired dockside. So it took *Fujian* 90 seconds to launch two aircraft. To launch and form up a single squadron of 18 aircraft, 15 minutes. To launch three squadrons, 45 minutes. Assuming both of the damned electronic catapult systems on *Fujian* cooperated fully. Which they rarely did.

To launch his counterattack, then, would take around an hour. He wouldn't wait an hour to send his squadrons on their way northwest, of course. Each squadron was sent off as soon as it had formed up. He went up to Primary Flight Control, or Pri-Fly, on the third level of *Fujian*'s superstructure, to supervise launch operations. His air boss was more than capable, but it saved time if he was at the man's elbow in case anything went wrong and new orders were needed.

Modern carrier operations still gave his blood a rush. There was still the same ballet of plane captains and deck crew as there had been since the dawn of steam catapults and piston engine fighters. But to that, *Fujian* added the roar of jet engines, and the chilling—no, awe-inspiring—sight of *pilotless* aircraft being manhandled across the decks, locked into catapults and fired off into the sky one after the other after the other. Wang knew that five decks down, the pilots for these aircraft were sitting in virtual cockpit pods, flying the aircraft as though it were their lives on the line, but he knew that was an illusion they created through training and discipline. Not one of the people below could actually lose their lives today. Lose their careers, yes. Lose their liberty too. They could be court-martialed and demoted or imprisoned for poor performance. But executed? Highly unlikely.

This change altered the dynamics of carrier operations *entirely*. The big debate at the start of the century had been about whether the era of power projection that the aircraft of the superpowers offered was over. Were they not simply huge, floating targets, vulnerable to everything from maneuvering ballistic missiles to sea-skimming hypersonic cruise missiles, surface drones or simple, run-silent, diesel-electric submarines?

No, they were not. A carrier could now stand even further back from the area of operations. It could send its drones in wave after wave against an enemy in one-way attacks that did not have to consider pilot attrition. *Fujian* could launch 54 fighters within an hour and lose every single one of them without losing a single pilot. As the first wave of "dead" pilots were climbing into the virtual cockpits of the next aircraft to launch, her next wave of fighters could already be on the way. As those were attritted, new machines could be flown in from the mainland, straight onto her decks, to be fueled, armed and turned around. China's drone-armed carriers were not islands in the middle of enormous lakes; they were stepping stones, skipping heavily armed machines from land to sea to sky.

China had been anticipating the American attempt to break the blockade for weeks and positioned its forces to respond to it on short notice. His squadrons, together with nearly 100 more aircraft launched from the Chinese mainland and the carriers *Liaoning* and *Shandong*, were ready to form a metal belt in the sky through which the Americans would have to pass. And they had enough aircraft to be able to rotate the blocking squadrons for several days or until the Americans gave up their foolish idea.

Short of opening World War III with a blizzard of missiles to blow a hole in the Chinese cordon, Wang could see no way through for the American cargo planes or their fighter escorts.

Turning his eyes from the deck of the *Fujian* to the large, ceiling-to-floor wall screen that showed a map of the operations area, Wang felt like he was looking at a computer game, so huge were the resources committed by each side. On the left of the map of Taiwan, Japan and the Chinese mainland, a continuous flood of blue icons for Chinese aircraft flowed over and around Taiwan to take up positions up and down the island's coast between Okinawa and Taipei. In the east, a similar flood of red icons represented the American carrier-launched fighters.

But the American flood was already ebbing.

A count on the side of the screen showed that though over 120 had been launched, they were not trying to push through the Chinese air defense zone. So far, they were only probing. The lead elements of the American force were

284

already turning back to Okinawa, followed by Chinese interceptors. As each flight of American fighters hit the red wall of Chinese fighters, it too was turning away.

It looked to Wang like the Chinese strategy was working. Until *Fujian*'s air operations officer pointed to the screen. "Here it comes," he said. "The American C-17 has been identified, entering the air defense zone."

Wang's eyes locked onto the icon for the American cargo plane. The tactical map showed it was flanked by a half dozen fighters, probably a mix of air-to-air and electronic warfare types.

He realized he was holding his breath and forced himself to relax. But what happened in the next few minutes could determine the course of history.

China was a country of 1.3 billion people. It had reached the peak of its military might at the time its population peaked in 2022, and it launched its third aircraft carrier, *Fujian*, that same year. Its navy peaked at 400 warships in 2025. Its armed forces had topped out at 4.1 million in 1995 and trended downward since, reaching a low of 2.2 million in 2038. It had made up for this decline in personnel by upgrading the quantity of its aircraft, armor and, most of all, its missile systems. Unlike all other branches of the armed forces, which were stagnant or downsizing, China's People's Liberation Army Rocket Force (PLA RF) stood up nearly 10 new brigades a year through the 2020s and 2030s, and by 2035 was over 50 brigades strong.

China's solution to every military problem in its modern history was to throw massed forces at it, like a storm breaking against a dike, looking for breaks through which it could flood.

The Operation Skytrain planners knew this. And though it looked like it, their strategy was *not* to try to match China fighter for fighter. Their first tactic was to test Chinese resolve, and here China had not been found wanting. The Chinese response had, if anything, surprised Operation Skytrain planners with the depth of its commitment. China was launching more aircraft, from more bases, covering more sky than they had expected.

Their second tactic was to pull a bait and switch. The C-17 approaching Taiwan from Okinawa in the northeast, in the company of F-35C fighters and EA-18G Growler EW aircraft, was empty. Instead, the US Air Force had launched a second and larger C-5 Galaxy, loaded with 280,000 lbs. of food and medicine, from Fort Magsaysay in the Philippines, 400 miles *south* of Taiwan.

Its skeleton crew of four—a pilot, copilot and two flight engineers—were volunteers. It was flying alone, 500 feet above the sea, and was just about to enter the radar field of the PLA Navy *Renhai* class cruiser, *Dalian*.

Flying out to meet it, just crossing the coast of Taiwan at its most southerly point at 35,000 feet, were six F-16V fighters of the Taiwanese Air Force, which would hit the self-declared Chinese air defense zone at *exactly* the same moment as the American Galaxy in the south and the C-17 Globemaster in the northeast.

And amid this chaos, oblivious to all of it, also skimming across the wavetops directly east of Taiwan, was the Black Widow of Karen 'Bunny' O'Hare.

Bunny was adjusting her course not based on any landmark or digital waypoint on her nav screen but according to the radar warnings she was getting on her RWR. She had a very strong naval search radar to her north: a high probability it was a *Renhai* class cruiser, which meant a high probability too that it would see her if she got too high, or too close.

There was another strong search radar, probably an airborne scanning array, and her AI classified that one as a probable carrier-launched KJ-600 early-warning aircraft. Of the two, that was the more dangerous, since it had "look down" capabilities that could probably sort a return from Bunny's Widow from the ground clutter of the surrounding waves, if she was not careful. So she optimized her stealth profile to avoid being picked up by the KJ-600 and trusted her ridiculously low altitude to protect her from the *Renhai* as she "threaded the needle" between them.

But they were too close together, and she couldn't see a bigger gap in the Chinese radar coverage anywhere. Sure enough, the radar signal from the Chinese early-warning aircraft changed from "search" to "search and track," indicating it had gotten a return off Bunny and was now working to isolate her. She still had four Peregrine air-to-air missiles in her payload bay, and she could launch one at the Chinese KJ-600 in radar-seeking mode for an almost-certain kill—but starting World War III was *not* in her mission orders. Today.

The Chinese radar painted her skin again, sliding off it like the clammy hand of a mermaid trying to drag a sailor to his death. She changed her angle to the threat, bringing her closer to the *Renhai* but making it less likely the airborne warning aircraft would …

A high, warbling tone sounded in her ears. *Locked!* The Chinese KJ-600 had a fix on her. It wasn't armed itself, but it would communicate her position to every Chinese unit in the sector.

There was no need to stay low and slow anymore, and she shoved her throttle forward, lifting her nose to bring her a few hundred feet higher. The extra height showed her a narrow sliver of coastline on the horizon that could only be Taiwan.

Now it gets interesting, she thought.

Major Tan was in Pri-Fly with Wang and monitoring screens of her own at the same time as she listened to multiple radio channels on a headset. Wang's squadron commanders were not operating under his orders anymore; they were taking tasking from the controller in the carrier *Shandong*'s airborne early-warning aircraft, which was coordinating interceptions in the northern air defense zone.

That was a frustration he just had to live with. But he still had a squadron northward bound that was under *Fujian*'s control. Ao Yin Squadron had just taken off, formed up and headed northwest to relieve one of the other squadrons that had been on patrol there for some time now.

"The American cargo plane and its escorts are deviating!" Tan said, holding a hand to one ear and listening intently. She looked up at the tactical map, which had not been updated for several minutes. "They tried jamming our radar but our interceptors are in visual range now and not allowing them to pass ..."

The plot on the map updated and Wang could see the heading of the American cargo aircraft had changed from southwest to south. It was *turning!*

His elation was short-lived. His air operations watch officer turned to him. "Message from *Liaoning*'s airborne control aircraft, in the eastern sector. Unidentified fast mover approaching Taiwan from Japanese airspace near Taketomi Island. Ao Yin Squadron is the nearest; they request permission to issue tasking."

Wang didn't hesitate. "Approved. Give them tasking authority."

Interesting. Someone was trying to sneak into Taiwan from the east while all attention was focused in the north? Clever. It could be anything from a Japanese military flight to a narcotics smuggler.

"New contacts!" his air operations officer announced. "Multiple. The Frigate *Lhasa* reports four fast movers, low level, heading south from Taiwan main island. Additional contact, low level, heavy, moving north out of Philippines airspace, on course to rendezvous."

Tan looked over to Wang. "The Americans are making multiple approaches," she decided. "They drew the bulk of our force north and are simultaneously trying to penetrate from the east and south!"

"What do we have in the south?" he asked her.

She consulted a tablet in front of her. "We're stretched. That sector is being covered by J-16s from Xiangyang. They were ordered to intercept the Taiwanese fighters. There is no one to cover the heavy."

He looked grim. "The *Lhasa* can easily deal with it. If it is allowed."

Chen and Mushroom were flying at the rear of the Ao Yin formation, tracking northwest to join the action there, when Bo broke radio silence. They were flying in a loose diamond formation, spread over about two miles to allow freedom of maneuver if needed.

"Ao Yin squadron, Ao Yin Leader. We have been tasked to intercept a contact, a single fast mover, bearing 198 degrees, altitude 1,000, range 20 miles. Estimated airspeed, 800. A KJ-600 is going to push us the data. Chen, Mushroom, you are closest; break and prosecute."

"Ao Yin Seven, good copy. Breaking." Chen acknowledged the order and rolled his Chongming left, turning toward the contact's bearing.

"Ao Yin Eight, good copy. Following," Mushroom said. She was a mile behind but soon caught up and joined him off his starboard wing. As she did, a tone sounded in his ears, and a new contact appeared on his tactical display, a steering cue for an intercept flashing up onto his helmet visor. He adjusted course slightly.

And did some quick math. They would not catch the target, whatever it was, before it reached Taiwanese airspace. What constituted Taiwanese airspace was a fluid thing these days, but the unidentified contact was booking and was now just 15 miles from the dotted line on his map that marked Taiwanese sky. They were 14 miles and closing. By Chen's calculation, they would get within visual range of the contact just as it reached the hypothetical safety of the Taiwan air border.

Chen passed his calculation on to Bo. "We're going to need orders, Captain," Chen told him. "Either we engage beyond visual range, or we let this one through. It got too close before it was detected."

"Maintain pursuit, Shredder," Bo told him. "Expect you'll be asked to visually ID it. I'll revert to *Liaoning*'s airborne controller."

Chen switched to the interplane channel. They might pick up the unknown aircraft on their own radars now, but that wasn't necessary and could give away their pursuit. They had good data on the contact being fed to them by the *Liaoning*'s early-warning aircraft. "What do you think, Mushroom? Private jet, or military?"

"Eight hundred knots? Got to be military. But whose? It came out of Japanese airspace maybe?"

"Makes sense. But we should have seen it."

"Could be a Japanese F-X stealth fighter?"

"Why would they send a *single* fighter?"

Chen could think of a dozen reasons. To probe Chinese defenses, to test their reaction time, to deliver a high-value package or person or just to distract Chinese patrols, which it was successfully doing.

And then it hit him. It should have been the first thing he thought of, but it had been a long day, he was on his third sortie, and the fact neither he nor Mushroom had seen the obvious told him they both needed to pinch themselves and wake the hell up.

"Our Black Widow," Chen said. "It could be our damn Black Widow." He checked the updated position on the contact. They were still going to intercept it too late if they had to make a visual ID, but they could fire *now*!

"No, it ... it can't be," Mushroom said. "Shredder, I *destroyed* it."

"You took the shot beyond visual range. You didn't see the wreckage," Chen pointed out. "It makes sense. How else did the bogey get in this deep before it was picked up?"

Bo came back on the radio. "Shredder, Mushroom, you will close to visual range and make an ID. It's just a single aircraft. But beware of Taiwanese land-based air defenses. Do not enter Taiwanese airspace, is that clear? The risk you get yourselves shot down is too high."

Casino was right of course. Every mile of the Taiwanese coast bristled with missile defenses. He could already see the radar signatures of at least two, almost directly ahead of him. In an invasion, they would be among the first targets China's air force would hit, but for now, they were still up and radiating and the only thing stopping them from locking up his Chongming already was its diminutive size and radar-absorbent skin. If they were detected within Taiwanese airspace, at a time like this, a volley of missiles would be their welcome.

"Ao Yin Leader, Ao Yin Seven. Understood." He switched channels again. "You get that, Mushroom?"

"It's not the Widow, Shredder," she insisted. "It *can't* be."

"Well, we're going to find out."

Commander of Water Dragon Commandos Detachment 23, Captain Yi Zhizhi, had searched every damn inch of the

Japanese facility, including in the sea under the dock, and could not find the scientist. But in the comms center, he'd found the answer to how the attack on his rib boat had been carried out: UFP mines. That much he could make out from the labels on the console he had just discovered. The console looked ancient, but the mines couldn't be. They weren't old-fashioned magnetic mines because his rib boat wouldn't have triggered those. So they had to be new-generation acoustic, programmed to home on the signatures of Chinese or other adversaries' vessels.

He'd overlooked the defensive systems console on his first entry to the station … getting ahold of the pilot had been his focus. Had it already been armed? No … if it had, their rib boat probably wouldn't have made it out of the reef chasing the decoy. So the pilot and professor had armed it *after* they took off on their wild goose chase, knowing they would return.

He should have killed them as soon as he found them. Now, it seemed, both were gone. It was entirely possible the pilot had taken the scientist with her. He was no aviation expert, but the American plane seemed to be quite large and the pilot herself quite small. Two people in such a cockpit didn't seem impossible.

Neither was he Japanese. He had no idea if the system was still armed or not. He thought briefly about putting a bullet through the console—he still had his sidearm—in the hope that would disable the system itself, but that seemed like a vain hope. It would just as likely trigger a failsafe that would arm the defenses.

He would have to contact *Three Zero* and report the failure of his mission and loss of his troops, then request a helo to lift him out. *Three Zero* had a helideck for emergency evacuations but not a helo of its own, or his squad would have used it to fly in earlier. Which meant he could be facing a stay of *days* at the station until a PLA Navy ship with a helo came to pull him out.

There was another problem. The encrypted radio with the frequency he needed to contact *Three Zero* was on the seabed with the commando who had been carrying it. If *Three Zero* was still jamming the Japanese Station's VHF radio and satellite links ... He reached for the VHF radio handset, switched the frequency to the maritime safety channel, turned on the unit and lifted the handset to his ear.

Clear reception!

"*Three Zero*, Captain Yi of Detachment 23 for XO of *Three Zero* ..." He repeated himself a couple of times, and the Executive Officer of the ship standing offshore soon came back.

"Yi, we have been waiting for you to report," the second-in-command of the spy ship said. "The target aircraft was destroyed by PLA Navy air. We are preparing to get underway. Are you and your men on your way back?"

What should he report? Not the truth, that was certain. But a version of it ... "*Three Zero*, we could not prevent the takeoff of the American aircraft. The Japanese site was protected by acoustic mines. Our boat was destroyed. I am the only survivor."

The naval officer sounded shocked. "Yi, please confirm. You lost your boat and your entire detachment is dead?"

Hearing the voice on the radio, it was as though the reality of what had happened was hitting home for the first time. He'd been so focused on making it back to the reef, so furious about what had happened, so embarrassed at his own stupidity, he had not allowed himself to dwell on the losses.

He swallowed hard. "Yes, *Three Zero*, I confirm. All Detachment 23 personnel were killed."

"That … where are you? What is the situation regarding the Japanese personnel at the facility?" the naval officer asked. Was he worried that Yi had gone on a murderous rampage and shot every Japanese scientist he could find? It was a reasonable fear—he probably would have.

"I am inside the Japanese facility, *Three Zero*. It is deserted …" Should he mention it wasn't deserted when he arrived? That he'd been duped by the pilot? Honesty wouldn't bring his men back. "We were hit coming in. An automated UFP defense system, I think. Our intelligence let us down. We should have known about it."

"Are you injured, Yi?" The man at the other end was slowly getting himself together, thinking of a rescue now. "Do you need an evac? We can send a boat …"

"No boat, *Three Zero*," Yi said quickly. "The defense system could still be active and I can't read the Japanese menus to shut it down." For a moment he wondered whether the *Yuan Wang Three Zero* was safe, moored off the coast of the atoll. But it was more than 10 miles out. There was no way Japanese engineers could sow a minefield so thick it could cover a perimeter nearly 100 miles around at that distance.

"We could—wait." Yi heard voices conferring at the other end. "We can deploy a drone to drop you a satellite phone with video capability. You send us a feed of this defense system console. We'll do the translation from here."

It was a good idea. And a quicker way off the reef than he was likely to get if he waited around for another ship to come and chopper him out. The island's owners could also be on their way back soon, if they weren't already. He did not want to be here if a heavily armed Japanese marine platoon dropped out of the sky.

"Good plan, *Three Zero*. There is a large open area on the roof above. I'll get up there now." He gingerly rolled his left shoulder. It had been cut up on the reef, but he'd also taken a beating in the explosion. It felt like he'd torn some muscles. "And yeah, get ready to send a medical team. Not sure what shape I'll be in when you get here."

"Alright, keep your eyes on the sky, Yi," the man said. "We shut down that defense system, and we can come and get you ... and the bodies of your men."

It was late afternoon and Kato was still curled into the small space in the weather station on the roof with his knees around his ears, sipping water so that he didn't pass out in the oppressive afternoon heat. The heat wasn't his only problem. He'd discovered a new torture. He needed to conserve water, so he still had about a quarter of the one-liter bottle left, but his bladder was bursting. He had the idea that he could drink the water and then piss in the bottle, waiting until the middle of the night before leaving his hiding place to go down to the mess and find some more water, grab some food, hoping the Chinese commando was asleep or gone.

Or dead from his injuries. That would also be fine. He hadn't looked too healthy as he swam toward the station—or not so much swam as stroked, with one arm flopping in the water.

Kato had waited just long enough to be sure there was only one man trying to get back through the reef before he hid his noodle bowl and chopsticks, filled a bottle of water and went up to the roof. There was a metal ladder leading up to a small hatch, which could be locked from both inside and outside, but Kato didn't lock it. He thought that could create more problems than it solved, since it might look suspicious and just make the commando curious.

The weather station was no more than a ventilated metal box on a stand on the roof, with a weathervane on one corner to measure windspeed, solar panels and a funnel for catching rain. It had a digital barometer inside and was probably intended to carry more sophisticated equipment at one point, but that had never been installed, which was why there was just enough space for a man to squeeze inside.

It was the absolute worst place for monitoring what was happening inside the building though, and he could do little more than sit in the cramped box, looking out through small vents at the roof in front of him and the blank sea on either side. Which he did now. His bladder was cramping. The roof was empty, the hatch from the building's utility floor closed. *Drop out quickly, piss in a corner of the roof,* he thought. *Get straight back in. Three minutes, maximum. Yeah, and how lucky do you feel? The way things have gone today so far?*

It was an interesting internal conversation, but it wasn't like he had a choice: his bladder was about to rupture. He reached for the panel by his left leg, which he'd jammed shut with a clothes-peg because there was no lock or handle on the inside. The wooden peg had swelled in the humidity and he had to work it back and forth to …

The hatch in the roof in front of him flew open. A hand appeared first, grabbing the square frame that ran around the building exit, and then a head appeared. The hand was holding a pistol.

Seriously? Just now?!

The commando paused to look around the roof and decided it was empty before he raised an arm and laid it on the roof, getting ready to pull himself up. To do so, he put his pistol down in front of him. A crazy image came into Kato's head of him running the 10 yards across the roof and slamming the hatch onto the head of the commando.

And then he was *doing* it. He kicked out the panel and rolled out of the box, landing heavily on his side as he fell the two feet to the roof, then he was on his feet and running toward the hatch. Or, actually, moving at a fast hobble, since his legs were cramping and his bladder was still about to explode and he was waving the water bottle like it was a goddamn *samurai* sword and screaming at the top of his lungs ...

Yi heard the Japanese scientist before he saw him. Heard the irregular thud of feet on the roof behind him, turned awkwardly because he was standing on a metal access ladder, holding on gingerly with his damaged left arm as he tried to lever himself up onto the roof with his right.

Where had he come from? The roof had been completely empty a second before, and there was nowhere up here to hide!

Then the man was nearly upon him, waving something in the air, looking like he was about to club him. Yi scrabbled for his pistol, but the Japanese scientist batted his hand away with a water bottle and then kicked the pistol away awkwardly before he grabbed the heavy metal trapdoor, swinging it over and down on Yi's head.

Yi tried to duck down, but the trapdoor slammed shut, striking him on the top of his head so that he fell back, hand scrabbling to hold on to the rungs of the ladder. He smashed into the floor, forced to use his damaged left arm to break his fall, and cried out in pain as he hit.

Looking up at the closed trapdoor, he heard a bolt sliding shut across it, and bellowed with rage.

Kato looked down at the trapdoor and the small bolt that was holding it shut. It was probably just there to hold the hatch closed in strong winds, in case you were working on the roof in a rain squall. It didn't look like it would last long against a determined Chinese commando.

The not-so-clever part of his not-actually-a-plan was that there was more than one way up to the roof. The fire escapes at each end of the building went up to the roof to allow people to be evacuated. Unless he had knocked him out, it wouldn't take long for the commando to get to one end of the building and come for him.

Except.

His pistol! It was lying on the ground near the hatch where Kato had kicked it, and he ran over and picked it up. It was *heavy*. He'd never held a pistol before. So he didn't know how to check if it was even loaded. Didn't pistols have safety catches? This one had a small catch at the top of the grip with a red dot showing, but he was afraid to move it in case it made the magazine drop out or something. He tried tucking it into the waistband of his jeans like they did in the movies, but then got worried it would discharge and blow his pecker off. Speaking of which, he still seriously needed to …

He relieved himself right there, on the hatch cover. There was no point hiding anywhere and he had to hurry. Then he zipped up his jeans and looked left and right. Which way? He was wracked with indecision again. *Pick a side, Kato. You know that guy who just kicked the ass of a Chinese commando? What would that guy do?*

He would do what the Chinese commando least expected, Kato told himself. Go after the soldier, threaten him with the gun and lock him up.

Yeah, right. That wasn't happening. Kato didn't even know how to be sure the thing was going to fire. The best thing he could do was to throw it into the sea so that the commando couldn't take it off him and shoot him with it. But first, he had to decide which way to get down off the roof.

Then where his next hiding place would be.

He had just decided he was going to go down the east side because there were no windows there through which the Chinese soldier could see him as he went down the fire escape—if he made it that far—which gave him a better chance of making it down and then …

He heard a high-pitched whining noise and looked up, trying to identify it.

Ah, great. A drone. And it was hovering about 20 meters away, with its camera pointed right at him. It had a small payload hanging from its underside. *The way this day is going, probably a bomb*, he thought. He looked at the pistol again. It had two buttons on it up near the barrel and he tentatively thumbed one, moving it up until it covered a red dot in the next position. Then he drew back the slide on top of the pistol and aimed at the drone with both hands holding the grip, like he'd seen in movies.

300

And fired! The gun jerked in his hand. He missed, of course, but he was jubilant. He'd achieved two things: worked out how to fire the gun, and in firing it, had scared the drone away. It had pulled back into the sky and was now just a small shadow about 200 yards out to sea.

He ran for the windowless side of the building.

16. 'So close, so many times'

He needn't have hurried. Still down on the floor under the hatch, Yi wasn't going anywhere just yet. He'd dislocated his injured left shoulder in the fall and had been levering himself painfully to his feet when liquid had started dripping on him from the hatch above. It wasn't rain from a clear sky, so he scuttled backward. The bastard up above was pissing on him!

An incandescent rage rose in his chest. He'd been deceived, lost his target, blown up, injured and rendered unconscious, his boat destroyed and squad decimated. Now he'd been disarmed, dislocated his shoulder and been *pissed on* by a Japanese nerd. He pushed himself up against a wall, lifted himself to his feet and then turned, hard, slamming his shoulder into the wall to push the joint back into place. The pain was excruciating, but he embraced it. He deserved it. He let it consume the red mist of fury that was fogging his brain and clouding his thinking.

Then he heard a shot from up on the roof, and the sound of feet, running to the east.

So now he knew two things. The Japanese a-hole had his gun and knew how to use it. And he knew which side of the building the professor had run to.

Knowing these things did not make him happier. He was unarmed and partially incapacitated. He needed to rebalance the equation in his favor. He needed to find a weapon.

Bunny O'Hare had at least two Chinese radars painting her: one airborne, one surface, probably a *Renhai* cruiser. Her RWR wasn't showing that either of them had a solid lock on her, but you only needed a solid lock if you were going to take a shot. They probably had more than enough data to predict her flight path and vector fighters onto her tail who could do the shooting for them.

Sure enough, new radars appeared behind her, and these were definitely locked on.

She laughed at herself. *You are a freaking ninja, and your shadow will be the only thing they see.* Her navigation screen showed she was about 30 seconds from Taiwanese airspace. Ah, hell, she'd nearly made it. She was already nudging Mach 1, and with nothing to lose, she shoved her throttle forward and pitched her nose a few degrees down to gain what little extra speed the Widow would give her.

She still had four missiles of her own. She could turn and fight, sure. But only if the Chinese fighters behind her fired first. Which ...

They weren't doing.

Every other time she'd been tagged by a Chinese fighter they had fired at her from beyond visual range. Now they were *chasing* her? That told her all she needed to know. She had a chance! The dotted line on her screen marking the Taiwanese air border ticked closer, second by second. An alert sounded in her ears as her DAS optical infrared system picked up two contacts behind her and put them on her heads-up display. Fighters, uncrewed, slowly reeling her in. She was down among the flying fish again and couldn't push the Widow any faster, so with a height advantage, they were catching her.

A chime—a glorious, unmelodious, long-awaited chime—sounded in her ears, telling her she had crossed into Taiwanese airspace.

But it didn't last long. A missile radar warning replaced it, and Bunny got ready to die again.

"Missile locked. I am within our air defense zone. Request permission to fire," Mushroom announced.

No one wanted the Black Widow kill more than Chen, not even Mushroom. But he dared not disobey orders. The dressing-down he'd received from Colonel Wang was etched into his skin. "You are within our air defense zone," Chen told Mushroom. "But he is *not*. He just crossed into Taiwanese air." The rebel island filled the entire horizon now. He'd never flown a machine so close to it before. The sight of it filled him with ... contempt? Or just anger? He pushed it away.

Their forward cameras were showing what they had feared they would show. The image of a fleeing Black Widow pursuit fighter, about 10 miles ahead of them. Zoomed and enhanced, the Widow looked like a UFO from the rear: a bulging ellipse with thin, tapered wings that bobbed up and down, riding the waves below.

They could so easily swat it from the sky.

"Damn, ground radar bearing two seven seven. They're painting my machine," Mushroom said. "Safing missiles."

"*Fujian* control, this is Ao Yin Seven," Chen said, switching to *Fujian*'s inter-ship channel. "We have a positive ID on the bogey. It is an American Black Widow. We have to break away now. We are being painted by Taiwanese ground radar." He changed channels again. "Turning to zero niner zero, Mushroom. Follow me around." The high-velocity chase had burned a lot of fuel. They would not be able to resume their mission and rejoin the rest of the squadron in the northwest.

He broke left, watching the American aircraft in his visor as it quickly turned from an ellipse to a disc to a dot again.

"Ao Yin Seven, *Fujian.* Good copy on your video feed, concur with your identification. You are near bingo fuel. Return to carrier, Seven."

"Seven and Eight, returning to *Fujian,*" Chen confirmed. They stayed outside Taiwanese air space, and the rebel's American-made Patriot missile battery radars followed them impotently back out to sea. The day would come when the PLA Air Force swept across the Strait to scour the rebels' radars and missiles from the face of the earth, Chen knew it. But that day was not today.

"So close, so many times," Mushroom muttered so quietly it was as though she was speaking to herself.

"If it was even him," Chen said. "Maybe we can get a tail number, or some kind of match on markings from the vision analysis."

"I don't want it to be him," Mushroom said. "But I know it was."

"You can't know. A short time ago you were certain it *wasn't.*"

"That was before I saw him," she said. "The chances of two Black Widows making a run for Taiwan at exactly the same time? The time elapsed since our last engagement fits perfectly. You know it too."

Chen knew it. But he swiped a hand across his main display to pull up a tactical map showing all known aircraft in the sector. He was limited to seeing only the data that *Fujian*'s operations analysts decided he needed to see, but it was enough. To port, Ao Yin was joining with the larger Chinese blocking force. To starboard, another engagement was taking place. Chen frowned. The screen was showing several red "adversary" aircraft surrounded by blue Chinese fighters. One of the red icons was a "heavy" of some sort.

But no missiles were flying. Then, as quickly as the data had appeared on his screen, it went blank again, as though every aircraft south of him had just dropped from the sky. He knew that wasn't the case; the veil of "opsec," or operational security, had just wiped the data from his screen. It was another sign their flying was done for the day.

Bunny's day was only just getting started. She lit up her Identification Friend or Foe (IFF) beacon to let any Taiwanese patrols in the air near her know she was a friendly, and contacted Taichung air traffic control to secure landing permission and directions. Then she tapped a button on her touch screen to flip up the Luneberg lenses on her airframe— small discs that popped from the skin of her machine on her ventral and dorsal lines—and went from being nearly invisible to being visible to just about every radar within 200 miles.

And hell, that felt good.

Because for the last few hours, she'd felt visible to every unfriendly radar in the sky and on the sea, and she had learned a few things that she was going to headline in the debrief she had never thought she would actually get to make.

One: China had a new stealth-busting radar that could lift the cloak on her Widow and vector intercepting fighters right to her. It had a pulse or beam so powerful it could jam her avionics and comms temporarily too. That effect lasted about five minutes, but when it cleared, more often than not, you had a drone or a damn missile coming at you so fast there was no time to think.

Two: Her nomination for the Most Likely To Be the Culprit Award went to that cruise-ship-sized vessel covered in satellite dishes that just happened to be anchored off the Japanese atoll. Which …

Three: Was too much of a coincidence for even the gullible Bunny O'Hare to believe. That ship and the complement of commandos it had sailed with had been placed right under her flight path, right next to the only emergency landing strip in hundreds of miles of open sea. Yes, sure, it *was* the only landing strip within hundreds of miles, so if you were going to pick a place to anchor, it was the obvious choice, but to do that you had to be in the neighborhood in the first place, which meant sailing hundreds of miles from Chinese waters, days or even weeks ahead of time, to be in exactly the right place at exactly the right time. So no, she didn't buy it. Which meant …

Four: China had a spy who had the details of her mission. Who knew her flight path, her mission plan, probably knew exactly what her payload was before Bunny even knew it. They had probably known way back, when the Galaxy carrying her, Salt and the three HACM carrier-killing missiles was intercepted off Wake Island. Which led her to something Salt had said.

Five: "The specifics of your mission are known to just a handful of people in the defense establishment, and half of them are in this room right now." She could rule out herself, but she'd like somebody to start ruling out everybody else.

A bad memory came back to her. Weird. Almost completely unrelated, but it was probably the *feeling* it evoked that called it back right now, rather than the memory itself. That feeling?

Betrayal.

<< *Twenty-three-year-old Bunny O'Hare was sitting in a lawyer's office. Two years earlier, while she was at the Defense Force Academy, her grandfather had been on his deathbed, dosed to the gills with morphine, and had signed over his cattle station lease to a multinational agribusiness conglomerate. He had died "intestate," that is, with no will. So the money from the sale had been frozen by a Government Probate Court while it established who was eligible to inherit. With his only daughter, Bunny's mother, dead along with her husband in the last epidemic, establishing Bunny's right to inherit should've been straightforward.*

It was, and it wasn't. A woman from the nearby city of Alice Springs came forward to claim that she had been in a relationship with Bunny's grandfather for 10 years. This was news to Bunny, who had never laid eyes on the woman before, never heard her grandfather speak of her, and never noticed her grandfather was particularly interested in traveling to Alice Springs more than once or twice a year.

"So what happens now?" she asked the lawyer. He was a mild man, with spectacles that sat low on his nose, wavy gray hair and a reassuring manner.

"Her legal representatives have advised they will take the matter to court. If she wins, she will get half of the value of the estate. You will get the other half," he said.

"Which is how much?"

"After outstanding debts and taxes are settled, the estate was worth about 12 million," he says. "You would get around six."

Bunny couldn't believe she'd heard right. "My share would be 6 million?"

"Less taxes and legal fees. Or, if she loses the court case, 12 million," he pointed out.

Part of her wanted to fight. She had no idea who this woman was, whether her claim was legitimate, and she'd suffered nearly 20 years of isolation and pain on that station. She deserved every single cent coming from its sale. But she was only a year from graduating from the Academy, a year from pilot training, two years from realizing her dream of flying fast jets. Did she want the distraction of years of court proceedings?

"You're saying I should fight it," Bunny guessed. "Go for the full 12?"

"No," he said. "Though this firm would make a fortune in fees, I am not. The other party's legal team has made an interesting offer you might want to consider."

"What's that?"

"They are willing to pay you a cash sum of 4 million dollars, net of legal fees and inheritance taxes, if you do not contest the matter."

Bunny leaned back, putting her arms behind her neck and staring at the ceiling. "So, I fight and lose, it takes years, and I maybe get 6 million ..."

"Less taxes and the additional legal fees."

"Right. Or I fight and win, and get 12. Or ... I take 4 million now and walk away."

"Yes, that is the offer on the table," he said. "Why don't you think about it and ..."

Bunny leaned forward again. "Five million, net, and I'll sign," she said. "In my account by the end of the month."

"That is considerably higher than ..."

"Either they want this deal, or they don't," Bunny told him. "If they want it, they'll pay 5 million to win an easy 12."

They threw numbers around a little longer, but Bunny walked out having decided to play the short game and get on with her life. Five million was still money, right? Enough to buy a house or a couple of apartments, rent them out, get a little income on the side to supplement her service pay. She wouldn't know what to do with 12 million dollars anyway. More money, more problems, right?

The deal went through, the promised money landed in her bank account, and Bunny got on with her life, quite happy.

Until she was sent an anonymous message on a social media app that said the nice man with the wavy gray hair had been playing both sides of the deal. He took fees and commissions from Bunny, and also a seven-figure kickback from the other party for getting Bunny to walk away. The message said there was no "mystery lady," just a fake persona and a series of shell corporations in a scheme concocted by corrupt lawyers over a bottle of wine. She did a little digging, and yeah, she'd been played. She imagined the nice man with the wavy gray hair toasting her stupidity over a bottle of expensive Shiraz, paid for by her inheritance.

She wanted to kill him. Literally. During her next leave from pilot training, she found herself outside his office in a secondhand car bought for cash in a fake name that morning, ready to run him down if he came outside and crossed the road. She was wearing a brunette wig and sunglasses. Gloves too, so she wouldn't leave prints in the car.

He never came out. But she had a lot of time to think, sitting in that car. And Bunny O'Hare drove herself straight from the street outside his

310

office to a private psychiatric clinic and asked to be admitted because if she wasn't, she was going to head to the nearest rail crossing, wait for a train to come through, and park her new secondhand car right in front of it, with herself locked inside.

She checked out a week later with a diagnosis of borderline personality disorder.

"Which is what, exactly?" she asked the doctor.

"It's a mental illness that severely impacts a person's ability to regulate their emotions. It is characterized by increased impulsivity, feelings of exaggeratedly high or low self-esteem, and untreated, it can negatively impact your relationships with others."

"How?"

"You may have difficulty forming attachments, trusting others …"

"No shit, doc."

He continued. "You may alienate people who try to get close to you, even if you love them."

Bunny stood. She'd heard enough. "You mentioned treatment? Drugs?" That wouldn't work, fast jets and drugs not being a good mix.

The doctor stood too. "Drugs aren't proven effective. Psychotherapy is."

"Therapy?"

He reached out and put a hand on her shoulder, squeezing it in a gesture that was probably supposed to be reassuring but just made her want to pull away. "Find a good therapist, Ms. O'Hare," he told her.

"I want all records of my visit destroyed," she said in reply.

As she walked away, she was thinking … Screw therapy. I just need to get myself into the cockpit of an F-35, that's what I need.

311

Having entered the pattern over Taiwan's largest airbase, Taichung, in central western Taiwan, Bunny was quickly given a landing slot and directed to a hangar at the edge of the airfield. Then ordered to hold in place on a taxiway before crossing the main runway.

As she watched, a gargantuan C-5 Super Galaxy with USAF markings came down the glideslope, seeming to float to a touchdown before it thumped heavily to earth in a cloud of tire smoke. Four Taiwanese Air Force F-16Vs streaked overhead and peeled away to the west like a departing guard of honor.

OK, looks like I wasn't the only one to make it through the Chinese blockade, Bunny thought. *Not much of a "ring of steel" if you can fly a beast like that through it.*

The Galaxy used the full length of the runway to pull up and then turned right, toward the main terminal building, which seemed a pretty strange place to park a cargo plane until Bunny's eye roved a little to the right, where there seemed to be a welcoming committee ... hundreds of people, MPs in white helmets holding back what looked like camera crews. The arrival of the Galaxy was being carefully stage-managed, she could see that. Operation Skytrain seemed to have succeeded.

At what cost? she wondered.

She could see Aggressor Inc.'s F-22 Raptors hangar across the other side of the airfield but still hadn't been cleared to proceed, so she opened a satellite link as she waited.

"O'Hare for Aggressors, Taichung, anyone home?" she asked, unable to keep the smile from her voice.

"Welcome to paradise, Bunny O'Hare," a familiar Welsh voice responded. The CO of Aggressor Inc.'s F-22 Squadron was an ex-RAF pilot with the somewhat impressive name of Anaximenes Papastopolous, which no one could pronounce, so he was only ever referred to by his call sign. He'd had to take US citizenship and qualify for the USAF Reserve to fly with Aggressor Inc., but he hadn't lost his Welsh lilt.

"Meany, old mate," she responded. "I thought you would have been arrested for something by now."

"Not yet, but there are a few of the finer establishments that no longer want my business," he said. "Pleasant trip over, I trust?" She knew the pilots of the stranded Aggressor squadron would have been briefed on her mission to some extent and in constant touch with Guam to follow her progress.

"Nothing to write home about," she told him.

"Thought not. Salt was spinning us a story about Chongming fighters and jamming and you being recorded missing or dead over some tropical island or other ... but we didn't believe a word of it."

She got approval to cross the runway at last and eased her throttle forward. "He's awake now, is he?" she asked. "Last time I tried to speak with him, he was having a lie-down."

"Awake and awaiting your debrief with intense interest. Especially the part where you explain how you lost *three* Valkyrie wingmen," Meany reported. "Now bring your machine in. I have some munition systems specialists here who are very interested to see what goodies you've brought us."

Wang had returned to his quarters to grab a couple of hours' sleep. It had been a very, very unsatisfactory day. Fortunately for him, unfortunately for China, the failure of the Navy special forces to achieve control of the Black Widow's weapons after his pilots forced it down was overshadowed by the bigger action of the late part of the day.

The American feint in the north, preceded by weeks of intelligence leaks about Operation Skytrain being launched from Okinawa, had drawn the bulk of Chinese air patrols and airborne radar resources to it, leaving the south poorly protected. American aircraft in the Okinawa-Taipei corridor had turned around as soon as they were met by Chinese fighters inside China's self-declared air defense zone, leading China to think it was winning the battle of wills.

And while it was, America pushed a C-5 Super Galaxy through the gap, which was met inside Taiwanese airspace by Taiwan's air force and escorted to safety. As Wang quit the bridge after a last conference with Vice Admiral Zhang, a screen on the wall was showing a Hong Kong news broadcast of the Super Galaxy taxiing up to the waiting press and its pilots giving a thumbs-up from the cockpit. To be followed no doubt by vision, ad nauseum, of Taiwanese aid organizations unloading ton after ton of food and medicine.

He doubted very much there would be any film crews filming the unloading of the HACM missiles from the Black Widow. And he couldn't help but wonder which of these two headaches was seen as the larger one in Beijing: the propaganda success and continuing problem of the American airlift, or the possible arrival on the island of nuclear-capable, if not nuclear-*armed*, "carrier-killer" missiles.

As he lay his head on his pillow, he knew which of the two was most likely to keep him awake. But then again, the bed he was lying in was one level below the flight deck of one of the carriers that the American missiles were designed to kill.

On Okinotori, Takuya Kato was also nodding off to sleep. He didn't want to, and he had tried desperately to stay awake, but his body had finally called time on his traumatic day, and as the sun slid toward the western horizon, dissolving in a red-gold blur, his eyes refused to stay open.

He'd found himself a new hideaway, one he should have thought of earlier. Various sets of rusted steps wound down around the former oilrig legs on which the platform supporting the research station building was bolted. They led variously to the sea-level dock, to the runway and hangar building, and one of the rusty sets of stairs led nowhere, just straight down into the water. It was never used except for fishing sometimes, if the prevailing wind was from the north. But that was how he had discovered the door into the inside of the support stanchion. It was a maintenance door to allow mechanics access to the hydraulic system inside the stanchion, which made the platform above "jackable," able to be raised or lowered as needed—for example, if one stanchion began to sink deeper into the seabed.

The door wasn't on any of the station plans mounted on walls around the building in case of emergencies, and it led into a large hollow space about 10 meters across, filled with pipes and hoses and pistons among which a skinny Japanese coral biologist could easily perch. It couldn't be locked from the inside, but it was so rusty it opened with a terrible screech, so there was no chance he'd be taken by surprise.

Like an opossum inside a hollow tree, he'd wedged himself between two pipes and was dozing with his head against the rubberized lining of the hollow stanchion, the slap of waves on the metal outside quite hypnotic. His head jerked and he realized he had fallen asleep. He gripped the pipe next to him in reflexive panic. He could easily have fallen.

This is not going to work, he decided. *You've got the gun; this is your station. It shouldn't be you hiding.*

Yeah, nice sentiment, but the smart thing would be to wait right here. Think about things for a minute.

Yi Zhizhi was not sleeping. He'd hauled himself carefully up to the roof, made sure the lunatic Japanese professor was not up there, collected the satellite phone from the drone that *Three Zero* had dispatched, and with the help of a Japanese-speaking PLA Navy officer, disarmed the Japanese UFP defense system.

A boat was on its way over to search the seas around the atoll for the bodies of his men and then pick him up. He'd asked, or more accurately demanded, permission to rig the Japanese building with explosives and drop it into the Philippine Sea along with the Japanese scientist hiding somewhere inside it with *his* sidearm, but that request had of course been denied.

But it would be quite some time before the boat arrived to collect him, and that had given him time to search the station, armed with a claw hammer he found in a toolbox. He was looking for the scientist, of course, but also for anything that might make a better weapon. And he'd found it. Against a wall in the comms room had been a small upright locker. It looked too narrow to hold uniforms or boots, but more importantly, it was *locked*. Which suggested to Yi that it either held something valuable, or something dangerous.

He had clawed it from the wall using the hammer and then bashed the less-protected back of the cabinet open. It wasn't a true weapons safe, just a lockable cabinet. But inside, he found a Miroku Arms over-and-under shotgun and a couple of boxes of shells. It took time to make the hole big enough to pull the shotgun out, but when he did, he couldn't help but stare at it in wonder. It was more of a work of art than a weapon. The machined steel barrels disappeared into a polished walnut fore-end and burnished metal receiver that was laser engraved with etchings of a pheasant on one side and a duck on the other. The stock was engraved too, and a sliding panel on the top allowed storage of shells. The shells were a mix of 12-gauge birdshot and rock salt, which was disappointing. Even buckshot would have been better, but he guessed the station personnel only kept a gun on the station to scare off birds and sea mammals and they probably didn't want to kill them if they could avoid it.

There was a particular mammal on the station that he very much *wanted* to kill, and disabling him with the beautifully engraved Miroku would just be the first step in that process. Actually, the first step was locating him, but he'd found help with that too. One level below the comms room was a computer room, filled with servers, but also home to a small PC that showed the feed from CCTV cameras scattered across the station. He had dragged a chair into the room, set himself up in front of the PC screen with his injured arm cradled in his lap and the Miroku shotgun in the crook of his other arm and started clicking through the cameras with a mouse. Most just showed empty offices and corridors, the hangar area, mess and sleeping quarters. But some were technical surveillance cameras, in place to allow staff to run a quick visual check on vital equipment, like air conditioning units, solar panel capacitors and …

The insides of what had to be the Japanese station's supporting legs. The images were dark and low resolution, and the first few he clicked on were festooned with what looked like very static images of cables, pipes and hydraulic pistons, but the third showed the unmistakable silhouette of a man, wedged between pipes up against one of the inside walls of one of the stanchions, busy with something behind one of the pipes.

"Hello, professor," he said quietly, not taking his eyes from the screen as he loaded two shells into the barrels of the shotgun and snapped it shut.

He visualized the layout of the station from his earlier circuits. There were only three sets of stairs that ran down the pontoon legs of the platform, which made searching for the man relatively easy. Disabling him so that he could be dealt an excruciatingly slow death would take some finesse.

But like prying a juicy oyster from its shell, that too was something he was very much going to enjoy.

Alright, we're doing this, Kato told himself. *We're going out there, we're going to take that guy prisoner and lock him away somewhere that really can't be opened from the inside.*

He had just the place. It had come into his mind when the commando had asked him for a place earlier, but he hadn't suggested it for obvious reasons. The station had a biosafe room, a double-doored sick bay where people with contagious diseases could be isolated. Every government building in Japan had to have one, after the various epidemics

318

of the '20s had ravaged the country. Both doors were lockable, the idea being you would unlock one, put food or medicine down in the space between the doors, and then go out again, sterilizing the room remotely before you opened the inner door to let the patient get their supplies. Then you locked them in and sterilized the space again.

It was checked annually to be sure the doors and seals were working, and the last check had been only a couple of months ago, not long after Kato arrived. It would be a perfect prison for a Chinese commando.

He climbed out from the tangle of pipes and onto the platform that went around the inside of the stanchion, pausing in front of the door to pull out the pistol from where he had it jammed into the back of his jeans. That had seemed like the best place for it, but he had been careful to push the button with the red dot back down and check that it wouldn't fire. Now he pushed the button back up.

He waited by the door, listening. All he heard were waves and seabirds. Behind him, and at the bottom of a 20-foot drop, black water slapped against the metal inside of the stanchion. He hesitated. This was such a dumb idea.

Come on, hero, it's now or never.

Yeah? How about never?

Pistol in his right hand, he put his left hand on the metal hatch leading out to the stairs and pushed.

Yi checked two of the staircases going down the side of the platform's support stanchions but found no way into them.

On the third, he got lucky. Down three levels, there was a landing about 20 feet above the water, right outside what looked like an access hatch. It had a simple latch on the outside that dropped into a lug to keep it closed.

The latch was open.

He bent closer to inspect it. There were scratches in the rust, lighter than the rusted metal around them. Someone had opened this hatch. Recently.

Lovely.

Yi took a step back, angling the barrel of the Miroku shotgun up so he could pull the door open, step through and fire. He'd loaded the birdshot, and he knew where the scientist was. Up in the pipes to the right. Had to be. He rehearsed the action in his head. *Step in, rotate right, fire one barrel, look for movement, and fire the second.* Move in, disarm him if he was still carrying the pistol. Drag his ass out into the evening sunlight.

And then the fun would begin.

Takuya Kato pushed on the access door at exactly the moment Yi Zhizhi pulled on it. The door flew outward, and they both stood there, open-mouthed, gaping at each other.

Then in a simultaneous crash of noise, *both men fired their weapons.*

17. 'Sky train'

April 5, 2038

The calls between Michael Chase, Pentagon deputy assistant secretary of defense for China, and his counterpart, Major General Huang Xueping, deputy director for the People's Liberation Army Office for International Military Cooperation, had become, if possible, even more strained since the arrival of the American C-5 Super Galaxy cargo plane on Taiwan.

The first had been a stream of invective and unspecific threats. The next, not much different. Now, it seemed an adult had intervened to provide the General with a script, which suited Chase better, since he had also been given a script.

"You heard the statement of our President, General Huang," Chase was saying. "These flights will not cease. They will in fact only increase in pace and volume until you lift your pointless embargo."

"Taiwan is not Berlin, and this is not the 1940s, Mr. Chase," the General said. "Taiwan is not 3 million people, it is 24 million. You cannot possibly sustain a population of 24 million with a few cargo planes."

"We shall see, General," Chase said. "I suspect if you were convinced of that, you would not be so violently opposed to Operation Skytrain."

The point hit home. On the screen, Chase saw the Chinese officer's lips tighten. He looked down at the paper in front of him. "I have a message for your Pentagon superiors, which comes from the most senior ranks of the PLA Air Force and, of course, with the full authority and resolve of the PRC Government."

Here it comes, Chase thought. *At last, the shouting is over.* "Please, go ahead, General," he said.

"The PRC Government in 2038 is not in the same position the Soviet government was in 1948—militarily inferior and easily cowed by the threat of a nuclear attack." That was his own editorial embellishment, Chase could see. Now he looked down at his paper again. "The State Council of the People's Republic of China, as authorized by the General Secretary, has ordered the General of the PLA Air Force to destroy any aircraft or vessel which attempts to enter the defense exclusion zone around Taiwan." He paused, looking up for a reaction, and getting none, continued. "This includes, uh … both military and civilian aircraft of the United States and its coalition partners."

"You will attack humanitarian flights delivering medicines and food?" Chase asked. It wasn't unexpected, but Chase knew Operation Skytrain planners had hoped to get a few more flights through before China reacted with the threat of military action.

Huang put his paper down. "Ah, but we both know that you have moved more than food and medicine to Taiwan, don't we, Mr. Chase?"

"I don't know what you are talking about, General."

The Chinese officer looked suddenly very pleased with himself. Not a good sign. He raised a finger. "Please, allow me to give you a preview of the presentation our Ambassador to the United Nations will soon make at a session of the UN Security Council." Huang looked offscreen and appeared to gesture to someone. His face was replaced by a montage of several images.

With a sick feeling in his gut, Chase immediately recognized what he was looking at. He'd received a report on the successful arrival of the Aggressor unit on Taiwan and its emergency landing on a Japanese atoll. The images showed the Aggressor Inc. Black Widow aircraft sitting on the runway of that atoll. Taken close up by a Chinese commando, no doubt.

"A nice set of photographs," Chase said, "showing absolutely nothing."

"But just the first," Huang said. The presentation clicked forward. Now it showed video footage of an airborne object, held in the sights of what was apparently a Chinese fighter's gun camera. The video was slightly blurry, but Chase knew it to be the rear aspect view of a Black Widow fighter. "The same aircraft, crossing into Taiwanese airspace, Mr. Chase." He clicked forward to pictures showing tail numbers from the aircraft on the ground, and others that looked like they were taken in the air. "The same aircraft, yes?"

"Again, showing nothing except how porous your so-called 'ring of steel' is, General," Chase offered. He had seen nothing to worry about yet. If this was all China had, then ...

The presentation clicked forward again. It showed what looked like a US Air Force document, marked SECRET: OPERATIONS ORDER. A section had been digitally cut out and enlarged.

Mission: Aircraft of The Contractor delivers the payload to Taiwan no later than 2400 May 24, 2038. Delivery by air is the only option available to satisfy broader strategic parameters.

Chase breathed a sigh of relief. Whoever had written the leaked, stolen or intercepted OPORD had the sense not to specify "the payload" in the document.

"That says nothing," he insisted. "A contract for an unspecified company to deliver an unspecified cargo to Taiwan ..."

"A US Air Force Operations Order, which coincides with the flight of *your* stealth aircraft from Guam to Taiwan."

"None of which is in contravention with any international law or treaty I am aware of, merely inconvenient for China," Chase continued, prevaricating. He had the feeling the General had at least one more card to play.

"So you say," Huang told him, reappearing on screen. "But I have not presented all the evidence in our possession. This was just a taste, Mr. Chase."

As I thought. It was well known in US intelligence circles that China claimed to have infiltrated the US military at almost every level, but to reveal that to the world in this way showed the level of concern China held about recent developments and America's involvement. It bewildered Chase that they had expected anything different when they announced their blockade. Had the US not been saying for decades it would come to Taiwan's aid if the island's democratically elected government was existentially threatened?

"Is there a specific message you would like me to convey to our military leadership, General?" Chase asked.

The Chinese officer leaned forward into the camera. "Yes, Mr. Chase. We *will* destroy any aircraft or vessel that enters our defense exclusion zone. There will be no more polite fencing. And one thing more, since we are being specific. If the USA, or any of its allies, use the hypersonic weapons you have now positioned on Taiwan, a state of war will be deemed to exist between the USA and China." He gave Chase a thin smile. "Good day, Mr. Chase."

Security Council? He needed to get on the line with State and send them a copy and transcript of the call. He wondered what they would make of it. China's rhetoric was always overblown and full of hyperbole, making it impossible to know which threats were just hot air and which were real. He was sure of one thing though. If China shot down any American aircraft involved in Operation Skytrain, the issue of the HACM missiles on Taiwan would become secondary.

The war China threatened would have started.

"They're letting the Brits take point?" Bunny asked, surprised. She turned to the pilot beside her and raised an eyebrow. He shrugged.

Two days had passed since she and her Widow had arrived on Taiwan. There had been no more relief flights arriving, and the C-5 Super Galaxy that had flown in just after her was still parked out on the other side of the airfield, completely isolated, in case China decided to make a point by dropping a precision-guided bomb or missile on it.

Bunny had spent quite a few of her waking hours trying to get anyone who would listen to understand that on a small atoll in the Philippine Sea, there was a lone Japanese scientist who needed rescuing. She had finally gotten through to an English-speaking duty officer at the Japanese Oceanographic Research Command who either did not understand, or did not appreciate, what kind of danger their employee was in.

He appeared to be more interested in the fact Bunny had landed at the base without getting prior authorization.

Bunny O'Hare was no diplomat. "Maybe it's my accent," she said, exasperated. "I'll try again. There is a Chinese spy ship moored off your research station. They sent a *commando* team ashore and took us prisoner, but I escaped. Your employee, Mr. Kato, is either still hiding, or he is a prisoner, or worse …"

"Yes. We have lost contact with the station."

Bunny sighed. "I know that. Your communications are being jammed. You need to get an aircraft …"

"We are sending a ship," the man said.

"A ship? That will take hours … days …"

"A navy ship," the man continued.

"I got that much. You need to send a plane!"

"No plane," the man said. "We sent a plane. Our plane was intercepted by the Chinese navy air force. We are sending a ship." He changed the subject. "Now, please explain how much aviation fuel you took from our facility and which type of aviation fuel please."

Bunny had contacts in the Japanese Self Defense Forces from a short posting to Okinawa and tried to impress them with the urgency of Kato's situation. They called her back to confirm a frigate was being sent to investigate the sudden silence of the station, and her intelligence about the Chinese spy ship had been passed to its Captain. They assured her there was nothing more she or they could do, since Okinotori was, after all, just a small civilian oceanographic research station and there were much bigger problems brewing to the

326

west of Japan, but she was left feeling it wasn't enough. Not nearly.

Now the Aggressor pilots had been called to an operational briefing by Meany.

Their squadron was being stood up as an official unit in the USAF Indo-Pacific Command: the 68th Aggressor Squadron. Part of the deal Aggressor Inc. agreed to in leasing fourth- and fifth-generation aircraft from the US government was that the aircraft, and any pilots who were USAF Reserve officers, could be deployed for active duty at any time. They'd been half expecting the call-up because it was pretty obvious no one was making any special effort to pull them out from behind the Chinese blockade, and it probably served a political purpose to have them stuck there.

Turning them from a private military contractor to an official unit of the US Air Force though—that *definitely* sent a political signal.

Several of the Aggressor Inc. pilots were not members of the USAF Reserve when the unit had been stood up and had the option to opt out. There were no hard feelings; most of the guys who declined had families and had left the regular Air Force for that reason, but it meant the unit currently had more aircraft than it did bodies: 12 aircraft, but only seven pilots, including Bunny.

Meany had taken a conversation with every pilot to deliver the news to them. Bunny's conversation with Meany before signing on for the extended duty had been a short one.

"So I'm required to tell you that as an active member of the USAF Reserve, you are being recalled on Presidential authority and you can be asked to serve for a period of up to 400 days …"

"Or longer if so ordered …" Bunny completed for him.

"Or longer if … right … but if you wish, I can request a posting to another unit where you …"

"Not necessary. Risk almost certain death for a hopeless cause like Taiwan v. China? Where do I sign?"

The shrugging pilot beside her had been brought in from the ROC Taiwan 34th 'Black Bat' Squadron to help fill the gap. His name was Jack Chang, and Bunny had formed an instant bond with him the night before over a game of eight ball that had degenerated into a series of more and more stupid wagers and ended with her putting an eight ball into a corner pocket off three cushions and Jack Chang flopping around on the floor barking like a seal. He was a lanky, rock-climbing American-Taiwanese guy from Colorado who had flown F-22s for eight years in the USAF before separating, after which he promptly got on a plane to Taiwan and joined up to fly F-16Vs for his grandparents' homeland.

Bunny liked that about him too.

Meany acknowledged the question. "Yes, the Brits are taking point, O'Hare, though the way it was told to me, they *insisted*, after the Chinese threatened to shoot down any aircraft trying to fly into Taiwan. The idea is to make the point to them that if they want a fight, they are taking on the whole Western alliance, not just the USA."

"*Just* the USA?" one of the other pilots quipped. "Like 'just the USA' couldn't whup China's ass without y'all's help anyway?" She reached up and took a 'hoo-ah' high-five from the American pilot next to her.

Bunny winced at the hoo-ah vibe. She knew the woman from exercises in Arizona, and they had *not* gelled. Charlene 'Touchdown' Dubois was Texas Longhorn heifer, and Bunny was Australian Brahman. Touchdown was cheerleader-blonde, ponytail-bouncing R&B while Bunny was crewcut, tattooed rock and roll. Ironically, both of them had grown up around cattle, and they probably had a lot in common that they would never, ever explore.

Of course, Touchdown wasn't one of the ones who opted out of this fight. *I couldn't be that lucky*, Bunny reflected.

Meany let the comment slide by. "So, the situation. China has been to the UN Security Council, accusing a certain pilot of a certain unnamed squadron belonging to a certain private defense contractor of smuggling 'strategic weapons' into Taiwan. Despite their best efforts to kill her, with which I am sure we all sympathize ..." —he paused for the groans and whistles, as Bunny ducked her head— "... she apparently succeeded in making the Chinese so pissed they have now threatened to shoot down any and every aircraft approaching their air defense zone."

"That might have more to do with the big-ass Galaxy sitting across the other side of the airfield," Touchdown pointed out.

"No," Meany corrected her. "I blame O'Hare. In any situation where I am unsure, I find it saves time."

Chang theatrically moved his chair a few inches away from O'Hare. His call sign was 'Magellan,' and he had refused so far to explain why, but the rumor was it had something to do with a lack of navigation skills.

"So," Meany continued. "Further questions or interjections? No? Mission brief. The next delivery by Operation Skytrain will be flown by the Brits. RAF 617 Squadron Tempests are going to escort their heavy from Kadena to the Chinese air defense exclusion border, at which point it will fly the next 20 miles unescorted until it reaches Taiwanese air space, where it …"

"I hope those Brits have made their peace with God, Major," someone said.

Meany continued. "… where it will be met by Magellan's buddies from ROCT 34th Squadron and escorted in. Our role … turn to your map package please … our role is *overwatch.* We will be in position inside Taiwanese airspace over Sandiaojiao on the east coast." He made a total mess pronouncing the Taiwanese place name but plowed on. "'A' Flight will cover the ROCT Vipers on their way out and the RAF Globemaster and its escort on the way in. 'B' Flight will cover 'A,' from back here over … uh …"

"Yuan-wang-keng," Magellan said from beside Bunny. "You guys putting your lives on the line for Taiwan, you should at least learn to pronounce a few things."

"Our job is to make the *other* guys give their lives, Chang," Meany said. "But thanks: Yuanwangkeng O'Hare in the Widow is our datahub and therefore quarterback and mission commander. She'll be with 'B' flight but up at 65,000 calling the plays, so you will take your tasking from her. I will lead 'B' flight; Touchdown will lead 'A.'"

"Going up with a full load of Peregrines too, if you need an assist," Bunny said. No one looked unhappy about that, not even Touchdown.

Bunny reflected on the mission plan. It was a pretty orthodox way to run an operation combining Taiwanese fourth-generation fighters, fifth-generation F-22 stealth fighters, the sixth-generation RAF Tempests and Bunny's Widow. The RAF fighters would lead the Globemaster in, making their presence known to the Chinese only as needed to try to scare them off, or if attacked, take out the Chinese

330

patrols. The ROC Taiwan fourth-gen fighters, unable to hide from Chinese radar, would lurk inside their own airspace and wait for the British cargo plane to come to them, with 68th Aggressor Squadron to protect them.

Bunny was completely at home behind the stick of a fighter like the F-22, playing beyond-visual-range hide-and-seek with an adversary, or down low, in a thrust-vectoring merge, guns on guns. But she also got a buzz from what she could do in a Widow that no F-22 pilot ever could—direct an engagement from on high, invisibly. Manage up to six drone wingmen, integrate data from a dozen sources, target up to 36 aircraft at a time with her own and her drone's missiles …

"Support assets," Meany continued. "Navy has positioned *USS Sam Nunn*, an Arleigh Burke destroyer, covering just about the entire operations area with its Aegis system, and you'll have ground-based anti-air missile coverage from ROC Taiwan air defense batteries up and down the coast." He flipped to the next screen of his tablet PC. "Comms frequencies …"

The communications portion of the briefing prompted Bunny to think of her last interaction with Salt, during the debrief on her Guam to Taiwan mission. She hadn't been stripped of her wings on landing as he'd threatened, because she had delivered the payload as ordered, despite significant challenges, and their USAF clients were more than happy about that. Air Force had seen the sacrifice of three low-cost drones as a small price to pay for the advantages of deniably positioning hypersonic missiles on Taiwan. For many reasons then, Salt had not been happy and spent the entire debrief on video link, doing what Bunny regarded as nitpicking.

They had gotten to her escape from Okinotori and Bunny had had enough. "Wait. You armed a Japanese UFP defense system, which resulted in the destruction and probable loss of a Chinese special forces team?" Salt said. "Do you realize what …"

Bunny interrupted, as diplomatically as she could since several others were listening in. "Colonel, the Japanese civilian in charge of the station, who had *also* been held prisoner with me, aided in constructing the decoy and instructed me in how to arm the UFP system. It was not a unilateral decision." He started talking again, but she kept going. "And can we get to the part of this debrief, please, where you ask how in hell China happened to have positioned an electronic warfare ship and naval special forces team offshore our only emergency landing option for about a thousand square miles?"

There was silence at the other end of the line.

"Or perhaps you were hoping to avoid that discussion by asking a million other pointless questions?" she asked.

"What are you insinuating, O'Hare?"

"I'm not insinuating, Salt. I'm saying as plainly as I can: someone leaked the details of the cargo manifest and probably the flight path for our flight to Guam, and we were intercepted. Someone leaked the flight plan for my flight to Taiwan, and I was not only intercepted, twice, but our mission plan was leaked in sufficient time for China to pre-position a naval vessel and special forces team. And probably other assets we weren't aware of."

"You're accusing *me*?" he asked aggressively. "If you are, just come out and say it."

Was she? No. She couldn't get around the fact it would have to be a very dumb Chinese agent who told his masters which aircraft he was riding on so they could shoot it down.

And Salt didn't strike her as the kind of guy who would happily commit suicide for any grand cause.

"No. But we do have a leak."

"I know you've been under pressure," Salt said. "You're seeing a pattern in a series of coincidences. But I'll have our internal security look into it."

"Have internal security report it to the FBI and Defense Intelligence, Colonel. Because I am going to."

A whirring noise from the front of the room broke her train of thought, and she focused on Meany again. He had moved to lean up against a wall as he continued. She'd known him so long that sometimes she forgot about the exoskeleton he moved himself around with. When she'd met him on deployment to Crete in an earlier life, he was already a bit of a local legend because of his tin legs, but also because no matter how drunk he got, the exoskeleton meant he never lost his balance.

He'd broken his back ejecting from a Tempest fighter over Syria, but that hadn't stopped him. He'd returned to flying after his rehab, risen to the rank of Squadron Leader, and it was O'Hare who suggested to Salt to headhunt him to head up Aggressor's F-22 squadron, since he'd flown Raptors on a posting to the USAF and he'd need no special physical considerations. Salt hadn't been sure about that, but five one-on-one air combat sorties in which Meany had scored 4-1 against Salt had convinced him.

Meany's RAF squadron buddies had given him the call sign 'Bader' after the World War II British ace who flew with prosthetic legs, but to O'Hare, he would always be 'Meany' Anaximenes.

He pointed to a Taiwanese meteorological officer standing at the back of the room. "Atmospheric conditions, if you please, Officer Xiao."

On *Fujian*, a very, very similar briefing, from a very different viewpoint, was also taking place.

"Situation please, Major Tan." Colonel Wang had assembled all the pilots of his air wing. He nodded to Tan to bring up a map on a large wall-mounted screen that showed the operations area.

"Yes, Colonel. The *USS Enterprise* carrier strike group remains within Japanese waters, here near Okinawa. Satellite images indicate the *Enterprise* has flown off nearly two-thirds of its fighters; they are now deployed at Kadena Air Base. *George HW Bush* is approaching Philippine territorial waters near the Babuyan Islands and now appears to be in the process of transferring aircraft to Fort Magsaysay Air Base."

"Explain your theory as to why the carriers are offloading their aircraft to land bases, Tan," Wang said.

"The US is moving a third carrier into the theater from Hawaii," Tan said. "The *USS Gerald R. Ford* left Hawaii three days ago. Photographs of its deck indicate it was carrying a full complement of aircraft, up to 70 fighters. It is currently 1,100 miles from Okinawa, and we believe it has already sent half its F-35C fighters to Okinawa, with the rest to be landed on either the *Enterprise*, the *Bush*, or both because their land bases will be at capacity."

"If this happens," Wang said, "The Americans will have more than 200 F-35 stealth fighters within range of Taiwan. The British have a squadron of Tempest stealth fighters on

Okinawa, as well as on their carrier, the *Queen Elizabeth*. The Australians, a squadron of F-35A stealth fighters at Fort Magsaysay. As you know, the US already has a 'training' squadron of F-22 fighters on the island of Taiwan itself. This brings the total of potentially hostile stealth aircraft arraigned against us to nearly 300." He paused to let this sink in and then did the math for them. "This is double the number of adversary stealth fighters in the Taiwan theatre than China has of J-20 stealth aircraft ... in our *entire* mainland air force."

Mushroom nudged Shredder. "Let's not forget Navy, right? The Western powers are not the only ones with stealth. *Shandong* has 30 Gyrfalcons, *Liaoning* 24, *Fujian* has 70 Chongming fighters ..."

"The Chongming is not a true stealth fighter, just small," he pointed out.

"Whatever. What the Air Force lacks, the Navy can make up, right?"

He didn't look convinced.

"This is not our only concern," Wang continued. He nodded to Tan, who paged to a new screen. It showed the flight corridor between Okinawa and Taiwan. "Signals intelligence indicates the adversary is preparing another attempt to land supplies on the rebel island," Tan said. "It could take place at any time."

"They can't keep the rebels from starving with a few cargo planes a day," Shredder said. "Not even with hundreds."

"Someone must think they can," Mushroom observed, "if they are planning to intervene. Come on, where do *we* come in?" she urged impatiently, but so that only Shredder could hear. They had spent two days filling out after-action reports, and only a few had been given any stick time. When they asked what was happening, they were simply told to enjoy the downtime, because it would not last. Rumors included everything from *Fujian* being withdrawn to Ningbo to the start of a full-scale attack on Taiwan. But Mushroom wasn't buying the idea they were being withdrawn to a mainland port. In the last two days they had sailed northwest and were now about 200 miles off the eastern coast of Taiwan, almost equidistant to the rebel island in the west, the Philippines in the south and Okinawa in the north.

Wang appeared to pick up on the impatience in the room and stepped forward. "Enough of the big picture. The mission of the *Fujian* Air Wing today: we will patrol between Taiwan and the anticipated launch point for aircraft deploying from Okinawa. They will be warned to return to their point of origin, and if they do not comply … they *will* be destroyed."

Mushroom gasped. "Holy shit." A general murmur swelled up across the room.

Tan spoke up. "We do not expect a large-scale engagement. The adversary's strategy is all about resupplying Taiwan by air, and if we prove this is impossible, we expect them to pull their aircraft back to avoid large-scale losses. If they do this, we have achieved our objective, which is to disrupt the adversary's efforts to supply the rebels."

Chen raised his hand boldly. "Last time, the Americans got a cargo plane through our southern defenses. What is being done to stop that this time?"

"The PLA Air Force Eastern Command has that responsibility," Wang said. "We will concentrate on ours. The operation will be executed by squadrons Xiu Snake, Fei Yi and …"

Come on, Mushroom urged inwardly.

"… Ao Yin," Wang finished. "Changfu Squadron is on carrier defense." He motioned with his hands to quell a wave of disappointed groans from the Changfu Squadron pilots. Tan raised a hand. "Please proceed immediately to your squadron ready rooms for pre-flight briefings."

Mushroom spun her chair and bumped fists with Shredder as he stood. "This is it. Today we get a meat kill. For sure."

"If we get a crewed aircraft in our sights," Shredder said, "it's mine. Alright?"

Mushroom raised her hands in surrender. As flight leader it was his call anyway, but she could hear he wanted her to acknowledge it. "Heard and understood, Lieutenant." It was fine by her anyway. Her confidence had been shaken by her first experiences in combat: letting the American Black Widow get away, because she was sure she had, but more particularly the experience of being shot down.

You could say what you wanted about drone pilots not putting their lives on the line in the way that crewed aircraft pilots did … thanks to the virtual-reality cockpit experience, the *psychological* trauma of a shootdown was intense. The sights and sounds of the warnings and alerts, the dizzying disorientation of violent maneuvering, the fear and panic as the enemy missile closed on you, and then the flash of orange and red light from the explosion, before all went … black. It was that blackness that was the most terrifying of all. How milliseconds earlier, her world had been a cacophony of noise and violence, to be replaced by … nothing. Horrible silence.

The silence of death.

The American's missile had killed her machine, but it had killed a little piece of her too. Mushroom didn't mind her call sign, even though she knew it was meant as a joke. If she could have, she would have continued living the life she was contentedly living in the darkened comfort of her own bedroom in Wuhan. Away from the light. Away from the noise and shouting and confusion that was the city outside her apartment. She'd had a cat, a bed and a kick-ass PC gaming setup. She'd had food delivered to her door and left only to see her doctor or drop garbage into the chute in the corridor outside. Her parents had died in a car accident, and she had no siblings to worry about.

Mushroom had been a game-coin miner. She made her living grinding in online games for in-game currency and then selling it at a discounted rate to rich gamers in the West. And she was good at it. A coder herself, she had perfected a system of AI bots that played all the major online games for her. Yes, she had to play through a game herself first and master it so that the AIs could watch and learn, but once that was done, she simply created accounts for them and let them loose to grind for coin. She didn't use cheats or hacks: her bots were indistinguishable from human players because they used the same mouse, VR goggles and keyboard inputs to control the games they played. But she could run up to 20 bots at a time from the PCs in her room and run them 24/7, changing from game to game to game every couple of hours so the stingrays on the game servers didn't get suspicious.

And while they were grinding, she was mastering whatever the newest number one global game was, preparing new bots to go to work on it as soon as she'd learned the most lucrative ways to earn in-game currencies.

The game developers hadn't shut her down; a People's Liberation Army Cyber Force algorithm had. Programmed to watch internet gaming traffic to identify China's heaviest and best gamers, it had of course flagged Min Sun, gaming tag "Teddy2034." When the PLA's cyber investigators realized what they were dealing with and that 21 of the best gamers it had identified were her and her AI bots, they were torn between reporting her to Wuhan cyber-crime authorities or recruiting her to their own ranks. They never got the chance. The PLA Air Force Uncrewed Aircraft Pilot Program had been given a list of the top 100 Chinese gamers for its newly accelerated drone pilot recruitment drive, and Min 'Maylin' Sun's name had been near the top of the list.

Refusing the call-up wasn't an option she'd been given.

She'd traded her bedroom for a drone cockpit pod, and Min 'Maylin' Sun became Second Lieutenant Sun, aka Mushroom, Ao Yin Fighter squadron, PLA Navy carrier *Fujian*.

Mushroom hadn't had the courage to tell the PLA that it had been her bots doing all the gaming. Sure, she was a competent enough gamer, and a hell of a good coder, but flying a Chongming drone required an amazing capacity for continuous partial attention so that you could soak up the competing high-volume streams of data, not to mention twitch reflexes so that you could really push the physical flight envelope of the drone.

Like Shredder had done in that amazing maneuver he pulled dodging the American missile. And like she ... hadn't. *Fear, alarms sounding, spinning vision, panic and blackness.* It kept replaying in a loop every time she closed her eyes.

Asien 'Shredder' Chen might act like he didn't even notice Mushroom's wheelchair, but the PLA recruiters had, and it had taken them a moment or two of blinking awkwardly at her when she had arrived at the interview location and had to call them to ask for help getting into their stupid no-ramp, no-lift building. But they'd adjusted quickly enough and quickly disabused her of any hope that her physical status might get her out of the conscription summons she'd received through the post. "If you can get yourself in and out of bed, you can get in and out of a drone pod," they'd said. Which was true enough.

Shredder looked back at her and frowned as they moved down a corridor to their ready room. "You deliberately going slow, or do you need a push?"

Less thinking, Mushroom told herself. *Time for action.* She sped up and overtook him, looking back. "You deliberately going slow, or do you want a ride?"

18. 'The least painful option'

Takuya Kato had seen a bright light, far away. He had reached out his hand, tried to move toward it, but all he felt was pain, and it didn't come any closer. Then he started coughing, his lungs full of water.

He was floating on his back, staring up at the open hatch, 20 feet overhead. His side was on fire, and just trying to look at it caused him to sink under the water, so he had splashed to the surface again and rolled onto his back looking up.

He remembered ... the man in the doorway, firing. Falling backward, falling ... then nothing. There was no ladder leading down the inside of the stanchion and the insides were just round, rusted sheet metal, so there was nothing to grip onto. There was a cable of some sort that had come loose and was hanging down, but it was still 10 feet above the water. He didn't even try to reach it.

He'd laid back, waiting to sink again, once and for all. He might have passed out again then, or at least couldn't remember the next few hours, because the next thing he was aware of was darkness.

Night had fallen. The moon must have been bright, because he could still see the sky through the open hatch, a less-dark oval in the darkness. And it seemed ... closer? Was that an illusion? No, the tide had risen and the water level inside the stanchion with it. Squinting, he looked for the cable he'd seen before. It was now just a couple of feet above the water. He paddled over until he was under it and reached up feebly, but it was still a good foot out of his grasp. His entire left side felt like someone had attacked it with a cheese grater, and he was pretty sure he had at least one broken rib.

From the moment the warning had sounded about the Chinese ship offshore, things had gone rapidly downhill. The universe clearly had a message for Takuya Kato, and it was simple. *Just give up.*

But ... what if there was help on the way? So many hours had passed, the Chinese commando *must* be gone by now. Maybe the ship too. He reached up and tried to measure the distance between his hand and the cable. Ten inches maybe?

You are going to lie here until you fall unconscious again and sink and drown because you couldn't jump 10 inches, that's what's happening here? It was the voice that had led him to charge out of hiding on the rooftop, the same one that told him he should leave the stanchion and go hunt the commando, and he tried to ignore it.

- *Yes. Yes, I am going to just lie here. That sounds like the least painful option.*

Or—here's an idea. Or ... you make just one almighty effort to kick up out of the water and grab the cable. How about that?

- No. Yes. No. *Do it!*

And before he could think another thought he was batting at the water and thrashing with his legs and scrambling up the inside of the stanchion, his fingers falling a few inches short as he fell back into the water and started to drown.

Do it!

He kicked again, bursting out of the water, gulping air, waving one hand wildly above him as something brushed against his palm and he held on literally for dear life to find himself swinging from the cable, wet hand slipping until it caught on some kind of metal connector near the end. He got two hands on it, and started pulling himself up, screaming at the pain in his side, pulling up a couple more inches, screaming again, until the pulling and the screaming became his entire world. There was only pulling and screaming until he got his feet up onto the metal connector at the bottom of the cable and then he was pushing, screaming, pulling and screaming, and his hand finally scraped across the metal grill of the landing and he hooked his fingers into it. After gathering his breath and before he could think about how much it was going to hurt, he swung one leg up onto the landing and got one arm and his chin up on it too.

Then he was rolling over onto it, on his stomach this time, looking *down* at the water.

Well, now I know what a spider in a toilet bowl feels like, he'd thought. And laughed weakly, but enough that his side felt like it was ripping open again. And he screamed.

That had been a day ago. He'd collected his energy and waited until the first light of dawn started coming through the open hatch. Levering himself to his feet, he'd sidled up to the doorway and looked out. There was, of course, no one there. If there had been anyone left on the station, they would have to have heard him hoot and holler and come to either rescue or kill him. He'd stumbled out of the stanchion and up the stairs to the sick bay, thinking he should get his shirt and jeans off and see how badly wounded he was.

But he'd only made it to the bed in the sick bay, which looked so pristine and clean and soft that he had just laid down on it, just for a moment, just to rest. He'd kicked off his sodden shoes.

And he'd slept for six hours.

When he woke it was midday, the sun through the sick bay window making the room so hot he was sweating, even though the building had solar-powered evaporative cooling. He sat up, wincing. And finally looked down at his side. He almost threw up. At and above his hip, the shirt and jeans were chewed up as though a dog had attacked him, and so was the skin underneath. In fact, that was exactly what it looked like. Like some huge bull mastiff with shark teeth had taken several bites out of him. He tried to pull his T-shirt off but couldn't get his arms high enough, so he got his feet on the floor and padded over to the medical cabinet to get some scissors and cut the shirt off. Then he undid his jeans and let them fall to the floor.

The saltwater thankfully must have slowed the bleeding while he was floating around, but he was bleeding again now, thin rivulets of blood from the cuts in his abdomen and hip and a hundred small holes that … what the hell? Fumbling for some tweezers in the medical cabinet he felt around one of the holes with a fingertip and then dug into it until the tips of the tweezers came across something *metal*. He got a good grip and pulled it out, holding it up in front of his face. A tiny ball bearing? He'd been shot with ball bearings. Well, that explained the other small holes in his side. They mostly seemed to be in his front left side, so he spent the next 30 minutes digging ball bearings out of his hide and counting them.

Twenty-nine.

There were probably some others in the more chewed-up parts of his hip and abdomen, and he knew he should try to

344

get those out as well, before infection set in, but even touching the flesh there made him feel like either puking or passing out, so he poured coagulating disinfectant powder on a bandage and wound it around his torso, pulling it tight.

There was a blue medic's shirt on a hangar on one wall, and he slowly dragged it on. He decided he was hungry. Wearing only the shirt and bloodied briefs, he made his way to the mess. Any worry that he might run into someone had vanished, and to be honest, he was beyond caring.

But he paused at the door to the mess when he saw a half dozen plates, bowls, cups, empty beer bottles and scattered cutlery on the table. He certainly hadn't left such a mess, and neither had the Australian pilot. Suddenly concerned again, he walked as quietly as he could to one of the tables and picked up a bowl. It had noodles stuck to one side, dried in the tropical heat. The liquid that had been left in the bottom had also dried out, leaving a thin film of spices and flavorings. Other bowls and plates looked the same.

Whoever had been here had probably eaten their meal during the day yesterday. Noodles, beer and soup weren't the kinds of things you would eat for breakfast. But then again, what the hell did he know about what Chinese commandos ate for breakfast? He had to be sure he was alone. There was a security room one level down where he could quickly check every floor on the station CCTV system, and he padded down there in his stockinged feet. Although "padded" sounded quite ninja; a better word was probably the Japanese equivalent of "schlepped."

The corridor from the stairs to the security room was empty and that floor sounded quiet. He went into the room and looked at the screen. It showed six cameras at a time and then cycled through each floor every two or three minutes. He didn't have the patience. He took the mouse next to the system's keyboard and clicked his way through every level of the station.

Nothing. No one. Either in the corridors, down on the boat dock or sleeping off their plundered beers in the living quarters. Good. He was alone.

He was about to stand and leave when the screen flicked to the next view, and he saw six views of the inside of the station's support stanchions. *Oh, for God's sake.* That's how the commando had found him? Hiding in plain sight? Actually, it made him feel better. As he made his way up to the comms level again, he reflected that if he hadn't been on the move when the commando had come through that door, he most definitely *would* have been killed. Or worse. As it was, he had been blown backward into the water and the commando had probably just left him for dead.

The pistol he'd been holding? Probably in the bottom of the stanchion under 20 feet of water. Or he dropped it as he fell and the commando picked it up. Did he vaguely remember firing it? Was it too much to hope he had killed the Chinese soldier? He was quite shocked to realize he hoped he had. He was a guy who believed every coral polyp had a right to life and felt true sorrow if any of his seedlings didn't take. Yet here he was, hoping he'd shot some random Chinese guy. Really?

He winced at the pain in his side. *Hell yes, he was.*

In the comms room, he went to the satellite communication console and tried to get a line out. *Signal not found.* He tried the VHF radio and got nothing but static. So his visitors had left the station, but they hadn't left the area.

He sighed. He was very, very tired. He should probably have another sleep. In a lot of ways, he was back where he had started a few days ago. All alone and cut off from the world around him. Nothing had changed.

One important thing had changed, but Takuya Kato was in no condition to realize it.

He was dying. He had taken most of the blast from the Miroku shotgun at a range of less than three feet. The acute pain he was feeling was torn flesh, but there was a deeper, less intense but more constant pain that he had not recognized yet. The birdshot from the shotgun had not stopped at skin and muscle depth. Several of the tiny pellets had penetrated through to his sigmoid colon and punched through it. As he slumped down in a chair in the comms room, chin on his chest and eyelids drooping, they were leaking intestinal fluid into his abdominal cavity.

Pain caused by punctures in the colon starts low and slow, then builds. As bacteria flood the abdominal cavity, sepsis or blood poisoning sets in. Then abdominal cramps, hyperventilation, fever and confusion.

Takuya Kato didn't need a nap. He needed a hospital.

Michael Chase needed a nap. He had slept little the past few days and in fact had set up a cot in his office so that he didn't waste time commuting to his apartment. His family didn't live in Washington; they were in Indiana—he didn't want to upset his teens' schooling—so sleeping and showering where he worked was the most practical thing right now.

347

With the world going crazy.

China had just accused the US in the UN Security Council of positioning nuclear weapons on Taiwan. They had shown the evidence General Huang had shared with him, plus a very nice illustration of a HACM missile with the word "NUCLEAR" stenciled beside its warhead. The only additional evidence they showed that Huang had not shared was a grainy photograph of HACM missiles being loaded into the belly of an airplane, which could have been any airplane, anywhere in the world, but which China was insisting was the same aircraft that had penetrated Taiwanese airspace. The most worrying thing about that photo, if you asked him, was that it wasn't shot from low-earth orbit by a satellite. It was taken at ground level. Probably by a human or a small drone, operated by a human. Which meant China had to have had a human agent in a position to do so.

The US had denied it all, from the existence of its stealth aircraft to transferring the HACMs, which was par for the course. But the stock markets had not reacted well, and Chase's stocks-heavy 401(k) had taken a hit, no doubt. Chase didn't know whether the missiles transferred to Taiwan were nuclear-armed or not—that was beyond his pay grade—but the way things were going, if the world survived long enough for him to worry about his retirement, that would be a fine thing.

The screen on his desk had been showing a logo. Now it showed the face of a Pentagon intern. "General Huang for you, Mr. Chase."

"Put him through." The Chinese General also looked to Chase like he had not had a lot of sleep. Chase took small comfort from that. "General Huang."

"Mr. Chase, are you recording this call?"

The Chinese officer had never started the conversation that way before. He saw no reason to dissemble.

"I am, General. I record all our calls so that I can faithfully relay any communication from you."

"Good." The General looked down at a piece of paper and read from it. "By order of the State Central Military Commission, China's participation in the US-China Defense Link is hereby terminated. All direct connections between the governments of the USA and the government of the People's Republic of China will be managed through the Chinese Ministry of Foreign Affairs." He folded his hands on the page. "Do you have any questions, Mr. Chase?"

The way he said it was almost a plea. As in, *please ask me a question, Mr. Chase.*

"Uh, yes, of course. Am I right that what you are saying means an end to our conversations on this line?"

"Yes." Huang's eyes flicked to his left and back again. He was not alone in the room.

A one-word answer. OK, Chase would have to fish some more.

"General, our predecessors created this hotline so that we could always keep an open channel between our militaries. That has proven its worth through multiple political and military situations. It distresses me to think China is closing this communication channel at a moment of heightened tensions between our militaries."

"Was that a question, Mr. Chase?" the man asked. He sounded frustrated now.

Try harder, Chase. "I ... How should our military leaders contact yours if an emergency arises?"

Huang lifted the page in front of him and read from it again. "*All* direct communications between the governments of the USA and the government of the People's Republic of China will be managed through the Chinese Ministry of Foreign Affairs. Is that clear?" He put the page down again.

Something ... there was something ...

"Yes, General, very clear."

"Thank you and goodbye, Mr. Chase. This channel is officially closed."

The screen went dead.

Chase scrabbled with his keyboard, trying to replay the recording of the call. He had never mastered that particular skill and walked to the door of his office, calling to the intern. "Park, get in here!"

The young man came running down the corridor. Chase pointed at his laptop. "Find me the recording of that call. The last one."

Of course, Park found it immediately. "This one?"

"Yes." Chase sat down. "Stay here."

Chase rewound the vision to the point at the end of the conversation where Chase asked the General how Pentagon officials should get in touch in an emergency. The General had basically replied with, "Read my lips; you can't." But as he did so, he picked up the script he was reading from.

And on the back of the page, a series of letters and numbers were faintly written.

Chase paused the replay and pointed at the screen. "There, that! What is that? Is it a phone number?"

The intern leaned forward, then tapped a couple of keys to take a screenshot, which he zoomed so that the text was clearer.

"Wow. Not a phone number. It's a Telegram ID."

"A what? An address to send a telegram?" Chase balked. Did the technology to send telegrams even exist anymore?

The intern smiled patiently. "No. *Telegram.* It's an encrypted messaging app. Its number one selling point is that no law enforcement or cyber intelligence agency has yet cracked it open."

Chase scoffed. "As far as they know. Like we'd tell them if we did."

Park crossed his arms. "I got a buddy who works for FBI Cyber Crime. He says it's not a boast; the app has on-device end-to-end encryption backed by cloud-based quantum keys …"

"Speak English."

"You write a message, the device scrambles it, then fetches a quantum-computer-generated code key from a Telegram server, attaches it, then sends it. Only the person it was addressed to can open it, and when they do, the Telegram app downloads the quantum key and decrypts the message. Then it tags the device it was opened on. Close the message, it can only be opened again by the user *and* the device it was sent to."

"So it can't be intercepted, it can't be cracked, and even if you get access to the person's device, unless they open it up for you while you are in the room, it can't be read."

"Correct. You can also set the message to autodelete itself when you close the app. Poof, gone forever."

"How is that even *legal?*"

"It's not, in the US and about 20 other countries. So you'll need a cyber agency to help you with this, I'm afraid."

"Alright, thank you."

When Park was gone, Chase slumped down heavily in his chair and spun around, thinking. China was officially closing down the deconfliction line, but Huang had probably just risked imprisonment, or worse, to keep a channel open to Chase.

Something very, very bad was about to go down.

Bunny O'Hare was back in the cockpit of her Black Widow. There had been a distinct lack of chocolate in the commissary at Taichung, but hey, the island was under a blockade, so she had filled her flight suit pockets with what the guy in the commissary had assured her were soft fruit jellies, at about 20 dollars a bag. "Siege prices," he said with a shrug. Then, probably feeling guilty at having ripped her off, he handed her a vacuum-packed bag of what looked like large black beetles. "On the house. Grandma's Iron Eggs," he winked. "Good for the eyesight."

She wasn't going near *them*.

After a rapid climb, she had just reached the waypoint at the start of her patrol, 65,000 feet over Taiwan's eastern Shuangxi district, about 10 miles from Taiwan's most easterly point. From this altitude, the extreme limit of the Black Widow's ceiling, the island looked tiny. Which it was—not much bigger than Florida's panhandle. But there were only

1.5 million living on the panhandle while 24 million were crammed onto Taiwan.

She was having one of those "calm before the storm" moments, the kind that made you think you had the best damn job in the world even though yeah, there were lethal downsides. From this altitude, right on the edge of the flyable atmosphere, she could see the curvature of the earth. To the south and east, sea fading into a hazy blue-white line and the blackness of space; to the north, the coast of China and the Chinese mainland at Wenzhou, rolling off into the distance as far as she could see. To the west, China's Fujian and Guangdong provinces, again rolling away into the distance until they merged seamlessly into the blackness of space.

When she looked at the impossibly small speck of land that was Taiwan, compared to the apparently infinite mass that was China, it struck her that geographic inevitability was not in favor of the tiny Republic. But then, if geography was all that mattered, Canada would be American and all of Eastern Europe would still be Russian, right?

She breathed deeply, enjoying the view, stretching the moment out. Reality intruded though. Unbidden thoughts. Like the conversation she'd had with Meany before she did her walkaround for this mission.

"Good luck up there," he told her. "By the way, we're getting additional support soon."

"Here?" she asked. "Someone else is going to try to run the blockade?"

"No, we only have one pilot crazy enough to do that," he said. "Salt, Flowmax and Flatline are bringing the rest of our Black Widows to the Philippines. They're going to be based at Clark Air Base."

"Attached to the 68th AGRS?" she asked.

"Yes, so they can be armed if need be. But they'll base out of the Philippines while things are hot. The owner apparently wants extra assets in the theatre in case the situation goes south and we need to get ourselves and our machines out under fire, as it were."

Bunny frowned. "This wasn't Salt's idea?"

"Don't think so. He likes his home comforts, right? An unlimited deployment eating adobo on Luzon would not be his idea of a good time."

Meany was right. She didn't take it as a good sign though. Aggressor Inc. was not one to waste money without reason and staging three fighters out of a foreign base "just in case" was not cheap. It wasn't just the aircraft, pilots and fuel; they would need to reimburse either the US or Philippine Air Force for staging and maintenance costs too.

"Wait, *three* Widows?" Bunny asked. "I thought we only had two mission capable ..."

"After you bent yours? Yeah, I heard about that." He grinned. "Salt is in your old machine. Apparently it was an easy fix, you put it down so gently."

"It didn't *feel* gentle," she said. "But, hey, the more the merrier."

"He said they're also trying to get Air Force to lease us a couple Valkyries, but they aren't so keen on account of how you wasted the last three they gave us, saving your own skin."

"Salt said that."

"He did. He's not a big fan, Bunny," Meany said. "You should work on that. It's not a good career move getting on your CO's bad side so often."

"You're my CO," she pointed out.

"Yes, but he's *my* CO, so therefore he is *your* CO. You remember how that works, right, Lieutenant?"

Yes, she did. But she was glad Salt would still be a few hundred miles away across the Philippine Sea.

It was time to go to work. She scratched her head, popped a mango fruit jelly (for the glucose, of course, but they were *damn* good) and, with one last look out the cockpit at the view, clocked on. She was already patched into the battlenet that comprised her Widow and the Arleigh Burke destroyer *Sam Nunn* as the primary nodes and linked her to three surveillance satellites, a Taiwanese Air Force Hawkeye airborne early warning and control system (AWACS) aircraft circling over central Taiwan and three Patriot Missile Batteries on the east and northeast coast.

Everything they could see, she could see, and in return, she was feeding *them* with the data flowing from the eight Aggressor F-22s now spread across the east island, their powerful radars reaching out into the seas between Okinawa and beyond, waiting to pick up the incoming British supply flight.

The picture on her tactical screen was a mess of icons, and though she had filtered as best she could, it still showed *dozens* of contacts. Over Taiwan, friendly ROC Taiwan Air Force standing patrols. To the west, a lot of US and Japanese aircraft but only one group she was interested in: the British C-17 Globemaster and, in front of it, its escort of six Tempest fighters. The flight had the unimaginative call sign of Skytrain 2.

Circling the island like buzzards around a dying corpse, there were so many Chinese aircraft that Bunny had her AI group them into flights or squadrons for simplicity. A counter in the lower left of her screen kept a tally of the total number of hostile contacts though, and currently it read … 76. She shook her head at the sort of burn rate China was throwing into its air blockade in terms of fuel, personnel and airframe hours. Keeping that many aircraft in the air around the island 24/7 was something few nations in the world could do. Sure, a lot of them were older aircraft, Cold War-era J-10s and J-11s with inferior radars and huge radar cross sections. But they fielded the latest Chinese missiles and would be backed by China's very capable J-20 "Mighty Dragon" stealth fighters if the missiles started flying.

Bunny knew the number on her screen was probably an underestimate too. It was very possible some of those J-20s were already prowling around the island, as invisible to normal radar as Bunny hoped she was at that moment. Only if they got very close, or Taiwan and its allies got very lucky, would the Mighty Dragon show itself. She pulled up the comms protocols to remind herself and configured her digital comms panel to allow her to quickly switch between speaking with one Aggressor flight, the other, or all, and to the other units in the battlenet. At that moment, she was patched into a common channel that all the unit mission commanders used to share intel.

It was the USS Sam Nunn who first spotted the coming attack. "Skytrain Commanders from Sam Nunn, we have new contacts. Multiple fast movers, estimate 50, bearing 170 from our position. Altitudes 5 to 30,000, range 32, heading north and northwest. Pushing to your screens … now."

Bunny put her aircraft into position-holding mode and focused on the new data pouring onto her screen. She saw three groups of aircraft moving in from the southeast.

Carrier launched, she decided, based on their direction of travel. Probably the *Fujian*. That made them uncrewed

Chongming fighters, which was how *Sam Nunn* was able to pick them up early. That, and the fact there were so damn many! She quickly pushed the data through to all Aggressor aircraft, but particularly to Touchdown, the leader of Aggressor's 'A' flight, and Meany, leading their 'B' flight on overwatch. An upgrade to the F-22's data distribution software meant they could individually send and receive data to each other and with Bunny but couldn't serve as data hubs themselves. She might not be the tip of the spear for this mission, but only Bunny's Next Generation Air Dominance Widow could do that.

"Widow for Meany and Touchdown," Bunny said. "New contacts. Fast movers, estimate 50, bearing one one zero from my position. Altitudes 5 to 30,000, range 49, heading north and northwest ..."

"Good copy your data, Widow," Meany replied.

"Touchdown copies."

"What are the Chinese blockade patrols doing?" Meany asked.

Bunny checked. "No reaction yet. Trying to act normal is my guess. Hoping we don't see their force in the south."

A laconic British voice came over the mission-commander net. "Skytrain Commanders, Skytrain 2. We are moving to intercept."

Bunny saw two of the Tempest fighters peel away from the British group and start south. The Tempest was a sixth-generation European-built stealth fighter very similar to the US F-35 but with one weapons system setting it apart. Instead of a cannon, it had a short-range directed energy weapon for use against enemy aircraft or missiles anywhere out to two miles in a 360-degree bubble around the aircraft.

357

Bunny had seen it in action over Syria, and she'd take it over her Air Trophy system any day because of its additional defensive range.

Bunny relayed what she was seeing to Meany and Touchdown. What they did with her information was up to them as tactical commanders, though it was her job to "call the plays." The Chinese aircraft were shaping to intercept the British flight while it was still technically inside *Japanese* airspace over Tarama Island, east of Taiwan.

Who was it who said you should never assume your enemy wouldn't do what you wouldn't do? she thought. *Because China is doing it.*

"Meany and Touchdown from Widow. RAF is moving to intercept. They will warn the Chinese off and, if necessary, defend. Recommend 'A' flight move east to the limits of Taiwanese airspace."

"'A' flight repositioning to Sector B32."

"'B' flight repositioning to Sector B33 as cover."

Bunny did the math. Four Tempests and eight F-22s with six medium-range missiles apiece, one Widow with 12 missiles. Fewer than two missiles for every Chinese fighter approaching them.

If the engagement got kinetic, and the Chinese patrols east of Taiwan joined in, it would not be enough.

She opened a channel to the Taiwanese AWACS coordinating Taiwan Air Force assets. "Hawkeye, Widow. Requesting you vector support to Sector … B34 … to cover B33 in case we need to engage."

"Acknowledge your request, Widow. Hawkeye will relay and revert." She didn't get support just because she asked for it, but she couldn't see any competing actions on her screen, so approval should just be a formality.

She checked the surrounding sky, ran her eye over her instruments to reassure herself all systems were nominal and returned her attention to the developing situation.

And said a quiet, nondenominational prayer to the gods of aviators. Things were about to get very, very hairy for their pilots to the east.

19. 'Invisible adversaries'

'Shredder' Chen could not believe their luck so far. There was no enemy radar on his Radar Warning Receiver, or at least none strong enough to light it up, which told him the enemy was still blind to the Ao Yin aircraft that were leading the Chinese attack.

Their adversaries had announced the next supply flight to Taiwan would be British. Shredder had been glad to see the news had not changed their orders. It was to be destroyed.

They were spread across a five-mile area in a staggered wedge formation, with Wang's aircraft out front and the rest of the squadron in three four-plane elements. Mushroom and Shredder were in 'Casino' Bo's four-plane with a fourth pilot with the call sign 'Iron Maiden.' Ao Yin Squadron was at high altitude, 35,000 feet. Fei Yi was at medium altitude, and Xiu Snake was down low, under 10,000.

There was no magical PLA Navy radar in position to find their target for them. They were going to have to use good old-fashioned airborne radar, but they were under orders not to reveal themselves by using their radars until they were hailed by the adversary and asked to identify themselves.

By then, the enemy would be in missile range, their attacking force would fill the sky with illuminating energies, and their target would be the one that was revealed.

Shredder's unshakeable faith in their mission plan lasted all the way from *Fujian* to the Japanese Tarama Islands, where a

British voice came in over the international guard emergency communication channel.

"Chinese aircraft over Tarama Islands, you are in Japanese airspace and are affecting aviation safety. Depart immediately or you risk provoking an armed response."

There were no adversary aircraft showing on their radar warning receivers or other passive sensors. But the radio call showed they were there, and they could see the Chinese flight. It was time to drop their cloak of caution.

Wang did not hesitate, coming onto the air wing interplane frequency immediately. "All *Fujian* aircraft, prepare to radiate on my order. Squadron leaders, I will call your targets." He gave his pilots a moment to set up. Shredder set his radar to scan a cone-shaped area in front of him and 20 degrees wide on every plane. His fellow pilots were doing the same. Together, *Fujian*'s aircraft would bathe the sky in front of them in radar waves and instantly share any returns. "Radiate," Wang called.

Bunny and the Aggressor fighters were not in the Chinese radar line of sight, but several of the units Bunny was pulling data from were. The massive wave of radar energy suddenly reaching out from the Chinese fighters lit them up, and the Skytrain mission command channel became a babble of coordinating voices, which Bunny listened to with her left brain while her right brain processed the images flooding onto her tactical screen.

The British Tempest flight commander remained impressively cool, even though his RWR must have been strobing insistently and warnings warbling in his ears.

"Chinese aircraft over Tarama Islands, you are in Japanese airspace. Depart immediately or we *will* fire on you."

Ao Yin Squadron included one Chongming drone that was configured for signals intelligence, or SIGINT. It had one job and one job only: to sort radio signals from background noise and triangulate the sender. The Chinese radar could not locate the British stealth fighters, which were still about 40 miles away, but it locked onto their first broadcast, and then its pilot turned his aircraft 90 degrees, to put as much separation as he could between his first contact and the next, if there was one.

He waited an anxious few minutes as Wang gave the order for his pilots to light their radars and the adversary stayed silent. Then the British broadcast again and he had a fix.

"Contact, bearing two eight four, signal strength indicates 30 to 50 miles," he said. He couldn't be more precise, but it was enough.

"Ao Yin pilots, arm missiles, autonomous seeker mode, aim 294 degrees …" Wang gave them a moment to set up the attack, counting backward from five in his head. *Three … Two … One.* "Launch."

Twelve missiles streaked out ahead of the Chinese drones across a five-mile front, all converging on the Tempest fighters that had just given away their location.

Bunny saw the wave of missiles lance out from the Chinese fighters and hit the Aggressor channel immediately.

"Touchdown, Widow, Chinese fighters engaging RAF Tempests your five o'clock. RAF escort moving to fully engage. Recommend you move to protective cover for incoming Globemaster."

The British cargo plane was 30 miles out, 10 miles from the coverage gap, but its escort of Tempest fighters was peeling away to assist its comrades and had called 68th Aggressor to take up the escort role. As Bunny watched the developing situation, the *Sam Nunn* launched a furious volley of 24 ground-to-air SM-6 missiles at the Chinese fighters.

Touchdown responded immediately. "Aggressor 'A' moving to join with Skytrain 2," she said.

"'B' flight moving to Sector B32," Meany announced, leading his flight into the gap on the coast Touchdown was leaving. "Touchdown, China will go for Skytrain 2. Prepare for anti-missile defense."

"Good copy, Meany. 'A' flight, bring your Sidewinders online."

Each F-22 carried four of the short-range infrared AIM-9X Sidewinders, which could lock onto the heat of incoming Chinese missiles. But with the missiles and their targets traveling at a combined closing speed upward of *five times the speed of sound*, the percentage probability of a kill was in the low 30s.

Touchdown's job now wasn't to kill Chinese fighters … the British Tempests were going about that job. Her pilots' role was to protect their Queen Bee, the lumbering Globemaster, and its volunteer crew.

With all respect for the Aggressor pilots moving to its defense, Bunny did not give the Globemaster a chance.

"Ao Yin Three is out."

"Ao Yin Eleven is out."

"Ao Yin Six is out."

Mushroom heard the despairing reports of her fellow pilots as they fell to the ground-to-air missiles from what had to be an American missile cruiser *they couldn't even see.*

"Continue your push, Ao Yin," Wang commanded. "Xiu Snake, cover the southeastern flank. Fei Yi, cover the southwest."

Mushroom's eyes dipped to her map screen. Wang was sending the other two squadrons toward the Taiwanese coast to support patrols already there and block any Taiwan Air Force fighters from interfering.

But Ao Yin had already lost six of its 18 aircraft and had no idea if its initial attack had destroyed the aircraft that had hailed them, because they had never gotten a radar lock on them.

The answer came a moment later as their optical-infrared sensors picked up incoming missile blooms. "Missiles. I count … eight …" Wang announced. "You will deploy decoys but continue your push."

He was sentencing several of the remaining Ao Yin pilots to a virtual death. Mushroom winced. She knew what that felt like. In a near panic, she watched the missiles track in her helmet visor, looking for the warning that one had locked onto her. She heard fellow pilots call out as they deployed chaff and flares to decoy missiles that had locked onto them.

Still, the adversaries firing them were invisible!

"Ao Yin Two, out."

364

"Ao Yin Nine, out."

"Ao Yin Four, out."

Bunny cheered and punched the Perspex above her head as first the *Sam Nunn*'s missiles and then the return salvo from the RAF Tempests hit home and Chinese icons began winking out.

But the joy was short-lived. A Tempest icon disappeared, to be replaced by the icon for an emergency locator beacon. One of the four Brits was down. The remaining three were flanking the Chinese fighters to their east, staying out of their radar detection zone as they fired another volley of missiles at them from a range of 20 miles.

The Chinese poured forward. Two swarms were breaking west to provide a blocking force, but the unit out front had pushed through, oblivious to the losses it was sustaining, heading straight for the Okinawa-Taipei air corridor. And why not? China was losing no pilots, only robots. Bunny did a quick eyeball calculation. If they continued on their current track, the Chinese spearhead could pick up the Globemaster at any second.

More missiles curved up from the *Sam Nunn* at sea, toward the cloud of Chinese fighters in the west this time.

Meany's voice broke into her cockpit. "'B' flight, target the Chinese force at zero eight zero. Widow, full salvo, same target. 'A' flight, wait for their attack; mop up any incoming."

Bunny's fingers tapped and dragged across her targeting screen, drawing a box around the Chinese spearhead. *Full volley?* She slid a finger down the screen, allocating all 22 of her missiles to the Chinese fighters pushing on the Globemaster.

She was circling over eastern Taiwan, at maximum range for her Peregrine missiles, 120 miles. It would take her missiles two and a half minutes to reach their targets. She wasted no time. As soon as the Widow told her it had assigned missiles to targets, she thumbed her firing button and, one by one, the missiles dropped from her payload bay, lit their tails and streaked away toward the horizon, at targets even they couldn't see.

"Ao Yin Five is out."

There were only eight Ao Yin fighters remaining. Xiu Snake had taken a broadside of sea-to-air missiles too, and only 12 of its 18 aircraft remained. None of the blizzard of missiles Ao Yin had flown through had come for Shredder's machine yet. Or Mushroom's, he noted.

Of course, the moment he had the thought, the situation changed. His missile radar warning started flashing and an audible warble in his ears grew more and more strident as it closed. Another wave of ground-to-air missiles out of the west!

"Ao Yin Seven, out."

"Twelve, out."

"Sixteen, out."

"Eighteen, out."

Now, they were only four.

"Ao Yin One has a contact, probable heavy, zero zero three degrees," Wang announced. "Altitude 20, range 15. All Ao Yin pilots, target and launch all missiles."

The cargo plane!

Fox three, Shredder thought, watching his missiles drop in pairs from his weapons bay and stream ahead of him. At the same time, he saw an enemy missile change course directly toward him.

With a sick feeling in his stomach, he realized he would not have time to evade the incoming missile and complete the launch of his missiles at the target. He was not going to get all his missiles away. He girded himself for the disorienting blackness that was about to fill his vision.

"Missiles inbound, Globemaster," Touchdown announced. "Positioning to intercept."

Bunny saw the Chinese missiles reaching out toward the RAF Globemaster and imagined the terror in the minds of the cargo plane's crew members as they heard the warning from Touchdown.

She barely registered as her own missiles and those fired by Meany's flight reached the Chinese formation and started batting Chinese fighters from the sky. Her eyes were on the hair-thin red lines trailing small glowing dots that were the Chinese missiles aimed at the Globemaster.

Between them, and the RAF cargo plane, were the four fighters of 68th AGRS.

Bunny quickly boxed the Chinese missiles and had her system do a count. *Twenty-two.* Touchdown's F-22s carried only 16 Sidewinders, and one out of three were likely to miss.

Bunny saw the Globemaster was diving now, nose down, heading for the sea, no doubt streaming decoys into its wake. She closed her eyes and began praying for the souls of its crew.

US President Carmen Carliotti was leaving the White House to board the Marine One helicopter, waiting on the White House lawn. She was being ushered along by her Chief of Staff and aides but paused and then walked between heavily armed Secret Service agents to the gathered press.

She had to yell to be heard over the shouted questions from the press corps.

"Ladies and gentlemen! I'd like to get a message to the American people," she said. "Following the incident over the Philippine Sea in which Chinese fighters shot down an unarmed British humanitarian flight, I have convened a meeting of our National Security Council to determine how we will respond. But I want to say this. Acts of naked aggression against defenseless aircraft show our adversaries for what they are, but they cannot dent the steel of American resolve, or that of our allies. I have spoken with the British Prime Minister to express our shock and dismay, and he has pledged that despite this criminal act, his nation will not give up its support for the operation to supply vital food and medicines to Taiwan. A new flight is being readied as we speak and we ... this time, we will provide it with every protection the Western alliance can muster. Thank you ..."

She turned to go, but the cacophony of shouted questions from the media stopped her.

"Madam President, do we know if any of the British aircrew survived?" A British-accented voice asked.

Her Chief of Staff leaned toward her to give her the answer, then she replied. "The rescue operation is still underway. We are hopeful some of the crew may have survived."

"Madam President, Madam President, China is saying missiles were fired by a US warship at its aircraft and may have struck the British plane. It claims several of its own aircraft were destroyed without provocation. What do you say to that?"

"I say that it may be the case China lost aircraft in this incident, but the accusation that the US fired first is a lie," Carliotti said, in typically undiplomatic fashion. "Allied units involved in this incident were only reacting in self-defense."

"How many Taiwanese or British aircraft were lost? Were any US or Japanese aircraft involved?"

She leaned in toward her Chief of Staff again. "Those details are still unclear. I'm sorry, we need to go. The National Security Council is waiting."

Shredder waited by Mushroom's pod until she got her Chongming into the landing pattern over *Fujian* and handed it over. As she cracked the pod hatch, he lifted it up for her and pulled her chair closer so it was easier for her to swing her legs into. He didn't offer to help her any more than that; he knew that would just earn him a scornful glance.

Both of them tried to keep deadpan faces, but Mushroom broke into a wide smile, causing Shredder to do the same.

He reached out a hand to give her a fist bump, but she batted it away, swinging her legs into her chair and levering her ass out of the pod, trying to wipe the smile from her face. "Stop grinning," she told him. "You're *dead*, remember?"

"No court martial this time," he told her, gesturing around him to where the other Ao Yin pilots were climbing out of their pods and high-fiving each other like teens after a football victory.

"Where is Wang?" she asked.

"First down, first out of his pod," Shredder said. "Probably up with the Vice Admiral already, drinking whisky."

"It's confirmed then?" she asked. "We knocked down the cargo plane?"

"And one British stealth fighter," he told her.

Two other pilots approached, bumping fists with Shredder and giving Mushroom crushing hugs that left her red-faced.

"You get a quarter of two kills," he told her. "Two *meat* kills."

"Not a quarter," she corrected him. "A lot more will share the first kill, and you should also get a piece of the second if you got your missiles away."

"New directive after our engagement over Okinotori. Didn't you read it?" She shook her head. "Only pilots who 'survive' an action will be credited with the victories." People were moving toward the debrief, and he gestured to the pod bay exit. "Come on."

She trundled alongside him. "How many losses?"

370

"The entire wing? I don't know, maybe 20."

"Twenty?"

"Xiu Snake and Ao Yin took the brunt," he said. "Fei Yi got challenged by a rebel patrol but Wang called them back before anything developed."

Mushroom shook her head. "But 20 machines? We can't sustain these losses."

She would be right of course, if *Fujian* had been all alone somewhere in the Eastern Pacific. But it wasn't. "What are you worried about?" he asked. "Replacement machines are probably already on their way from Ningbo. The adversary is going to be licking its wounds now, bleating at the United Nations, thumping tables in its Congresses and Parliaments. By the time it resolves to do anything, we will have a full complement of machines again."

The mood in the ready room of the 68th Aggressor Squadron was not the same. Not even close.

It mattered to no one that the squadron could claim at least a dozen uncrewed aircraft kills. The US Navy, probably the same number for *USS Sam Nunn*. The RAF pilots were also claiming six kills, but the reality was so many missiles were flying, it would prove almost impossible to tally all the calls, let alone correctly attribute them. Estimates of Chinese losses in the incident ranged from 20 to 35.

On the other side of the ledger, the British had lost just two aircraft. But both were crewed. The pilot of the Tempest destroyed in the first minute of combat had been pulled alive and largely uninjured from the sea after baling out. But all

371

three members of the C-17 Globemaster crew were still missing, presumed dead.

Touchdown's last-ditch defense had beaten the odds, her pilots' Sidewinder missiles destroying 12 of 22 Chinese missiles. But at least 10 had struck the Globemaster, the first hits shearing off a wing, sending it spinning violently toward the earth before the remaining explosions turned it into a fireball of metal and flesh that struck the sea at near the speed of sound and spread quickly into a flaming debris field nearly a square mile across.

As soon as its missiles hit home, every Chinese drone turned and fled southeast for its carrier again. Taiwanese and Chinese patrols on either side of Taiwan's air border eyed each other warily, but none were interested in taking the fight further, and they quickly settled back into the routine blockade positions.

Bunny found what was becoming her usual seat, at the back, beside 'Magellan' Chang. He looked at her with a strained expression as she sat. Bunny felt his pain personally. "Hey, the next flight will get through," she said. "The odds won't always be against us. Brits are moving the *HMS Queen Elizabeth* back into the theatre."

Charlene 'Touchdown' Dubois was in the seat in front of her and turned around, putting her arm over her chair. "For whatever good that does," she said. "Until we start moving *serious* assets into this theatre, we're always going to be going up there outnumbered and outgunned."

"Way to boost morale, Touchdown." Bunny shot a look at Chang, who was pulling on his lip thoughtfully.

"You were part of the US force involved in the Pagasa Incident, right?" he asked, referring to the short sharp air conflict between the US and China over a Philippine island that had left both air forces with heavy losses.

"Why?"

"What happens now?" he asked. "The US didn't go to war then. Is it going to go to war with China now?"

Bunny was no politician. But neither was this her first rodeo. "Politicians don't seem too fussed if a few airplanes get knocked down, unless the other side starts parading wounded pilots in front of cameras ..." she said.

"But the Brits ..."

"Aren't going to declare war on China on their own. They'll be pissed, and they'll be thinking of a million different types of payback, from cyber to financial, but they aren't going to war over a cargo plane."

Chang nodded. His right knee was jerking up and down with a staccato rhythm, the adrenaline of the recent engagement still washing out of his system. He'd been in Touchdown's flight and had watched the Globemaster go down. "So, we're still on our own," he said. "We" being his ancestral island of Taiwan, Bunny guessed.

Bunny nodded at the other pilots in the room. "Does it *look* like you're on your own?"

He didn't look ungrateful, but he didn't look reassured either. "We don't need a handful of stealth fighters, we need *squadrons*. We need brigades of US Marines. We need hundreds of anti-ship and anti-air missile batteries. We need thousands of drones and artillery shells and barrels. We need submarines in the Straits between us and China ..."

"The West has been arming Taiwan for decades," Bunny pointed out. "Anything you need that you don't have already, I'm sorry ... but it's too late."

"I know," he said. "China is really coming this time, right?"

What should she say? Maybe not? Maybe all sides would suddenly see sense now and pull back and start real negotiations? It had happened before, right? The Cuban Missile Crisis came to mind. But the world was different then, and so were world leaders. World War II was still fresh in their minds, the fear of global nuclear Armageddon at its peak. Leaders had been desensitized to extremes since then, each global outrage outdoing the next until it seemed like nothing short of total war was regarded as unacceptable.

And now, even that seemed like a line the superpowers were willing to cross.

"Look," Bunny said. "It all depends on what happens next. Does the US coalition escalate, or does it pull back?"

20. 'Did China just declare war?'

A bunker in the Offutt Air Force Base in Nebraska—the US strategic air command center—was not where Michael Chase expected, or wanted, to be when he got up that morning. He'd assumed that with China pulling the plug on the deconfliction line, he'd be temporarily a deputy assistant secretary of defense for China "without portfolio." But looking at the people in the chairs lined up behind the Cabinet secretaries and advisors ranked around the table in the ad hoc situation room, he realized President Carliotti had ordered her staff to assemble just about everyone in Washington who had any kind of take on what China's leadership was thinking. He saw the US Ambassador to China on a wall screen, and beside him the CIA head of station, Taipei. On chairs opposite he saw academics from a range of think tanks and universities, and beside him sat the Defense Intelligence Agency's, or DIA's, Senior China Analyst.

The rules had been explained as the President entered and the meeting of the National Security Council began. Speak only if you are asked a question by name. If you interrupt, even if you disagree with what is being said, you will be asked to leave the meeting. They were rules Chase could live with. He couldn't sit quietly if someone in the room was saying something dangerous or stupid, and he didn't want to be there anyway.

The topic of the moment was a question from Vice President Bendheim: Was the attack on the British aircraft a de facto declaration of war, or something less? The room seemed equally divided on that. Defense and the various security and intelligence agencies were convinced it was. State and several China analysts did not believe so and were arguing for back-channel diplomacy.

"Goddamn it, how many red lines does China need to cross? We have a *duty* to act," the Secretary of Defense was complaining. He held a piece of paper in front of him and read from it. "Any effort to determine the future of Taiwan by other-than-peaceful means, including by boycotts or embargoes, is considered a threat to the peace and security of the Western Pacific area and of grave concern to the United States. The United States shall provide Taiwan with arms of a defensive character and shall maintain the capacity of the United States to ..." —he thumped the table to emphasize his words— "... to *resist* any resort to force or other forms of coercion." He glared around the room. "Taiwan Relations Act, 1979, ratified 2022. China has fulfilled every criterion for a military response, from boycotts to embargoes and now to military action against a humanitarian air bridge. What more do we need?!"

"I need to believe, Ervan," Bendheim said firmly, "one thing. That today's events really were the opening shots in an invasion of Taiwan, and not just what China is saying: an isolated response to what it saw as an effort to challenge its illegal air defense zone."

"Our RIMPAC allies still have their assets in theatre," Holoman pointed out to him. "We need to move to DEFCON 2 in the Indo-Pacific and request the Brits, the Australians and the Japanese to move their carrier strike groups into position to support Taiwan. We have just spent a month rehearsing with them for this day even though *no one* in this room wanted it to arrive. But arrive it has, and now we must act!"

President Carliotti coughed, loudly enough that everyone stopped talking. "Thank you, Ervan. I hear you." She looked at her intelligence heads. "Let me summarize. You are all telling me China has the capacity and intention to launch an invasion, and that we have evidence of the active preparation needed for moving troops across the Strait." Now she turned to the Defense Secretary. "You are asking me to move our forces in the Indo-Pacific to DEFCON 2 and announce with our coalition partners that we are ready to provide immediate military support to Taiwan, which by the way, Treasury says would cause a global run on stock markets and banks. And finally, I have State and several of the learned colleagues in the bleachers saying China's regime appears very much to want to keep political channels open and has just proposed some kind of off-ramp, even if it is closing down military channels like our deconfliction hotline. Which leads us to you, Mr. Chase."

Chase had been happy to be behind the President and out of her line of sight, but his ears pricked up when he heard the President's last words. So far, he had not been called on to speak. To his dismay, she turned her head, looking over her shoulder, straight at him. "Mr. Chase, I have been briefed on your nearly daily conversations with General Huang. You seem to be the best placed to have an informed and up-to-date understanding of China's military mindset at this very moment. I want your opinion."

Chase swallowed. "On what, specifically, Madam President?"

"Did China just effectively declare war shooting down that airplane?"

377

"Yes, Madam President," he said, without hesitating. There was a murmur around the room and a lot of glowering. "I ... the Chinese military doesn't make a move without political direction. This was not some small-scale accidental misunderstanding. It was an unambiguous head-to-head confrontation between Chinese and Western forces, in which our own Aggressor unit on Taiwan was knowingly engaged. The order for that shootdown had to have come from the highest levels and is a clear sign China has decided to go to war over Taiwan."

"Or as *they* say, simply that they intend to enforce their blockade," Bendheim insisted. "While they seek a peaceful resolution."

Chase thought again of the look in Huang's face as he held up the paper and covertly flashed his contact details to Chase. His words were angry, but his face said something else. It was a desperate attempt to keep a line of communication open, knowing what was about to happen. "My interactions with my counterparts in the People's Liberation Army have taught me that the Chinese military knows two things. It knows that any war over Taiwan will be long and bloody and even 'victory' on Taiwan would leave China's military and economy crippled. Its air and missile forces would be gutted, the core of its navy lying at the bottom of the South China Sea. Partisan rebels on Taiwan would continue an armed insurgency and China's other regional competitors, like India, Russia, Korea and Japan, would start picking away at the rotting edges of its corpse, with China's military too weak to respond."

"Then why in God's name would they *want* war?!" Bendheim exclaimed. "If it will lead to their ruin?"

"I said the Chinese military knows two things, Mr. Vice President. The second is that, like Japan in 1940, their politicians have walked them to the edge of a cliff over the Taiwan issue and we, in the West, have left them with no option but to jump."

The Defense Secretary glared at him. "Your 1940 analogy is out of place here, sir. But since you raise it, let me remind you of what the Japanese Vice Admiral Yamamoto said after the attack on Pearl Harbor. *I fear all we have done is to awaken a sleeping giant and fill him with a terrible resolve.* China would do well to heed his words."

Chase could not let that one pass. "Actually, that is a Hollywood-inspired myth, Mr. Secretary. Yamamoto never said those words. The screenwriters of that Pearl Harbor film stole a line from Napoleon Bonaparte. The actual quote from Napoleon was, 'China is a sickly, sleeping giant. But when she awakes, the world will tremble.' Perhaps we should heed Napoleon's words?"

The President smiled patiently. "Assume the sleeping giant has woken then. What would your advice be, Mr. Chase?"

Did she really want it? He felt that after the Vice President's intervention, the room had been leaning toward appeasement and de-escalation. But he took a chance. After all, he would only be telling them what they already knew, right? "Madam President, China's invasion force across the Strait is in place. It is evacuating civilians from its coastal cities. It has expelled foreign tourists and businesspeople from its Eastern provinces. It has militarized ship-building facilities and ports up and down the coast. It has commandeered civilian housing to garrison nearly 300,000 troops, mobilized a 100,000-strong militia to direct traffic and control internal dissent in its megacities. Under the cover of this 'blockade,' it has assembled 300 landing ships, 2,500 air and seaborne drones, 500 mobile missile launchers and moved enough satellites into orbit to give it 24/7 coverage of the operations area. It has put 75 missile destroyers, submarines and cruisers into the Taiwan Strait and Philippine Sea, placed its three carrier strike groups in a ring around the island and placed its entire Eastern Command Air Force on alert. The Chinese military has clearly been ordered to use force to achieve China's political objectives, and we just saw it fire the first shot. We need to act accordingly." He took a deep breath. "If we really are committed to defending the democracy of Taiwan, we need to stop looking for 'off-ramps' that do not exist, because *we are now at war.*"

He sat back, shocked at himself. Was he really this much of a hawk? No, he was not. He was a realist, and yes, the last couple years of dealing directly with the Chinese military had convinced him of what he had just said.

The President was silent, lips pursed. He had no idea if it was the answer she had hoped for. In any case, she turned back to the table without further comment. As she did so, an aide entered the room and, spotting the Secretary of Defense, went quickly to his side and placed a message in front of him. With all eyes on him, he read it carefully, then looked up.

"Uh, Madam President, I recommend all non-core NSC members leave the room now but remain available ..."

Carliotti nodded. "Clear the room please, people. Only core NSC to remain."

Chase got a few dirty looks from the other assembled China "experts" as they all gathered up their things and filed out, as though the decision to kick them out was his fault. They repaired to a mess next door.

The DIA China analyst, an owl-eyed, portly academic called James Burroughs, brought him a cup of coffee and sat down opposite, looking at him with a smile. "It's refreshing to meet someone who doesn't care about their career," he said and toasted him with his paper cup. "The Vice President is a dove, as you might gather, and a powerful one—he wouldn't have appreciated your long-winded slap-down …"

Chase took the coffee. "I've got two children growing up with their mother in a different city," he said glumly. "The worst the Vice President can do is give me the opportunity to spend more time with them."

"That's the spirit," Burroughs said, clapping him on the shoulder. "For what it's worth, nothing you said was—factually—wrong."

Two hours later, when the NSC meeting disbanded and he was released, he packed his things and walked out of the mess, unclear about what, if anything, had been decided. Reflecting on his conversation with Burroughs, Chase had decided he'd call his kids. See if they'd like to come and visit soon. He had a feeling he was about to have some time on his hands. But as he left the room, he found the President's Chief of Staff waiting for him outside.

"Mr. Chase, a moment?" He motioned to Chase to return to the conference room.

HR Rosenstern was a pure political appointment, the former chairperson of the President's party caucus, a man whose chief talents were keeping the President's rambunctious party in line and raising inordinate amounts of money for her election campaigns. Chase had never had reason to speak with him alone before.

The room was empty now, except for Rosenstern and the Secretary of Defense, who waited for him to sit and then spoke. "With the military deconfliction hotline shut down, Chase, is there any way you can still get a message to your PLA contact?"

Chase thought of the Telegram ID. "There may be. What is the message?"

"That the USA is going to pause Operation Skytrain immediately and the President will tonight address the nation to reaffirm our commitment to a *peaceful* resolution of the One China question," the Secretary said.

Chase frowned. "We're reversing our position on Taiwanese independence?"

"Reversing, no," Rosenstern said. "Nuancing, yes."

So, the doves won the day, Chase thought. Peace talks? It might buy time, and it was probably good for Chase's 401(k), but he still felt it was just delaying the inevitable. "Alright, can I get the message in writing, please?" he asked. "Just, you know, so I get it right."

"Of course."

"When do you want it sent?"

The two men exchanged a quick glance. "Immediately, if possible," Rosenstern said. "We need to put a lid on this situation before it boils over. You can use the room next door. We'll send an Air Force comms specialist to get you whatever you need."

Chase had never used Telegram before, but he was given a clean smartphone with the app loaded onto it. The young specialist stood by in case he needed any help, but as far as he could see, all he needed to do was start a message thread and input the ID the Chinese General had shown him.

He had the phone in one hand and the message he was asked to pass on in the other. He had no idea how to begin.

He didn't know who, if anyone, would be at the other end of the link. Should he ask for some kind of identifying information? What would be the point of that? Since the idea was simply to get a message to the PLA hierarchy as quickly as possible, as long as the message was received by someone, his job was done. And if Huang's phone was now in the possession of Chinese intelligence, he was sure his wouldn't be the only channel being put into play that day.

He started the conversation naturally.

> *Hi. Just checking this ID is correct. MC.*

There was no reply immediately, so Chase got up, fetched himself and the specialist some coffee and then sat down again. Still nothing. Had he misread the …

>> *Yes you have the correct channel. I am relieved we still have the chance for dialogue. I am may not always reply quickly but I will check this channel as often as possible. Do you know how to automatically delete communications so they cannot be recovered from your device? H.*

No, he did not. He showed the question to the specialist. "You want to do that, sir?" the man asked. "I mean, we can, but since you aren't being clandestine, I'm like, why do it? You know?"

The young man was right, of course. It might be important for Huang, but it wasn't for Chase.

> *Yes. I have a message for you to pass on. You can attribute it however you like.*

>> *Go ahead.*

Chase picked up the page and thumbed the paragraph there into the app.

> *The US President will give an address to the nation tonight about events of today expressing regret at the loss of lives on both sides. She will*

announce Operation Skytrain is to be paused and reaffirm US government commitment to the PEACEFUL resolution of the One China question. She will invite Chairman Xi to a meeting at a neutral location to discuss. A visible gesture of de-escalation from China's side is requested. Message ends.

He hit "send" and waited, trying to guess the reaction at the other end. Relief, he expected. After all, China had gambled and won. The US and its allies, especially the UK, could just as easily have gone ballistic over the China attack. Chase was certain an angry British PM had demanded a more forthright response than the one Chase had just delivered.

>> *Message received. I will ensure it reaches Beijing promptly. Communication ends.*

Chase stared at the screen another couple minutes, but there was no more. That was it? He handed the cell phone to the specialist again. The arrangement was that it would be monitored around the clock from now on and any new messages flagged to Chase immediately for a response. It struck him that Huang, if it really was him at the other end of the link, was probably risking his life to keep the channel open, whereas Chase was doing so openly and with the full knowledge of his government.

Which kind of said it all, really, didn't it?

The message from Michael Chase did reach Beijing quickly. And like a rock thrown into a pond, it immediately created a series of ripples across the globe that magnified as other sources sent similar messages through other channels to other contacts within the Chinese State apparatus. All the messages confirmed that the US was walking back its commitment to Taiwan.

Within an hour, a filtered form of the message had reached *Fujian*'s flag officer, Vice Admiral Zhang Weili, along with new orders for the *Fujian* strike group and its air wing. Zhang had gathered the air wing's senior officers in his flag quarters. He had indicated to Wang that he should sit immediately to his left, which Wang took as a very good sign, since it was the place of honor.

A wardroom attendant went around pouring tea into small cups, and when all had been served, Zhang invited Wang to "taste the steep," or test that the tea had been brewed properly. He stood, took in the tea's aroma, and then sipped it. He nodded and sat, and the steward poured for the rest of the guests.

The fact they were served tea was the first sign to Wang's officers that the day's business was not yet done. After a successful mission, a Vice Admiral or other officer might show appreciation to his officers with a glass of whisky, but only if they were not required for further operations that day, since a glass could easily become several bottles. The serving of tea indicated the day was not over.

When all officers had sipped from their cups, Zhang stood. "I have received a message of commendation from Fleet Command Ningbo for the execution of the order to disrupt the adversary's attempt to provide material support to the rebels." He smiled beneficently. "They have received reports that because of our action today, the main enemy has canceled its plans for an air bridge to the rebels, and the American President will soon go on American television to recognize China's goal of unification with Taiwan." There was an enthusiastic round of applause around the table, and he held up his hands to quell it. "On the advice of Colonel

Wang, I have recommended to Fleet that Ao Yin Squadron be recognized with the *Sword of Deep Blue*."

Wang was pleased to see the pride on his officers' faces at news of the commendation, especially that of Casino, Ao Yin's squadron leader. They would need to bottle that feeling and draw on it in the days ahead.

The Vice Admiral sat and nodded to Wang. "Colonel, you may take over the briefing."

Wang stood, looking down on faces that had quickly changed from proud to alert. "Today's success is just the first. We must continue our stranglehold on the rebel island until it submits and exploit the timidness of our main enemy. *Fujian* will move west, behind the two US carriers which are currently skulking in the waters of Japan and the Philippines. When they see themselves flanked to the north by *Liaoning*, to the south by *Shandong* and to their east by *Fujian*, they will withdraw to Hawaii or Guam and will no longer be a concern …"

A pilot raised her hand. Wang recognized the woman he had given a dressing-down earlier. Not afraid to ask a question? Good, he liked that. "Yes, Pilot Officer Sun?"

"Colonel, we have three other carrier strike groups to our north and east—the British, Japanese and Australians—who were in the Western Pacific on exercises. Do we have any update on their … intentions?"

Wang looked to Major Tan, standing beside him, and raised an eyebrow.

"Yes," Tan replied. "The adversary carrier groups were moving west at flank speed but have now slowed down. Another good sign. Given the American message that they wish to open peace talks, we expect they will be called back to their home ports."

Wang nodded. "Now, new aircraft are being flown from the mainland. You will prepare your crews to receive them tonight and make them ready for operations tomorrow." He looked around the table, seeing only affirmation and resolve in his officers' faces. "You are dismissed."

Wang waited as his officers filed out. Zhang pointed at a chair. "Sit, please, Colonel. I have news for your ears only."

Wang sat. "Yes, Vice Admiral."

The old man looked younger. There was a light in his eyes that Wang had not seen for some time. An energy in his voice. He had been short-tempered and curt after the failure to intercept the American stealth aircraft, but he was a different man today. *Success is a powerful tonic,* Wang reflected.

From a pocket in his jacket, the old man pulled a small flask and pointed to a sideboard where there were plastic cups. Wang was surprised, but jumped to his feet and fetched two cups. The Admiral handed him the flask, and Wang poured them both a draught of what smelled like whisky before handing a cup to the Admiral, who raised his glass in a toast to his air wing commander. *"Ganbei!"* Zhang said, and drained his cup, with Wang following suit. The Admiral indicated Wang should refill their cups.

"There will be no peace talks. *Fujian* is moving west to do more than pressure the Americans to pull back," Zhang said when their cups had been refilled. "Tomorrow, our Marines and airborne forces are going ashore on the Taiwanese Matsu Islands and Kinmen. *Fujian* will guard against any reaction by the Americans to these actions."

Wang balked. The Matsu Islands were a chain of small islands and islets just a few miles off the Chinese coast near the province of Fujian and home to about 10,000 Taiwanese. They were of symbolic, but not military, value. Kinmen, however, was a much larger island, again nestled up against the Chinese mainland, but home to 140,000 rebels, including a thousand strong military garrison. It had a special and unfortunate place in Chinese military history since China had attempted to take it back at the height of the Cold War in 1958, even landing troops at one point. With the help of the USA, the rebels had repelled the attack both on land, sea, and in the air, and Chinese forces suffered 500 dead or wounded, losing several ships and as many as 31 aircraft.

"A bold move, Vice Admiral," Wang said. "It sends a clear signal to the rebels."

"The main enemy is weak, Wang," Zhang said. "They quail at our resolve and beg for meetings with our Chairman. They will not intervene in this operation. It takes place too close to Chinese territory. Their aircraft, ships and submarines will be useless. When Kinmen falls, the rebels will see they stand alone, and they will capitulate."

Wang was not so sure, but it was the obvious next step in ramping up pressure on the rebel government. "You mentioned our role?"

"Yes. We expect the rebels to ask the Americans for air support. They will be tempted to use the assets they have now positioned on Okinawa, Luzon and perhaps launch from the decks of their carriers hiding in Japanese and Philippine waters. Your aircraft will create a threat vector near the American carriers which they cannot ignore, limiting their ability to deploy aircraft to Matsu and Kinmen. Our mainland-based aircraft will deal with any attempt by the rebel air force to intervene."

It was a simple and sound plan. "We need to resupply with fuel and ordnance, as well as the aircraft that are flying in," Wang said, thinking out loud.

"Of course. Planning is underway for replenishment at sea. And we will also be reunited with an old friend of yours."

Wang raised an eyebrow. "Yes?"

"The *Yuan Wang Three Zero* will soon get underway from Okinotori Island. It will join the Strike Group and provide us with unparalleled detection capabilities during operations against the American carriers."

"It *was* very effective," Wang said. "The failure to prevent the American aircraft reaching Taiwan did not belong to *Three Zero*."

"No," Zhang agreed. He reached over to take back his flask and this time poured a draught for the Colonel. "*Suiyi*," he said, toasting again. "It is well you admit that, Wang."

Takuya Kato was not feeling well. He had woken from a restive sleep with a fever. *Should have gotten all those pellets out. What were you thinking? You're infected now.*

He looked around the bunk room, a little confused. *What was the ...?* He was about to go and do something, right? Maybe it would come to him if he stood and got dressed. So he did that. He pulled on the blue medic's shirt that was lying there, couldn't find any trousers and so just slipped his stockinged feet into some shoes and walked out into the corridor.

His feet felt wet. His socks were wet, his shoes too.

Oh, yeah. That damn commando shot him. Fell into the dark sea. Crawled out. He remembered.

His side hurt, and his guts too. He looked down, saw a bandage around his abdomen, and blood. He'd done that. Bandaged himself. There was something more. Painkillers? He grabbed a couple and realized his mouth was too dry to swallow them. He was thirsty. Needed water.

He went down the corridor until he came to a bathroom and went inside. He relieved himself and drank from the tap. It tasted saline. Drinkable, but it tasted bad. *You aren't supposed to drink from the tap Takuya,* he told himself. *Potable water in the mess, remember?* He went back out to the corridor, got to the stairwell and stood there looking at the steps. Steps going up, steps going down.

Where was he headed? He leaned against the doorway, shaking his head. *Snap out of it, Kato.* Yes, a message. He had to get a message out. Call for help. The Chinese were here, or … they had been? Someone had to know. He looked at the stairs. Up or down? He started climbing up the stairs. The comms room was up. Probably. He noticed his bare legs, skinny knees taking a step at a time. He should ask for some trousers, that's what he should do. The thought amused him and he chuckled out loud, his voice echoing up and down the stairwell. He did it again, louder, faking a laugh, listening to the echo.

When he got to the next level, he saw the comms room and went over to the long console full of buttons and switches, collapsed into a chair on wheels and sat there, staring at it. What was that noise? He put his hands on his ears, lifted them away again. *His heart, the blood pounding in his ears from taking the stairs.* Man, he was seriously out of shape. He should start gym sessions again at the station gym again.

Takuya Kato had a temperature of 103 degrees, systolic blood pressure in the low 90s and falling, and he was breathing at 24 breaths a minute. He didn't know it, but he was about to go into septic shock.

He was just sitting, staring at the console. He was going to do something. Supposed to do ... something. In front of him was a panel labelled UFP 1, UFP 2, UFP 3 ... Ah, he knew what to do. The switches under the labels were down. They should be *up*. He fixed that. The monitor screen blinked to life. Three rings around a triangle in the middle of the screen. He knew this game! You had to click the little dots. Something about boxes and crosses. His hand jerked, clicking randomly on the screen. *Hard game; not easy to hit those dots.* He concentrated, got most of them, waited for a score.

His hand fell from the mouse and hung limply beside him as he sat there, panting.

So weak, just from one flight of steps. He really had to hit that gym.

Asien 'Shredder' Chen had grabbed a few hours' sleep, hit *Fujian*'s gym for a two mile run and showered before reporting for duty—a solo mission to provide air cover for a ship that was going to be joining the *Fujian* strike group. He'd grimaced as he'd seen what ship and where it was sailing from.

Okinotori Reef. That damn island was like a magnet, constantly drawing him back. Scene of his first aerial kill, yes, but not one he associated with success. No one had come out of that particular operation smelling of roses.

He reached the island and put his machine into a racetrack pattern around it, using his distributed aperture system to scan the sea below while his radar scanned the skies. No trouble was expected, but the big space-tracking ship below, *Yuan Wang Three Zero*, was particularly valuable, and particularly vulnerable, and tensions were high. Hence, he was orbiting over the top of it.

He was up at 20,000 feet but gradually dropped down to 5,000. Probably good for the crew's morale if they could see and hear his Chongming, see that he was up there, standing guard.

"*Fujian* Control, Egret flight in position over Okinotori," he reported. "No contacts. All clear here."

The Japanese UFP outer ring surrounding Okinotori was not made up of acoustic mines. The defensive ring had a circumference of 125 kilometers, or nearly 80 miles. It would have taken hundreds of mines to guard a perimeter that long. So instead, the Japanese Self Defense Force Naval Engineers tasked with securing Okinotori against an invading force that approached by sea chose a more economical solution. Instead of hundreds of mines, they anchored 10 Japanese "Long Lance" torpedoes to the seabed. Named after an experimental torpedo developed by Japan before World War II, the 21st Century version of the Japanese Long Lance was a high-speed torpedo with an autonomous active/passive sonar seeker-head, 600 lb. warhead and a 40-mile range. The only modification made to the Long Lance torpedoes that Takuya Kato had unknowingly activated was that their range had been limited to just 10 miles, to avoid them running out into nearby sea lanes and sinking commercial shipping.

But a 10-mile range was more than enough. All they needed was for a target from their acoustic signature database to move within range, and once armed, they would launch.

There was a Japanese destroyer headed toward Okinotori at speed to investigate why it was not responding to attempts to contact it. But its acoustic signature was registered in the database of the Long Lance torpedoes, so even if it blundered into an active UFP field, it was in no danger.

The Vortex crew aboard *Three Zero* had just stowed their arrays and discharged their capacitors, readying their system for the passage ahead. The Vortex crew chief had been saving a bottle of champagne for the moment they were stood down, and now he pulled the champagne bottle out of the bag he'd hidden it in and took some paper coffee cups from a drawer by his feet. His crew had performed well; they deserved to celebrate.

It didn't matter that the champagne was warm. Hell, that would just make the cork popping more impressive. So would the shuddering of the deck beneath their feet, as *Three Zero* redirected its turbine power to its screws and got underway at last.

"Ladies and gentlemen!" he said, standing and holding the bottle in air. "Shall we toast?!" He had debated with himself whether to hold the celebration at all, given the rumors that had filtered down to him from fellow officers. Apparently their away team had struck a mine and all had been killed, except for the commander, who had been recovered, but with a bad gunshot wound.

Their departure had been delayed while their passage away from the atoll had been checked for other mines, but none were found, so they were finally on their way.

He held the bottle above his head, thumb ready to send the cork flying. Then the ship shuddered and rolled. Which was ... strange.

He heard a noise up forward, like steel grinding on steel. *What the ...?*

21. 'Her long ponytail trailing behind her ...'

None of the Long Lance torpedoes in the UFP outer ring were under the route that had been checked for mines. The closest lay two miles to port. But it had lain too long on the seabed. It launched, acquired the *Three Zero* very quickly, and its armored warhead drove itself into the ship's 20 mm bottom plate at 38 knots, penetrating deep into one of the ship's lithium battery storage compartments.

The fuse on its warhead was defective and didn't explode. Not straight away. That would happen later, as seawater poured into the battery compartment and interacted with the damaged lithium batteries.

A second Long Lance torpedo came at the ship from five miles out on its starboard side, stern quarter. It too buried itself deep inside the ship's hull. It struck the crew chief of the Vortex radar system right in the chest. The champagne bottle flew into the air, and the violent spin was too much. The cork flew out of the bottle as champagne fountained outward.

There were no cheers from the horrified Vortex crew. No time for anything, really. A millisecond later, the 600 lb. warhead of the second Long Lance exploded, tearing a hole the size of a family car in the stern of the *Yuan Wang Three Zero*.

From its radio room, the radio operator began sending a panicked mayday.

Shredder looked down on the crippled ship in horror. He'd heard the distress call from the ship on the guard radio frequency while he was five miles away on an outbound leg of his patrol route and immediately made speed for the ship's position. The radio operator reported that they'd seen at least one torpedo before they were hit. They were calling for help, at the same time warning all Chinese shipping in the area to beware and to approach with extreme caution.

He had his Chongming circling overhead and was watching with his DAS cameras zoomed in on the sea below. Should *he* have spotted the submarine down there, or whatever had attacked the ship?

No, of course not, that was ridiculous. He was there to watch the skies. Which were completely clear. No aircraft had launched those torpedoes. Right?

He couldn't help feeling he was somehow responsible though. He opened a channel to the Air Operations Control Room.

"*Fujian* Control, Egret. I picked up a mayday from PLA Navy ship *Yuan Wang Three Zero*. My aircraft is over the ship now. It has been hit by some kind of munition and is taking water." He watched with dread fascination.

"Egret One, relay your vision to Operations."

"Patching vision through."

The *Three Zero* was going down in the shallow waters by the stern. It seemed to him it had stopped and then started

396

sliding backward, but now it had settled, hadn't it? About a third of the ship from the third satellite antenna and backward was underwater, but the rest was still above the water. Maybe the water there wasn't so deep. Maybe the stern of the ship had hit the sea floor and just stuck there? Wouldn't that mean the sailors who were still alive were safe?

He'd seen them trying to lower lifeboats before, and they were still doing that. There was a hole in the front of the ship too, its bow stuck about a hundred feet up in the air. But it was a smaller one, some wisps of smoke drifting out of it. Now he noticed the crew up at the bow. They were *jumping* off and into the water. That made no sense, unless …

He zoomed his camera in on the hole in the forward part of the hull, just below the waterline. It was elevated now and wouldn't be taking any more water. But there was a … what *was* that? A milky white vapor pouring out of the hole now, like those slow-motion videos of waterfalls.

A *lot* of milky white vapor.

Lithium reacts intensely with water, forming lithium hydroxide and highly flammable hydrogen. Damaged batteries overheat, creating "thermal runaway," or the spontaneous explosion of the battery thanks to a buildup of heat in the cells inside.

Several minutes had passed since the *Three Zero* was torpedoed. Since hydrogen is lighter than air, as the bow of *Three Zero* rose into the air, the hydrogen being released by the damaged lithium batteries immersed in seawater floated forward, filling six watertight compartments in the bow.

Usually, leaking hydrogen disperses in the air, so it isn't dangerous. Unless it can't escape.

Exploding batteries plus flammable hydrogen in a constrained environment?

These are Not A Good Thing.

Hydrogen is odorless, colorless and tasteless, so humans can't detect it. Until they start choking. Those members of the crew too slow to make their way out of the hydrogen-flooded compartments were rendered unconscious by the sudden huge volume of hydrogen displacing most of the air.

They were the lucky ones.

As Chen watched, the entire forward third of the enormous vessel turned into a fireball 100 yards high and wide. Burning debris and people on fire flew through the air and hit the water.

He was still down at 5,000 feet and was right above the fireball. He flicked his flight stick right and spun his machine away from the rising flame and smoke. Once he'd settled his machine again, he checked the sky around his machine was still clear and returned to the vision of the ship below.

The entire bow section of the ship had disappeared. Fire and smoke were pouring from the gaping hole forward of the large bridge superstructure. The water around the ship was full of debris, and there was the unmistakable sight of bodies floating in the water. He saw a few people splashing or waving, and those who had made it down in lifeboats were already paddling toward them or throwing life preservers.

It was carnage. He felt bile rising in his throat and coughed, trying to hold it down.

He watched a flaming sailor tumble down the deck, over the side and into the water. Then another. A woman. He could see her long ponytail trailing behind her as she fell. It was on fire. "Control, there are people *burning* ..."

"Egret flight! Hold station over the vessel. We received the mayday too. We are coordinating rescue operations. Control out."

Chen reached forward, tapping icons on the screen in front of him to better frame the vision from his Chongming for the Operations Room overhead. He sat frozen in place, unable to move, unable to tear his eyes away from the scene below. He watched until he couldn't watch anymore. Putting his machine on AI control, he pulled his virtual cockpit visor off, lowered his head and began weeping.

It was about an hour later, as President Carliotti was preparing to go live on national networks to address the nation, that her Chief of Staff appeared at the door to the studio, looking ashen faced. A makeup artist had been working on Carliotti's face and Rosenstern clicked his fingers to get her attention. "Sorry to interrupt," he said, motioning to the woman. "Outside please. We need a moment."

The makeup artist put down her brush and hurried out. Rosenstern closed the door behind him and leaned up against it.

"What is it?" Carliotti asked.

"The Japanese just sunk a Chinese space-tracking ship," he said. "Big. Size of a cruise liner. Crew of 400. No word on casualties, yet."

"They *what*?!"

"This doesn't impact the timeline," he said. "Indo-Pacific Command has been moved to DEFCON 2. Taiwan's ground attack aircraft are on the wing. *USS Bougainville* with 1,800 Marines has deployed from Okinawa, with escorts."

Carliotti thought hard. Rosenstern hadn't been completely honest with Michael Chase. In fact, he'd told him a lie, and asked him to pass that lie on to the Chinese General Staff. It was the same lie that dozens of other government officials and influential businesspeople with access to China's elite had been briefed to pass along: that the US was looking to de-escalate the Taiwan situation and willing to pause Operation Skytrain to achieve that.

The reality was entirely the opposite.

In the two hours after Chase had left the National Security Council meeting, the cabinet members were presented with new intelligence by the Secretary of Defense. Satellite imagery showed that China was preparing a small invasion force near the port of Xiamen, adjacent to the Taiwanese island of Kinmen. A flotilla of *Yuyi* class landing hovercraft had been gathered, and images showed troops and light-armored vehicles being loaded. Each of the hovercraft could hold 50 troops and a tank or infantry-fighting vehicle. They were specifically designed to sail up onto land, *over* the obstacles Taiwan had strewn across beaches and potential landing zones. Additionally, mobile artillery units had been spotted in columns on roads in the nearby Jimei district and signals intelligence confirmed an unusually high volume of traffic between PLA Army, Navy and Air Force units in the surrounding Fujian province.

Taken with the brazen attack on the British humanitarian flight, the information had been sufficient to solidify the NSC's agreed direction. It had been agreed that a message would be fed to Chinese sources through back-channel contacts that the US was seeking to *de-escalate*.

But the message the US President was about to deliver to the American people was something completely different.

"I want updates on that Chinese ship, right until I go live," Carliotti said. "And a meeting with the Japanese Prime Minister the minute we are done."

"You got it." Rosenstern pulled out his cell phone. "I have your speech here; let's see if this changes anything."

Carmen Carliotti, Address to the Nation Regarding Taiwanese Military Action in the Taiwan Strait

Just one hour ago, Taiwanese air and naval forces began attacks on military targets on the Chinese mainland bordering the Taiwan Strait to repel a planned Chinese invasion.

These attacks continue as I speak. US forces are not actively engaged. The Taiwanese government's action follows incontrovertible evidence, which will be presented to the UN Security Council in an emergency session, that China was hours from beginning an invasion of the Taiwanese islands of Kinmen and Matsu. This followed the unprovoked attack by China on a British humanitarian aid flight carrying food and medicine to that besieged island.

Taiwan does not stand alone. As I report to you, US forces, together with those of our allies—which include the nations of Great Britain,

Australia, Canada, France, Belgium, the Netherlands, Colombia, Ethiopia, South Africa, New Zealand, Turkey, Greece, Thailand, the Philippines and Luxembourg—are preparing to support Taiwan in preventing a Chinese invasion of their island.

If necessary, we will eliminate the ability of Chinese forces to invade Taiwanese territory. If forced to, we will sink their assembled invasion ships. The artillery guns and missile launchers that China plans to use in this invasion will be destroyed. Offensive preparations by the Chinese Air Force will be disrupted. Any operations we conduct will be designed to protect the lives of Taiwanese citizens and soldiers by targeting only China's assembled invasion arsenal. Other targets in China will not be attacked, only those directly related to invasion preparations.

I have spoken with the President of Taiwan, and the objectives of Taiwan as he explained them to me are clear: to eliminate China's ability to invade Taiwan, now, in relation to the islands of Kinmen and Matsu, but if needed in the future, in relation to any attempt by China to assemble an invasion force to invade the main island of Taiwan. The US and our allies will do whatever is necessary to defend the right of the people of Taiwan to resist such an invasion and freely and democratically choose their own destiny.

And we will continue, in every way possible, to try to provide critical humanitarian assistance to the people of Taiwan. In that regard, the Secretary of Navy has ordered the USS Bougainville *to sail for Taipei immediately from Japan.* Bougainville *is equipped with a full Navy field hospital, medical personnel and 2,000 tons of food and medical supplies. Let me assure the families of the crew of* Bougainville, *we are providing them with every protection as they carry out their urgent humanitarian mission. More ships are being readied to continue our efforts to supply Taiwan in the face of the Chinese blockade, and we will defend them with the full power of our Navy and Air Force and with the complete and total support of our coalition. Tonight, as our forces fight, they and their families are in our prayers. May God bless each one of them, and the coalition forces at our side, and may He continue to bless our nation, the United States of America.*

In the sitting room of his DC apartment, Michael Chase had been following the President's address like 200 million other Americans, and let out the breath it felt like he had been holding for the last five minutes.

OK, that did not go in the direction I expected.

Preemptive attacks on Chinese mainland forces and positions? Dispatching US ground forces for Taiwan? These were exactly the things he had counseled the President to consider and never for a moment believed she or the other members of the NSC would do. He had in fact been lobbying inside Defense for Pentagon strategic planners to include preemptive strikes in their Taiwan war-gaming for a couple of years now, but he was sure his voice had gone unheard. He now knew also that he had been duped by the President's Chief of Staff, suckered into delivering a classic piece of strategic misdirection through Huang, to lull the Chinese military into the belief their aggression had forced their adversaries to reevaluate their position and convince them to walk away from Taiwan, not pile on.

Chase's telephone rang, and he leaned forward to his coffee table to pick it up. He was still deputy assistant secretary of defense for China, and his duties had been broader than just managing the dialogue with General Huang. He expected the call to be from one of his staff but was surprised to see the contact's name flashing on his screen.

HR Rosenstern.

He took the call. "Chase."

"Rosenstern," the man said. There was no preamble. "The President is creating an Executive subset of the National Security Council to manage strategic issues during this crisis. I proposed and the President agreed for you to be a part of the Executive."

He balked. "Of course, but why me?" Chase asked.

"You speak Chinese. You have been in near daily contact with the highest ranks of China's PLA for three years. I've read the memos you wrote predicting that China would invade Taiwan and that it was just a matter of when, not if. In several of those memos, you proposed we develop the capability and position the assets to allow us to conduct preemptive strikes on Chinese targets to disrupt their capacity to invade Taiwan, or at the very least support Taiwan to do so ..."

"I wasn't aware anyone was paying attention," Chase admitted.

"You didn't need to be made aware, but yes, we *were* listening, and yours was not the only voice. We started moving those assets into place as soon as China threw up its blockade. We have been preparing diligently with our allies, as you would have seen in the RIMPAC exercises. What you just saw the President announce was a direct result of contingency planning for exactly the kind of strikes you were calling for. Now if we are done making you feel sufficiently important, please get your ass to Edwards Air Base, where ExCom will convene in ... 40 minutes."

Vice Admiral Zhang Weili had reassembled *Fujian*'s senior officers, and the ready room they were meeting in featured wall screens on which the captains and executive officers of every ship in the *Fujian* strike group were joining by satellite link. Beside him were Wang, Major Tan and *Fujian's* Captain and senior officers. Wang could not help note that Zhang looked considerably less good humored now than he had the night before.

He nodded to Major Tan to begin her briefing. She was seated at a desk behind a bank of screens as the entire briefing was digital. A briefing window projected from her PC appeared on all the wall screens.

"Thank you, Vice Admiral. At 0415 this morning, Taiwan launched up to 175 long-range land attack missiles, believed to be of the Hsiung Sheng type, at targets along the coast. Their warheads included both high-explosive and dispersal-type munitions, including cluster bombs, land and sea mines. Most of these missiles were intercepted by our air defenses, but some damage was sustained and 23 aircraft were destroyed on the ground." Murmurs broke out around the room, but Tan continued. "Between 0420 and 0500, there were numerous combat engagements between Taiwanese and Chinese fighter aircraft in the Chinese air defense zone. Five Chinese aircraft were lost, and more than 50 Taiwanese aircraft destroyed. Some naval skirmishes took place between Taiwanese Navy and Chinese vessels, but no Chinese vessels were lost. Two Taiwanese Navy submarines were, however, destroyed."

Impressive, Wang thought wryly. *So we shot down a quarter of their entire air force for the loss of only five of our own? And no naval vessels?* Somehow he doubted that.

"At 0430, F-16 fighters of the Taiwan Air Force attacked our air patrols in the vicinity of Xiamen and Fuzhou, near the islands of Kinmen and Matsu. The attack was a precursor to intensive air-to-ground attacks by Taiwanese aircraft, targeting our air defense batteries on the coast covering these sectors. Most of the Taiwanese attackers were destroyed, but some damage to air defenses was sustained ..."

Tan changed the screen and looked up. She gave the participants time to digest what she was saying. She flipped to a map showing a number of Chinese missile battery locations and PLA Air Force bases.

"At 0430, a second wave of cruise missiles and swarming drones, estimated to be around 500 in number, struck our amphibious forces at the ports of Xiamen and Fuzhou. These ports were the embarkation point for troops positioned to retake the islands of Kinmen and Matsu."

Flying Fish drones, that was Wang's guess. Taiwan produced the small ground-launched kamikaze drones locally and each one carried a warhead equivalent to 10 antipersonnel grenades. They were almost impossible to jam because they could be inertially guided and used onboard cameras and AI to identify targets. Flying just above the ground in swarms of 20 to 50 units, they were hard to detect and even harder to destroy. Taiwan would have sent the drones in first to overwhelm air defenses and followed up with a barrage of Hsiung Sheng cruise missiles.

"Casualties from the attack on our staging areas are currently unknown, but the amphibious landings on Kinmen and Matsu islands have been delayed," Tan said. "Air defense installations along the coast were also targeted."

In other words, our amphibious landing force was decimated, Wang decided. The landings were planned to be small in scale—a demonstration more than anything else. Even Kinmen, the most ambitious of the two operations, involved only 5,000 troops landing in two waves after the island's defenders were rendered insensible by an intensive artillery and missile bombardment.

Wang was listening intently. He had learned long ago to take the damage estimates of his intelligence colleagues with a grain of salt, along with reports of success in intercepting enemy missiles. If Tan said 23 aircraft had been destroyed, the real number was probably at least double that number. If she said most of the enemy missiles and drones had been intercepted, then how was she able to be so clear about what warheads they had been carrying?

The real message she was conveying was that China had been caught with its pants around its ankles. No one had seriously expected *Taiwan* would open a war with China, and Wang knew it would never consider doing so on its own.

Tan paused, and Vice Admiral Zhang stood. Wang knew they were saving the worst news for last, and not all the officers in the room would be aware of it. He was, because he had personally reviewed the vision from his aircraft over Okinotori.

"Thank you, Major," Zhang said. The vigor he had presented with just a couple of hours earlier had evaporated. Now he looked every one of his 62 years. "There is more troubling news. As some of you have heard, the satellite tracking vessel, *Yuan Wang Three Zero*, was torpedoed off the coast of the Japanese-claimed atoll of Okinotori, simultaneous with the attacks Major Tan has just described. The *Three Zero* has been sunk, and casualties are estimated in the hundreds. A rescue is being organized."

He waved a hand to Tan, who killed the presentation. "In addition, we have seen potentially threatening movements by the carrier strike groups of Britain, Japan and Australia in the Western Pacific. Taken together, the events today confirm our worst fears. The People's Republic is under attack by the combined nations of the Western Alliance, from Taiwan and the USA to Japan, from the UK to Australia, in a coalition that includes the Philippines and Korea ..."

Wang felt a rage rising inside him. It was as they had always feared. A world determined to hold China down, to stop it from taking its rightful place among the great nations. And it must have been planned long before the small fracas of the previous day in which the British aircraft was destroyed. Before even the transfer to Taiwan of hypersonic missiles, though that had clearly been a precursor to the current attack. Multiple nations did not muster the forces needed for a combined air and sea attack on targets up and down the Chinese eastern seaboard without months of preparation. Of course, China had been watching the preparations for years—Japan extending the American leases on its bases, allowing it to deploy stealth fighters from Okinawa and continue to base its strengthened Seventh Fleet there; Australia purchasing surplus US-made *Los Angeles* class nuclear-powered attack submarines while it partnered with the UK to build its own version of the *Astute* class. US strategic bombers being moved out of bases in the US, on permanent rotation to Guam and Darwin. The sale of increasingly advanced weapons systems to Taiwan and support for its indigenous defense industry. Congressional vote after congressional vote reaffirming the US duty to defend Taiwan's "democracy."

The portents were clear, and had made the timetable for reunification all the more urgent.

Wang was convinced in his own mind that his leaders had not wanted war. That they had always taken only the minimum steps necessary to nudge Taiwan in the direction of historical inevitability. First, economic and political incentives, political pressure from China-aligned parties on Taiwan and diplomatic pressure from without. Then economic pressure in the form of sanctions, tariffs and embargoes. Peaceful military pressure from naval and air incursions into Taiwan's unrecognized "air defense identification zone." And finally, all of this having failed, rather than an invasion, an air and sea blockade.

Even the planned operations to retake the Kinmen and Matsu territories were an expression of minimalism, intended only as a warning, a demonstration of a future that could still be avoided by negotiations between rational actors.

But the West was *not* rational. The US government had said for decades it supported the One China policy and the eventual reunification of Taiwan and Hong Kong into one Chinese nation. Yet at the same time, it had prepared for war, and now, it had unleashed it.

Well, China had prepared too.

Zhang motioned to Wang. "The People's Republic is under attack by the US and its allies, but we were ready for this day. Colonel Wang?"

Wang stood. He needed no slides or presentation, not for this briefing. Formal briefings would be held in combat centers across the strike group and in ready rooms on *Fujian* in the decks underneath his feet. His message was simple.

"The rebel puppets would never have conducted this attack without the express support of the Western Alliance. Today, we, the combined aircraft carriers of the PLA Navy, will be the key that opens the door to an attack on the American Seventh Fleet from which it will never recover," he said. "As you know, we have replenished our squadrons with aircraft, ordnance and fuel. Every available aircraft except those required for fleet defense will be launched at 0700 hours. *Fujian*'s target is the *USS Enterprise*, currently sailing in

Philippine waters off the coast of Luzon. As we attack the *Enterprise*, our carrier *Shandong* will attack the *USS George HW Bush* in the waters off Okinawa. The *Liaoning* will attack the Amphibious Landing Ship, *USS Bougainville*, which is currently en route, under escort, to Taipei."

He placed his hands on the back of the chair in front of him and stared into the conference camera. "We will not attack alone." He heard voices behind and beside him whisper, as the officers around the table realized what was coming. The attack plan was one the strike force had trained on and rehearsed in exercises multiple times, over several years. "Our comrades in the submarine and strategic rocket services will be part of the operation, but *we* are the spearhead," he continued. "The American carriers are surrounded by air warfare cruisers and destroyers. They field advanced long- and short-range anti-air missiles, close-in kinetic and laser defense systems and orbiting defensive air patrols with jamming and anti-missile capabilities. Our role is to open the attack and distract and overwhelm these defenses. *Fujian*'s missiles and aircraft will drain the American strike group of defensive weapons, overrun its pickets, jam its radars and render it vulnerable to a killing blow."

They were only being told what they absolutely needed to know. But Wang had participated in enough exercises simulating an attack on an American carrier to know success could only be assured by a multipronged attack—from the air, under the sea and ... from space. "Our attack will coincide with an intensive missile and rocket barrage of military installations on the rebel island, which will inhibit the ability of the Taiwan Air Force to interfere in our mission."

"That concludes this operational briefing," the Admiral said. "Unit mission briefings will now begin."

Fifty miles north-northwest of Okinotori Island, the Captain and crew of the *JS Haguro*, a *Maya* class missile destroyer of the Japanese Self Defense Force Navy, had been plowing through the water at flank speed toward the Japanese Oceanographic Research Station that had gone ominously silent.

The *Haguro*'s Captain Shinji Kagawa was no ordinary naval officer. He was a blood relative of Mitsuko Naishinnō, the first Empress in the history of the modern Japanese Empire. As children, they had played games at each other's birthday parties. Kagawa particularly remembered a game of Fuku Warai on his sixth birthday: a game where a child places a blank mask over their face and then, with instructions from the other children sitting in a circle around them, tries to place eyes, nose, mouth and eyebrows on it—a kind of facial "pin the tail on the donkey." The children were, of course, not particularly helpful, and fell about laughing when he was finished, his face completely upside down and cross-eyed. Kagawa hadn't really seen the fun in the game and had started crying. His cousin Mitsuko, just a princess at that time, had ordered everyone to shut up, then put the mask on herself. "Anyone want to laugh now?" she asked loudly.

No one did. Kagawa loved her for that small act of kindness.

It was also Mitsuko, by then *Empress* Mitsuko Naishinnō, who had been behind the decision to dispatch the *JS Haguro* to investigate why the Japanese island had fallen silent. She was *not* a ceremonial Head of State; in fact, she had come to power by exercising her ancient right to dismiss the sitting government—a populist cabal of war-mongering criminals—and rule in its place until new elections could be held.

Nonetheless, Kagawa had been surprised when he had received a call in his stateroom from the Comms watch officer in *Haguro*'s CIC. The man had stumbled. "Captain, I … Captain, you have a call from … from an eminent person."

He had been poring over a map, reviewing the course being recommended for the next day, which was taking them away from the recent RIMPAC exercises they had been a part of toward a friendship port call in Brisbane, Australia. After which they were supposed to conduct anti-submarine exercises against one of the newly leased *Los Angeles* class nuclear-powered submarines that had been loaned to the Royal Australian Navy. "What 'eminent person'?" he had snapped at the man. Like every other officer aboard the vessel, he had seen the US President's announcement that Taiwan had opened hostilities with China with a surprise attack and had contacted his fleet base to ask for new orders. He was still awaiting a reply but was certain they would not be playing war games with the Australians.

"Captain, your … it is the Empress Mitsuko Naishinnō, Captain! A voice call."

Mitsuko, calling him *here*? This could not be good. He had not spoken with her for nearly a year. Their distant blood ties won him no special privileges, and she was, after all, completely occupied with matters of State. "Put her through, please, Lieutenant."

The voice was as he remembered it. It was as though she always spoke with a soft smile, whether she was meeting with school children, or announcing on radio that she had ordered police onto the streets of Tokyo. Kagawa knew that in political circles she was known as "the smiling assassin," not that anyone would use that sobriquet in front of him.

412

He picked up the handset on his desk. "Empress, this is Captain Shinji Kagawa. How can I serve you?" he said.

"Shinji, it is so good to hear your voice," the woman said. She was 25 years old but still sounded like the girl he grew up with. "It calms me at this time to know we have people like you in charge of our defense."

"Hardly in charge, Empress," he said. "I am a small man in a small ship in a very big sea," he told her.

"But still, an important command," she insisted. "I am calling you because I have been indiscreet again and annoyed your Admiral."

Oh, no. Mitsuko's "indiscretions" were becoming legendary. The Palace was supposed to stay out of affairs of State, and it was certainly not supposed to interfere in military matters. And, technically, it could be said that since the "Palace coup" of some years ago, she had not directly interfered. But she had a habit of asking questions of her ministers and generals, and it soon became apparent that many of them were rhetorical. To not act on her concerns was to lose favor with the Palace, a career-ending form of tone deafness.

She continued, "I wanted to speak with you before his staff contact you, in case there was any misunderstanding."

"Of course, Empress," he said. "Would I be right in guessing you asked him a question?"

"Why, yes," she said. "My military counsel has been keeping me up to date with developments concerning Taiwan, and it occurred to me that some days ago, I was told we lost contact with one of our island outposts. It is called ..."

"Okinotori," he said. "Yes, I read a report. The Navy dispatched an aircraft to investigate, I think."

"And it was turned away by Chinese fighter planes," she said. "I asked the Admiral what *more* was being done to investigate. I was told there is a single scientist on the outpost on the island because the rest of the personnel are back home for Golden Week. I got the impression the Admiral saw this as inconsequential and did not appreciate the full implications of the situation."

He silently shook his head. She was the Empress of Japan, a country of 126 million people, covering 2,000 miles of sea from the Kurile Islands in the north to Okinotori in the south. Yet it was typical of her to be concerned about the fate of a tiny island and a single man. "I see," he said.

"Yes, so I asked the Admiral whether it might not be a good idea to send a vessel to investigate, and imagine my delight when I was told the *JS Haguro,* with my dear cousin aboard, is the nearest vessel to Okinotori!"

Kagawa was not so sure the delight was mutual. "I will prepare to investigate the situation at Okinotori," Kagawa assured her. "We will respond as soon as we receive the order."

"That is wonderful, cousin. You have seen the news, I assume," she said, sounding more serious now.

"Taiwan's attack on China? Yes. I was expecting to receive new orders tonight anyway," he said.

"Be careful, Shinji. You are sailing into uncharted waters. We all are," she said.

That troubled him. What did she mean? "Empress, may I … no, nothing."

"Ask, Shinji," she told him. "If you have a question, you may ask as my cousin, not as a Captain in my Navy."

414

"Mitsuko," he said, feeling suddenly awkward using the name he had used all through his childhood. "Are we going to join this war against China?"

She was quiet. Weighing what to say? No, more likely weighing *how* to say it. "If I have any influence, yes, Shinji. If China succeeds in taking Taiwan by force, no disputed territory will be safe, nor any nation that opposes China. But our Prime Minister and his cabinet may have other opinions. I find myself dealing with the consequences of my earlier actions, ironically. In the elections after I dismissed the corrupt fools of the last government, I gave my support to a peace candidate who I thought would bring stability to our fractured relations with the West. He did that, but he is a pacifist at heart. He will never be a wartime leader. You can expect a period of … well, turmoil I suppose, as we work through this. You understand me?"

If I have any influence … False modesty, or just innocent understatement? Whichever, the response did not bode well for political harmony. "Yes, Mitsuko. I will serve in whatever capacity you require."

"I know. But for now, just keep your mind on the man on that station, yes?"

"Yes."

"Our government and our Navy may think it is an insignificant coral atoll, but it is our southernmost possession, and right now, it may be completely undefended except for a lonely scientist. Make haste."

22. 'Why isn't that reassuring?'

April 6, 2038

Bunny was just stepping out of the debrief that followed their early morning sorties. Considering the rain of chaos surrounding the island, the 68th AGRS' first mission of the day had been smoothly executed. The unit's 10 pilots, with Bunny's Widow on overwatch, had flown invisibly to 20,000 feet over central Taiwan and identified the Chinese air patrols in the Strait that were between the main Taiwan island and Kinmen Island on the Chinese coast. They identified nearly 50 aircraft. The Chinese patrols, mostly last-century J-11 and J-16 fighters, were between 50 and 70 miles away, staying out of range of Taiwan's shore defenses but well within the range of the Aggressors' Peregrine missiles.

In what was one of the opening salvos of the conflict, as one, the F-22s locked their targets and fired 60 missiles at the Chinese patrols. As they did so, Taiwan fired its first volley of ground-launched cruise missiles at the Chinese mainland. Simultaneously, nearly 40 Taiwanese F-16V multirole fighters dropped out of their normal defensive air patrol patterns and stormed in behind the wave of cruise missiles. Twenty of the Taiwanese fighters were configured for air-to-air operations, the rest for air-to-ground.

Bunny could almost read the minds of the Chinese pilots watching their reactions on her tactical monitor high over the island's central mountain range. They saw the Taiwanese F-

16s first and turned to meet them, expecting perhaps a large-scale provocation but nothing more. They had not seen the Aggressors' Peregrine missiles closing on them, much less the F-22s behind them, guiding them to their targets. As the Aggressors' missiles got to within five miles, closing at *3,000 miles an hour*, they switched to active homing to guide them through the last seconds of their attack. Now the Chinese saw them and scattered, desperately maneuvering to avoid the blizzard of air-to-air missiles coming at them.

Those few who survived were quickly engaged by the 20 Taiwanese fighters storming in behind the Americans' missiles. At no point was any Chinese aircraft engaged within visual range by the US Aggressor squadron. Bunny doubted that little piece of deniability would have any credibility in days to come, since anyone must know that the intelligence informing the Taiwanese attack could only have come from the US, and the US administration would have had to give a green light to using it.

The action blew a 50-mile-long hole in the Chinese air blockade over the Taiwan Strait, the location chosen because of a lack of anti-air naval vessels underneath it, through which came the second wave of 20 F-16V fighters, which were carrying high speed anti-radar missiles. Their targets were Chinese air-defense radar installations along the coast around Kinmen. A similar operation was underway in the north, at the Matsu Islands. Most of the Chinese radar operators were figuratively or literally asleep at their command posts at that early hour, months of minimal air activity from Taiwan having dulled their wits. They felt almost redundant behind the belt of fighter aircraft their country had patrolling up and down the Strait.

They were slow to detect the incoming Taiwanese fighters, slow to react, and they reacted offensively, trying to track,

417

lock and fire at the incoming aircraft, rather than do what they should have done, which was to expect a HARM attack as the first move in any air war, shut down their radars and hide.

Fifteen of 22 missile batteries were taken out of action in the Taiwanese attack, and six F-16s lost. Their HARM missiles delivered, the remaining Taiwanese F-16s banked sharply and fled for home.

The sky around Kinmen Island was clear. The air defenses up and down the coast north and south of it were blind. And over the horizon came the second wave of Taiwanese cruise missiles and swarming drones. The missiles and drones skimmed the sea as they flew at wavetop height for their run in on the Chinese mainland. In the middle of the Strait, they split north and south. Nearly half targeted the Chinese port of Xiamen, and the landing hovercraft, supplies and troop concentrations gathered there for the planned invasion. Fifty thousand lbs. of high explosives rained down on the port as the drones attacked lightly armored vehicle targets, supply dumps and troop concentrations. The cruise missiles scattered cluster bombs and mined the harbors with anti-shipping mines. Rapid satellite damage assessments, made when the smoke cleared, showed the Chinese hovercraft, along with the embarked troops dozing in their seats aboard them, had been obliterated, and fuel and ammunition depots were ablaze.

Bunny had also heard Taiwan had surprised the Chinese navy at sea. It had no surface navy to speak of, but it had eight locally made, super-silent diesel electric submarines, based on a Dutch design, each of which could fire six Harpoon anti-ship cruise missiles. She'd heard six Chinese destroyers had been sunken or damaged, but she had no news on how many of the submarines had survived. Her guess would be very, very few.

The naval anti-ship missile strikes had gone in while Bunny and the Aggressor F-22s were already on their way back down at Taichung Air Base to refuel and rearm.

As high-value assets, Aggressor's F-22s were refueled immediately, then directed to underground revetments: small, two-plane hangars dug into the earth in the southwest corner of the air base away from fuel and ordnance stores. They were fronted with Metalith blast-deflecting barriers that could be raised in seconds to block the entrance and covered in 10 inches of reinforced concrete under six feet of earth.

Each bunker was connected by a tunnel to the next in line, and they had rudimentary facilities such as independent power and plumbing. But no fuel, and no ordnance. Refueling and rearming had to take place outside. The Aggressors' new "ready room" was a corner of one of these underground hangars, and as she and Magellan stood, the hydraulically operated barrier at the opening to the hangar deployed. It whirred into place, sealing the entrance.

"Why isn't that reassuring?" Bunny said.

"Uh, because just about any bunker-busting bomb dropped at just the right angle would punch through that and incinerate everything and everyone inside?" he offered.

"Thanks for putting that into words."

"You're welcome. But I'd still rather be in here than out there when the hard rain falls."

They made their way over to a folding table lined with mostly empty coffee jugs and lifted several until they found one with some lukewarm coffee in it, then poured it into paper cups. "How soon before China hits back, you think?"

"A few hours, maybe longer, but definitely today," he said. He leaned against a wall and drank a mouthful of coffee. "We took a bite out of them but now they'll try to smash us with everything they can muster. We'll know it's starting when they try to take down our air defenses. Then their ground attack and air supremacy fighters will move in, swamp us, trying to knock out everything with wings and every airfield. They already cut our internet cables, but now they'll go after our satellite links, jam or just plain shoot the satellites out of the sky. After that, sky is going to rain rockets and cruise missiles. For days."

"So we'll be hit, for sure?"

"For sure." He nodded toward a nearby F-22. "They know we're here. They'll have the GPS coordinates of these hangars locked in." He stared bleakly into his cup. "We've got half of our aircraft in hangars like this or buried in tunnels in the mountains, but in war games they destroy 30 percent of our air force and anti-air defenses in the first three days. The Patriot and NASAM batteries the US sold us make all the difference. What's left of our air force will keep fighting."

Bunny shivered. Being entombed in a concrete cave with a rampaging enemy roving overhead with impunity really didn't feel like such a great idea.

Meany had come up to get coffee too and was listening to their conversation. "I don't expect us to still be here when that happens. Like Magellan says, this has been war-gamed to death. Taiwan's air force will stay and fight as long as it can, but *we'll* support from offshore." He frowned as he poured from the last remaining coffee jug and only a mouthful of coffee came out. Bunny handed him what was left of hers. "Thanks. I'm expected to get the order to bug out any minute. I was talking to Salt before we went up; they're putting the

420

pieces into place to move us to Okinawa. He'll meet us there with the other two Widows."

"They're going to keep us on the line?" Bunny asked, a little surprised. The 68th AGRS' pilots and ground crews were, after all, only reservists and their aircraft only on contract. She'd thought of the move to stand up the 68th as an official USAF Aggressor squadron as a political one, not a tactical military one. "I've got a haircut booked in Phoenix for Saturday," she said. "You know how hard it is to get an appointment with my guy?"

Meany pointed at her stubble with his cup. "Probably charges a bomb. I reckon I could do that with some garden shears, *and* you could pay me in bourbon." He drained the coffee and crushed the cup, throwing it in a nearby trash can. "They'll keep us on the line. China is going to throw everything at us now, and whatever assets we've got in theatre, they aren't going to be enough."

Once again, Michael Chase found himself sleeping on a cot in clothes he hadn't changed since yesterday. But this time he was under the West Wing of the White House, so he'd been asked for shirt, shoe and trouser sizes, and clothes were being bought. Which sounded more glamorous than it was, because a basement is a basement, and this one was crammed with a lot of people in a few small rooms. In the quiet between the Taiwanese preemptive strike and the inevitable Chinese retaliation, he'd grabbed a power nap, shaved and had some overdue breakfast. Then he'd called home and tried to reassure his family they were as safe in rural Indiana as anywhere in the country, but what could he really say? At this point, nothing. Chase had heard that the Secret Service had tried to persuade Carliotti to get out of DC to somewhere like Nebraska, or NORAD in Colorado, in case China went suddenly and unexpectedly nuclear, but she had shut that down straight away. "People see me holding press conferences from inside a fallout shelter, it's game over for the stock market, the economy and civil order," she said.

NSC ExCom, the small subset of officials Carliotti had gathered around her, was in permanent session, and Chase was still surprised to find himself there. Carliotti had pared the group to an absolute minimum. It comprised the President, Vice President Mark Bendheim, Homeland Security Secretary Emily Harvey, Defense Secretary Ervan Holoman and her Chief of Staff, Rosenstern. Plus himself, of course.

They each had the role of feeding into ExCom input from the outside world. They weren't supposed to be just giving their own opinions. "Whenever you open your mouth, I want pros and cons; I want for and against. I want you to represent the voices who disagree with you as well as those who agree. If I think you aren't, you don't belong here, is that clear?" Carliotti told them in laying out her ground rules. "You are all experts on each other's business in here. There is no patent on the truth. I chose some of you because I don't necessarily agree with you. I don't want groupthink here. We argue, we weigh the odds, then we decide. And if we can't agree, *I* decide."

Chase's role was to be the voice of the China experts assembled earlier. They were an eclectic bunch of military, security, intelligence, political, economic and academic thought leaders he was tasked to pull together via video link whenever input was needed. He'd just come from a meeting with his "expert group" and rejoined the ongoing ExCom meeting, which had just been given a download on the

422

preliminary damage assessment from the early morning preemptive strike.

The meeting of the China Expert Panel, as he'd suggested they call themselves, had neither started, nor ended, as he'd planned.

There were nearly 20 people in the room when he'd arrived, including several he had not invited but whom others had pulled in. He'd had to scramble to get a few of them security clearances. He had a speech prepared, including the brief he'd been given by Rosenstern. He also had an agenda for the meeting: some things he wanted input on immediately, some things he wanted them to go away and get advice on.

A plan never survives contact with the enemy, he reflected. The minute he walked into the Pentagon conference room, and while he was still looking around, trying to work out exactly who the hell everyone was, the DIA's James Burroughs took him aside. "Can we have a word before we get started with whatever that is?" he said, looking pointedly at the folder Chase was holding. "A few of us have a suggestion for you."

Chase had frowned, looked at his watch, felt the ground shifting underneath him. "Uh, sure. Outside," he said, trying to regain a little control. They commandeered a two-person room nearby. "What's up?" Chase asked.

"China Expert Panel," Burroughs said.

"What about it?"

"The name suggests you're going to come in with a list of things you want advice on, we'll talk, you'll listen, and then you'll distill what we said and present it to the National Security Council. About right?"

"Yeah, pretty much. I'm your voice on the NSC. I'll do my best to represent all views and ..."

"Not the best use of everyone's time, Michael," Burroughs said. "Not the best way to tap into the collective brainpower of those people and the organizations they represent."

"About that," Michael said, letting his own stress and frustration surface. "There are at least 20 people in that room, half of whom I don't know and didn't invite. Do you know what a P.I.T.A. it was getting them all cleared for this?"

"I do. I'm sorry," Burroughs said disarmingly. "I should have checked it with you. But unless I'm mistaken, this nation is now at war, and the NSC needs more than the usual DC 'expert panel' to help it navigate the months ahead."

"Yes, you should have cleared it with me," Chase agreed. "So before I kick you off this team, tell me what you were thinking."

Over the next 10 minutes, Burroughs laid out his idea to Chase, explaining exactly who he had invited to the party and why. The biggest shock had been that one of the man's precious invitations had been extended not to a person at all, but to an AI.

"HOLMES?" Chase had asked, puzzled by the acronym.

"Heuristic Ordinary Language Machine Exploratory System," Burroughs had explained. "An NSA AI. For the last few months they have had it studying every single known deliberation, decision and action of every member of the Chinese Communist Party Central Committee since its inception in 1927, cross-referencing these with the known historical record based on both public sources and intelligence from every Five Eyes intelligence and security organization."

"Should I be impressed?" Chase asked, still somewhat annoyed at Burroughs for going off reservation without consulting him. "So, NSA has an AI that can read."

"No," Burroughs told him. "NSA has an AI that is freaking *spooky*. It has been predicting every move of the Chinese leadership in this crisis since before it began its blockade of Taiwan. We need it on the 'red' team in this thing, role-playing China."

Chase couldn't argue against that. Inside 30 minutes, they'd agreed how to proceed. Chase hadn't sent anyone home.

Back at the first meeting of the Executive Committee of the NSC, formalities had not lasted long. Most of the others referred to each other by first names, though they still called Carliotti Madam President. Chase wasn't anywhere near first names with the others yet, though they were calling him Michael. Ties and shirt collars had been loosened, jackets thrown over the backs of chairs. Both the President and Emily Harvey had kicked off their shoes.

Carliotti waited until Chase sat down. "So, Michael, the Defense Secretary has just updated us on the military situation in the Strait, but in a nutshell, China has pulled its aircraft back for now but has gone on the attack at sea, targeting any and all Taiwanese military and civilian shipping while it hunts for the U-boats that hit its destroyers. The Taiwanese attack seems to have taken them by surprise, and we suspect China's generals are urgently seeking direction from Beijing on how to respond. So what does your brains trust predict they are going to do next?"

"JWC, Madam President," he said. "Not 'brains trust,' not even 'expert panel.'"

"Sorry?"

"What they've called themselves: Joint Wargaming Council. They've decided to war-game everything we put to them. Defense Intelligence is hosting and providing the support resources; all arms of the forces and intelligence agencies are contributing data and intel; State and Academia the political and cultural angles. Cybercom is providing AI support to present and synthesize all the inputs. ExCom plays blue; the JWC are playing red."

"That's a damn smart approach Michael," Emily Harvey said. "We've been talking about having a joint agencies war-gaming capability for years, and you just went and did it."

"Not me. They came up with the idea themselves while I was … having a nap," he demurred.

Carliotti smiled. "Anyone else would have taken the credit. That's the kind of honesty I want to see, Michael. So, your 'JWC,' what does it say China will do?"

Chase looked at his notes. "Try to shape the information space to make it look like they are the victims of an unprovoked attack and justify retaliation. Hit back at Taiwan. *And* they are going to go for our aircraft carriers."

Chase could see frowns and stunned looks around the room. "Our carriers?" the Defense Secretary asked. "My people are saying attacks on Taiwan's air defense system and airfields, attempt to achieve air dominance, destroy Taiwan's air force, and then bombard the island with rocket and missile attacks on military and infrastructure targets …" He frowned. "This is Taiwan's war for now. Why would they go immediately on the front foot with attacks on US forces?"

"Because, respectfully, the President announced that Taiwan's war is our war, and China is big enough to walk and chew gum. It can take on Taiwan and try to scare the US and our allies from piling in," Chase said. He stood and walked to a floor-to-ceiling map of the Operations Area. "We currently have two carriers, one here east of Okinawa, and the other here, southeast of Luzon in the Philippines. Both are within range of Chinese carrier-based aircraft."

"No, they are *outside* the range of PLA Navy aircraft," The Defense Secretary, Holoman, corrected him. "Besides, we flew off most of our combat aircraft. And our carriers are protected by land-based missile batteries as well as their own pickets. We aren't that careless."

"They are outside the range of PLA Navy aircraft planning a *return* trip," Chase said. "Which is how we would think. We would make our plans around the need to get our pilots back alive and conserve our forces. The JWC plan is to attack the US carriers with aircraft they are sending on a *one-way* trip." Chase moved a little and pointed to a point in the Philippine Sea east of Taiwan. "And we have to remember, China has 60 or 70 aircraft here, on the carrier *Fujian*, which are all *uncrewed*. No pilots to lose." Chase sat down again. "JWC predicts they will swarm us with kamikaze aircraft, launch cruise and anti-ship missiles to strike the pickets and degrade air defenses, and finish with DF-26s."

"Which are?" Vice President Bendheim asked.

"Ballistic carrier-killer missiles," Chase said, folding his hands in front of him on the table to stop them shaking. He wasn't used to speaking so long, in front of such an audience. With the risk of being so, so wrong. "Like the HACM missiles we just shipped to Taiwan, which China knows about. Ballistic missiles may be less accurate, but they're much harder to intercept. China knows if they can hit even one of

427

our carriers—cause mass casualties—public opinion will waver, Congress will be split, our allies will lose confidence …"

"Wait, we put *hypersonic* missiles on Taiwan?" Carliotti asked Holoman, surprised. The look on his face told her the answer. "Forget that for now. Would this change anything?"

Carliotti waited for her Defense Secretary to chew through the implications. He was a former Secretary of Navy. It didn't take him long. "I need to put it to the Joint Chiefs, but I'd say we have to move the *Enterprise* and the *Bush* further back. I know I haven't heard about any massed kamikaze attack scenario being run. But moving our flat-tops further away from Taiwan would make them unavailable to directly support operations there."

"Which is why we flew their aircraft off anyway, right?" Carliotti asked. "We *know* they're vulnerable."

"I guess. This … I need to confer with the Joint Chiefs," Holoman said and stood. But then he stopped and addressed Carliotti. "Madam President, this 'Joint Wargaming Council'—how seriously am I supposed to weigh its predictions around what China will do?"

Carliotti looked at Chase, then back to Holoman. "They just found a flaw in our strategy and made a uniquely Chinese plan to exploit it. So I'd say 'high probability' for now," she said. "Until they are consistently proven wrong."

Holoman left. Carliotti wasn't finished with Chase. "China won't attack our bases on Japan or the Philippines yet?"

"Not yet. They'll be wary of widening the war to other nations too quickly. They want to scare our allies away, not go to war with them yet."

428

"Japan just sunk a Chinese warship," Vice President Bendheim pointed out. "I'd say they'd be pretty upset at that."

"Japan is already wavering," Carliotti said, frowning. "I spoke with the Japanese PM. The Chinese ship was sunk by automated defenses, and they have no idea how or why they were triggered. He's considering making an 'expression of regret' to the Chinese Chairman."

"*What?*" Bendheim said. "We've got half of our forces on Okinawa, and he's thinking of kowtowing to Beijing?"

"He said he was happy to support Operation Skytrain," Carliotti said. "And humanitarian operations. Not so happy to support Okinawa being used as a base for offensive operations against Chinese mainland targets."

"We can't afford to lose Japan. We can't contain China just with forces based in the Philippines, *especially* if we need to pull our carriers back out of range." Bendheim stood, picking up his cell phone. "I'll call the Japanese PM too. It might help to remind him that if China doesn't accept his apology and starts raining cruise missiles on Japanese cities, he's going to need a friend."

Rosenstern's cell phone buzzed, and he picked it up. "Chinese aircraft forming up over East Coast bases," he said. "Storm is about to break."

Mushroom and Shredder were already locked into their pods, their aircraft orbiting over the *Fujian* and waiting for the rest of Ao Yin Squadron to form up. Operational security meant they were observing radio silence, but that didn't stop them speaking with each other over the fiber-optic network that snaked between their pods. Another advantage of virtual cockpits was that pilots speaking "aircraft to aircraft" or contacting their carrier didn't need to leak any radio energy.

Mushroom ran an instrument check and swiveled her head, checking the virtual sky and position of the surrounding aircraft. It was a gray, overcast morning. There was a tropical storm front moving over the top of *Fujian*, dark thunderclouds between 10,000 and 20,000 feet all the way to the target. That seemed appropriate somehow. She opened a channel to Chen's pod. "Hey, Shredder. We're really doing this."

"We are. You know that crate of San Miguel I owe you?"

She became instantly suspicious. "Yeah, why?"

"How about double or nothing that I get a kill and you don't?" he teased.

She didn't like that bet. He was flying air-to-air cover in Bo's flight. Her Chongming had gone up armed with two Eagle Strike anti-radar missiles, her mission objective to take out one of the carrier's anti-air missile defense pickets. Her machine had little to no chance of even getting its missiles away, and Shredder knew it. "I got a better one. How about double or nothing you die first," she said. That one had a better chance. He was going in first, to engage the carrier fighter screen. The American stealth fighters would probably swat him from the sky before he got within 50 miles of them. She, on the other hand, would be down on the deck, following him in, launching two sea-skimming supersonic missiles at her target as soon as anyone in the squadron got a fix on it.

"Alright," he said. "I got eight missiles; you got two. I like those odds."

Mushroom smiled. There was a reason he owed *her* a crate and not the other way around.

Secretary of Defense Holoman had returned from consulting the Joint Chiefs with their recommendation for dealing with the threat of an imminent attack on the US Seventh Fleet carriers.

Strike the Chinese carriers first. Senior officials in the State Department were aghast, muttering that it was the equivalent of the Japanese attack on Pearl Harbor since there was no evidence that China really was planning to attack US Seventh Fleet vessels. They were referred to the shooting-down of the British Globemaster and told to stop trying to find reasons for inaction, and instead to put themselves on a war footing.

They had positioned the HACM missiles on Taiwan for a reason, and there was a very strong possibility that they would not survive the coming high-explosive rain that was about to be unleashed on the island. The Joint Chiefs had agreed there was a possibility China would target their carriers with naval aircraft and ballistic missiles, and the carrier strike groups were ordered to pull back and put their defenses on high alert.

Two US attack submarines were currently in position to be able to launch anti-ship missiles against Chinese carrier strike groups. None were in torpedo range. Given the limited number of missiles each carried, it was decided they would be used to degrade the surface-to-air defenders of the Chinese carriers *Liaoning* and *Shandong*, going after their air warfare destroyers. With Chinese vessels now on high alert, their chances of a successful attack were rated as low, but they would at least serve to distract the carrier groups from the primary attack vector: air.

431

B-21s out of Guam, Okinawa and Darwin were already airborne. Each carried 16 AGM-158 air-to-surface missiles, armed with 1,000 lb. warheads. The two from Guam were moving into position to launch on the *Shandong* carrier group, the two from Okinawa would attack *Liaoning*, and four from the Australian base of Darwin would launch on *Fujian*'s strike group. The targets of their 128 missiles were not the carriers themselves but their air warfare escorts.

A subsonic cruise missile would never get through to the carrier at the center of a strike group. Which was why the Hypersonic Attack Cruise Missile had been developed.

Two of the HACM missiles would be loaded onto Taiwanese F-16s. Pilots who had been trained in their use on ranges in the USA would carry out the attacks. They would launch from inside Taiwanese airspace, targeting *Liaoning* at the northern entrance to the Strait and *Shandong* in the south.

The third missile was being loaded into the payload bay of Bunny O'Hare's Widow. It was the only option, since *her* target was currently 617 miles east of Taiwan, and reaching it required the pilot launching it to weave their way through the strengthened Chinese combat air patrols watching Taiwan's eastern skies. A non-stealth aircraft would never make it through, and Aggressor's F-22s could not carry the HACM. The Operational planners had weighed their options for an attack on the *Fujian*: a swarming attack with cruise missiles launched from B-21 Raiders and submarines or a low-level solo penetration by a stealth aircraft. They had gone with the latter because their B-21s had been used in the opening attack on Chinese mainland targets and weren't available, and the available submarines were either not in position or not able to bring enough missiles to the attack.

Having only one HACM in her weapons bay this time meant she had room for six medium-range and four short-

432

range air-to-air missiles, but that was little comfort. If she needed to use them to defend herself, it meant she had been discovered and she was pretty much screwed anyway.

A lot was being done to make sure she would get a clear run in which to take her shot. The British carrier HMS *Queen Elizabeth* was the closest of the RIMPAC carriers to *Fujian* and its pilots were aching for payback after the takedown of the RAF Globemaster.

Meany had pointed to its current location on a screen during their mission planning. "The Lizzie is here, northeast of the Fujian. They'll engage her outer perimeter patrols, try to draw the carrier's air defenses into a fight in the northeast." He pointed at the route and ingress point they'd plotted for her. "You approach from the southwest, fast and low; get as close as you can to reduce the missile's run time. Hopefully they won't see you, and if they do, you're just one plane, right? You'll be in range by the time they spot you anyway, so get your missile away and bug the hell out."

Her machine had been towed out under the open sky again so it could be armed. Bunny had a hard time tearing her eyes away from those skies, every bird or speck on her vision looking to her like an incoming missile. Mentally, she was still trying to shake the shadow of their recent failure in protecting the British Globemaster crew, and was squatted on her haunches watching the ordnance specialists at work on her machine. There was something about the sense of order and purpose of ground crews at work that relaxed her. It was the opposite of the chaos that was the mind of Bunny O'Hare. She had never mastered the whole business of order and purpose, had in fact been kicked out of the RAAF nest after her first combat posting in Syria—theoretically for insubordination, but in reality simply because she was not now, and had never been, adapted to the necessary business of executing orders she disagreed with.

So had begun her life as a contractor, most often with DARPA, the US weapons research agency, but more recently with Aggressor Inc., because at the end of the day, what she burned for was still the same thing she had burned for as a 17-year-old: the opportunity to fly fast jets, whether sitting in a cockpit or in-silico, in a virtual cockpit a hundred miles away. As she walked past a line of Taiwanese Teng Yun drones—local copies of the venerable US MQ-9 Reaper—she was pulled back to the time she had first been offered the chance to fly combat drones.

<< *Bunny O'Hare was sitting in a lockup on Crete after slugging her CO with her flight helmet—a longer story—when a DARPA project manager by the name of Shelly Kovacs arrived with a cup of tea and a question.*

"Lieutenant O'Hare, have you heard of the F-47B Fantom?"

"The Navy drone?" Bunny had nodded. She hadn't had many visitors in the brig. Shelly was the highlight of her day. "I heard of it. Haven't seen one. It's like the Russian Okhotnik, right?"

Kovacs leaned forward, a gleam in her eyes. "You engaged an Okhotnik flight, didn't you? I read your combat report and pulled the data logs. You ..."

"I know what I did. I nearly got killed by one of those bat-winged mothers."

"You destroyed one. Your CO destroyed two. But in your final dogfight you used an unorthodox evasive maneuver that went directly against the algorithm your AI was telling you to follow, and it ..."

"Would have got me killed, if that Okhotnik had been carrying missiles. But it wasn't."

"How could you know?"

"The flight profile of that Okhotnik flight suggested they were recon birds."

"Suggested?"

"Yeah. It was a gut thing. We bet on them not carrying missiles."

Kovacs looked disappointed.

"You DARPA types don't like pilots telling you it's a gut thing, am I right?" O'Hare guessed. "You can't program that."

"Oh, we can. Except it isn't gut. It's probability theory, not gut or instinct. Or you can call it what it is, a wild ass guess."

O'Hare had laughed. "Fair enough. But you aren't here to talk about those Okhotniks," she guessed. "So why are you here?"

Kovacs looked suddenly serious. "You're right. I'm here to talk about how you overrode the command-and-control protocols for six Boeing Airpower Teaming System Loyal Wingman drones, took command of them in flight and then used them to engage a wave of Russian OVOD cruise missiles."

"I was out of missiles myself. They were the only platforms airborne and available."

"You commandeered six drones by hacking my software mid-dogfight!"

"That was your software? Sorry. If you didn't want me to, you shouldn't have built it so I could."

Bunny smiled at the memory. Kovacs had gotten her the job at DARPA, organized the paperwork for dual citizenship and her acceptance into the US Air Force Reserve, helped her land several good roles at DARPA and the defense industry afterward. That had been the start of a wonderful friendship with Shelly Kovacs. One of the few she hadn't screwed up and could look back on without regret.

"You don't have to do this," a voice behind her said. She twisted her head around and saw Meany there.

"How long have you been staring at my butt?" she asked, standing.

He ignored her. "It's a volunteer mission. If you don't want to fly it, they'll find a Taiwan Air Force F-16 to fly it."

"And he or she will get killed before they've gone feet wet," Bunny predicted. "Not my style."

He held out a hand to help her stand, the actuators on his exoskeleton whirring audibly as he crouched. Most of the time she didn't even notice anymore, but up close like this … he'd been damn lucky to even survive taking a hit over Syria, let alone to be able to *walk* again. "We're bugging out, like I thought," he said. "Just got the word. Okinawa. You'll join us there."

"I'll need to tank," she pointed out. They were both going through the motions, like it was going to happen. Like she *wasn't* going to die sometime in the next hour.

"It's being organized. And that's not all. Assuming you make it out of here, I was just told you'll have support on this mission. Salt, Flowmax and Flatline are going to rendezvous with you at the first waypoint. You'll have *three* Widows watching your six. You just do what you have to, get your butts to Okinawa. First bourbon is on me."

Salt, Flowmax and Flatline? Well, Black Widows were the only machines in the Aggressor Inc. inventory with the range to escort her anywhere. *The more the merrier,* Bunny thought.

The ordnance crew pulled out from under her machine and the payload bay doors closed. As she watched, one crew dog plugged her fighter into the power grid and another who had climbed up inside the cockpit began the boot procedure for her avionics.

Before going out to her machine, she turned to Meany. "I wasn't actually thinking about what would happen if I *didn't* succeed. I was thinking about what would happen if I *did.*"

"Well, that's ... typical you, I guess," he decided.

She clapped him on the shoulder and took a step toward her machine to do a last walkaround. As she did, air raid warning sirens began wailing across the base.

"Come on!" Meany said, setting himself in motion toward the hardened concrete shelters about 200 yards away.

Bunny ran in the opposite direction. She slid under the wing of her Widow and came to a stop under the hatch leading up into the cockpit. The crew dog inside was still in the cockpit and about to shut the avionics down again.

"Don't kill those systems!" she yelled up at him. "Get down here while I start the engines, pull the power cable, get the chocks off the wheels and then get yourself into cover!"

"Ma'am, that's an air raid warning," the man yelled back, hesitating. "You can't ..."

"That was an *order,* airman," she yelled.

She moved out of the way as he slid down and ran to the side of the machine to grab some ear protection while she climbed up inside the Widow, strapped in and booted the engines to life. When she waved to him, he ran over to disconnect the power and pull away the wheel chocks. How much time did she have? Minutes? Seconds? There was no time for running checklists. She did a quick scan of the engine readouts, looked out the starboard side of her machine to see the ground technician backing away from her machine with wheel chocks in hand and gave him a salute. He saluted back, indicating she was clear to roll, though he didn't look happy about it. She eased her throttle forward, the Widow jerked and began moving, and he ran, bent double, for the hangar Meany was still clomping toward.

Bunny's Widow had been parked on a circular turning apron to refuel, and she had first to exit the apron, get onto a taxiway and then point her machine toward the main runway.

"Taichung Tower, this is Aggressor Black Widow, no call sign, requesting permission for immediate takeoff."

Bunny could hear yelling in the background and could imagine the controlled pandemonium going on up there. "Negative, Aggressor, we have incoming. Get out of that machine and get to cover."

Bunny didn't bother to respond. As she looked over to the runway to check for traffic, she saw a shadow in the corner of her eye, a low-flying object that crossed the runway from behind her and slammed *right into the control tower.* It dissolved in flame and glass, the cupola toppling onto the international air terminal building beside it.

Forget this, Bunny thought. There was a narrow taxiway ahead of her, and apart from a few dozen people running pell-mell for the illusory safety of nearby buildings, it was clear of vehicles and aircraft. She gripped her flight stick, kept her toes on the wheel brakes and pushed her throttles all the way forward. The engine note changed to a whine, and then a scream. The airframe began shaking so hard her teeth were rattling, and she made one last check to each side and ahead of her. She saw Meany stopped by the entrance to the bunker, watching with a look of disbelief on his face.

Yeah, I get that a lot. Bunny lifted her feet from the wheel brakes and the Widow leaped forward.

Five hundred yards ahead of her, the panicked driver of a small fuel truck stopped his truck right on the taxiway, jumped from his cab and ran for his life.

Oh, shit, Bunny thought.

23. 'Meat kill'

Meany heard the engines of the Widow crank up and turned at the entrance to the bunker to look back out across the airfield. As he did, a ground crew technician ran past him into the bunker, pausing only to say, "That woman is crazy, sir."

He couldn't disagree. As he watched, the Widow taxied off the turnaround apron it was parked on and rumbled over the concrete taxiway toward the runway.

She's not …

She was. He saw the Widow pause before crossing over to the main runway. Taichung had two parallel runways, and the nearest was still 100 yards from her machine. As it waited there, Meany heard the whine of a jet engine low overhead, looked up and saw the slim outline of a subsonic cruise missile scream right over him. He watched in horror as it flew right across the airfield … and buried itself in the control tower.

He ducked, backing inside the doorway to the hangar. The blast doors were already up, and he knew he should get inside, but he looked for the Widow again and found it now. O'Hare had swung it around and pointed it along the taxiway, and as he watched, she lit the pursuit fighter's tail and *accelerated*.

And for a minute, it looked like she was going to make it.

Then he flinched as more explosions began to ripple across the air base, he saw a panicked truck driver abandon

440

his truck right in front of Bunny's Widow, and then a Chinese missile struck right behind the fuel truck. The concussion from another explosion nearby flung him back inside the bunker and laid him flat.

Bunny saw the truck 500 yards ahead, saw that she wouldn't have the airspeed to even hop herself over it, and pulled her harness tight, reaching for the ejection handle between her thighs. She grabbed it in both hands ...

And then the truck exploded in a roiling black ball of flame, and through it, she could see the taxiway ahead of her was suddenly clear. Or mostly. The blast tried to shove her machine sideways, and taking her hands off the ejection handle, she put them back on throttle and stick. She twitched her stick to get her nose pointed right at the cloud of smoke that had been the fuel truck and ... closed her eyes.

The Widow blasted through the smoke, Bunny saw the carcass of the flipped truck flash past on her port side, and she had only beautiful, clear tarmac ahead of her. Her airspeed rocketed up through 150 knots, and she eased the stick back, banking away to the right, toward the forested mountains of central Taiwan. She eased her throttle back and took stock. The stink of burnt fuel filled the cockpit.

It smelled like death.

Miss is as good as a mile, she told herself as her landing gear tucked itself back up into her airframe with a thud. Her eyes scanned her instruments for signs of damage, and seeing none, she checked the skies. If China was counterattacking with cruise missiles now, there was no guarantee its fighters weren't trying to penetrate Taiwanese airspace. She checked

441

her radar warning receiver and, sure enough, it showed hostile search radars all around her. She was flying into a high-explosive metal shitstorm.

Her nav screen was tracking her position and it showed a highway ahead that snaked along the north of a ridgeline, from west to east across the island. Highway 8? *Hope somebody installed an automatic toll chip on this baby,* she thought. She dropped her Widow down to treetop and billboard height, just above the powerlines that bordered the two-lane highway, and focused on threading the needle through the valleys, under any Chinese fighters overhead, and over the small ridges that would take her to the east coast.

She began muttering to herself without even realizing it. *THIS is where you live. THIS is your time. You OWN the sky. You are a freaking NINJA, and your shadow will be the ONLY thing anyone will see.*

"Ao Yin pilots, we have an airborne radar bearing two eight two degrees, range 80 to 100," Casino announced. "AI is calling it a US Navy Sentinel. The Sentinel will be well behind the carrier fighter screen, which means they are probably less than 50 miles ahead. They may already see us. 'A' flight will prosecute the contact. 'B' flight, maintain course and monitor passive sensors. 'C' flight, stay in trail; arm missiles."

'Shredder' Chen felt the muscles in his abdomen tighten and tried to relax. Bo had divided their 18 aircraft into three flights of six. 'A' and 'B' flights were armed for air-to-air combat. His machine was in 'A' flight with Casino. Mushroom's machine was about 10 miles behind, in 'C' flight. They were spread across the sky in a front about 20 miles wide, with 'A' flight high, at 40,000 feet, expecting to be the first ones discovered by the American radars. 'B' and 'C' flights were down with the fish, skimming the wavetops, trusting in their stealthy form factors and the curvature of the earth to hide them from their enemy.

Chinese satellites crisscrossing the operations area in low earth orbit were constantly updating the American carrier strike group's position and feeding it to the *Fujian*. They didn't have perfect information—the data was always crucial minutes old—but they had a pretty damn good idea where the skyscraper-sized American carrier and most of its air warfare pickets were. It now lay 120 miles ahead of them. What they couldn't see was the stealth fighter patrols protecting it. He was prepared for the less stealthy X-47B drones, but was hoping for the ubiquitous F-35C Panther.

The *crewed* American fighter.

Only a meat kill would be worthy of the memory of his sister, Li.

His brief combat history told Shredder the Americans would probably see his Chongming before he saw them, even, or especially if, he was using his own phased array radar. The tightly focused radar beams would be nearly invisible to any lesser opponent, but the technology had been invented in the west, and it seemed the American fighters like the F-22, F-35 and Black Widow were a generation ahead of the Chinese in this regard. His Chongming had other advantages. It was more maneuverable than any of the American aircraft, more adept at evading their missiles, which were shorter ranged than his PL-15s. And unlike a crewed aircraft, it was not flown by pilots who would lose their minds in terror as the enemy closed on them. No matter what happened to his Chongming, Shredder was going to end his mission by

443

popping the hatch of his pod, going to his debrief and grabbing a cup of tea.

His US pilot adversaries could not say the same.

He locked in the radar contact Casino had reported, checked his position in the formation and then opened a line to Mushroom. "Going to get a little busy now," he warned her. "Just wanted to say good luck."

Asien Chen wanted to say more than that. He wanted to tell his comrade Mushroom he loved her like the sister he'd lost. Maybe even more than Li. Li had been older, absent, the golden child whose accomplishments he could never match. Mushroom was more real, more a friend than Li had ever been. He loved watching the way she cut down anyone who showed her the slightest sign they thought she was weaker than them. Loved the way she looked up to him even though she was a better, more disciplined, more all-round pilot than he would ever be. Chen had instincts, sure, and better reflexes, but Mushroom knew her machine inside out and could command it to do things Chen didn't even know it was capable of.

"Nah, you want to distract and jinx me," she replied. "You aren't getting that San Miguel, boy. Just try to keep your machine alive as long as you can, alright? If the Americans are shooting at *you*, there's less chance they're shooting at me."

Mushroom wasn't feeling anywhere near as cocky as she was trying to sound. Her nav screen showed her flight, spread out across the sea in line-abreast formation about two miles apart. A hundred twenty miles ahead, it showed the last known position of the American carrier group. The carrier's outer pickets, anti-air and anti-submarine warfare destroyers were also plotted. Her task was to be able to tell one from the other—though her RWR software should do that—and to launch her missiles at the radar signals from one of the air-warfare pickets. She was already within missile range, but she needed a target, and then she needed to follow her missiles in for as long as possible so that she could keep feeding them data on the target and they wouldn't need to turn on their onboard radars too soon. Twelve missiles would be directed at the same target she fired on, closing simultaneously from different aircraft spread across a 12-mile front.

Chang Fu and Fei Yi squadrons were executing identical missions but attacking from different vectors to the southeast and east of the American carrier strike group. Together they would hit the American defenses with 36 anti-ship missiles and then move into jamming mode, adding whatever remained of their 54 aircraft to the attack the Americans were trying to defend against. She knew one of the American Arleigh Burke destroyers held up to 96 anti-air missiles, which could be ripple fired, but they had been briefed that most of the missile types fired by the American air warfare destroyers were required to keep a data link to their ship in order to track their targets.

That made them susceptible to jamming.

Flying in behind their missiles, radiating jamming energy into the sky ahead of them—exercises on ranges in China against Chinese technology similar to the Americans' had shown the American missile defenses could be spoofed, and some of the Chinese missiles would get through.

That might not matter in the grand scheme since *Fujian*'s attack was only a decoy, to deplete and degrade the American defenses so that other attacks could succeed. But it mattered to Mushroom. She wanted to get missiles on target.

She had a bet to win.

If getting into Taiwan had been a nightmare, getting out again had proven an amble in the park. Bunny had stayed low, twisting and turning with the contours of the landscape over Taiwan and, once she got feet wet, using her Radar Warning Receiver to navigate through the belt of Chinese fighters patrolling up and down the coast.

She stayed low, held her speed at 600 knots and made no radical turns, using vertical stabilizers to yaw her machine around the patrols overhead. Down against the dappled-blue sea, her Widow's mottled, matte-gray skin was near invisible to the eye and radar. The most dangerous part of the egress was the 20-mile-wide band being patrolled by Chinese fighters, but she crossed in under two minutes, and once the radar warning indicators fell behind her, she started to breathe normally again for the first time.

A message appeared in her visor, and she checked the data that had just downloaded to her nav computer. Twenty minutes to the waypoint where she was due to meet Salt. She adjusted her heading slightly south. He was going to be up at 25,000 feet. That would not do. She flashed a message back for him to meet her down under 5,000. There was no knowing what naval assets China had out in front of her right now and it would be just her luck to run into a *Type 055* air warfare destroyer or that damn spy ship that had tracked her halfway from Guam.

An uneventful 20 minutes followed though. The only thing breaking her concentration was a brief radar signal off her forward starboard quarter. Only a tingle, then gone again.

Chinese J-20 stealth fighter? Could be. She adjusted her course to make sure she went nowhere near it.

Five miles to the waypoint. She didn't want to use her radar or radio but figured she'd pick him up on optical-infrared sensors if he was where he was supposed to be. She closed on the rendezvous position. *OK, Salt, where are you?*

The momentary flash of radar energy Bunny O'Hare had picked up was not a Chinese J-20 Mighty Dragon stealth fighter. Nor a *Type 055* air warfare destroyer.

It wasn't the *Yuan Wang Three Zero*, which lay broken on the seabed off Okinotori Atoll.

It was Salt Carlyle, making a brief scan of the sky where he expected Bunny O'Hare to be and finding her right on course and on time. He shut down his radar again for the same reason O'Hare was avoiding using hers. He had no desire to run into a Chinese patrol either.

There had been a chance she would not make it off the island and through the Chinese air patrols, but then again, he couldn't be that lucky. She'd plagued his existence since the moment Aggressor Inc.'s billionaire owner, Mark Aaronson, had signed her, and his patronage had ensured she had survived multiple incidents that would have ended the career of any other pilot. He knew what old man Aaronson saw in O'Hare because he'd actually asked him, the first time he'd recommended she be dismissed.

"She has no discipline around deportment," he had told the man, having saved up a list of beefs. "Reports for preflight briefings with about a dozen earrings in her damn ears, studs in her damn nose, eyebrows, cheeks ..."

"That must be painful under a flight helmet," Aaronson had said with a smile. He was a former pilot himself, had made his pile after leaving the Swedish Air Force, running a private charter company that over the next 20 years he'd turned into a private air force.

"She takes them out when she flies; that isn't the point," Salt said, exasperated. He went on to list the other 10 things that irritated him about O'Hare as Aaronson patiently listened.

"You have said nothing about her competency as a pilot," Aaronson observed when he was finished.

He had scowled. "She's competent enough, I guess."

"She's more than that," Aaronson said. "She's rated on about 10 aircraft, including rotary. She's been a DARPA test pilot, even helped design some of the drone wingmen we fly with and against. I was told she can fly anything with wings. No?"

"Yes. But give me a middling pilot with the right attitude over a great pilot with a bad attitude any day."

"Perhaps it is her CO who needs an attitude adjustment," the old man said with a twinkle in his eye. "None of the other pilots have complained to me."

"They're too damned scared, probably. You say something to her, you never know if she is going to laugh or throw a punch," Salt responded. "I don't understand why you took her on."

"She reminds me of my granddaughter," he said simply, and the conversation was done. After that remark, Salt did some digging and found out Aaronson's granddaughter had committed suicide at 20. And suddenly his misplaced affection for the troubled Bunny O'Hare made a weird kind of sense.

"Alright, O'Hare, come to papa," he said out loud. He'd marked her position on his tac screen and banked left, away from their rendezvous waypoint. He was still up at 20,000 feet and wanted to put about 20 miles between himself and the Australian pilot when she hit the waypoint, get on her six before he hailed her.

It struck him as more than passingly ironic that he was flying "her" Black Widow, just back from having its nosewheel repaired and the stealth anti-radar coating reapplied to its otherwise undamaged nose section. Her ground crew had used the opportunity to paint a tiny Playboy bunny along with her name above the Aggressor Inc. squadron badge on the Widow's nose.

Shame she was unlikely to live long enough to thank them.

It was looking like 'Shredder' Chen would not live long enough to collect on his bet with Mushroom.

They had been closing on the American AWACS drone, but as none of them were carrying homing anti-radar missiles, they had been trying to close to visual identification range so that they could engage without giving their position away. Knock out the carrier group's eyes and ears, and every other element of their attack would have a better chance of success. That was Casino's logic, and no one challenged it.

Except it was a damned trap. As they'd moved within 20 miles of the Sentinel, about 70 miles farther east than the main body of the carrier group, a surface radar had suddenly lit the formation up, and seconds later, a volley of ground-to-air missiles rose toward them from the sea almost directly below.

Shredder hadn't needed Casino's order of *"Break, break, break!"* in order to react. He already had two PL-15 missiles aimed down the bearing to the Sentinel's radar, and he fired them in autonomous targeting mode, just like Mushroom had taught him, barely waiting for the second missile to drop out of his payload bay before he flung his Chongming onto its back and pointed it vertically at the sea.

Right at the source of the attack. He could see the American missiles rising up to meet them, streaming tails of white smoke. He flew his Chongming straight at them. At a closing speed over Mach 5, he had barely seconds to react before the missiles struck. As the proximity warning sounded in his ears, he shoved his flight stick fully forward and held it there and fired decoys into his wake.

His aircraft flipped like a pancake through the air, tail over nose, spraying decoys in a sphere around itself.

Not only did he decoy the missiles aimed at him, but he pulled two more missiles into his cloud of chaff and flares, where they detonated harmlessly.

He was still "alive," but pulling his machine out of its head-over-heels death dive was going to be easier said than done. It was falling toward the sea now, almost completely out of control. He tried pulling his stick back to reverse the rotation of the machine, but the momentum was too great. He still had some horizontal control authority though, and he tilted his stick back and hard right, trying to disrupt the near gyroscopic spin of his Chongming. Eventually it rebalanced and he got control back, flattening out only 500 feet over the sea.

Directly ahead of him, beam on, was the American destroyer that had fired on them. It was a low, gray silhouette on the horizon, and as he screamed toward it at a speed near Mach 1.3, a line of tracer fire from its close-in weapons snaked toward his machine. Shocked, he watched the tracer float almost lazily toward him until suddenly it was whipping past his virtual cockpit like bolts from a laser. He swerved left. The tracer was following him, so he put his machine into a corkscrewing roll, its nose still pointed at the destroyer, horizon rolling sickeningly, tracers whipping past on all sides now but unable to lock on him because of the insanity of his maneuver—acrobatics that no human pilot would have been able to achieve.

The American destroyer grew closer, and time dilated. *I can't make it,* he decided. *I might get past the ship, but it will tag me as I pull away. It can't miss.*

Then it occurred to him that this was one of the carrier pickets 'C' flight was intended to attack. He'd gone up to find and kill American fighters, but here was an American destroyer, right in his sights! The acid words Colonel Wang had burned into his skin suddenly came to him again. *I need pilots who are not mindless robots, blindly executing orders. I need pilots who can think.*

He focused on the center of his screen, ignoring the dizzying, nauseating, roller-coaster roll of his machine to stay focused on the narrow gray shape in the center of his cockpit view that was growing larger and larger. He aimed his fighter at the middle of the ship, the box-shaped superstructure holding its bridge and antenna arrays. In his payload bay were six PL-15 missiles, each with a 100 lb. HE warhead. It would have been impossible for him to do anything in the wildly gyrating Chongming if he had been physically inside the cockpit, but he was not. He reached out with his left hand

and calmly armed his missiles. He had nearly a third of a tank of fuel remaining. His machine was a kamikaze missile flying at nearly one-and-a-half times the speed of sound ...

It buried itself in the destroyer's superstructure ... and his screen went black.

'Casino' Bo had also survived the ambush by the destroyer. Two of his aircraft had not. He was trying to gather his pilots, at the same time expecting at any moment to hear or see another volley of ground-to-air missiles come at them from the vessel below.

Which ... he still had the missile radar warning warbling in his ears, so why was the ship no longer engaging them?

He banked his machine, searching for the vessel with his optical infrared cameras until ... there!

Tian ä! What in the hell?

As he watched, a Chongming fighter closed on the destroyer. The ship was firing its radar-guided autocannon at the Chinese fighter, but the Chinese machine was corkscrewing like a firework, throwing chaff clouds into the air behind it, just feet above the sea. A missile lanced out from the ship toward the Chinese fighter, but it was too low, and the missile didn't track.

It would be hit, any moment now. It had to be. It was flying through a hail of cannon fire.

But then it reached the ship, smacked into its superstructure, and detonated, a gout of fire bursting out of the other side of the ship's bridge. The explosion flipped the entire top section of the superstructure into the air, slamming it into the antenna mast just aft. The mast heeled over sideways, the ship heeling with it from the hammer blow of the supersonic fighter striking it side-on. Then the ship righted itself, trailing smoke.

"A4 is down," Casino heard Chen's voice report. "Anyone see if I hit that bastard ship?"

The missile radar warning alarm in Casino's helmet stopped warbling.

"Sentinel *down!*" he heard Chen's voice again. The man was breaking protocol. "Dead" pilots were supposed to quit their pods and debrief. "I fired two missiles in autonomous mode before I was destroyed; the Sentinel is down!" Chen said, his voice both elated and tinged with disbelief at what he had just done from beyond the grave.

Chen had single-handedly blinded the carrier's eyes and ears in their sector. Casino opened a channel to the command-and-control center on *Fujian*. "*Fujian*, Ao Yin Leader. We have opened a gap in the carrier's defenses. Sending my coordinates; recommend you vector all surface attacks through this sector." Casino did not celebrate yet. The American carrier had multiple layers of defense, both on the sea and in the air. They had simply poked a small hole in one of them. It would be up to their ground-attack aircraft to exploit it now.

"A2 is down!" one of his pilots reported. "Missile ... I didn't see it ... air-to-air missile. From the east."

Casino quickly checked his tactical screen. They were being hunted now, picked off, no doubt by US stealth fighters. The adversary was not completely blind after all. 'A' flight was now down to four aircraft. The attack had come from the east, the opposite direction to the US carrier. A decoy, intended to pull them away to search for their attacker?

But their mission was not to tangle with the carrier's fighters. It was to draw fire from the surface defenders.

He made a decision. 'Ao Yin all flights, go nap of the earth and push toward the carrier,' he ordered. He rolled his machine onto its back and pulled it into a half loop that took his machine down to wavetop level and pointed toward the last known position of the *USS Enterprise*.

'Casino' Bo's snap judgment proved fateful. Wang took his advice and poured his three squadrons into the gap Chen had blown in the carrier's outer perimeter. The F-35C fighter patrol covering that sector had moved east to engage the Chinese aircraft from their flank, on the premise that the prize of the Sentinel would lure the Chinese to it, and the Arleigh Burke destroyer, *USS John Basilone*, would knock many of the Chinese fighters down, leaving the F-35s to deal with the stragglers. The Sentinel was giving them almost perfect vision of the Chinese attacking force, allowing the F-35s to attack without revealing themselves.

But now their Sentinel was down, and the *John Basilone* was out of the fight.

What Bo didn't know, but the commander of the *USS Enterprise* did, was that the only other ship directly between the carrier and the Chinese fighters was the unarmed replenishment vessel, *USNS Alaska*. He ordered his surface escorts to the northeast and southeast to swing around into the gap, ordered a new Sentinel into the air and pushed two combat air patrols down the bearing to the Chinese attack, but the Chinese fighters had dropped off their radars. The F-35s were chasing, closing on them from front and back, but it was a flat-out foot race now. And his Aegis crews had not only to locate the incoming Chinese aircraft but keep their eyes on the skies above for the ballistic missile attack he'd also been alerted to.

Forewarned was forearmed, but he was being swarmed. His strike group and others had trained this scenario a hundred times, against swarming aerial and surface drones, swarming crewed vessels, swarming missiles. He had faith in his men, in his sensors, in his aircraft, in his layered defenses. But the commander of the *Enterprise* had insight into classified information most of his subordinates didn't.

In those exercises against swarming attacks, the carrier did *not* always survive.

Salt was 20 miles behind O'Hare and 20,000 feet above, in clear skies. He had her on his DAS optical-infrared cameras, a slightly blurry dot skimming across the sea. Oblivious.

She had not seen him yet. He decided to enjoy the moment.

"Bunny, Salt, approaching waypoint," he announced. He brought up his targeting interface, drew a box around the Widow ahead of him and locked it up.

"Hey boss," O'Hare replied. "Nice to have you along for the ride. Was getting a little lonely up here."

"I bet," he said. "Battlenet chatter is things are getting hot on Taiwan. Any trouble getting out?" *Twelve miles.* Salt armed two CUDA missiles in optical-infrared mode. He'd gone up with a full load of off-boresight shorter-range missiles because they were highly maneuverable and unlikely to be detected when launched. They had the added advantage they could be decoyed but not jammed.

"Chinese tried to test my calm demeanor on the way up. No drama after that."

The good thing about even new-generation air-to-air missiles was that space inside the missile was at a premium. Every square inch was needed either for sensors, explosives, fuel or control actuators. They had no Identify Friend or Foe detectors that might allow them to tell the good guys from the bad.

Not that Bunny was one of the "good guys." Not to Salt Carlyle.

Salt had been the child of American expats in Hong Kong, arrested for participating in an illegal pro-democracy protest. His parents had been locked away in a work camp deep inside the Chinese mainland. They had no family lobbying Congress about them; their company soon lost interest in their welfare. Forgotten by their government, they languished there for more than a decade. The last time he had seen them had been 30 years ago. Salt had no idea if they were still alive.

He'd been taken from them at age five, raised by adopted parents and schooled at Chinese military schools as part of China's extensive "sleeper agent" program. The trauma of being separated from them was replaced by a narrative he was told over and over. They were criminals, they had abandoned him, and the Chinese State had rescued him. The Chinese State, his teachers, his dormitory supervisor—*they* loved him. At military school, Salt was given an American high school education. He mixed only with other Western children. They called themselves "the orphans" even though most weren't, but they had no contact with their parents or with the world outside their high school compound. They made field trips to

Hong Kong for exposure to the modern world, to "Western ideas and values." These trips were always followed by intensive de-programming. They spoke English, were educated almost exclusively in STEM subjects and ate a Western diet. When they graduated, they were provided with false papers from an anonymous Midwestern secondary school.

At 18 years of age, Salt returned to the USA with a false passport in his real name to live with a false uncle and aunt. He applied to several military entry colleges and universities and was accepted by the US Air Force Academy, starting a lifelong career of providing high-grade intelligence to his Chinese Ministry of State Security handlers—his uncle and aunt—on US military doctrine, training methods, strategies and tactics, and then detailed information on the specifications, systems, strengths and weaknesses of its military aircraft.

Bunny had been right, suspecting that someone had passed information on the transfer of HACM missiles to Taiwan, right down to the detail of which flight would ship them to Guam and how they would be smuggled onto Taiwan from there. And she had been right that he was shaken when that flight, *with him on it*, was attacked. He'd called his uncle and aunt, furious. They had sympathized on the open line, then sent him a coded message to tell him it was a mistake, an operational oversight.

He had chosen O'Hare for the mission, fully expecting she would screw it up. Of all his pilots, she was the least reliable, the most erratic. Also the most aggressive. He knew all he had to do was put her in a situation where she felt threatened, and she would try to fight her way out of it, giving China's forces a politically palatable excuse for shooting her down. He was assured that sufficient assets were being put in place to ensure she would be intercepted and her escape would be "impossible." Salt had made the mission plan that routed the flight path near Okinotori and ensured it was the nominated emergency landing field for that segment of the mission. He did everything he could, as early as he could, to ensure there was *zero* chance O'Hare would survive. And even if she did, that the HACM missiles would be destroyed.

They had screwed up, and she had made it off Okinotori, with the missiles.

He was then ordered to look for every opportunity to interfere with the missiles' deployment, ideally by gaining access to and destroying them. No opportunity presented itself until planning began for the exfiltration of the Aggressor squadron. He requested, but was denied, permission to try to penetrate Chinese defenses and join his unit on Taiwan. His success would have been assured by his Chinese handlers, but the request was denied by the USAF. Instead, he requested Aggressor Inc. move their two available Widows to Luzon so they could be available to support the evacuation of the team there. He flew there himself and waited for a chance to present itself …

And finally, it had. One of the missiles was in the aircraft right in front of him. And so was Bunny O'Hare. Salt Carlyle was all alone in the sky behind O'Hare. The two other Widow pilots, Flowmax and Flatline, had never been part of the plan, their inclusion in the package just another lie he had told Meany.

And then he was done with lying. When this last task was done, he was going to deliver Aggressor Inc.'s P-99 Black Widow to the Chinese air base on Woody Island in the Paracel Islands group.

Five miles.

After several days of acute frustration, it was a sweet, sweet moment. He wanted to share it with her.

"Well, I'm glad to hear you made it out of Taiwan with your famous Bunny O'Hare demeanor intact," Salt said. He jabbed his thumb down on the missile launch trigger. "Fox two, O'Hare."

24. 'Breathe, alright?'

There was one thing that defined the famous Bunny O'Hare demeanor more than any other. Distrust. Bunny had her head on a swivel anytime she was in the badlands, constantly checking her sensors, instruments, then the skies around, and back again, and again. Years of looking over her shoulder in case her grandpa was there, looking over her shoulder in case one of the cattle-mustering crew was about to spring a practical joke on her, looking over her shoulder at the Defense Academy for fellow students, in Red Flag missions for adversaries, then in combat for real enemies, trying to kill her.

She'd picked Salt up on DAS as he slid in behind her, and watched as he closed before he hailed her, and she had only one thought. *Asshole.* She tried to convince herself that he was just going to play a joke on her, see how close he could get before he said "boo." But something was wrong. Where were Flatline and Flowmax? They should be flying formation with him. She let him come, preparing a few comebacks. But when he started the casual chitchat, she knew something was seriously messed up. Then again, she'd known that for a while, right? Just hadn't wanted to see it.

Choosing her for this mission and not one of his preferred pilots. The mysterious intercept on their Galaxy transport off Wake Island as if China knew who and what was aboard. His shocked, drunken reaction at what China had done with that information, nearly killing them both. Ordering her down on

Okinotori, right into the lap of the Chinese special forces. Showing up on Luzon "just in case," when he usually did everything he could to avoid deploying. The final clue: him volunteering to cover her back for the *Fujian* mission.

That really should have gotten her alarm bells pealing.

You blind idiot, O'Hare. She had her camera zoomed in on him, hands resting on throttle and stick, missiles up and armed though she didn't intend to use them. Her primary weapon was going to be non-kinetic. The Black Widow was absolutely not a dogfighter, but she wasn't up against a dogfighter; she was up against another Black Widow. The playing field was level. This was not going to be about which machine was better, but which pilot.

Salt was up high, with a big altitude advantage, but it also gave her a perfect view of his fuselage. As she saw his payload bay doors drop open, before she even saw the missile drop into his slipstream and light its tail, she had split her throttles, sent her machine into a high-speed skidding turn and was firing infrared decoy flares behind her. In a millisecond, she had spun her machine to face his, pushed both throttles through the gate and was accelerating away, *underneath* him.

His missiles couldn't follow her. One bought the decoys and exploded among them, and the other buried itself almost vertically in the sea behind her.

As he passed above her, Bunny hauled her nose up and around. Her reaction had caught him flat-footed, but he was recovering. She was too close to launch a radar-guided missile—it wouldn't have time to drop, ignite, acquire—but she had another plan. He was banking hard, trying to bring himself around to take another shot while he still had separation, but he was moving too fast to turn tightly, and she turned inside him.

461

Tapping her sensor system screen, she lit him up with *every erg of radar energy her Widow could radiate.*

One second, O'Hare was floating across the waves, her machine boxed nicely in the targeting zone of his helmet visor ... The next, she was skewing across the sky, her machine spewing infrared decoy flares. His missiles barely had time to clear his aircraft and launch, and she was *already disappearing* under his nose?!

She'd spoiled his moment. No matter. Whoever had the height had the fight. It was the oldest rule in basic fighter maneuvers. He dropped his nose and banked hard, putting the Widow into a tight diving turn. His CUDAs could acquire a target as far as 70 degrees off his nose. He just had to ...

His heads-up display flickered, the targeting reticle jerking randomly across his vision. The multifunction display on the instrument panel in front of him blanked and then reappeared. Red warning text began flashing in his visor.

CPU_N failure. Backup system engaging. Reboot Y/N. CPU_N failure. Backup system engaging. Reboot Y/N.

The neuromorphic chip? She'd fried his damned AI?!

He tried to break away, get separation, but his controls and the readouts in his helmet-mounted display no longer matched. His backup systems had not yet kicked in. He pulled harder on his stick, making a wild-assed guess about his angle of attack and airspeed, trying to tighten his turn and get the hell out of her kill cone ...

Meany had told Bunny that one of the Widows Salt had ordered deployed to Luzon was hers. Repaired, sure. But she had bet it still had that piece-of-shit first-gen neuromorphic chip in it. So when she saw him slide in behind her, and saw the fresh skin on the nose of his machine glinting in the sunlight, she quickly decided to punch him in his weak spot: the neuromorphic chip.

She blasted his machine with raw, high-powered, close-range jamming energy, and sure enough, she took that piece-of-shit chip offline.

Bunny saw Salt's Widow stagger. She was still turning inside him. He tried to reverse on her, tighten his turn to get inside her, get away for a missile solution, but that just caused him to bleed airspeed. He no longer had the AI telling him how to fly his machine right to the edge of its flight envelope. He dropped his nose, tightened his turn more, trying to turn his height into energy based on what his AI was still showing him. It wasn't showing him reality. He should have been increasing separation; instead, he was pulling his machine closer to her.

Bunny wasn't relying on AI. She was using 10 years of mistakes made in basic fighter maneuvers that had nearly got her killed, both virtually and in real combat. She had her throttles forward, her twin engines pouring fire, her nose pointed where Salt was going to be in just a couple of seconds' time. Straining against the force of her acceleration, she tapped her control panel, and ensured the Widow's Trophy defense system was armed.

CPU_N failure. Backup system engaging. Reboot Y/N. CPU_N failure. Backup system engaging. Reboot Y/N.

The message was still flashing across his vision, and Salt canceled it. He nearly had her. Two could play that game! He pulled up his electronic warfare menu and sent a chip-killing beam of energy at O'Hare's Widow. What was good for the goose …

She was going to go across his nose and underneath him again, but that would only protect her for the next few seconds. He would blow past her, get some separation and set up a missile shot with his CUDAs before she …

He never completed the thought. He heard a sound like hail drumming on a tin roof, his controls went dead in his hands, and his machine rolled onto its back. From horizon to horizon, all he could see out of his cockpit was sea.

THUNK THUNK THUNK …

There was no live neuromorphic chip in Bunny's machine for Salt's electronic warfare attack to kill. And her Air Trophy defense system didn't care whether it was a missile or a drone or a friendly aircraft moving in; when armed, it was designed to kill anything that looked like a threat. And Bunny had done her best to make sure Salt's aircraft looked like a big, ugly target to her Trophy turret.

He passed right over her at more than 700 knots, less than 50 feet overhead. As he moved into range, the turret fired three bursts of hundreds of explosively formed penetrators into his path. They shredded his machine from nose to tail, destroying control actuators, slicing open hydraulic hoses and flaying the shiny skin from the Widow's belly.

Bunny kept her machine turning, one wingtip toward the sea, following Salt's Widow down, flame flickering along the side of its fuselage.

Two hundred feet above the waves, his cockpit canopy flew off, but no ejection seat blasted out. No ejection, no chute. The Widow hit the water with its right wingtip, cartwheeled across the sea and went under, leaving only foam, oily smoke and a small trail of fuel and debris.

She circled briefly to see if he'd somehow made it out, but she saw no life vest, no one struggling on the surface. No emergency distress signal either. It was like the sea had simply swallowed him and his machine. The idea did not make her sad.

She refreshed the data on her nav screen, dropped a waypoint over the launch point for her HACM and pointed her nose northeast.

Toward the PLA Navy aircraft carrier *Fujian*.

Pilot Officer Maylin 'Mushroom' Sun of the PLA Navy carrier *Fujian* had felt a surge of pride listening to Chen claim the Sentinel kill. She had seen the vision of his attack on the American destroyer and had cheered out loud as he opened the gate, allowing the pilots of *Fujian*'s air wing to pour through it.

They weren't left alone for long.

"A9, down."

"B15, down."

"B2, down."

"C11, down."

The calls came thick and fast as the aircraft at the edges and rear of the low-flying swarm of Chongming fighters were picked off, either by surface-to-air missiles fired from their flanks or the F-35s hunting them from behind now. Ao Yin wasn't the only squadron taking losses; the other two were as well.

"Stay low, *dammit*," Bo ordered his pilots. "Disengage laser terrain following. You get above 200 feet, you die."

The automated laser-guided terrain following systems of the Chongming had a 200-foot safety limit. She wasn't using it anyway; she was flying manually and couldn't get any lower. The fuselage-mounted cameras on her machine's underbelly were blurring from salt spray kicked up by the whitecaps underneath her.

There were search radars in the sky all around them now. And staying low wasn't enough, not when you had American fighters above and behind you. That reality became apparent a moment later.

"A1 is down," Casino announced. "Ao Yin Leader is down, taking control of … C4."

Mushroom squirmed in her seat. A squadron leader was not out of the fight until every last machine was down. Bo could commandeer any aircraft in his squadron at the push of a button, cutting out the pilot in control and taking over. And he'd just chosen to drop into the Chongming on Mushroom's wing.

Tense minutes passed. More comrades fell. How many machines could they have left? There was no time for her to check.

"'C' flight, Ao Yin Leader. We are approaching launch point," Casino said as he adjusted to his new reality. "Reengage terrain following; set to 500. Arm Eagle Strike Missiles. Refresh combat net data."

Mushroom put her machine back onto automated terrain following, felt it bump higher, but there was no choice. The Eagle Strike missile had to be launched at a minimum safe altitude of 500 feet. She manually refreshed the data on the last known location of the American carrier, and the updated position was transferred automatically to the guidance system of her missiles. They used GPS to guide themselves during the first phase of their attack or, if that was jammed, fell back on inertial guidance, which couldn't be jammed. As they entered the terminal attack phase, they began zigging and zagging erratically to avoid interception as they searched for their target using optical-infrared imaging. Their onboard AI matched the images the missile was seeing with a dataset containing every known adversary naval vessel class, and if it found a match for the chosen vessel type, it homed on that target. If it didn't, it chose the nearest and largest hostile target instead.

They were 50 miles from the American carrier now.

"'C' flight, launch, launch, launch," Casino ordered.

Mushroom triggered her missiles, felt a slight dizziness as her machine bumped up and quickly down again, and watched from her virtual cockpit as the two long, light blue missiles streaked away in front of her. She had time now and checked the counter on her tac display that showed how many friendly aircraft it was tracking. There had been 54. There were 38 now.

Her missiles dropped lower, toward the sea, until all she could see were their contrails. They were low supersonic, only slightly faster than her own machine, and there was a reason for that.

"All Ao Yin aircraft, down on the deck again; initiate jamming," Casino ordered.

As one, the remaining aircraft of *Fujian* put their radars into electronic warfare mode and began filling the sky ahead of their missiles with jamming energy. The frequencies of their missiles and their aircraft were deconflicted so that the missiles could still pull down satellite data on their target's location, but the jamming was designed to disrupt the radar of the American Standard surface-to-air missiles.

"Follow them home, Ao Yin pilots," Casino said. "You know what to do."

She knew *exactly* what to do. Shredder had shown them the way.

Fujian's pilots had not been briefed on the entirety of China's attack on the *Enterprise*, only their part in it.

From their maximum operational range of 30 miles, northeast and southeast of the *Enterprise,* two Chinese *Shang* class nuclear attack submarines began launching their YJ-82 cruise missiles. Fired through the submarines' torpedo tubes, they sped to the surface and then blasted out of their cannisters and into the air. At near the speed of sound, they skimmed about 20 feet over the waves.

As they did, they established a link to an overhead satellite and downloaded updated targeting data.

Each *Shang* class submarine could fire six of the missiles, and inside a minute, 12 of the missiles were arrowing in on the *Enterprise*.

In the CIC of the *USS Enterprise*, their frantically launched Sentinel was aggregating data from the carrier's picket destroyers even as it climbed to operating altitude and the resulting image of the developing air battle was projected onto a widescreen on the wall.

It showed no fewer than 30 Chinese aircraft boring in on the *Enterprise* from about 70 miles out, and they had just launched 26 missiles. From the northeast and southeast, more missiles were inbound, probably sub launched. A total of 38 missiles were headed directly for them.

That gave the networked Aegis defense systems of the *Enterprise* strike group a collective silicon sigh of relief. A single Aegis destroyer could handle 38 missiles. Fed targets by every radar in the group, the remaining four picket ships could together manage both the missiles *and* the aircraft that fired them without breaking a sweat.

Dozens of SM-2 and SM-6 missiles erupted from the vertical launch tubes of the four destroyers and converged on the incoming missiles and aircraft. There was just one problem, which China's tactics exploited. To guide themselves to their targets, the US Standard Missiles needed to keep a data link to the ship that launched them. The Chinese jamming broke that link as soon as the missiles got within 10 miles of their targets.

Most of the US missiles flew wide. The SM-6 missiles that stayed on course switched to infrared targeting and looked for heat signatures to home on. Copying Shredder's corkscrew maneuver, the Chinese pilots spun their machines like whirling dervishes, sending infrared decoys showering around them.

The intense heat and pattern of the decoys lured most of the SM-6 missiles to them.

A counter on the CIC screen counted down the remaining incoming missiles and aircraft. It still showed *12 missiles and 14 aircraft*. Another volley of missiles erupted from the decks of the carrier's pickets and the short-range Sea Sparrow missile launchers on the *Enterprise* itself began searching for targets. Crew on the *Enterprise*'s deck had long finished tying down everything on the deck that could possibly move, slide or crush and were left to stare east. As they watched, a line of lights appeared on the horizon—a mix of missile plumes and flares fired into the air by the incoming Chongming kamikaze fighters.

Across every deck of the carrier, the "incoming missile" alarm began sounding.

Then the carrier began heeling over as it started a flank-speed hard turn to starboard. As it did so, missiles punched out of the Sea Sparrow launchers mounted above the *Enterprise*'s flight deck. A Phalanx radar-guided autocannon opened up, firing at maximum range, but the sudden and violent pitch of the carrier's deck sent its spray of cannon fire up into the sky.

Further out, new missiles burst from the decks of the air warfare destroyers. But they weren't the anti-aircraft missiles the destroyers had been firing so far. They were SM-3s, missiles designed for one purpose: to destroy *ballistic* missiles.

China had launched so many ballistic missiles as part of its opening barrage on Taiwan that the launch of its carrier-killer hypersonic missiles had been hidden in the mass of heat signature blooms. Four of the DF-26 missiles had just been detected descending from orbit, and they were falling on the *USS Enterprise* at nearly *20,000 miles an hour.*

Either the missiles the *Enterprise's* pickets had just launched would intercept them in the next 30 seconds, or the carrier and every one of the 5,400 crew members aboard would die.

Bunny O'Hare was maintaining an emissions and signals blackout. That meant she only opened her comms system for the time it took for a satellite to squirt a data update down to her before she closed the channel again.

I am a ghost, a cipher, a black hole in the emissions firmament.

Up ahead, she had just picked up the signal of a Chinese KJ-600 airborne warning aircraft. It would of course have defensive air patrols up too. And a ring of *Type 055* destroyers protecting it. Although she didn't know it, the US attack vector for taking out the Chinese carriers couldn't have been more different than the Chinese. China had chosen to overwhelm the American defenses with a bewildering volume and variety of attacks. The USAF had chosen to send in a single, almost invisible attacker.

But in one thing they were the same. Both nations were relying on hypersonics to do the job.

Bunny was 100 miles from the *Fujian*. At a velocity of Mach 5, it would still take her HACM missile more than a minute to reach the Chinese carrier. Too long.

She had to push in further. One thing niggled at her. Bunny O'Hare was in an emissions blackout, so she could only trust that the British fighters from the *HMS Queen Elizabeth* were playing their part in the attack on *Fujian*. She needed them to draw the carrier's air pickets away and give her clear air for her HACM attack.

She needn't have worried. Through the 2030s, British and Italian aircraft and avionics designers had partnered to create the Tempest, the newest and most advanced sixth-generation fighter on the planet. Beyond anything China, Russia or even the US had produced, it was the ultimate flying death machine. The naval variant, a short-takeoff, vertical-landing machine like the F-35Bs that had first shipped on the British carrier *HMS Queen Elizabeth* and which had later been sold to Australia for use on its helicopter landing docks, involved a few compromises. For example, it did not feature the rear-firing laser missile defense of the Tempest-A or Air Force variant. But the Tempest-N was the same in every other respect: a sleek, dolphin-nosed aircraft where the boundary between pilot and machine was almost invisible. Supported by a "deep learning AI" that adapted to an individual pilot's preferred flying style, a Tempest pilot was freed from all the mundane and attention-sapping tasks of normal fast jet management and left to do what his or her masters wanted them to do. Penetrate enemy airspace. Find enemy aircraft.

And destroy them.

Fleet Air Arm Squadron Leader 'Two-Tone' Jules Hamilton was the polar opposite of Karen O'Hare, and not just because of his ancestral West Indian skin tone. Nor because of the rather remarkable mixed colors of the irises that gave him his call sign—one brown, the other a piercing blue. Where Bunny O'Hare was uncorked chaos, Two-Tone Hamilton was buttoned-down efficiency. He wasn't a robot, that wasn't it. For example, as his two-plane element went about the business of quietly identifying every Chinese fighter in the *Fujian*'s outer perimeter of air patrols, a silent fury was burning deep in his gut.

Two-Tone had been flying carrier defense when his comrades escorting the doomed RAF Globemaster had been engaged by the swarm of drones from *Fujian*. He hadn't known the pilot from the *Lizzie* who had died that day, but that didn't matter. He was a brother in arms, the first among them to die in combat, and every pilot or sailor aboard the *Lizzie* had felt the loss.

But Two-Tone had a place where he contained that anger. A chamber in his heart that pumped the blood to the brain that he used when he was airborne. It was nuclear fuel that, unlike Bunny O'Hare, didn't blind him with rage but rather kept him clear eyed and goal focused. Like now.

Two Tempests may not seem very many to be going up against at least 10 Chongming drones, maybe more, but the two UK Tempests approaching *Fujian*'s outer air perimeter were not alone. Each was accompanied by two Mosquito uncrewed wingmen, and in the payload bay of the four Mosquitos was an adversary no Chinese pilot had ever met and which no amount of training could prepare them for.

Some Tempest pilots gave their AIs customized voices and call signs or names. Two-Tone indulged his pilots but had no time for such nonsense himself. The deep learning AI designed by British Aerospace's AI engineers was known as VIPR—Virtual Interactive Polymorphic Recurrent neural network—so that was what Two-Tone called it.

"VIPR, prepare all Mosquitos for offensive penetration," he said into his helmet mic. The view from his helmet showed three simulated wide-screen monitors superimposed on the sky around his machine. He saw no cockpit, no airframe. He was a disembodied soul soaring through the sky over the western Pacific Ocean, and at that moment, the fact he was sitting in a jet fighter blasting through the sky at 600 miles an hour in the company of two greyhound shaped supersonic drones was irrelevant.

Targets identified. Mosquitos armed and ready for penetration operations, the AI replied in a neutral tone.

"VIPR, open channel to Oryx Two."

The AI opened a radio channel to his wingman. "Oryx Two, Oryx Leader. Preparing Mosquitos for offensive penetration. You have your targets, Chippie."

"Good copy, Oryx Leader. Two has targets; Mosquitos armed and ready on your command." His wingman, 'Chippie' McDormand, replied.

Two-Tone made one last check. On the tactical screen in the center of his helmet display, he saw 10 Chinese fighters, at ranges from 80 to 100 miles distant. He knew he was invisible to the Chinese aircraft, which had no idea they were about to be attacked.

That would soon change, because the two Mosquito drones flying on his port and starboard wings were not stealth aircraft like his Tempest. If they were lucky, the first Chinese fighter would pick them up while they were anywhere from 20 to 50 miles distant. But that would be too late.

He checked that he had a solid lock on every one of the Chinese fighters and that his wingman had the same. He ran his eye over the virtual screen to the left of the tactical display, which showed everything he needed to know about his Mosquito wingmen. He saw only green indicators across the board. One last flick of his eyes to the screen on his right showed the strategic situation, with the Chinese air and naval pickets plotted, and his own carrier 500 miles behind him, steaming out of the Indian Ocean toward Japan. More importantly, the Chinese carrier *Fujian*, 200 miles to his southwest, heading north, toward Taiwan.

For an unforgiveable moment, he felt hatred. He pushed the errant emotion back down. He had no hatred for the people aboard the Chinese vessel. Not really. They were just journeymen and -women like himself, doing what their country demanded of them. Hatred had no place in his cockpit. It was a humanizing emotion that might make him think twice about what he was about to do. And besides, the aircraft he was about to attack were just machines—carbon fiber, silicon and metal. He could no more hate them than he could hate a vending machine that refused to deliver a soda can.

Behind them though. Behind them was an aircraft carrier carrying 4,300 souls that might soon lie at the bottom of the Philippine Sea, if he did his job right.

He shook his head, wiping the thought away.

"VIPR, release all Mosquitos," he commanded.

The order was enough to send the Mosquito drones of both him and his wingmen shooting ahead of them. Accelerating from their cruising speed of 600 miles an hour to Mach 1 within 30 seconds, the contrails of the four drones soon merged into a single white line on the horizon.

Their job was done. He knew that somewhere to his southwest, there was a lone American pilot who would soon deliver a payload of their own if all went well. But there was nothing more he could do to help them.

He prepared to bank his machine to port and turn back for the *Lizzie*. "Oryx Two, Oryx Leader. Good job, Chippie; let's head home."

He wiped the tactical map and reset it to show the sky around him. It was quite an anticlimax, really. A 500-mile flight, a few minutes mapping targets, another couple of minutes of tension around weapons release and then a 500-mile flight home.

It didn't feel like they'd just unleashed the hounds of hell, but there you go; that was modern warfare.

Mushroom was flying through hell. She knew she had to push in further, had to keep pushing on the American carrier, but she was feeling sick. Physically sick.

She was trying to copy Chen's corkscrew maneuver, but her vision kept locking on the horizon and she would lose her sense of up and down. She felt control of her Chongming slipping away from her. A missile blew past her starboard side, exploding behind her so close the flash filled her virtual cockpit and momentarily blinded her onboard cameras. She hit autopilot, the Chongming flattened out and then camera vision returned and she started corkscrewing again, infrared decoys spraying out around her machine like some kind of insane teenager's idea of a New Year's Eve party.

She touched her throat mic. "Shredder, I can't hold it!" she cried out.

She knew he wouldn't have left to debrief; he would still be there, listening for her. Watching out for her.

"You got it, girl," he said calmly, soothingly. "Any minute now, you'll see the target. Breathe, alright? You have got this."

Her nose swung down, toward the sea. She jerked it up as she was spinning, rising high, too high ... "I can't, I'm going to puke ..."

"Command copy mode," Shredder's voice said in her ear. "Hit it."

The Chongming's "command copy mode" was a flight aid designed to help pilots who were feeling suddenly sick or mission incapable. It happened, even to drone pilots in their pods. An alternative to a standard autopilot, it recorded the pilot's most recent control inputs, and as long as they didn't pose a risk to the machine, it continued them until the pilot either recovered or was relieved. *Focus, Mushroom,* she told herself. She kept her nose fixed on the spinning horizon, letting the sea, sky, sea, sky turn as she kept her altitude level and punched infrared decoys into her wake. Then she hit the button combination on her flight stick for "command copy."

Her AI took over, and Mushroom closed her eyes, letting the bile in her throat sink, panting to get as much oxygen into her lungs as she could. She opened her eyes, but instead of focusing on the gyrating horizon through her virtual cockpit view, she pulled up her tactical screen and focused on that. It was ridiculously calming. She knew that in the real world, her Chongming was screaming low across the waves toward an American aircraft carrier like a roman candle attached to a child's spinning top, tracer fire and missiles exploding around it.

But in front of her was a simple multifunction display, and it showed that insane world to her in basic, easy-to-digest glowing lines and icons.

It showed her the American carrier, five miles ahead. Flicking her eyes to her cockpit view, she could just see it on the horizon, a tiny gray spinning sliver. The screen showed her how many Chinese missiles were still tracking. *Four.* It showed her how many of her comrades were still "alive." *Two.*

She had to read the number again before it sank in. Only *three* aircraft left from 54, including her?

As she watched, another of their missiles was knocked down. *Three missiles, three aircraft now.* But the furthest of the missiles was merging with the icon for the target. She tore her eyes off the screen, trying to focus on the spinning carrier in her cockpit view. As she watched, the missile reached the carrier.

Nothing. No explosion. Nothing!

"C4, down. I'm out." Casino's voice. Casino had been knocked down again. It was over. They had done what they could, and it hadn't been enough.

The carrier crept closer. Now it felt like every gun in the world, every missile launcher, was firing just at her. She reached out in front of her to the virtual space that was the Chongming's cockpit glass, as though just by placing a hand on it, she could stop the machine 600 miles away from killing her fighter.

Something in the corner of her eye. A bright flash. Her screen went dark.

The *USS Enterprise* took down the last two Chinese drones, but two Chinese missiles buried themselves in its sloped hull. One was the missile launched by 'Mushroom' Sun; the other was a missile from a *Shang* class submarine. Both struck within milliseconds of each other, on either side of the Enterprise.

It didn't flinch. Mushroom's missile penetrated deeply before it exploded, which was why Mushroom saw no explosion. It exploded inside one of *Enterprise*'s aircraft elevators, taking it out of action, but miraculously killing no one. But because of the radical angle at which the *Enterprise* was heeling over, the second missile slammed into the aft hull below what normally would have been its waterline. It punched through the officers' baggage store, into the low-voltage distribution department, where it detonated, killing a dozen crew.

The hole it made was still above the water, thanks to the carrier's radical turn.

That would change.

China's four DF-26 hypersonic ballistic missiles used optical guidance for their terminal attack. In testing, China had determined that despite the insane air pressures and temperatures they were subjected to, the Dong Feng warhead's sensors could discriminate between a ship and the surrounding sea. Whether moving at 10 knots or 40, sailing in a straight line or maneuvering wildly, their onboard processors could make the minute adjustments to their trajectory needed to calculate an impact point in the middle of the target.

Give or take 100 yards.

Two of the *Enterprise* pickets' SM-3 missiles slammed home, taking out half of the Chinese hypersonic attack.

The rest didn't.

The two remaining missiles were a millisecond from impact. They were both locked onto the same gray target against the blue sea below, and their 2,000 lb. high-explosive warheads were armed.

One struck beside its target, exploding as it hit the surface of the water, creating a steaming crater in the sea 500 yards across and sending a gout of water 200 feet into the air. The concussion alone would have been enough to rupture the eardrums and internal organs of anyone caught on deck nearby. The second hit its target about 20 yards forward of the bridge superstructure. It smashed through the vessel's deck like it was made of balsa and exploded deep in the ship's guts, the power of its impact alone snapping the ship's back like a twig before the missile detonated and flung the two halves of the massive vessel into the air.

In that one strike, the 103 sailors aboard the fleet replenishment vessel *USNS Alaska* instantly perished.

The *Enterprise* hadn't deliberately used it as a decoy. In fact, the carrier had turned starboard to avoid colliding with the *Alaska* or putting its highly explosive fleet oiler in danger.

But China's DF-26 missile targeting software wasn't sophisticated enough to tell the difference between the 780-foot-long oiler and the 1,000-foot-long carrier, when the oiler was *exactly* where it had been told its target would be.

Give or take 100 yards.

Bunny was ignorant of anything happening in the world outside her cockpit.

She knew Taiwan was under a rain of fire. Probably would be for days. She knew that on both sides of the Taiwan Strait, aviators, sailors, soldiers and civilians were dying. She had never become immune to the horror of that, but there was a compartment in her heart where she locked it away when the time came for her to play her own small part in the messed-up history of the world.

If she did her job right, many people were going to die. She knew that. And she took that thought, plucked it out of her mind like a rotten apple from the bough of an apple tree and tossed it away.

At these times, there was solace in numbers.

She was *50* miles from the *Fujian*. She had *six* radars around her, but none tracking. She did the math. Launch now, the HACM would have around *40* seconds to run. She would launch at *30* miles. That would give it a running time of *30* seconds at *Mach 5*, or *63* miles a minute.

She pulled up her ordnance screen and armed the HACM. Green lights showed on all systems.

THIS is where you live. THIS is your time. You OWN the sky. You are a freaking NINJA, and your shadow will be the ONLY thing anyone will see.

Forty miles. She moved her finger to the missile launch button on her flight stick.

Above *Fujian*, the commander of the KJ-600 early-warning aircraft circling the carrier was also doing math. Like Mushroom, he had been following the engagement to the northeast and watching the attrition of *Fujian*'s fighters in horror. Wang had launched three of four squadrons against the US carrier, leaving only 18 to provide air defense for *Fujian*. Two of these were out for maintenance, so make that 16. Only half were airborne at any one time, so make that eight, because for no reason he could see, China didn't do odd-numbered aircraft elements. One of the strike group's *Type 055* destroyers was experiencing problems with its phased array radar too, which left a gap in *Fujian*'s sensor coverage that could only be met with the available Chongming fighters.

All this meant that, according to his math, there was an almost solid gold certainty that something would go horribly wrong on his watch, and sure enough …

"Four contacts! Fast movers, bearing zero two five degrees, altitude 30,000, range 72, speed Mach 1," his tactical director announced.

"Vector fighters to intercept," he said calmly. He had eight fighters in that quadrant, and two behind them in reserve. They would deal with such an insignificant threat easily. "And move up the patrols in the south and east to fill the gap." An attack from the northeast? What was out there? He checked his map screen. Ah, the British carrier, *Queen Elizabeth*. British stealth fighters perhaps. *Not so stealthy after all.*

The radar warning receivers aboard the British Mosquitos picked up the Chinese radar painting them and lit up their own scanning array sensors. Like their World War II namesakes, the Mosquito drones were designed to penetrate deep inside enemy airspace at high speed and create havoc.

The Chinese radar triggered the algorithm in their small silicon brains that told them to go about doing exactly that. They armed the weapons in their internal payload bays and continued flying toward the *Fujian*.

Seconds later, they were painted by the first radar from a Chongming fighter. They didn't wait for the missile that would surely follow the moment the Chongming got a lock on them.

As one, the four Mosquito drones opened their payload bays, and one by one, the Alvino swarming drones inside the Mosquitos fell through the air, their small, missile-shaped bodies lancing through the air unpowered until they reached 10,000 feet above the sea. At 9,999 feet, X-shaped wings snapped out of their bodies, and they began gliding. At 1,000 feet, the small rocket engines in their tails lit up, accelerating them to 200 miles an hour as they fell to just 200 feet above sea level.

The Mosquito aircraft from which they had been released were twisting and turning now, trying to avoid the missiles that had been fired on them by the Chinese Chongming defenders, but whether they survived or not was immaterial now. Each Mosquito had launched 100 of the small Alvino swarming drones.

Each Alvino carried the equivalent of a 40 mm grenade in its nose section. And in their tiny brains was the last known position of the PLA Navy aircraft carrier *Fujian*. They quickly established jamming-proof laser links with one another, and the four swarms oriented themselves southwest.

"New contacts! Four … but …" the Chinese airborne warning aircraft's tactical director hesitated. "The AI is calling them chaff clouds," he said. "But they are moving against the wind. Designating as groups A2 to A5."

"Show me," the AWACs commander said. He stepped to the man's shoulder and looked at his screen. It showed four blurred contacts, the sort that usually represented metallic chaff clouds fired by aircraft. But these were too far away, and they were moving. *Toward Fujian.*

"Drone swarms," he decided. "Alert *Fujian*. They have four incoming drone swarms, estimate anywhere from 200 to 300 munitions." He clicked his fingers. "Time to impact?"

The TD ran a calculation. "Twenty-three minutes." It sounded like an eternity, but it was anything but. Intercepting a missile was a simple matter of calculating an intercept and sending ordnance into its way, either another missile, a high-powered laser beam or fragmentation shells from a radar-guided cannon. Intercepting a drone swarm comprising hundreds of small aircraft was another matter entirely. Missiles had trouble seeing them; their HE warheads could destroy tens, maybe dozens at a time, but as soon as they detected an attack, they spread out, and the rest pushed on unscathed. Laser beams were even less effective, and autocannons? Useless. Optical and radio jamming was the only defense, and China had not yet perfected that technology.

The only positive was that a swarm usually comprised hundreds of drones with tiny warheads, only a few kilograms of explosive in each. They were lethal against massed troops formations and lightly armored vehicles, but they were not fatal to capital warships like the *Fujian*. They might destroy aircraft parked on the flight deck, kill any crew unlucky enough to be caught out in the open, damage fragile radar and radio antennas, but they could not sink her.

He looked at the sensor returns. They were very *large* swarms. "Update that estimate to 500 munitions," he said. It was better to be cautious.

"Yes Commander. I ... New contacts! Twenty ... no ... *30-plus*, bearing one eight nine, altitude approximately 500, range one thirty-five, velocity 600, heading one nine nine ..." His TD conferred with his team. "AI is calling them cruise missiles, AGM-156 or 158s. Designating target group 'B!'"

A swarming attack. They were being pushed by waves of attackers, first from the northeast, now from the southwest. He didn't panic, but he had just moved his patrols *out* of the sector the cruise missiles had appeared from. "Push that data to *Fujian!*" he yelled. He reached for his earpiece and changed his channel so that he could speak directly to the air boss on *Fujian*. "*Fujian*, this is Angel Two. You have multiple incoming. Thirty-plus vampires approaching from the southwest, speed 600 knots, reaching your position in 13 minutes. Four drone swarms from your northeast, speed 200 knots, closer in, but reaching your position in 20 minutes. Launch everything you have, *Fujian*. I recommend sounding general quarters." He turned to his Fighter Allocator. "Push everything you can into that gap. I want aircraft in position to pick up any missiles the pickets miss."

He did his numbers. The cruise missiles were potentially more dangerous but easier to intercept. One or two might get through, but no more. The drone swarms were harder to intercept, but less lethal. Many drones would get through the carrier's defenses, but the damage they caused *should* be light.

He breathed a sigh of relief. If this was the worst the Western Alliance could do, it was not going to be such a bad day after all.

Bunny was doing numbers too, but this time it was a countdown. She had started at three minutes. It kept her focused.

At two minutes 45 seconds she picked the first of them up on her DAS. Right on schedule. As though they had been following her in, the cloud of JASSM cruise missiles fired by the four B-21s behind her crept into view. They were only going marginally faster than her and took a few seconds to reel her in. She was relieved to see they were going to pass by close to her, but not *too* close.

She whistled as they overtook her. The cruise missile formation passing her was four wide and about a half mile long. *Holy crap. So that's what a volley of 64 cruise missiles looks like in flight.* They were flying slightly higher than her, about 500 feet above sea level, and left no contrails.

The KJ-600 radar must have seen them by now, and if it could see them, then it was possible it would see her. But the missiles were her cover, and she gently pulled back on her throttle. Though every fiber of her being was shouting at her to go faster, she needed the sensor operators protecting the *Fujian* to be 100 percent focused on the missiles ahead of her and not looking for or worried about the lone stealth fighter trailing behind them. Let them think she was just another cruise missile if they found her. She checked her airspeed: 400 knots. Minimum safe launch velocity for HACM missile.

The last cruise missile passed her.

Twenty seconds to release.

Chinese air defense destroyers would be launching at the cruise missiles already. Screening fighters would be inbound. She increased the gain on her radar warning receiver. Sure enough, new radars off her nose, left and right, and one on her flank, slightly behind her. Their KJ-600 had shown them where she was; now they were reaching out with their own radars like children playing a deadly game of blindfold tag.

Ten.

The HACM was a two-stage missile. The conventional first stage boosted the missile to Mach 3, then a scramjet engine kicked in, taking it hypersonic. Counterintuitively, the scramjet had to be booted first to be ready when needed. She sped through the startup procedure for the scramjet, then checked the status on the first phase boost engine.

The scramjet showed red, then orange, then green. The first phase engine, also green.

Five.

Final arming procedure for the warhead. Nuclear/non-nuclear? It wasn't an option, just a setting that impacted whether the targeting mode was hit-to-kill or airburst. She'd heard rumors among the 68th Aggressor ground crews that they'd been told she might be bringing nukes with her. A few people had lost money on that bet. She hit the toggle. *Non-nuclear.* She bumped her machine 200 feet higher and moved her thumb to the missile release.

Three ... two ... one ...

Missile away!

She didn't wait for it to light its tail. She was a fox surrounded by a pack of hounds, and picking a gap in the radar signatures around her, she angled her machine gently toward it. In seconds, the nearest threat was on her six, and she was moving away from it.

Her combat AI kept a projection of the missile track on her helmet visor though, so she could watch it run. The missile kept a link to her and a satellite above for as long as it could, but if that link was cut, it would move to optical targeting. Unlike the Chinese HF-26, the HACM could tell the difference between a fleet oiler and an aircraft carrier. It could even choose where on its target it would hit.

Give or take *10* yards.

Bunny watched the timer on her visor run down, pushing her throttles forward and banking gently to starboard. She didn't want to be anywhere near the scene of this particular crime.

When Mushroom cracked the shell of her pod, the first sight that greeted her was a grinning 'Shredder' Chen. He reached in and hugged her, causing her to blush, then pulled back, as though realizing a boundary had been crossed. The grin didn't disappear from his face though.

"You got a carrier strike!" he yelled as she disconnected her VR rig. "A *carrier* strike!"

"Don't know for sure it was my missile," she said. "Could have been anyone's."

"Part of a carrier strike then. How *crazy* is that?"

"You got a solo destroyer strike," she said. "With your Chongming. They're going to name that wild-ass corkscrew maneuver after you, you know that. *That's* crazy."

"And a Sentinel," he said, sticking his thumbs under the armpits of his flight suit like they were braces. "Don't forget that one." He looked around for her chair. It was behind her pod, and he bent down to unlock the wheels. "Here, for once let me help you out."

She looked down, reached for the buckle on her harness. And hesitated. She would never know why. It was like she *heard* something. But that would have been impossible ...

Bunny's hypersonic sea-skimming HACM missile was fired at such a close range, it reached the *Fujian* before any of its picket or ship-board defenses could be brought to bear. It struck the ship 20 feet above the waterline, at an angle that would drive it deep into the *Fujian's* innards, one deck above the carrier's Hangar Forward Bay.

Otherwise known as the Pod Bay.

Mushroom heard a crash, saw the wall behind Shredder lift off the deck and move straight at them like the maw of a supersized garbage crusher. Then flame boiled around it, Shredder turned, Mushroom ducked down into her pod, and her world dissolved into a cacophony of noise, fire and blood.

25. 'How do I look?'

White House Situation Room, April 7, 2038

Defense Secretary Ervan Holoman had just returned from a meeting with the Joint Chiefs, and the mood was grim.

Chinese land-, sea- and air-launched missiles had attacked the carriers *USS Enterprise*, *USS George HW Bush*, and landing helicopter dock *USS Bougainville*. All had taken damage and casualties. China had sunk the *USNS Alaska*, which went down with all hands. All surviving carriers were being pulled back, out of the theater, and there was no news on when they would be combat capable again.

The US did not have carrier-killer ballistic missiles in its arsenal, but its attacks on the Chinese carriers had borne fruit. *Fujian* had been hit by a HACM missile and was changing course, heading southwest, trying to put as much distance as it could between it and US land-based aircraft in the Philippines and Japan. China had moved it into a position to flank Western forces around Taiwan, but that left it alone in the Western Pacific, with no obvious route back into Chinese home waters. Its speed had fallen to 10 knots, a clear sign it was badly damaged.

China's first aircraft carrier, the ex-Soviet *Liaoning*, had been caught moving north for the safety of the East China

Sea and the HACM missile launched by Taiwan's air force struck it in the stern, damaging its rudder and at least one screw. It was continuing to limp north, trailing smoke, toward the port and fleet base of Ningbo. The Taiwan Air Force had lost 13 aircraft in the attacks, but two of China's three carriers were effectively already out of the fight.

The attack on the *Shandong* in the South had been unsuccessful. All Taiwanese attacking aircraft had been destroyed either by Chinese patrols over Taiwan or by the *Shandong*'s air warfare picket destroyers. Submarine-launched cruise missiles had all been intercepted. The Taiwanese Air Force had not even launched the HACM missile intended for *Shandong*. The F-16V fighter carrying it had been shot down shortly after taking off from Taichung Air Base. But satellite intel showed the *Shandong* too was being withdrawn, heading southwest to the relative safety of Hainan and the South China Sea.

"Sum it up for me, Ervan. This series of carrier strikes—do the Joint Chiefs think we came out on top?" Carliotti asked.

He shook his head. "*Bush*, *Bougainville* and *Enterprise* all need repairs, with *Enterprise* hit below the waterline. We took the *Liaoning* and *Fujian* out of play, *Liaoning* perhaps for good; *Fujian* might be capable of air operations again if it can repair the damage it took at sea. So call it two for three."

"We promised those service families *Bougainville* would be protected," Chief of Staff Rosenstern pointed out.

"It was protected," Holoman insisted. "Or it would not have survived, and it *will* make port in Taipei in about two hours. Thank God we lost very few lives in any of the Chinese attacks. The missiles that got through our defenses were not as accurate as our worst-case projections."

"We lost *Alaska,* with near all hands," Carliotti reminded him. "So let's be careful what we label as 'few.'" She hadn't meant to rebuke Holoman and saw a pained look on his face. "I know you didn't mean it that way. What now?"

"We continue to reinforce Taiwan. *Bougainville* is putting a battalion of Marines ashore, mobile anti-air, medical personnel and supplies. She's in the company of a *Zumwalt* and an Arleigh Burke, but after the Chinese attacks, they need to be resupplied with missiles. They'll be able to hold their own, for now, and supplement surface-to-air cover over most of the capital, Taipei. We'll have a fast-attack submarine offshore Taipei by tonight and several more in the operations area within three days to protect her. China tried to air-drop mines around Taipei harbor, but Taiwanese air defenses knocked their aircraft down. They'll probably try again at other ports." He paused and looked at a tablet PC in front of him. "Taiwan's air force is taking a battering, but they won't accept our offer to move their aircraft to Japan. Probably because their air defenses are still at 70 percent and our Okinawa- and Luzon-based aircraft have pushed Chinese fighters back west of the island. We lost two aircraft this morning in those actions; China lost upward of 20. China still has air superiority over the Strait, but not over the island yet."

"What about our unit on the ground there? The F-22s?" Rosenstern asked. "Any losses?"

"No. We were going to pull them back to Okinawa, but they're still operating and providing valuable support to the ROC Taiwan Air Force. Now that we have put boots on the ground, they'll support and protect the Marines and our ships from air attack." Holoman paused, then pushed the tablet away from him, looking directly at the President. "The Joint Chiefs want to move to DEFCON 1, in all theatres preferably, but at the very least the Indo-Pacific."

"What? Why?" Carliotti asked. "Have we seen any indications China is going nuclear?"

"Not yet, but they assess the likelihood China will use battlefield tactical nuclear weapons to support an invasion is high."

"We just *canceled* their invasion, Ervan," Vice President Bendheim said. "You told us this morning their ability to move on the two Taiwanese islands without carrier support is zero."

"We put them back in their box," he admitted. "Made them realize we aren't going to wait for them to start sailing troops across the Strait before we act. But they are still massing forces along the Strait: army, navy, air. As you know, our plan is to hit those assembly points too, if it looks like they are mounting up, but if we do, it's another escalation and China starts to run out of plays. The nuclear option becomes more appealing ..."

"No. We're still several levels of escalation away from pushing China into that corner," Carliotti said, then hesitated. "Aren't we, Michael? What does JWC say is China's next move?"

Michael Chase knew the question would be coming. He was still adopting a "speak when spoken to" approach in the NSC meetings, mostly just listening to the arguments in the room because after all, he didn't have the same skin in the political game as the others. But he had an update on the thinking from his Joint Wargaming Council.

The JWC had moved out of its cramped conference room and taken over a third-floor canteen and its private dining rooms. The 20-strong team assembled by Burroughs had now been supplemented with nearly the same number again: of intelligence analysts, AI programmers, linguists and agency liaison officers. Including, not least of all, a bespectacled, bewhiskered guy called Carl Williams, who was the human face of HOLMES, the AI role-playing the Chinese leadership.

The canteen was their war-gaming room, a huge, old-school theatre map of the western Pacific Ocean and Taiwan Strait filling the center of the room, covered in wooden blocks with scribbled military unit designations on them for infantry, armor, artillery, navy, space and air assets. Around the walls of the dining room were high-resolution, floor-to-ceiling screens, where the information from the physical theatre map was broken down in more granular detail around specific geographic areas or tactical issues. The dining rooms on one side of the canteen had been taken over by the "blue" team of Western allies, who were taking the input from the NSC and Joint Chiefs and translating it into actions in the larger war game. They were also able to tap into the collective intelligence apparatus of a dozen agencies across the US defense and intelligence network.

The rooms on the other side of the canteen had been taken over by the experts playing the "red," or Chinese, side. They were not only able to leverage the intelligence flowing in from signals, cyber, satellite and human sources about Chinese military developments but had a battery of predictive AI engines they were able to use to run scenarios and evaluate consequences, just as China's strategic planners would be doing. One of the AI engines, which Burroughs had brought to the project, was based on actual Chinese strategic decision support code stolen by a CIA agent just two years earlier.

Where the "blue team" had the NSC and Joint Chiefs making decisions for it, the "red" team had a group of individuals role-playing China's Politburo Standing Committee, reviewing every recommendation from the "red" military actors through a party-political lens based on a deep historical, political and structural understanding of Chinese culture.

It was the combination of the stolen Chinese AI code engine, and the filter provided by the individuals role-playing the Chinese political hierarchy, that was providing a lot of the breakthrough thinking regarding China's responses to Western initiatives, and it had so far been uncannily correct.

Chase had watched the two teams at work with a mixture of frustration, fascination and, occasionally, horror.

As he mulled over how to answer the President, one interaction came back to him.

He'd been sitting with the "red," or China, team, as they processed the results of the damage assessment from the attacks on the US and Chinese aircraft carriers. The Chinese side had perfect information about the damage to their own carriers (as best the US could estimate) but imperfect information about the damage they had caused to the US carriers.

They were living themselves into their roles with gusto. And they were furious. The DoD analyst representing the PLA Navy was red faced as he addressed the room. "This is a declaration of all-out war! We must respond with all means at our disposal, and that includes nuclear!"

"What are you suggesting?" the DIA senior analyst Burroughs asked him. He was playing "moderator," trying to structure the interactions of both sides. "Please be clear."

"I am suggesting ..." the man said, "... a demonstration of our intent that the US cannot ignore."

Another "red" player waved a hand dismissively. "You're talking nukes. Our weapon of last resort. PRC policy is to

495

conserve our nuclear arsenal for the moment the unity of the state is threatened. We are far from that moment."

"No, I know I said nuclear, but I am not talking about atomic weapons; I am talking about going nuclear on the economic front," the man insisted fervently. "We have the capability to bring the US economy to its knees, to deal it a blow that would take it a generation to recover from. I propose we show that we are willing to use that power!"

The group discussed that proposal for nearly an hour, with Chase listening in, becoming increasingly terrified. Then they put their proposal to HOLMES, their Chinese Communist Party Central Committee role player.

The discussion with and decision from HOLMES had not eased his troubled soul.

Back in the NSC situation room, the pressure of several pairs of eyes all looking at him was a little too much, and he stood, going for coffee. "Well, Madam President, right now, Beijing is more worried about geopolitics than military strategy," he said. "Their superficial response to our actions is straightforward and needs little thought because they already have the plan. An air campaign to degrade Taiwanese air defenses and try to win air dominance. Drone, artillery and missile strikes on military targets, infrastructure, ports. They'll regard their attacks on our carriers as unsuccessful: even though we've had to pull back, they didn't get the big PR kill they were hoping for. They'll be thoughtful about how vulnerable their own carriers were; those ships are big prestige projects for them, and we *have* taken them off the board, for now. And there's the space-tracking vessel Japan destroyed. Bottom line, the PLA Navy has taken all the big hits, and it wants blood …"

"You talk like you've got a source on the inside," Rosenstern said. "Be careful being so confident of what you think you know."

Chase swallowed. The Chief of Staff was right. But ... "JWC has access to CIA, DIA, CyberCom and NSA reporting and AI support tools, sir," Chase said. "If they have high confidence that the PLA Navy wants blood, then it's because they've seen sufficient intelligence to suggest that."

"Point made. Go ahead," Carliotti said.

"China's navy will look to make the seas in the OA impassible for Western shipping, military *and* civilian. Expect them to step up submarine activity. Don't be surprised if they attack Western-flagged cargo shipping. JWC expects them particularly to be looking for *Japanese* targets."

"Because Japan took out their spy ship," Rosenstern nodded.

"More than that," Chase said. "They're worried about geopolitics right now, remember? To them, it looks like Japan is all-in supporting the attack on China. It torpedoes their spy ship, it is allowing the US and allies to base fighters on Okinawa. But China's diplomats are telling them what we know is the case: the Japanese PM is wavering, probably others in his cabinet too. The attack on the spy ship was probably a badly timed mishap. China wants to make very clear to Japan what the price of its support for Taiwan will be, and the PLA Navy has the submarines needed to exact that price. Eight nuclear-powered attack submarines, to be exact—and we only know for sure where four of them are." Chase sat down again. "China's next moves? Keep up the air and missile attacks on Taiwan, and send a big message to Japan: most likely sink Japanese shipping, or unleash a cruise missile blitz on Okinawa, a few other Japanese ports ..."

497

Carliotti turned back to Holoman. "It sounds to me like we are a quite a few steps away from China throwing tactical nuclear grenades, Ervan," she said. "Tell the Joint Chiefs no. We stay at DEFCON 2 for now. And have State pass on a warning to Japan."

"There's more, Madam President," Chase said. He could sense Carliotti was mentally moving on. He had to keep their attention a little longer. He realized there was a risk he was placing too much store in the JWC process, but then again, his brief was to pass its thinking directly to the NSC. Holoman and Rosenstern began talking with each other, ignoring him now. He raised his voice. "An existential threat to the United States."

That stopped everyone.

"Go on," Carliotti told him.

"Our PLA military role players have proposed to their political masters that they proceed with a plan to isolate mainland USA from the rest of the world by attacking our undersea internet cable and orbital satellite networks."

"A *cyberattack?*" Holoman said dismissively. "We're prepared for that particular scenario. Long-term damage will be minimal."

"Not cyber," Chase said quickly. "Kinetic. China has the undersea drone capability to sever the main optical fiber cables linking the US eastern and western seaboards to Europe and Asia. In space, it has been mapping every object in near-earth orbit with its *Yuan Wang* class tracking ships for years. It has launched several hundred hunter-killer mini satellites that can physically disable so many of our military and civilian communications satellites as to render satellite communications with US forces outside of the US effectively non-operational. Our Chinese military players just asked for permission from their Politburo Standing Committee to execute these options."

Holoman saw Carliotti turn toward him and stammered. "That ... that's an absolute worst-case scenario," the Defense Secretary said. "The economic equivalent of mutually assured destruction. They would cripple our military communications capabilities, but more importantly, they would collapse our economy, and the global economy with it." He looked pained. "Ma'am, we discussed this exact scenario when we agreed to stand up to China. Yes, it has the potential to go after our communication infrastructure, just as it has a nuclear strike capability. But to use it already ..."

Carliotti held up a hand to stop the Defense Secretary and focused on Chase. "You said the JWC Chinese military team asked for a political green light to bring our economy down. What was the decision?"

"The decision from the 'red team' Central Committee was no," Chase told her. "But they were also told to ensure the appropriate assets were in place to execute the takedown if the decision changed."

"Ah, *come on*," Chief of Staff Rosenstern exclaimed. "We can't operate like this. This ... this ... think tank of policy wonks can throw doomsday scenarios and hypotheticals at us all day long, and we're supposed to take them seriously?"

Chase thought of how right the JWC and in particular its AI overlord HOLMES had been so far. "If you want to win this war, yes," Chase snapped back. And immediately regretted it.

Carliotti narrowed her eyes, but she was mercifully still looking at her Chief of Staff. "How many carrier strike groups do we currently have in the Western Pacific within range of Taiwan, HR?"

"I ... none, Madam President," Holoman admitted. "They're all being pulled back to northern Japan, Guam or Pearl."

"But we owe their continued existence to the forewarning we got from Mr. Chase's ... what was it ... 'think tank of policy wonks'?" she said without rancor. She addressed Holoman. "Ervan, please have your people immediately re-examine our contingency planning around an attack on either our subsea cables, satellite networks or both, assuming it might come *earlier* than we currently expect."

"Yes, Madam President," Holoman said. Chase was careful not to meet the glare from Holoman that followed, because he was pretty sure it would have blowtorched his soul.

Rosenstern had already moved on. He looked at his watch. "Madam President, we need to get ready for the press."

Carliotti stood. "I'll be out for an hour," she said. "Get some food; hydrate; take a walk. I need you all fresh for the next 24 hours. It's going to be hell." She crooked a finger at Chase. "Michael? Walk with me."

Oh, shit, Chase thought. *I smart-mouthed the President's Chief of Staff in front of everyone. Like a jerk.*

Rosenstern didn't appear particularly perturbed. The moment he stepped out of the situation room, he started working his phone as he walked toward the West Wing elevators. The President, however, stopped outside the corridor.

She leaned against the wall, looking at him for a moment before she spoke. It was an "I'm looking at you" kind of moment. He felt very, very uncomfortable. "I want you to give my thanks to your JWC," she said. "They called that

500

carrier attack. China hit us hard, but we were prepared. And we gave as good as we got."

The praise surprised him. "I'll pass that on, ma'am."

She nodded. "I want you to keep feeding in their thinking, without fear or favor. I know they won't always get it right. I'll make sure you and they aren't punished for every prognosis that flies wide."

"That's good to know."

"But don't be a smart-ass about it," she said. "You don't have the stripes."

He reddened. "No ma'am."

She softened. "You have family?"

"Uh, wife and kids in Indiana," he said, surprised again at the change in direction and tone. "I'm … my wife and I are separated. The commuting never really worked out." It was more complicated that, but he wasn't about to get into that with the President of the USA.

She put a hand on his arm. "Sorry to hear it. HR is recently divorced too. We ask a lot of our people, more than we really have a right to …"

Rosenstern was holding the elevator, looking annoyed now. "Madam President?"

"See you on the other side of this presser," she said with a grimace. She pushed her hair behind her ears. And then, for a few quick seconds, she looked human, even vulnerable. "I'm about to go and tell the world what it already knows … that we are at war with China. How do I look?" she asked him, turning her head from side to side. "Commander-in-Chief, or Victim of Events Spinning Out of Control?"

He smiled. "Definitely Commander-in-Chief, Ma'am."

501

"Good, because I also have to tell about 150 families they lost their loved ones today when the *Alaska* was hit. People need to believe we have a plan, and these sacrifices will be worth it." She turned, waving at Rosenstern. "Coming, HR. Do *not* give me that look."

Chase watched her go. *And what do you believe, Chase?* he asked himself. *The fight against China has been brewing for nearly 50 years. But is now the right time, and is Taiwan the right place? Do we have a plan? Will the sacrifices be worth it?*

Well, since he believed in the right of all people to decide their own destiny and not have it decided for them by autocrats and despots, yes. To all those questions.

But after the events of the last 24 hours, he hoped the right people on the other side were asking themselves the same questions.

Maylin 'Mushroom' Sun was asking herself exactly the same questions as she lay in *Fujian*'s sick bay. But the way she was feeling, she was probably not the right person.

Why Taiwan? Why now? Do we have a plan? And is it worth what we have already sacrificed?

She'd had a lot of time to think, lying on her side staring at the wall. She'd received burns to the back of her scalp and upper back where her clothes and skin had been in contact with the pod shell. The doctors said her hair would grow in again, but her back would have scars. Her body was full of pain, but her mind was full of mutiny. It was the morphine, she told herself, and let herself think. *Just don't say anything out loud*, she reminded herself. *Don't talk in your sleep.*

Her Chongming control pod was blast- and fire-proofed, and she'd been quick to duck when the wall exploded. The pod hatch cover had slammed shut over her, and she had no idea how, but it had saved her. Had Shredder done that? Had his last act been to save *her* life? The top of the pod had been crushed and she'd been buried, bent double, face between her legs, but for once she was glad she had no feeling in her legs from the waist down. She didn't cramp up, or at least, couldn't feel it. Her biggest problem had been breathing, with compressed lungs and smoke filling the air inside the pod as the filtration systems inside the pod eventually failed.

It had taken a long time for rescuers to reach her. A very long time. After she had been freed, she found out why. The enemy missile had delivered a shattering blow to *Fujian*, but about 20 minutes after it, hundreds of kamikaze drones had exploded across the exposed decks of the carrier, teeming with emergency personnel trying to deal with the fires and carnage caused by the hypersonic missile strike. Hundreds of explosions equivalent to fragmentation grenades had detonated across the length and width of the carrier, taking out personnel, parked aircraft, fire direction and navigation radars and communications antennas.

If there had been a follow-up hypersonic missile attack, *Fujian* would have been completely vulnerable. The only blessing of the day was that there had not been.

She went back to her ruminations. *Why Taiwan?* That was obvious. No one disputed the logic of it, even though Taiwan had variously been ruled by the Dutch, the Spanish, the Japanese, the Han Chinese and then the Kuomintang. It was its destiny to be Chinese. Even the main enemy accepted that—or said it did. Events of the day notwithstanding.

Why now? That was harder to answer. China had been patient with the rebels for 90 years. Why not another 10? It was just as easy to ask, why 90? Or why not? She was no general; she did not have insight into her military's relative strengths and weaknesses versus the adversary. She had to trust that when her government announced the blockade of Taiwan, it could be the precursor to war, and that it was ready for that war.

Do we have a plan? That was unclear to Mushroom too. The plan to blockade Taiwan had seemed sound enough. If the rebels would not listen to reason, then let the threat of starvation and economic ruin test their resolve. Taiwan's attack on their forces on the mainland had come as a shock, but had something like it not been expected when China had thrown up its blockade, and then attacked the adversary's aircraft to enforce it? It seemed obvious to Mushroom the rebel's allies would react poorly to the blockade, and if threatened, would lash out with brute force, as always. And now that open war had been joined, what next? Invasion?

It was hard to imagine how that would be possible now, especially with *Fujian* out of the fight and hiding in the Western Pacific. The carrier had been mortally wounded by the hypersonic missile attack and could do no more than crawl through the ocean at present. Nor could it launch and recover aircraft until the damage from the swarming drone attacks was repaired. Mushroom wasn't privy to how long that would take, or whether it was even possible to repair the damage without returning to port. And where could they dock?! *Fujian*'s strike group was isolated now. Its only way to reach a port in China was to run a gauntlet of unfriendly skies and seas past Taiwan or Japan. It hadn't escaped the crew's attention that they were in fact crawling *south*, away from China, into the Philippine Sea. There was a route to China through non-aligned Indonesia, past Vietnam, but that would

504

take *weeks*. Micronesia? There was a Chinese-owned port there. Could they be headed to Micronesia?

The conflict had entered a strange phase, as though neither side knew exactly what to do next. The preemptive attack on Chinese amphibious forces by Taiwan had derailed the plans China had been laying for months, if not years. She had no idea if other carriers had been struck too. She had to assume the Americans had tried. There would be no surprise seaborne landing by China anymore; that was obvious. Any attempt to concentrate its forces for a landing would be met with airstrikes and missiles from the Western Alliance before Chinese troops could embark. An airborne landing then? She knew China had been building up its airborne forces to allow an airborne operation, but only to support a larger seaborne invasion, surely not alone. The next step in China's "plan" was obscured to her.

And finally, *Are we willing to make the sacrifices that our country asks of us in the name of this war?*

That was an easier answer. No. For China the State? No, and a hundred times no.

I have lost my friend Asien. Taken from me in a storm of metal and fire. His body turned to mist, only the ghost of his smile remaining. No. This war is going to take the best of us and leave only the wounded and the crippled.

Like me.

He had lived long enough to truly honor the memory of his sister, Li. But who now would avenge Asien Chen? His parents had no other children; there were no uncles or aunts to mourn their children with them or seek atonement for their deaths. Maylin would not offer her life for China. But she *would* offer it in the name of her friend, Shredder. For his family. For his sister's memory.

505

She would heal. And then she would avenge him.

Bunny O'Hare was looking for answers too.

She'd made it back to Taichung without incident. She'd kept an emissions blackout the whole way back since she had no idea whether the skies she was flying through were hostile or friendly. She had only opened her comms to send a brief text message back to Taichung. *Package delivered. Carlyle KIA. Flowmax and Flatline no show. Will refuel and RTB. Pls advise, Okinawa or Taichung.*

She'd pondered what to say about Salt. A blue-on-blue kill. The inquiry, and there would be one eventually, was going to be ugly. Luckily for her, the entire engagement was captured on her black box, from their radio interchange to the DAS camera images of the dogfight. It didn't matter how clear-cut things looked from where she was sitting though; she had shot down a Colonel of the USAF Reserve. She was going to need an excellent lawyer. Not for the first time, she was glad Aggressor Inc. had an owner with deep pockets and an inexplicable soft spot for Bunny O'Hare.

The message that came back included a question. *RTB Taichung. Pls confirm Carlyle KIA, no beacon located, search and rescue not viable.*

What should she say to that? She sent two words: *Confirmed. KIA.*

The return journey had been easier than her egress, in fact, because the blizzard of Chinese missiles had waned and coalition fighters based on Japan and Luzon, together with Taiwan's own air force, had won back air superiority in the skies over and to the east of Taiwan.

The 100-mile-wide Taiwan Strait was still No Man's Land, with both sides dueling for control. There, China had a definite advantage, since most of its key airfields were inland and had not been targeted in the initial Taiwanese strike. Its aircraft, covered by ground and naval air defenses, prowled up and down the coast. But they couldn't approach Taiwan itself too closely, since doing so would see them targeted by the surviving Taiwanese Patriot batteries or the Coalition stealth fighters now running overlapping patrols up and down the length of the island.

Only one runway at Taichung was open; the base itself was a moonscape of smoking craters and destroyed buildings. She found Meany and the 68th in their revetments on the far side of the airfield after she landed. The underground hangars had escaped largely unscathed, only one near miss jamming a blast door in place and stopping them from being able to remove the aircraft inside. A Taiwanese engineering crew was working on the door.

Meany had been standing beside them. He didn't waste time on greetings. "What happened to Salt?"

"I'll give you the full report. Did we lose anyone here?" she asked. Her first question, of course.

"No. Touchdown hit a crater on her last landing, broke a gear strut. No airframe damage; no injuries. We'll have that bird flying again in no time. Lucky we have a couple more machines than pilots. She's back on patrol already." He returned to his own question. "Salt?"

She told him. It didn't take long. Their entire dogfight had been about three minutes from start to end. Explaining her suspicions around his motives took a little longer. "The attack will be on my Widow's black box," she said when she was finished.

"Air Force will send a ship out to try to recover his Widow to stop the tech falling into the wrong hands, but if they find it, they'll also have his black box, to corroborate your assertion he fired first." She'd expected Meany to react with disbelief. Or shock. Instead, he'd simply said to her, "Come with me."

In the back corner of the hangar that served as their ready room, he went to a desk and picked up a tablet PC. He handed it to her. "This came from internal security while you were on your way back. I guess that report you wrote got a reaction."

CONFIDENTIAL: EYES ONLY

To: Squadron Leader Anaximenes Papastopolous, 68th AGRS.

From: Aggressor Inc. Internal Security Division, Director Harlan Elliston.

If Lieutenant Colonel K. Carlyle lands your location after current operation, please contact base security immediately, <u>without his knowledge</u>. You will assist Taichung base security as needed to take Colonel Carlyle into custody. Colonel Carlyle should not be allowed access to any aircraft or vehicle. He is a flight risk and should be considered dangerous. Physical precautions are recommended.

"Damn," Bunny said. "They couldn't have sent this *before* I took off?"

"You know what this tells me?" Meany asked.

"Salt is a traitorous swine who deserved to die?"

"That, and … FBI already had their eye on him. Our internal security can't investigate anything this fast. Your report triggered FBI to move on him."

"FBI let a Chinese spy operate inside Aggressor Inc.? Why?"

"Who knows why spooks do what they do. Shits and giggles? Not enough evidence? I don't know," Meany said. "Or maybe you just killed one of their best double agents."

"Who was trying to protect his cover by shooting *me* down?" Bunny said. "Nah. You've seen too many action movies. He was just a dirty spy who sold his soul for a few yuan."

"I guess we'll never know," Meany said. "But it probably means you're off the hook for killing him."

"In self-defense."

"Sure." Meany held out his hand. "You owe me 100 bucks."

Bunny frowned.

"What?"

"Salt owed me 100 bucks. You killed him. So now *you* owe me 100 bucks."

"Go screw ..."

She didn't finish the sentence. She was just winding herself up when air raid sirens started wailing across the base again.

Takuya Kato was going home.

When the mayday went out from the *Yuan Wang Three Zero*, Shinji Kagawa aboard the *JS Haguro* was just 40 miles away.

Having received the order to investigate Okinotori, as expected, he directed his crew to make flank speed toward the island and brought the ship to general quarters. They were soon plowing through the water at 30 knots, with every eye

509

and ear on the ship fixed to a sensor or screen, watching for danger. Kagawa had shown some false modesty himself when he had described himself as "a small man in a small ship." The Maya Class *Haguro* was equipped with the US Aegis air defense system and formidable anti-ship, anti-submarine capabilities. It was in fact one of Japan's most powerful vessels.

The first thing they saw, as soon as they turned their attention in the direction of Okinotori, was a significant amount of air activity over the island, and none of it friendly. Kagawa immediately put their Firescout drone into the air and sent it ahead of them to extend their sensor range, then got on the internship comms.

"This is Captain Kagawa. As you would have heard, hostilities have been initiated between Taiwan and China. We have also received information that US and Coalition forces have been involved in action against the PLA Navy. Our nation is a part of that Coalition. We will remain at general quarters, and you will treat any adversary ship or aircraft contact as hostile. The decision to engage hostile vessels or aircraft will be mine, however. You will keep cool heads and execute your duties diligently. That is all."

Dropping sonar buoys in their path, their Firescout picked up no subsurface or surface contacts, and the aircraft over Okinotori also disappeared. He frowned at that. They had simply dropped right off the radar. He had to assume they had landed on the island's runway; there was no other explanation. Not a promising piece of intel. He had reported it immediately to fleet command and was ordered to assume he was entering hostile waters and to prepare an *armed* away team to investigate the island.

Then the mayday call had been received, and he had vectored his Firescout to the source. It sent back vision of a

Chinese *Yuan Wang* class vessel, split in two, its front section burning with phosphorescent fury. There was no sign of other Chinese vessels, aircraft or, more importantly, rescuers.

When the *JS Haguro* arrived at the position the *Yuan Wang Three Zero* had broadcast from, it found chaos and carnage. The exposed parts of the Chinese ship were still smoking from internal fires. A few dozen crew members were clinging to the wreck or floating on debris in the water. Many were badly burned. There were a lot of bodies in the water.

Haguro spent most of the morning rescuing the Chinese sailors. Those who were injured were treated. Those who were not were put into a makeshift brig under armed guard. The *Haguro*'s Captain decided it wasn't his job to decide who was friend and who was foe. That could be sorted out when they made port again.

As soon as he could spare it, the Captain sent a rib boat to the facility itself. If there was still a scientist on the station, they hadn't been able to raise him. Their hope was that his radio or sat comms were just dead. But some of their prisoners had told them Chinese commandos had been sent to the island. Reports said a couple of these had come back, but they were wounded. He'd ordered his men to check the prisoners again to see if there were any in Commando uniforms, and they found one, in the ship's infirmary. He was in no condition to talk. He had been shot in the chest and had an endotracheal tube down this throat.

But Kagawa couldn't be sure all the Commandos were accounted for, so he sent a party of armed Marines to check the facility, just in case it was not empty of all Chinese. And he held out hope that they would find the coral biologist there.

They did.

511

The man's dead body was not in good shape. Tropical heat and insects had taken their toll, and he had a large seeping wound in his abdomen. The ship's medic sent with the boat party had declared it to be a gunshot wound, delivered at close quarters. Probably a shotgun, judging by the damage.

The Marines found his dead body near the armed UFP defense system. They disarmed it and discovered it had been fired not once, but twice—both acoustic mines and torpedoes had been deployed. That was an investigation for another time, but it seemed that the man had singlehandedly defended the Japanese territory from an overwhelmingly superior Chinese assault.

As the biologist's body was brought aboard and news of his death spread, any sympathy the Captain and crew of the *JS Haguro* might have had for the Chinese commando in their sick bay evaporated very, very quickly. Kagawa had put an armed guard outside the infirmary, for his enemy's protection.

The incident was to have a profound effect on the officers and crew of the *JS Haguro*, and the role they were to play in the war that was to come.

/END VOLUME 1

Next

Coming Summer 2023, the second novel in the Aggressor series: Beachhead.

With US troops and aircraft on Taiwanese soil, and missiles flying across the Taiwan Strait, the world prepares itself for the war that has been building since the turn of the century …

Will China back down, or double down? Will the fragile Western Coalition hold? Will regional conflict tip over into a global war? And what's next for the newly raised 68th Aggressor Squadron and the personnel of Aggressor Inc.?

Beachhead is told through the eyes of six combatants from multiple nations, fighting to survive as the two superpowers clash.

Only one will be alive by the end of the week.

Featuring a plot taken from tomorrow's headlines, cutting-edge technologies that are on the drawing board today, and characters you will never forget, the Aggressor series delivers guaranteed page-turners for military fiction enthusiasts.

PRE-ORDER 'BEACHHEAD' ON AMAZON TODAY AND
LOCK IN THE LOW PRE-LAUNCH PRICE …

Author note

I hope you enjoyed AGGRESSOR.

Western military strategists and think tanks have spent a lot of resources war-gaming a Chinese invasion of Taiwan. And, we know from leaked reports, so have Chinese planners. In preparing to write this novel I reviewed every publicly available war game readout and they generally *all* reach the same conclusion: if China attempts to invade Taiwan, a long and ruinous war will result. In these war games, China usually manages to get ground and airborne forces across the Taiwan Strait and achieve a foothold on the island, but once the US and allies pile in, Chinese troops are either limited to their beachhead or pushed back into the sea.

In the process, both the US and China lose one or more aircraft carriers, hundreds of ships and aircraft, tens of thousands of soldiers. The war pulls in regional powers, rocks the global economy and risks escalating into a nuclear confrontation.

The assumptions used in almost all these war games are critically flawed, and I became so frustrated at this that the AGGRESSOR series is my personal attempt to show what could happen if we use an alternative set of assumptions to those that have become the "accepted wisdom." That "wisdom" is summed up in the introduction to the Center for Strategic and International Studies (CSIS) Taiwan war game, which looked at 25 sets of assumptions, nearly all of them assuming Chinese superiority and incompetence in the Taiwanese military. As the CSIS introduction says: "The invasion always starts the same way: an opening bombardment destroys most of Taiwan's navy and air force in the first hours of hostilities. Augmented by a powerful rocket force, the Chinese navy encircles Taiwan and interdicts any attempts to get ships and aircraft to the besieged island. Tens of thousands of Chinese soldiers cross the strait in a mix of military amphibious craft and civilian roll-on, roll-off ships, while air assault and airborne troops land behind the beachheads."

Let's look at the most used and typically flawed assumptions from a range of war games:

1) China takes Taiwan and Western powers "by surprise" with a "lightning attack." Usually this assumption runs like this: China has positioned invasion forces along the coast opposite Taiwan for military exercises intended to intimidate Taiwan and its allies. But, in a bewildering leap of logic, an opening air and missile attack destroys most of Taiwan's air force and navy, leading to a "lightning invasion," which manages to land tens of thousands of troops on beaches on Taiwan. Even more unbelievably, this lightning attack is often assumed to take place after China has already begun an economic blockade of air and sea traffic around Taiwan in which it has moved considerable naval and air assets into the area around Taiwan without any military reaction from Taiwan or its allies.

The experience of the Russian invasion of Ukraine illustrates the massive flaws in these assumptions. Russia telegraphed its invasion of Ukraine well ahead of time and the US administration called out the invasion loudly and publicly for weeks, if not months, before the first Russian paratroopers landed on Ukrainian soil. A Chinese invasion of Taiwan would *completely* dwarf the Russian invasion of Ukraine and the signs would be evident months in advance.

Firstly, China would need to mass hundreds of thousands of troops, tens of thousands of transport ships, reposition its air force and send hundreds of naval vessels into the Taiwan

Strait to achieve an invasion. The 2022 leaked report of an invasion rehearsal conducted by military and civilian authorities in the "Southern War Zone of the PLA Guangdong Province" showed that, for the first phase of the invasion, China's Eastern and Southern Theater Command planned to mobilize 300,000 combat troops and 140,000 support personnel, 953 ships of various types and 1,653 drones. The drone supply was flagged as a critical issue, with only 2,000 "pieces of high-tech equipment," 480 drones and 70 unmanned boats available. The conclusion was that 90 civilian industrial facilities would need to be militarized to produce the necessary drones.

To move this massive force would require the support of 20 airports and docks, six repair and shipbuilding factories, 14 emergency transfer centers and forward positioning of resources such as grain depots, hospitals, blood stations and fuel and oil depots. To support logistics above what it had available itself, the military would need to requisition 10,000-ton trains with 588 train carriages, 64 ships, 38 aircraft, and civil buildings to house personnel.

The invasion fleet itself would comprise no fewer than 365 ships, which would need to be "weaponized" within 45 days of the invasion order being issued. But only 72 ships were already prepared, meaning the rest would have to be found, transported and made ready. Chinese authorities identified 90 capable ship repair and construction enterprises in the whole Eastern Command district but reported that only 280 ships could be "weaponized" within the 45-day warning timeframe, much less than the 365 ships needed. This effort alone would therefore take several weeks!

A huge security operation would be initiated involving 26,000 armed police and 7,000 armed militia in 17 cities "utilizing the combined power of the Chinese Communist party, government, military, police and civil as a whole, to help guard 61 important military targets and 276 important civilian targets." It was acknowledged in this leaked transcript that current personnel levels would be inadequate to meet these demands and a massive mobilization program would be needed in advance. Of particular concern was the risk of foreign-influenced civil unrest in the "megacities" of Guangzhou and Shenzhen, so foreigners would be rounded up and ejected.

No "military exercises" can mask these kind of preparations. And yet so many of these war games assume that all the preparations flagged above are going to somehow take place under the noses of the intelligence services of Taiwan, the US and its allies and they are going to be "taken with their pants down."

Sorry, not a chance.

2) Assumption two in almost all these war games is that Taiwan and its allies will mysteriously take no preemptive military action to thwart an invasion but will instead just build up their defenses (usually inadequately) and wait for the invasion to start. The US and allies might increase surveillance and move one or more submarines or aircraft carrier strike groups into the theatre, but little more. It would therefore take days or even weeks for Taiwan's allies to come to its aid, during which Chinese forces would decimate Taiwan's defenses and get a foothold on Taiwan itself.

There are *so* many things wrong with these assumptions too. Remember the Chinese rehearsal allowed a 45 day 'war alert' in which to get forces ready for an invasion. This alert state would be evident to every Western intelligence service. Why then do none of these war games assume that the US administration of the time, and its allies, might make a preemptive strike against Chinese invasion forces? In fictional accounts of this potential conflict, the US administration is often portrayed as weak, docile and incompetent.

In AGGRESSOR I make the opposite and, I believe, more realistic assumption—that a US administration, *not* asleep at the wheel, has seen war coming and prepared for it. That it has put assets into the theatre in expectation of Chinese aggression, conducted exercises of its own intended to ensure those assets—from several allied nations—are trained, available and ready. And that the administration has both the means and the will to take preemptive action to prevent a Chinese invasion force from even leaving Chinese shores. In AGGRESSOR I assume a US administration that might keep the door to peace open but that will be prepared for war.

3) Assumption number three is that China's strategic missile and air forces will decimate Taiwanese defenses, leaving it wide open to invasion before Taiwan's allies can rouse themselves from their sleep and come to the island's aid.

China has formidable missile forces and a numerically superior air force compared with Taiwan. The war gamers who propose this assumption, however, overlook every lesson from the Russian invasion of Ukraine, where even a year after the invasion, the numerically vastly superior Russian Aerospace Force was unable to achieve anything *approaching* air superiority over Ukraine. Instead, it was so humiliated by losses in the first months of war that it was banned by its President from participating in the usual Victory Day flyover. After a year of war it was visually confirmed to have lost more than 300 frontline aircraft, versus 129 lost by Ukraine.

The reason? Modern anti-aircraft systems are highly effective against fourth-generation aircraft (which comprise the bulk of China's air forces) and are very difficult to degrade.

Ukraine fielded Russian-made, high-altitude S-300 surface-to-air missile defenses, which Russian anti-radar missiles proved unable to destroy, and which prevented high-flying Russian aircraft from entering Ukrainian airspace. These were supplied with Patriot and NASAMs systems, which made the skies over Ukraine even more lethal. In addition, a proliferation of low-altitude anti-air cannon, man-portable missiles and radar-guided autocannons prevented Russian ground attack helicopters and jets from operating at low level, reducing their ability to provide close air support to Russian troops.

Yet for some reason, in Taiwan war games, the assumption is that, unlike the combat-tested Russian Air Force, the *untested* Chinese air force will somehow dominate the skies over a Taiwanese enemy armed with the latest in Western-made ground-to-air missile and radar-guided cannon defenses, including long-range Patriot and medium-range NASAMs Missile Batteries!

True, Taiwan has no fifth-generation stealth aircraft, and China will have a limited number of these available. Chinese stealth fighters can probably be used to launch stand-off attacks against Taiwan with near impunity. But China has no stealth ground attack aircraft and will not have in the foreseeable future. The same tactics that turned Ukraine into a porcupine the Russian Air Force could not attack would have exactly the same effect on Chinese air forces over Taiwan.

Chinese missiles would rain down on Taiwanese airfields, but the idea Taiwan's air force and air defenses would be wiped out in this initial attack is highly suspect. Taiwanese defense planners are not idiots who, with an invasion imminent, will stupidly leave precious military aircraft parked out in the open for China to destroy. Taiwan has already invested heavily in underground storage and hangars for its air force and supporting logistics, burying these facilities deep in the mountain ranges that run down the middle of the island. There will be no "surprise missile strike" by China that wipes out half of the Taiwanese Air Force in a single night, allowing China to sail its ships and land its paratroops without aerial or naval interdiction. (If anything, it is US aircraft based on Guam and in Japan that are at greatest risk from Chinese missile strikes.)

Instead, it is highly likely that, just like Russia's air force, China's air force is relegated to launching standoff missile attacks from within Chinese airspace on the other side of the Taiwan Strait, and its main weapon of choice for trying to degrade Taiwanese anti-air and anti-ship defenses will be cruise and ballistic missile attacks, which Taiwan will be well prepared to counter. Many Chinese missiles will get through, of course, and the military and civilian toll will be terrible, but as we have seen in Ukraine, these sorts of attacks alone cannot win wars.

4) Certain powerful weapons systems are not available to the US side but *are* available to China.

In this leap of logic, the Western technological advantage in weapons systems is negated so that the battle for Taiwan becomes one of quantity, not quality, thus favoring China again. In the CSIS war game the US side was denied the use of the JASSM missile system, probably the most potent cruise missile in the US armory of the future. This is not a prototype "future weapon"; more than 2,000 have already been delivered to the USAF. Yet its use was denied to the blue side in the CSIS war game. And yet the Chinese were allowed the use of their hypersonic carrier-killing ballistic missiles because allowing the US side to use JASSM would have tipped the balance of power too far in favor of blue.

Ya think? Just like HIMARS tipped the balance of the ground war against Russia in favor of Ukraine? Advanced weapons systems impact the outcome of wars. Excluding them from war games to give the adversary a chance is nonsensical. Enough said.

5) Assumption five is that China *will* get troops ashore, create a foothold and may even break out of its beachhead to attack targets in inland Taiwan. But by the time it does, Taiwan's allies will arrive to rescue it and Chinese troops will not make or take Taipei. They will either be pushed back to their beachhead or be forced to withdraw entirely.

This assumption again presumes no preemptive action by the US or Taiwan, but even allowing that, just how is China supposed to land anything except a token force on Taiwan's coasts? Sufficient airborne troops will not exist to support a purely airborne invasion, and as already discussed, China will not have the air superiority allowing it to insert a meaningful paratroop force.

Since Taiwan's air and missile forces will not have destroyed them all, the motley fleet of "weaponized" Chinese vessels and their escorts trying to ferry troops across the Strait would be attacked as they are forming up and from the moment they came within range of Taiwan's anti-ship missile defenses. Let's assume some of these missile defenses have been degraded by Chinese precision missile strikes. Under cover of China's *Type 055* missile destroyers and fighter jets, let us also assume that some of the Chinese landing ships make it to the Taiwanese coast.

Taiwan is not Ukraine, with thousands of miles of border through which an enemy can invade. There are only a dozen possible landing sites for Chinese ground troops, and these will be fortified with anti-air and anti-ship missile defenses, and physical defenses in depth. Taiwanese military planners would have weeks of warning of an impending invasion, and ground defenses would be prepared, thousands of troops dug in near these landing zones, artillery ranged. Any ships that managed to approach the shore, any troops that managed to make landfall, would be hammered mercilessly with massed artillery and Taiwanese close air support because China's air force will *not* have air superiority.

And then, far sooner than most war game planners allow, US and allied forces would join the counter-offensive against China's navy, air and land forces. Hundreds of aircraft flying from Japan and the Philippines, and off the decks of US carriers far out in the Philippine Sea to the east, would fly around-the-clock sorties against any Chinese troops who made it ashore. US and allied naval vessels and submarines would launch hundreds of cruise missiles at Chinese targets, initially those trying to reach Taiwan, but then inevitably also at logistics and supply nodes up and down the Chinese east coast.

At this point, the paper-thin assumptions of most war gamers become irrelevant since the war would enter a completely different and much less predictable phase. Would China withdraw to lick its wounds? Would it have the resources for a new offensive? Would it draw on support from allies of its own—Russia, Iran, North Korea—to place political or military pressure on Taiwan and its allies? Would China open a new front elsewhere in an attempt to split the focus and resolve of the US and its allies? Or would the US open a new front to draw Chinese focus away from Taiwan?

These questions and more will be explored in the coming volumes of the AGGRESSOR series!

In the writing of AGGRESSOR I am deeply indebted to the strong beta reading team which came together to advise on the manuscript. Among the team were current and former service personnel from the armies, navies, Marines, air forces and intelligence services of the US, UK, France, Australia, India and Israel. If you find the novel authentic, it is thanks to them. Any technical errors you might find are entirely mine!

And finally a word of thanks to my best mate and long-suffering wife, Lise, who had to sacrifice a couple of weeks of summer holidays so I could get this novel started.

Now, on to the next novel in the AGGRESSOR series, 'BEACHHEAD,' which is coming summer 2023 and can be preordered today!

FX Holden

Copenhagen, April 2023

Glossary

For simplicity, this glossary is common across all FX Holden novels and may refer to systems not in this novel. As such, it is useful as a reference beyond this book! Please note, weapons or systems marked with an asterisk* are currently still under development. If there is no asterisk, then the system has already been deployed by at least one nation.

3D PRINTER: A printer which can recreate a 3D object based on a three-dimensional digital model, typically by laying down many thin layers of a material in succession

ADA*: All Domain Attack. An attack on an enemy in which all operational domains–space, cyber, ground, air and naval–are engaged either simultaneously or sequentially

AI: Artificial intelligence, as applied in aircraft to assist pilots, in intelligence to assist with intelligence analysis, or in ordnance such as drones and unmanned vehicles to allow semi-autonomous decision making

AIM-120D: US medium-range supersonic air-to-air missile

AIM-260* Joint Advanced Tactical Missile (JATM), proposed replacement for AIM-120, with twin-boost phase, launch and loiter capability. Swarming capability has been discussed.

AIS: Automated identification system, a system used by all ships to provide update data on their location to their owners and insurers. Civilian shipping is required to keep their transponder on at all times unless under threat from pirates; military ships transmit at their own discretion. Rogue nations often ignore the requirement in order to hide the location of ships with illicit cargoes or conducting illegal activities.

AIR TROPHY*: 'Trophy' is an Israeli-made anti-projectile defense system using explosively formed penetrators to defeat attacks on vehicles. It is currently fitted to several Israeli and US armored vehicle types. In 2023 the US Navy announced it was testing the Trophy system for naval defense. Use as an air defense system is speculative.

AGGRESSOR/ADVERSARY: Fighter squadrons that provide training against adversary aircraft are known as 'Aggressor' squadrons. The US Air Force has several in-house Aggressor Squadrons (including F-16s and F-35s) which it uses to train fighter pilots and joint tactical air controllers. In the US Marines and Navy these are known as 'Adversary' units. In 2022, the USAF confirmed that Aggressor aircraft in Alaska had been used to intercept Russian aircraft off the coast of Alaska, and Aggressor squadrons had been used to backfill regular USAF squadrons deployed overseas. Many air forces including the USAF and RAF, also use private contractors to provide these services, and several large private military aviation contractors exist, fielding recently retired F-16 and F-18 fighters. The most advanced private air force in the world, Air USA, claims to be able to field three Aggressor Squadrons including 46 ex-RAAF F/A-18 Hornets.

ALL DOMAIN KILL CHAIN*: Also known as Multi-Domain Kill Chain. An attack in which advanced AI allows high-speed assimilation of data from multiple sources (satellite, cyber, ground and air) to generate engagement solutions for military maneuver, precision fire support, artillery or combat air support.

AMD-65: Hungarian-made military assault rifle

AN/APG-81: The active electronically scanning array (AESA) radar system on the F-35 Panther that allows it to track and engage multiple air and ground targets simultaneously

ANGELS: Radio brevity code for 'thousands of feet'. Angels five is five thousand feet.

AO YIN: Legendary Chinese four-horned bull with insatiable appetite for human flesh

APC: Armored personnel carrier; a wheeled or tracked lightly armored vehicle able to transport troops into combat and provide limited covering fire

ARMATA T-14: Next-generation Russian main battle tank

ASFN: Anti-screw fouling net. Traditionally, a net boom laid across the entrance of a harbor to hinder the entrance of ships or submarines. Can also be dropped from a fast boat, or fired from a subsea drone to foul the screws of a surface vessel.

ASRAAM: Advanced Short-Range Air-to-Air Missile (infrared only)

ASROC: Anti-submarine rocket-launched torpedo. Allows a torpedo to be fired at a submerged target from up to ten miles away, allowing the torpedo to enter the water close to the target and reducing the chances the target can evade the attack.

ASTUTE CLASS: Next-generation British nuclear-powered attack submarine (SSN) designed for stealth operation. Powered by a Rolls Royce reactor plant coupled to a pump-jet propulsion system. *HMS Astute* is the first of seven planned hulls, *HMS Agincourt* is the last. Can carry up to 38 torpedoes and cruise missiles, and is one of the first British submarines to be steered by a 'pilot' using a joystick.

ASW: Anti-Submarine Warfare

AWACS: Airborne Warning and Control System aircraft, otherwise known as AEW&C (Airborne Early Warning and

Control). Aircraft with advanced radar and communication systems that can detect aircraft at ranges up to several hundred miles, and direct air operations over a combat theatre.

AXEHEAD: Russian long-range hypersonic air-to-air missile

B-21 RAIDER*: Replacement for the retiring US B-2 Stealth Bomber and B-52. The Raider is intended to provide a lower-cost, stealthier alternative to the B-2 with expanded weapons delivery capabilities to include hypersonic and beyond visual range air-to-air missiles.

BARRETT MRAD M22: Multirole adaptive design sniper rifle with replaceable barrels, capable of firing different ammunition types including anti-materiel rounds, accurate out to 1,500 meters or nearly one mile

BATS*: Boeing Airpower Teaming System, semi-autonomous unmanned combat aircraft. The BATS drone is designed to accompany 4th - and 5th-generation fighter aircraft on missions either in an air escort, recon or electronic warfare capacity.

BELLADONNA: A Russian-made mobile electronic warfare vehicle capable of jamming enemy airborne warning aircraft, ground radars, radio communications and radar-guided missiles

BESAT*: New 1,200-ton class of Iranian SSP (air-independent propulsion) submarine. Also known as Project Qaaem. Capable of launching mines, torpedoes or cruise missiles.

BIG RED ONE: US 1st Infantry Division (see also BRO), aka the Bloody First

BINGO: Radio brevity code showing that an aircraft has only enough fuel left for a return to base

BLACK WIDOW (P-99)*: Concept aircraft. Several companies were competing in 2023 for the Next Generation Air Dominance air superiority initiative. The Black Widow is a purely speculative platform combining what is known about the requirements issued and the designs in testing. NGAD is described by the USAF as a "family of systems", with a stealth fighter aircraft as the centerpiece of the system, and other parts of the system likely to be uncrewed escort aircraft to carry extra munitions and perform other missions. In particular, NGAD aims to develop a system that addresses the operation needs of the Pacific theater of operations, where current USAF fighters lack sufficient range and payload. The successful NGAD aircraft is therefore unlikely to resemble current US stealth fighters such as the F-22 Raptor or F-35 Panther.

BLOODY FIRST: US 1st Infantry Division, aka the Big Red One (BRO)

BOGEY: Unidentified aircraft detected by radar

BRADLEY UGCV*: US unmanned ground combat vehicle prototype based on a modified M3 Bradley combat fighting vehicle. A tracked vehicle with medium armor, it is intended to be controlled remotely by a crew in a vehicle, or ground troops, up to two miles away. Armed with 5kw blinding laser and autoloading TOW anti-tank missiles. See also HYPERION

BRO: Big Red One or Bloody First, nickname for US Army 1st Infantry Division

BTR-80: A Russian-made amphibious armored personnel carrier armed with a 30mm automatic cannon

BUG OUT: Withdraw from combat

BUK: Russian-made self-propelled anti-aircraft missile system designed to engage medium-range targets such as aircraft, smart bombs and cruise missiles

BUSTER: 100% throttle setting on an aircraft, or full military power

CAP: Combat air patrol; an offensive or defensive air patrol over an objective

CAS: Close air support; air action by rotary-winged or fixed-wing aircraft against hostile targets in close proximity to friendly forces. CAS operations are often directed by a joint terminal air controller, or JTAC, embedded with a military unit.

CASA CN-235: Turkish Air Force medium-range twin-engined transport aircraft

CBRN: Chemical, biological, radiological or nuclear (see also NBC SUIT)

CCP: Communist Party of China. Governed by a Politburo comprising the Chinese Premier and senior party ministers and officials.

CENTURION: US 20mm radar-guided close-in weapons system for protection of ground or naval assets against attack by artillery, rocket or missiles

CHAMP*: Counter-electronics High Power Microwave Advanced Missiles; a 'launch and loiter' cruise missile which attacks sensitive electronics with high power microwave bursts to damage electronics. Similar in effect to an electromagnetic pulse (EMP) weapon.

CHONGMING CH-7 Rainbow*: A stealthy flying-wing uncrewed fighter aircraft similar to the US X-47B, with a 22-

meter wingspan and 10m length, and a maximum take-off weight of 13 tons. Reportedly able to fly at 920 km/h or 571 mph, with an operational radius of 2,000 km or 1,200 miles. Can carry air to air or air to surface missiles in an internal bay. Production was due to begin in 2022 but deployment has not yet been confirmed.

CIC: Combat Information Center. The 'nerve center' on an early warning aircraft, warship or submarine that functions as a tactical center and provides processed information for command and control of the near battlespace or area of operations. On a warship, acts on orders from and relays information to the bridge.

CO: Commanding Officer

COALITION: Coalition of Nations involved in *Operation Anatolia Screen*: Turkey, US, UK, Australia, Germany

COLT: Combat Observation Laser Team; a forward artillery observer team armed with a laser for designating targets for attack by precision-guided munitions

CONSTELLATION* class frigate: the result of the US FFG(X) program, a warship with advanced anti-air, anti-surface and anti-submarine capabilities capable of serving as a data integration and communication hub. The first ship in the class, *USS Constellation*, is expected to enter service mid-2020s. *USS Congress* will be the second ship in the class.

CONTROL ROOM: the compartment on a submarine from which weapons, sensors, propulsion and navigation commands are coordinated

COP: Combat Outpost (US)

C-RAM: Counter-rocket, artillery and mortar cannon, also abbreviated counter-RAM

CROWS: Common Remotely Operated Weapon Station, a weapon such as .50 caliber machine gun, mounted on a turret and controlled remotely by a soldier inside a vehicle, bunker or command post

CUDA*: Missile nickname (from barracuda) for the supersonic US short - to medium-range 'Small Advanced Capabilities Missile'. It has tri-mode (optical, active radar and infrared heat-seeking) sensors, thrust vectoring for extreme maneuverability and a hit-to-kill terminal attack

CYBERCOM: US Cyberspace combatant command responsible for cyber defense and warfare.

DARPA: US Defense Advanced Research Projects Agency, a research and development agency responsible for bringing new military technologies to the US armed forces

DAS: Distributed Aperture System; a 360-degree sensor system on the F-35 Panther allowing the pilot to track targets visually at greater than 'eyeball' range

DFDA: Australian armed forces Defense Forces Discipline Act

DFM: Australian armed forces Defense Force Magistrate

DIA: The US Defense Intelligence Agency

DIRECTOR OF NATIONAL CYBER SECURITY*. The NSA's Cyber Security Directorate is an organization that unifies NSA's foreign intelligence and cyber defense missions and is charged with preventing and eradicating threats to National Security Systems and the Defense Industrial Base. Various US government sources have mooted the elevation of the role of Director of Cyber Security to a Cabinet-level Director of National Cyber Security (on a level with the Director of National Intelligence), appointed by the US

President to coordinate the activities of the many different agencies and military departments engaged in cyber warfare.

DRONE: Unmanned aerial vehicle, UCAV or UAV, used for combat, transport, refueling or reconnaissance

ECS: Engagement Control Station; the local control center for a HELLADS laser battery which tracks targets and directs anti-air defensive fire

EMP: Electromagnetic pulse. Nuclear weapons produce an EMP wave which can destroy unshielded electronic components. The major military powers have also been experimenting with non-nuclear weapons which can also produce an EMP pulse–see CHAMP missile

ETA: Estimated Time of Arrival

F-16 FALCON: US-made 4th-generation multirole fighter aircraft flown by Turkey

F-35: US 5th-generation fighter aircraft, known either as the Panther (pilot nickname) or Lightning II (manufacturer name). The Panther nickname was first coined by the 6th Weapons Squadron 'Panther Tamers'. There is much speculation about the capabilities of the Panther, just as there is about the Russian Su-57 Felon. Neither has been extensively combat tested, though the F-35 has reportedly been used in combat by the Israeli Air Force.

F-47B (currently X-47) FANTOM*: A Northrop Grumman demonstration unmanned combat aerial vehicle (UCAV) in trials with the US Navy and a part of the DARPA Joint UCAS program. See also MQ-25 STINGRAY

FAC: Forward air controller; an aviator embedded with a ground unit to direct close air support attacks. See also TAC(P) or JTAC

FAST MOVERS: Fighter jets

FATEH: Iranian SSK (diesel electric) submarine. At 500 tons, also considered a midget submarine. Capable of launching torpedoes, torpedo-launched cruise missiles and mines

FELON: Russian 5th-generation stealth fighter aircraft, the Sukhoi Su-57. There is much speculation about the capabilities of the Felon, just as there is about the US F-35 Panther. Neither has been extensively combat tested.

FINGER FOUR FORMATION: a fighter aircraft patrol formation in which four aircraft fly together in a pattern that resembles the tips of the four fingers of a hand. Three such formations can form a squadron of 12 aircraft.

FIRESCOUT: an unmanned autonomous scout helicopter for service on US warships, used for anti-ship and anti-submarine operations

FISTER: A member of a FiST (Fire Support Team)

FLANKER: Russian Sukhoi-30 or 35 attack aircraft; see also J-11 (China)

FOX (1, 2 or 3): Radio brevity code indicating a pilot has fired an air-to-air missile, either semi-active radar seeking (1), infrared (2) or active radar seeking (3)

GAL*: A natural language learning system (AI) used by Israel's Unit 8200 to conduct complex analytical research support

GAL-CLASS SUBMARINE: An upgraded *Dolphin II* class submarine, fitted with the GAL AI system, allowing it to be operated by a two-person crew

G/ATOR: Ground/Air Oriented Task Radar (GATOR); a radar specialized for the detection of incoming artillery fire, rockets or missiles. Also able to calculate the origin of attack for counterfire purposes.

GBU: Guided Bomb Unit

GPS: Global Positioning System, a network of civilian or military satellites used to provide accurate map reference and location data

GRAY WOLF*: US subsonic standoff air-launched cruise missile with swarming (horde) capabilities. The Gray Wolf is designed to launch from multiple aircraft, including the C-130, and defeat enemy air defenses by overwhelming them with large numbers. It will feature modular swap-out warheads.

GREYHOUND: Radio brevity code for the launch of an air-ground missile

GRU: Russian military intelligence service

H-20*: Xian Hong 20 stealth bomber with a range of 12,000 km or 7,500 miles and payload of 10 tons. Comparable to the US B-21.

HACM*: Hypersonic Attack Cruise Missile. A two-stage missile with solid fuel first stage boosting the missile to supersonic velocity after which a scramjet engine takes over to drive the missile to speeds of Mach 5 and above. The contract to develop HACM was awarded to Raytheon in September 2022.

HARM: High-speed Anti-Radar Missile; a missile which homes on the signals produced by anti-air missile radars like that used by the BUK or PANTSIR

HAWKEYE: Northrop Grumman E2D airborne warning and control aircraft. Capable of launching from aircraft carriers and networking (sharing data) with compatible aircraft.

HE: High-explosive munitions; general purpose explosive warheads

HEAT: High-Explosive Anti-Tank munitions; shells specially designed to penetrate armor

HELLADS*: High Energy Liquid Laser Area Defense System; an alternative to missile or projectile-based air defense systems that attacks enemy missiles, rockets or bombs with high energy laser and/or microwave pulses. Currently being tested by US, Chinese, Russian and EU ground, air and naval forces.

HOLMES*: A natural language learning system (AI) used by the NSA to conduct sophisticated analytical research support. The NSA has publicly reported it is already using AI for cyber defense and exploring machine learning potential.

HORDE*: Drones, missiles or smart bombs with onboard AI and the ability to coordinate their actions with other drones while in flight, either autonomously or using preselected protocols. 'Horde' tactics differ from 'swarm' tactics in that they rely on large numbers to overwhelm enemy defenses. See also SWARM

HPM*: High Power Microwave; an untargeted local area defensive weapon which attacks sensitive electronics in missiles and guided bombs to damage electronics such as guidance systems

HSU-003*: Planned Chinese large unmanned underwater vehicle optimized for seabed warfare, i.e. piloting itself to a specific location on the sea floor (a harbor or shipping lane) and conducting reconnaissance or anti-shipping attacks. Comparable to the US Orca.

HYPERION*: Proposed lightly armored unmanned ground vehicle (UGCV). Can be fitted with turret-mounted

50kw laser for anti-air, anti-personnel defense and autoloading TOW missile launcher. See also BRADLEY UGCV

HYPERSONIC: Speeds greater than 5x the speed of sound

ICC: Information Coordination Center; command center for multiple air defense batteries such as PATRIOT or HELLADS

IED: Improvised explosive device, for example, a roadside bomb

IFF: Identify Friend or Foe transponder, a radio transponder that allows weapons systems to determine whether a target is an ally or enemy

IFV: Infantry fighting vehicle, a highly mobile, lightly armored, wheeled or tracked vehicle capable of carrying troops into a combat and providing fire support. See NAMER

IMA BK: The combat AI built into Russia's Su-57 Felon and Okhotnik fighter aircraft

IR: Infrared or heat-seeking system

ISIS: Self-proclaimed Islamic State of Iraq and Syria

J-7: Fishbed; 3rd-generation Chinese fighter, a copy of cold war Russian Mig-21

J-10: Vigorous Dragon; 3rd-generation Chinese fighter, comparable to US F-16

J-11: Flanker; 4th-generation Chinese fighter, copy of Russian Su-27

J-15: Flying Shark; 4th-generation PLA Navy, twin-engine twin-seat fighter, comparable to Russian Su-33 and a further development of the J-11. Currently the most common aircraft flown off China's aircraft carriers.

J-16*: *Zhi Sheng* (Intelligence Victory); 4th-generation, two-seater twin-engine multirole strike fighter. In 2019 it was announced a variant of the J-16 was being developed with *Zhi Sheng* Artificial Intelligence to replace the human 'backseater' or copilot.

J-20: 'Mighty Dragon'; 5th-generation single-seat, twin-engine Chinese stealth fighter, claimed to be comparable to the US F-35 or F-22, or Russian Su-57

JAGM: Joint air-ground missile. A US short-range anti-armor or anti-personnel missile fired from an aircraft. It can be laser or radar guided and has an 18 lb. warhead.

JASSM: AGM-158 Joint Air-to-Surface Standoff Missile; long-range subsonic stealth cruise missile

JDAM: Joint Direct Attack Munition; bombs guided by laser or GPS to their targets

JLTV*: US Joint Light Tactical Vehicle; planned replacement for the US ground forces Humvee multipurpose vehicle, to be available in recon/scout, infantry transport, heavy guns, close combat, command and control, or ambulance versions

JTAC: Joint terminal air controller. A member of a ground force—e.g., Marine unit—trained to direct the action of combat aircraft engaged in close air support and other offensive air operations from a forward position. See also CAS

K-77M*: Supersonic Russian-made medium-range active radar homing air-to-air missile with extreme maneuverability. It is being developed from the existing R-77 missile.

KALIBR: Russian-made anti-ship, anti-submarine and land attack cruise missile with 500kg conventional or nuclear warhead. The Kalibr-M variant* will have an extended range of up to 4,500 km or 2,700 miles (the distance of, e.g., Iran to Paris).

KARAKURT CLASS: A Russian corvette class which first entered service in 2018. Armed with Pantsir close-in weapons systems, Sosna-R anti-air missile defense and Kalibr supersonic anti-ship missiles. An anti-submarine sensor/weapon loadout is planned but not yet deployed.

KC-135 STRATOTANKER: US airborne refueling aircraft

KRYPTON: Supersonic Russian air-launched anti-radar missile, it is also being adapted for use against ships and large aircraft

LAUNCH AND LOITER: The capability of a missile or drone to fly itself to a target area and wait at altitude for final targeting instructions

LCS: Littoral combat ship. In the US Navy it refers to the *Independence* or *Freedom* class; in Iran, the *Safineh* class; in other navies it may be considered equivalent to a frigate or corvette class. Has the capabilities of a small assault transport, including a flight deck and hangar for housing two SH-60 or MH-60 Seahawk helicopters, a stern ramp for operating small boats, and the cargo volume and payload to deliver a small assault force with fighting vehicles to a roll-on/roll-off port facility. Standard armaments include Mk 110 57mm guns and RIM-116 Rolling Airframe Missiles. Also equipped with autonomous air, surface and underwater vehicles. Possessing lower air defense and surface warfare capabilities than destroyers, the LCS concept emphasizes speed, flexible mission modules and a shallow draft.

LEOPARD: Main battle tank fielded by NATO forces including Turkey

LIAONING: China's first aircraft carrier, modified from the former Russian Navy aircraft cruiser, the *Varyag*. Since superseded by China's Type 002 (*Shandong*) and Type 003 carriers, the *Liaoning* is now used for testing new technologies for carrier use, such as the J-20 stealth fighter.

LOITERING MUNITION: A missile or bomb, able to wait at altitude for final targeting instructions

LONG-RANGE HYPERSONIC WEAPONS (LRHW)*: A prototype US missile consisting of a rocket and glide vehicle, capable of being launched by submarine, from land or from aircraft

LS3*: Legged Squad Support System—a mechanized dog-like robot powered by hydrogen fuel cells and supported by a cloud-based AI. Currently being explored by DARPA and the US armed forces for logistical support or squad scouting and IED detection roles.

LTMV: Light Tactical Multirole Vehicle; a very long name for what is essentially a jeep

M1A2 ABRAMS: US main battle tank. In 2016, the US Army and Marine Corps began testing out the Israeli Trophy active protection system to provide additional defense against incoming projectiles. Improvements planned for the M1A3 are to include a lighter 120mm gun, added road wheels with improved suspension, a more durable track, lighter-weight armor, long-range precision armaments, and infrared camera and laser detectors.

M22: See BARRETT MRAD M22 sniper rifle

M27: US-made military assault rifle

MAD: Magnetic Anomaly Detection, used by warships to detect large artificial objects under the surface of the sea, such as mines, or submarines

MAIN BATTLE TANK: See MBT

MASS: Marine Autonomous Surface Ship, or autonomous trailing vessel

MBT: Main battle tank; a heavily armored combat vehicle capable of direct fire and maneuver

MEFP: Multiple Explosive Formed Penetrators; a defensive weapon which uses small explosive charges to create and fire small metal slugs at an incoming projectile, thereby destroying it

MEMS: Micro-Electro-Mechanical System

METEOR: Long-range air-to-air missile with active radar seeker, but also able to be updated with target data in-flight by any suitably equipped allied unit

MIA: Missing in action

MIKE: Radio brevity code for minutes

MIL-25: Export version of the Mi-25 'Hind' Russian helicopter gunship

MOPP: Mission-Oriented Protective Posture protective gear; equipment worn to protect troops against CBRN weapons. See also NBC SUIT

MP: Military Police

MQ-25 STINGRAY: The MQ-25 Stingray is a Boeing-designed prototype unmanned US airborne refueling aircraft. See also X-47B Fantom

MSS: Ministry of State Security, Chinese umbrella intelligence organization responsible for counterespionage and counterterrorism, and foreign intelligence gathering. Equivalent to the US FBI, CIA and NSA.

NAMER: (Leopard) Israeli infantry fighting vehicle (IFV). More heavily armored than a Merkava IV main battle tank. According to the Israel Defense Forces, the Namer is the most heavily armored vehicle in the world of any type.

NATO: North Atlantic Treaty Organization

NAVAL STRIKE MISSILE (NSM): Supersonic anti-ship missile deployed by NATO navies

NBC SUIT: A protective suit issued to protect the wearer against Nuclear, Biological or Chemical weapons. Usually includes a lining to protect the user from radiation and either a gas mask or air recycling unit.

NORAD: The North American Aerospace Defense Command is a United States and Canadian bi-national organization charged with the missions of aerospace warning, aerospace control and maritime warning for North America. Aerospace warning includes the detection, validation and warning of attack against North America whether by aircraft, missiles or space vehicles, through mutual support arrangements with other commands.

NSA: US National Security Agency, cyber intelligence, cyber warfare and defense agency

OFSET*: Offensive Swarm Enabled Tactical drones. Proposed US anti-personnel, anti-armor drone system capable of swarming AI (see SWARM) and able to deploy small munitions against enemy troop or vehicles while moving.

OKHOTNIK*: 5th-generation Sukhoi S-70 unmanned stealth combat aircraft using avionics systems from the Su-57 Felon and fitted with two internal weapons bays, for 7,000kg of ordnance. Requires a pilot and systems officer, similar to current US unmanned combat aircraft. Can be paired with Su-57 aircraft and controlled by a pilot.

OMON: Otryad Mobil'nyy Osobogo Naznacheniya; the Russian National Guard mobile police force

ORCA*: Prototype US large displacement unmanned underwater vehicle with modular payload bay capable of anti-submarine, anti-ship or reconnaissance activities

OVOD: Subsonic Russian-made air-launched cruise missile capable of carrying high-explosive, submunition or fragmentation warheads

P-99 Black Widow (Pursuit Fighter)*: Concept aircraft. Several companies were competing in 2023 for the Next Generation Air Dominance air superiority initiative. The Black Widow is a purely speculative platform combining what is known about the requirements issued and the designs in testing. NGAD is described by the USAF as a "family of systems", with a stealth fighter aircraft as the centerpiece of the system, and other parts of the system likely to be uncrewed escort aircraft to carry extra munitions and perform other missions. In particular, NGAD aims to develop a system that addresses the operation needs of the Pacific theater of operations, where current USAF fighters lack sufficient range and payload. The successful NGAD aircraft is therefore unlikely to resemble current US stealth fighters such as the F-22 Raptor or F-35 Panther.

PANTHER: Pilot name for the F-35 Lightning II stealth fighter, first coined by the 6th Weapons Squadron 'Panther Tamers' due to the unpopularity of the official name 'Lightning II'. There is much speculation about the capabilities of the Panther, just as there is about the Russian Su-57 Felon. Neither has been extensively combat tested.

PANTSIR: Russian-made truck-mounted anti-aircraft system which is a further development of the PENSNE: 'Pince-nez' in English. A Russian-made autonomous ground-to-air missile currently being rolled out for the BUK anti-air defense system.

PARS: Turkish light armored vehicle

PATRIOT: An anti-aircraft, anti-missile missile defense system which uses its own radar to identify and engage airborne threats

PEACE EAGLE: Turkish Boeing 737 Airborne Early Warning and Control aircraft (see AWACS)

PENSNE: See PANTSIR

PERDIX*: Lightweight air-launched armed microdrone with swarming capability (see SWARM). Designed to be launched from underwing canisters or even from the flare/chaff launchers of existing aircraft. Can be used for recon, target identification or delivery of lightweight ordnance.

PEREGRINE*: US medium-range, multimode (infrared, radar, optical) seeker missile with short form body designed for use by stealth aircraft

PERSEUS*: A stealth, hypersonic, multiple warhead missile under development for the British Royal Navy and French Navy

PHASED-ARRAY RADAR: A radar which can steer a beam of radio waves quickly across the sky to detect planes and missiles

PL-15: Chinese medium-range radar-guided air-to-air missile, comparable to the US AIM-120D or UK Meteor

PL-21*: Chinese long-range multimode missile (radar, infrared, optical), comparable to US AIM-260

PLA: People's Liberation Army

PLA-AF (PLAAAF): People's Liberation Army Air Force, comparable to the US Air Force, with more than 400 3rd-generation fighter aircraft, 1,200 4th-generation, and nearly 200 5th-generation stealth aircraft

PLA-N (PLAN): People's Liberation Army Navy

PLA-N AF (PLANAF): People's Liberation Army Navy Air Force, comparable to the US Navy Air Force and Marine Corps Aviation, it performs coastal protection and aircraft carrier operations with more than 250 3rd-generation fighter aircraft, and 150 4th-generation fighter aircraft.

PODNOS: Russian-made portable 82mm mortar

PUMP-JET PROPULSION: A propulsion system comprising a jet of water and a nozzle to direct the flow of water for steering purposes. Used on some submarines due to a quieter acoustic signature than that generated by a screw. The most 'stealthy' submarines are regarded to be those powered by diesel electric engines and pump-jet propulsion, such as trialed on the Russian *Kilo* class and proposed for the Australian *Attack* class*.

QHS*: Quantum Harmonic Sensor; a sensor system for detecting stealth aircraft at long ranges by analyzing the electromagnetic disturbances they create in background radiation

RAAF: Royal Australian Air Force

RAF: Royal Air Force (UK)

ROE: Rules of Engagement; the rules laid down by military commanders under which a unit can or cannot engage in combat. For example, 'units may only engage a hostile force if fired upon first'.

RPG: Rocket-propelled grenade

RTB: Return to base

SAFINEH CLASS: Also known as *Mowj/Wave* class. An Iranian trimaran hulled high-speed missile vessel equivalent to the US LCS class, or the Russia *Karakurt*-class corvette

SAM: Surface-to-Air Missile; an anti-air missile (often shortened to SA) for engaging aircraft

SAR: See SYNTHETIC APERTURE RADAR

SCREW: The propeller used to drive a boat or ship is referred to as a screw (helical blade) propeller. Submarine propellers typically comprise five to seven blades. See also PUMP-JET PROPULSION

SEAD: Suppression of Enemy Air Defenses; an air attack intended to take down enemy anti-air defense systems; see also WILD WEASEL

SENTINEL*: Lockheed Martin RQ-170 Sentinel flying wing stealth reconnaissance drone

SIDEWINDER: Heat-seeking short-range air-to-air missile

SITREP: Situation Report

SKYHAWK*: Chinese drone designed to team with fighter aircraft to provide added sensor or weapons delivery capabilities. Comparable to the planned US Boeing Loyal Wingman or Kratos drones.

SKY THUNDER: Chinese 1,000 lb. stealth air-launched cruise missile with swappable payload modules

SLR: Single lens reflex camera, favored by photojournalists

SMERCH: Russian-made 300mm rocket launcher capable of firing high-explosive, submunition or chemical weapons warheads

SPACECOM: United States Space Command (US SPACECOM or SPACECOM) is a unified combatant command of the United States Department of Defense, responsible for military operations in outer space, specifically all operations above 100 km above mean sea level

SPEAR/SPEAR-EW*: UK/Europe Select Precision at Range air-to-ground standoff attack missile, with LAUNCH AND LOITER capabilities. Will utilize a modular 'swappable' warhead system featuring high-explosive, anti-armor, fragmentation or electronic warfare (EW) warheads.

SPETSNAZ: Russian Special Operations Forces

SPLASH: US Navy and Air Force Radio brevity code showing a target has been destroyed. In artillery context splash over means impact imminent, splash out means rounds impacted.

SSBN: Strategic-level nuclear-powered (N) submarine platform for firing ballistic (B) missiles. Examples: UK *Vanguard* class, US *Ohio* class, Russia *Typhoon* class.

SSC: Subsurface Contact Supervisor; supervises operations against subsurface contacts from within a ship's Combat Information Center (CIC)

SSGN: A guided missile (G) nuclear (N) submarine that carries and launches guided cruise missiles as its primary weapon. Examples: US *Ohio* class, Russia *Yasen* class.

SSK: A diesel electric-powered submarine, quieter when submerged than a nuclear-powered submarine, but must rise to snorkel depth to run its diesel and recharge its batteries.

Examples: Iranian *Fateh* class, Russian *Kilo* class, Israeli *Dolphin I* class.

SSN: A general purpose attack submarine (SS) powered by a nuclear reactor (N). Examples: HMS *Agincourt*, Russian *Akula* class.

SSP: A diesel electric submarine with air-independent propulsion system able to recharge batteries without using atmospheric oxygen. Allows the submarine to stay submerged longer than a traditional SSK. Examples: Israeli *Dolphin II* class, Iranian *Besat** class.

STANDOFF: Launched at long range

STINGER: US-made man-portable, low-level anti-air missile

STINGRAY*: The MQ-25 Stingray is a Boeing-designed prototype unmanned US airborne refueling aircraft

STORMBREAKER*: US air-launched, precision-guided glide bomb that can use millimeter radar, laser or infrared imaging to match and then prioritize targets when operating in semi-autonomous AI mode

SU-57: See FELON

SUBSONIC: Below the speed of sound (under 767 mph, 1,234 kph)

SUNBURN: Russian-made 220mm multiple rocket launcher capable of firing high-explosive, THERMOBARIC or penetrating warheads

SUPERSONIC: Faster than the speed of sound (over 767 mph, 1,234 kph); see also HYPERSONIC

SWARM: Drones, missiles or smart bombs with onboard AI and the ability to coordinate their actions with other drones while in flight, either autonomously or using preselected protocols. 'Swarm' tactics differ from 'horde' tactics in that swarms place more emphasis on coordinated action to defeat enemy defenses. See also HORDE

SYNTHETIC APERTURE RADAR (SAR): A form of radar that is used to create two-dimensional images or three-dimensional reconstructions of objects, such as landscapes. SAR uses the motion of the radar antenna over a target region to provide finer spatial resolution than conventional beam-scanning radars.

SYSOP: The systems operator inside the control station for a HELLADS battery, responsible for electronic and communications systems operation

T-14 ARMATA: Russian next-generation main battle tank or MBT. Designed as a 'universal combat platform' which can be adapted to infantry support, anti-armor or anti-armor configurations. First Russian MBT to be fitted with active electronically scanning array radar capable of identifying and engaging multiple air and ground targets simultaneously. Also the first Russian MBT to be fitted with a crew toilet. Used in combat in Syria from 2020.

T-90: Russian-made main battle tank

TAC(P): Tactical air controller, a specialist trained to direct close air support attacks. See also CAS; FAC; JTAC

TAO: Tactical action officer; officer in command of a ship's Combat Information Center (CIC)

TCA: Tactical control assistant, non-commissioned officer (NCO) in charge of identifying targets and directing fire for a single HELLADS or PATRIOT battery

TCO: Tactical control officer, officer in charge of a single HELLADS or PATRIOT missile battery

TD: Tactical Director; the officer directing multiple PATRIOT or HELLADS batteries in ground air defenses, or interception operations aboard an AWACs aircraft.

TEMPEST*: British/European 6th-generation stealth aircraft under development as a replacement for the RAF Tornado multirole fighter. It is planned to incorporate advanced combat AI to reduce pilot data overload, laser anti-missile defenses, and will team with swarming drones such as BATS. It may be developed in both crewed and uncrewed versions, and a version for use on the two new British aircraft carriers is also mooted.

TERMINATOR: A Russian-made infantry fighting vehicle (see IFV) based on the chassis of the T-90 main battle tank, with 2x 30mm autocannons and 2x grenade or anti-tank missile launchers. Developed initially to support main battle tank operations, it has become popular for use in urban combat environments.

THERMOBARIC: Weapons, otherwise known as thermal or vacuum weapons, which use oxygen from the surrounding air to generate a high-temperature explosion and long-duration blast wave

THUNDER: Radio brevity code indicating one minute to weapons impact

TOW: US wire-guide anti-tank missile, fired either from a tripod launcher by ground troops or mounted on armored cavalry vehicles

TROPHY: Israeli-made anti-projectile defense system using explosively formed penetrators to defeat attacks on vehicles, high-value assets and aircraft. It is currently fitted to several Israeli and US armored vehicle types.

TUNGUSKA: A mobile Russian-made anti-aircraft vehicle incorporating both cannon and ground-to-air missiles

TYPE 95*: Planned Chinese 3rd-generation nuclear-powered attack submarine with vertical launch tubes and substantially reduced acoustic signature to current Chinese types

UAV: Unmanned aerial vehicle or drone, usually used for transport, refueling or reconnaissance

UCAS: Unmanned combat aerial support vehicle or drone

UCAV: Unmanned combat aerial vehicle; a fighter or attack aircraft

UDAR* UGV: Russian-made unmanned ground vehicle which integrates remotely operated turrets (30mm autocannon, Kornet anti-tank missile or anti-air missile) onto the chassis of a BMP-3 infantry fighting vehicle. The vehicle can be controlled at a range of up to 6 miles (10 km) by an operator with good line of sight, or via a tethered drone relay.

UDV: Underwater delivery vehicle. A small submersible transport used typically by naval commandos for covert insertion and recovery of troops.

UGV: Unmanned ground vehicle, also UGCV: Unmanned ground combat vehicle

UI: Un-Identified, as in 'UI contact'. See also BOGEY

UNIT 8200: Israel Defense Force cyber intelligence, cyber warfare and defense unit, aka the Israeli Signals Intelligence National Unit

UPWARD FALLING PAYLOADS (UFP)*: A DARPA research project of the 2020s, now shelved, to develop deployable, unmanned distributed systems that lie on the deep-ocean floor in concealed containers for years at a time.

These deep-sea nodes could be remotely activated when needed and recalled to the surface. In other words, they "fall upward." Payloads could include sensor packages, cannister-launched aerial drones, mines or torpedoes.

URAGAN: Russian 220mm 16-tube rocket launcher, first fielded in the 1970s

U/S: Un-serviceable, out of commission, broken

USO: United Services Organizations; US military entertainment and personnel welfare services

V-22 OSPREY: Bell Boeing multi-mission tiltrotor aircraft capable of vertical takeoff and landing which resembles a conventional aircraft when in flight

V-280* VALOR: Bell Boeing-proposed successor to the V-22, with higher speed, endurance, lift capacity and modular payload bay

V-290* VAPOR: Concept aircraft only. AI-enhanced V-280 with anti-radar absorbent coating, added rear fuselage turbofan jet engines for additional speed, and forward-firing 20mm autocannons

VALKYRIE (XQ-58)*: an experimental uncrewed stealth fighter designed and built by Kratos Defense and Security Solutions to support a USAF requirement to field an uncrewed wingman cheap enough to sustain losses in combat but capable of supporting crewed aircraft in hostile environments. In January 2023 it was announced the USAF had purchased two Valkyrie demonstrators for $15.5m USD, shortly after which the US Navy announced it had done the same.

VERBA: A Russian-made man-portable low-level anti-air missile with data networking capabilities, meaning it can use data from friendly ground or air radar systems to fly itself to a target

VIRGINIA CLASS SUBMARINE: e.g., *USS Idaho*, nuclear-powered, fast-attack submarines. Current capabilities include torpedo and cruise missiles. Planned capabilities include hypersonic missiles.

VORTEX*: 'Quantum Radar' technology that generates a mini electromagnetic storm to detect objects. First reported by Professor Zhang Chao at Tsinghua University's aerospace engineering school, in Journal of Radars, 2021. A quantum radar is different from traditional radars in several ways, according to the paper. While traditional radars have on a fixed or rotating dish, the quantum design features a gun-shaped instrument that accelerates electrons. The electrons pass through a winding tube of a strong magnetic fields, producing what is described as a tornado-shaped microwave vortex.

VYMPEL: Russian air-to-air missile manufacturer/type

WIDOW*: P-99 Black Widow (Pursuit Fighter). Concept aircraft. Several companies were competing in 2023 for the Next Generation Air Dominance air superiority initiative. The Black Widow is a purely speculative platform combining what is known about the requirements issued and the designs in testing. NGAD is described by the USAF as a "family of systems", with a stealth fighter aircraft as the centerpiece of the system, and other parts of the system likely to be uncrewed escort aircraft to carry extra munitions and perform other missions. In particular, NGAD aims to develop a system that addresses the operation needs of the Pacific theater of operations, where current USAF fighters lack sufficient range and payload. The successful NGAD aircraft is therefore unlikely to resemble current US stealth fighters such as the F-22 Raptor or F-35 Panther.

WILD WEASEL: An air attack intended to take down enemy anti-air defense systems; see also SEAD

WINCHESTER: Radio brevity code for 'out of ordnance'

X-95: Israeli bullpup-style assault rifle. Bullpup-style rifles have their action behind the trigger, allowing for a more compact and maneuverable weapon. Commonly chambered for NATO 5.56mm ammunition.

YAKHONT: Also known as P-800 Onyx. Russian-made two-stage ramjet-propelled, terrain-following cruise missile. Travels at subsonic speeds until close to its target where it is boosted to up to Mach 3. Can be fired from warships, submarines, aircraft or coastal batteries at sea or ground targets.

YPG: Kurdish People's Protection Unit militia (male)

YPJ: Kurdish Women's Protection Unit militia (female)

YUAN WANG class tracking ships: Ships of 18-21,000 tons displacement, used for tracking and support of ballistic missiles and satellites, aircraft and for signals interception.

Z-9: Chinese attack helicopter, predecessor to Z-19

Z-19: Chinese light attack helicopter, comparable to US Viper

Z-20: Chinese medium-lift utility helicopter, comparable to US Blackhawk

Made in United States
Orlando, FL
05 April 2023

31791334R00303